R0085452829

11/2017

W9-AXB-224

CLOSE CONTACT

LORI FOSTER

CLOSE CONTACT

HQN™

Dear Reader,

I'm so excited to introduce the third book in my Body Armor series, featuring hot alpha males whose überprotective instincts are put to good use in their roles as elite bodyguards.

Miles Dartman, the latest MMA fighter to join the elite Body Armor personal security agency, has learned through his time as a heavyweight contender to always expect the unexpected. But he never imagined Maxi Nevar, the casual fling he can't stop thinking about, would suddenly show up at Body Armor needing his help...or that getting to know her would only intensify their already sizzling connection. Now keeping her safe is more than just a job—and convincing her to trust him with her heart is the most important mission of his life.

I hope you enjoy Miles and Maxi's romance. And of course, you're always welcome to reach out to me. I'm active on most social media forums, including Facebook, Twitter, Pinterest and Goodreads, and my email address is listed on my website at www.lorifoster.com.

Happy reading!

Lori Foster

CHAPTER ONE

Maxi opened her eyes to a black velvet sky pierced with shimmering stars. A balmy breeze drifted over her skin. She frowned, her head aching horribly, her mouth as dry as cotton, her body heavy...every part of her hurt in one way or another. She stared at the sky, trying to make sense of it.

It took an extreme amount of effort, but she lifted up and winced at the sharp pain in her elbow and back. A strange sense of dread crawled over her.

What the hell? *Gravel?*

How was she on gravel? In dirt and clumps of dried grass... With her head now swimming and her stomach trying to revolt, she paused, closed her eyes and concentrated on not throwing up. When everything somewhat settled, she pried her eyes open again and slowly looked around.

Realization doused her in ice, followed by a wave of prickling heat.

Good God, she was outside, lying in a dry, rocky field.

Her heart rapped painfully hard, confusion gripping her so tightly that she couldn't think. She didn't know the time; she didn't even know the day.

Where am I and why?

Past the confusion, expanding fear brought a sob up her throat. But sobbing would require sound, and she was too scared to make any noise.

Forcing her sluggish body to move, she shifted slightly and peered around. She recognized a tree, a fence… Okay, so she was on the farm that she'd inherited from her grandmother. The hard earth, dry from a long August drought, sent bristly weeds sticking into her skin.

She looked down at herself and recognized the sleep shirt and cutoff shorts she'd changed into after her shower. Each minuscule movement made her head throb in agony and sent acid burning through her stomach. She put a hand over her mouth to stave off the sickness.

Off to the side, something moved in the encircling darkness.

Frozen, her eyes wide in an effort to see, Maxi held her breath and waited. Another breeze moved the branches of the tree, allowing a splinter of moonlight to penetrate.

Yellow eyes came her way—and she realized it was a black cat strolling cautiously toward her.

Relief brought a rush of hot tears to her eyes. "Oh, baby, you scared me." The cat, recognizing her voice, sat beside her. The moonlight slid away, but the cat's yellow eyes remained visible, unblinking.

Because she needed to feel something real, Maxi pulled him into her lap and stroked his long back. "What am I doing out here?"

No answer. She heard only the rustling of the wind and a rumbling purr from the cat.

What should I do? How far away was she from the farmhouse? Trying to figure it out left her more frustrated. Tears spilled over to her cheeks and she dashed them away. Crying now wouldn't help her.

She had to *move*.

With an effort, still clutching the cat, she got to her feet and turned a slow, clumsy circle. Once she moved away from the tree, the scant moonlight helped orient her. She was near the two-acre pond. Judging by the tall reeds that grew at the back of the pond, she needed to circle around to the dock, then go up the hill.

Tunnel vision distorted what the night didn't hide, forcing her to feel her way in near blindness. It seemed every third step she found a rock or thistle that cut into her heel or tender arch. Once, she tripped and almost fell. She did drop the cat, but the dear thing didn't leave her. In fact, she used him as a guide, following close behind as he meandered up the slight incline to the back porch. He, at least, had no problem seeing his way.

The house, dark inside and out, appeared as a looming gray structure that left her decidedly uneasy. She felt as if she approached danger rather than shelter.

The darkness didn't make sense. She always left on the outside lights in the evening. A power outage? Maybe during a storm, but they hadn't had one of those in a good long while.

Besides, an outage couldn't explain why she'd awakened outside.

Nervousness and fear coalesced into real terror. While she gulped in the clear evening air, she belatedly realized why.

Someone did something to me.

How, she didn't know. Thinking made her head hurt worse. She summoned only a vague memory of drinking a glass of wine on her sofa while reading a book. That had to have been hours ago. What had happened after that? Folding her arms around her stomach, she again fought the sickness.

Could there be an intruder in her house? *Oh God, oh God, oh God.*

Pausing near the back porch, she strained to listen for unfamiliar sounds, steadying her shaky limbs with a hand planted on the outer wall. More cats joined her. The isolated farmhouse her grandmother had left her came with too many cats to count—and a distinct lack of nearby neighbors. At about eight miles away, Mr. Barstow would be the closest, but at seventy-nine, he wouldn't be much help if a threat remained.

She was too far from town to walk anywhere, and her car keys were in the house.

What to do?

Desperation decided for her.

Her chest tight with dread, she crept up the porch, carefully turned the doorknob and found the back door unlocked, then slipped inside while making sure to keep the cats out. The last thing she needed was to try to distinguish their movements from any other sound.

Her heartbeat pounded in her ears and her blood rushed, making her dizzy.

The back of the house opened into a short hall. Stairs to her right led up to the bedroom she used, a small study and a bathroom. To her left was the main floor bedroom, but it had been her grandmother's, and other than packing up the belongings and keeping it clean of dust, she didn't intrude into that room.

Her keys hung in the kitchen straight ahead, but her purse, which had her wallet, would be in the living room on the desk. She couldn't leave without money.

Each creeping step sharpened her nervousness until a scream built in her throat. Gasping each silent breath, she lacked her usual grace, moving like someone suffering a killer hangover. In the dark, she groped around, being as silent as possible. She didn't dare turn on a light; what if she did and she found someone standing there? She shuddered at the thought.

When she finally located her purse, her knees almost gave out. She hooked the strap over her head and across her body to ensure she wouldn't drop it. Her eyes adjusted to the darkness so that now she could make out vague shadows.

Somehow that seemed even eerier.

Anxious to escape, she made her way back through to the kitchen. Praying she wouldn't drop them, or even rattle them, she grabbed the keys in her fist. Next, she slipped her feet into the rubber boots she wore when going to the barn and, because she couldn't stop shaking, she snagged the flannel shirt off the hook. She felt sick with trepidation by the time she got back out the door.

And she still didn't feel safe.

Dawn cast a gray hue over the horizon, telling her it was almost morning. *How long had she been outside?* No, she wouldn't tax herself by thinking about that now. Her number one priority was getting away until she could figure out what had happened.

She wanted to run to her car, but not only was she unsteady on her feet, she feared that once she started to run, hysteria would set in. She needed to stay calm, so she took one deliberate step after another, constantly checking her surroundings.

At her car, she hesitated. If anyone was watching for her, the light when she opened her door would give her away.

As to that, what if someone was *in* the car?

She dug out her cell phone and, willing to risk it, used the softer light to look into the front and back seat.

Thankfully empty.

All but diving into the driver's seat and then locking the doors, she fumbled until she got the key in the lock and started the engine.

Breath held, she turned on the headlights.

A dozen sets of cat eyes reflected back at her, but she saw nothing more sinister than that. She quickly looked behind her, too, but saw only shifting shadows that further intimidated her.

She put the car in Drive and, because she remained a little muddled, carefully pressed on the gas. Down the long drive to the main gravel road, she drove slowly, well aware that the cats often showed up out of nowhere.

As she cleared the property line, she knew what she had to do.

He might not appreciate seeing her again, not after such a long absence without a single word from her, but she could explain that if necessary.

She knew where he worked. She knew he was more than capable of helping.

And thanks to her recent inheritance, she could even afford him.

Miles Dartman, heavyweight MMA fighter turned bodyguard, the sexiest, and most sexual, man she'd ever known, was about to be in her employ.

It was the only upside to a very rough two months.

Miles rode the private elevator in the Body Armor agency to his boss's very upscale office. The early-morning summons left him confused and he didn't like it. He'd been in the shower when she'd called at 7:00 a.m. Her message said only that he was to get there as quickly as possible. She had a *surprise* for him.

Of course, he'd called her back, but she'd told him she'd explain everything once he made it to the office.

He'd finished his extensive training only a few weeks ago, learning enhanced computer skills and practicing his shot with a variety of guns. He'd settled on the Glock as his preferred weapon, but he carried a few other toys, as well.

So far, he'd had two cases, both of them pretty routine. He'd helped to control pushy fans at a sporting event for a baseball player during a PR stint, and then he'd escorted a big-time author with a new movie deal to some local signings around the area.

Easy peasy.

He missed competing, damn it. Missed the cage and the physical exertion. If fate hadn't played him a dirty hand, he'd be at it still, fighting his way to a championship belt.

The loss of his fight career was only one of many regrets he suffered lately, and as usual, he shoved it from his mind, determined to live in the here and now.

The elevator opened and he stepped out, going straight to Sahara Silver's posh office. As he passed Enoch Walker, Sahara's personal assistant, he said, "She's expecting me."

"Indeed she is," Enoch said without looking up from his PC screen. "Go right on in."

Did he detect an unusual note in Enoch's voice? Hard to tell when Enoch stayed focused on his task.

Miles liked Enoch a lot. He was a little dude with a will of iron and mad organizational skills. Always friendly, incredibly smart and damned reliable.

Because the door was closed, Miles knocked, and a mere second later it opened, almost as if Sahara had been waiting for him.

Oozing satisfaction, she smiled. "Miles."

He paused, suddenly on guard. So far, his boss had been something of an enigma. On the outside, she was a real looker, a shapely five feet eight inches of sass with glossy mink-brown hair, direct blue eyes and the demeanor of an Amazon. On the inside, she probably wrestled alligators and won. Always polished, always in killer heels and always sporting attitude.

"That's a different smile for you," he noted. "Why do I feel like I'm about to be offered as a sacrifice to angry gods?"

The smile widened, then she stepped back to allow him to enter. "Thank you for getting here so quickly."

"You didn't leave me much choice with that cryptic message."

"I'm never cryptic."

"No? Then what was so urgent that I—" That was when Miles saw her. His eyes flared as he noted her huddled position in a padded chair, a steaming cup of coffee held in both hands. "Maxi?"

When he said her name, she straightened but didn't look at him.

"What are you doing here?" For two months, he'd waited for her, hoping she'd get in touch again.

She hadn't.

From the start, she'd made it clear that he was a convenient booty call and nothing more. That should have worked great for him, but instead it had driven him nuts.

He'd finally, well, *almost*, put her out of his mind with the job switch and move to a new apartment. Now here she was, at Body Armor of all places.

A slow burn started, making him blind to Sahara standing close, at least until she said, "Your friend has had something of an ordeal."

"And she came to me?" Umbrage churned, made sharper by other losses at the same time. He fashioned a sarcastic grin. "Surprising, since she walked away without a goodbye."

Maxi looked at him then. Those dark eyes he'd always found so mesmerizing were now glazed and somehow troubled.

And they stared at him like a lifeline.

It dawned on him that she looked terrible, when he hadn't thought that possible. One of the very few things she'd ever revealed to him was her occupation as a personal stylist, a job that seemed to suit her, since the lady had always looked very put together.

Not this time, though. Dried leaves clung to her long, tangled blond hair. Gone were the trendy clothes, and instead she wore an oversize flannel shirt, faded cutoffs and bright green rubber boots dotted with yellow ducks. The ridiculous clothes made her look endearing.

Concern sharpened his tone. "What the hell happened to you?"

When she didn't answer, he went to one knee in front of her, resting his hands on her slim thighs. A few months ago they'd been in a similar position, both naked. But she hadn't looked wounded then. No, she'd been soft and hot, moaning his name.

Blocking that memory seemed imperative. His tone didn't lose the edge. "Maxi?"

Pale slender fingers curled around the cup of steaming coffee. She swallowed audibly, met his gaze again and muttered, "I'm not sure."

"What does that mean?"

Sahara strolled up behind him. "Sometime before dawn, Ms. Nevar woke up in her yard, feeling very sick and with no memory of how she got there."

Miles looked back at Sahara, his voice stern with surprise. "What are you talking about?"

"She was a fair distance from her farmhouse but made it to the back porch. Needless to say, she wasn't keen on going back inside, not without knowing what might await her. The house was dark and her property is isolated with no close neighbors."

Miles sat back on his heels in disbelief. He didn't know jack shit about her property, but he put that aside for the moment. "Drunk?" He hadn't figured her for a big drinker, but then, what did he really know about her—except that, for a time, she'd enjoyed using him for sex.

As if to convince him, Maxi stared into his eyes. "I'd only had one glass of wine. At least, that's all I can remember."

All she remembered? "Could you have drunk enough to black out?"

She took that like a physical hit, flinching away from him and making him feel like an asshole.

Brisk now, Sahara said, "Despite being disoriented, she had the forethought, and guts I might add, to enter the unlit house to get her purse, car keys and those adorable boots."

Adorable? They belonged on a ten-year-old, not a grown woman.

"Staying there was out of the question, and she wasn't sure where else to go." Sahara propped a hip on the desk. "Since she remembered that you work here, this is where she came."

So she finally had a use for him again? No, he wouldn't be that easy, not this time. But he had questions, a million of them.

Looking back at his boss, Miles said, "Give us a minute, will you?"

She smiled down at him. "Not on your life."

He recognized that inflexible expression well enough. Sahara Silver did what she wanted, when she wanted. The lady was born to be a boss. In medieval times, she probably would have carried a whip. Still, he tried. "If she's here to see me—"

"She's here to hire you."

Hire him? He turned back to Maxi and got her timid nod. Skeptical, he clarified, "As a bodyguard?"

"Yes."

Since when did a woman need to be protected from a hangover? Did he want to be involved with that?

Now that he worked at the Body Armor agency, did he have a choice?

Sahara ruled with a small iron fist and she, at least, seemed taken with Maxi's far-fetched tale. If Sahara took the contract, he might not have much say in it.

And who was he kidding? Much as he'd like to deny it,

territorial tendencies had sparked back to life the second he saw Maxi again. In his gut, he knew he was happy—even relieved—to again have her within reach.

Maybe because she was the one who got away, or the one who hadn't been all that hung up on him in the first place.

His ego was still stung, that was all.

It didn't help that her disinterest had piled on at a low point in his life, making her rejection seem more important.

She'd come on to him hot and heavy, they'd gotten together three separate times, had phenomenal sex that, at least to him, had felt more than physical, and then she'd booked. She'd guarded her privacy more than her body, and other than her name and occupation, he hadn't known much about her, not where she worked, or lived, or anything about her family...

As to that, maybe getting smashed and passing out in her yard were regular things for her. If so, he'd count himself lucky that she'd cut ties when she had.

Yet, somehow, that didn't fit with his impressions of her.

First things first. He had to get a handle on what had actually happened. "Where is this farmhouse?"

"In Burlwood."

"Never heard of it."

"Few people have. It's a really small town forty-five minutes south of here, close to the Kentucky border."

With that answered, he went on to other details. "So you woke up outside?"

"Yes."

"In your front yard?"

She shook her head. "A good distance away, on the far side of the pond."

"Like a little decorative pond?"

"It's two acres."

Wow. Okay, so not close to the house, then. "How long were you out there?"

Her brows pinched together and her hands tightened. "I honestly don't know. The last thing I remember is opening a book to read." She drew in a deep, shaky breath. "That's it. Just reading. Then I woke up with a splitting headache, some bug bites and gravel digging into my spine."

"What were you doing before opening the book?"

Staring down at her hands, she gave it some thought. "I remember cleaning the kitchen."

"Before that?"

She shook her head. "It was an all-day job."

Who spent all day cleaning one room? He didn't know Maxi's habits, but maybe she'd never done any cleaning if tidying up dinner felt like a big chore to her. Hell, all he really knew about her was that she made him laugh, he enjoyed talking to her and she burned him up in bed.

Yeah, not a good time for that particular memory.

"Did you have company?"

"I don't think so."

"You don't remember?"

"I can't remember much of anything."

"Then how do you know—"

"No one comes out to the farmhouse," she snapped. "But I already told you, if someone did, I do *not* remember it." Temper brought her forward in her seat. "I can't remember *anything*. Especially not how I ended up sleeping on the ground in the middle of the night!"

Okay, so he had to admit, all in all that sounded like more than alcohol. Hell, had someone actually drugged her? If so, how and when? Most likely on a date.

Or had she trolled another bar?

Narrowing his eyes, Miles said, "I know you haven't been to Rowdy's lately." *Where they'd met.* It was a nice place, small and with enough regulars that spiking a drink wouldn't go unnoticed. That brought up another idea. "Switched to a less reputable bar?"

Still breathing hard from her rant, she settled back, and after visibly collecting herself, she shook her head. "No."

That clipped voice didn't deter him from his questions. "Any boyfriends been around?"

She gave another sharp shake of her head. "I don't have a boyfriend."

"No one?"

Glaring, she repeated, *"No one."*

"Did you piss off your newest bed partner, then?"

"Miles," Sahara chided mildly.

"It's a legitimate question."

Maxi scowled at him. "No bed partner."

"You're telling me that in the two months since I've seen you—"

"There's been no one." Belligerent now, she muttered, "Not since you, and you were a long shot. Sort of a last hurrah."

She kept saying the craziest things. "I have no idea what that's supposed to mean."

Sahara interrupted with "Look at yourself, Miles. With all her new obligations, she obviously didn't mean to get involved, but then, I'm sure she didn't expect to meet you."

"Exactly," Maxi stated, as if vindicated.

His temples started to throb. "Exactly *what?*"

Helpfully, Sahara explained, "Oh, sweetie, you were supposed to be a one-night stand. Not a repeat performance."

Maxi nodded. "But what woman could resist coming back?"

Raising her hand, Sahara said, "I could, but then, I'm used to being surrounded by—" she flapped her hand at Miles as she searched for the words "—by temptation. Body Armor is *the* place to go for sexier protection, you know." Then sotto voce, she added to Maxi, "I'm trying to cement that brand for the agency. So far, I'm meeting resistance."

Sahara's typical blunt approach might have insulted someone else; after all, she now knew something very personal and private about him. He couldn't blame Maxi for sharing, not when Sahara had a way of getting the details out of people. Plus, Maxi was obviously out of sorts, therefore easily susceptible to Sahara's not-so-subtle digging. At the moment, though, offense was the last thing he felt. Everyone at the agency was used to Sahara's informal and often intrusive manner. It went hand in hand with a lot of caring, making her a most unusual but likable boss.

After rolling his eyes at Sahara, Miles turned to Maxi. He wanted to believe everything she said, he really did. He'd even admit that she looked sincere.

Problem was, he knew her sex drive matched his own, and he sure as hell hadn't been celibate.

Maybe this time she'd hooked up with the wrong man. Had she played around and then tried to call it quits, but unlike Miles, the new guy knew where to find her and, in a sick way, had insisted?

He hated that thought. His natural instinct was to protect women, never to abuse them. His reaction to Maxi had honed that instinct to a razor's edge.

Still, facts were facts. Why would a total stranger drug her only to leave her outside? That didn't make any sense.

But a pissed-off lover? That at least explained a motive, if the guy had only wanted to fuck with her.

Miles gently lifted her chin. Caution filled her big dark eyes, but she didn't pull away. Checking for any other signs of injury, he tipped her face first one way, then the other. He didn't see any bruises, but that didn't mean much. He hated to ask, but he had to know. "Are you hurt anywhere else?"

Her tongue touched over her dry lips. "I don't think so."

Did she understand what he was asking? "I mean—"

"I know what you mean." She spared a brief glance for Sahara, then lowered her voice. "I don't think anyone...touched me. Not *that* way."

Matching his voice to hers, he whispered, "You checked?"

She nodded. "As best I could. I mean, I was still wearing my shorts. And my...my panties weren't twisted or anything." She bit her bottom lip. "If anything like that did happen, I'd know, right?"

"I assume so." Miles wanted to check for himself, but he could just imagine how that'd go over.

Sahara probably wouldn't give him the privacy for it anyway.

So if she had been drugged—then what? She'd have to open up first instead of denying any involvement, but if he could find the guy, he'd annihilate him, no problem.

Because he didn't want this to get personal, he told himself he'd feel the same for any woman. "You're sure you don't remember anything else? No other clues? No one I should check out?"

Nodding at Sahara, Maxi said, "Nothing that she hasn't already told you." Shivering again, she sipped the hot coffee.

It wasn't cold in the office. In fact, beneath his hands her thighs felt warm. Reaction, then. To the upset of thinking she'd been roofied, or because she *had* been roofied?

The urge to gather her close strained him. Only the hard reminder that she'd left his life as quickly as she'd entered it kept him somewhat impersonal. "We'll find out what happened."

Relief washed over her, making her go limp. She looked down, gulped a few quivering breaths and nodded. "Thank you."

The tears in her voice nearly undid him.

It must have affected Sahara, too, because even though she'd refused to give them privacy moments before, she now said softly, "I'll be right back," and then she slipped from the room, closing the door behind her.

Silence stretched out.

As Miles watched, Maxi banked the desperation and forced herself to calm. It surprised him when she said, "You've gotten bigger."

He lifted a brow. Now that they had a moment alone, that was all she had to say to him? Or was she just hoping for a distraction? "I'm not fighting anymore. Now I eat what I want."

"But you're not heavy." Her warm gaze moved over his shoulders. "You're still as chiseled as ever. Just...bigger. Bulkier."

He shrugged. "True." He'd had plenty of time to exercise and lift weights, especially since the Body Armor agency kept a state-of-the-art gym with every type of equipment a fitness buff could want. After all, bodyguards had to stay in shape. Plus, beating a heavy bag helped rid him of his anger.

Or so he'd told himself.

At the moment, the anger seemed dangerously close to the surface. "A lot can change in two months."

Guilt brought color to her face, so she didn't appear as pale. She turned away before saying, "I should apologize—"

"You made it clear there was no commitment." That was usually how he liked it. Just not this time.

"I know, but... It's just that I had so much to deal with and..." She blew out a breath. "I was tempted to lean on you."

He waited, but when she said nothing else, he frowned. "That would have been so bad?"

She choked. "You can't tell me you'd have wanted that."

"I don't think you have a clue what I wanted." Mostly because she'd never bothered to ask.

"Look at yourself," she said, almost in accusation.

Sahara had said the same, and he still didn't know what it meant.

"You can have anyone you want. I had no reason to think you'd want me, especially with all my…chaos."

Chaos? He started to ask, but she cut him off.

"I figured it was better to go before I got rejected."

With quiet anger, Miles said, "I wouldn't have rejected you."

"You can't know that when you don't understand what my life is like."

He'd already said too much, more than he'd meant to, so Miles shook his head. "Suit yourself. But now that you've explained and had your coffee, you need to go to the hospital."

She groaned.

"If what you said is true—"

Insulted, she asked, "You still doubt me?"

"—then you know someone probably roofied you." Yeah, he had doubts. Too much of her story didn't add up. If she claimed to have an angry ex, or if she'd been in a club, it'd make more sense. Either way, they'd know the truth soon enough.

Until then, he had an opportunity to turn the tables on her. He'd be accessible, he'd help her, but she'd be the one left wanting.

Sahara reentered with a soft throw blanket. Miles had no idea where she'd found it, but she handed it to Maxi.

Miles drew it over and around her shoulders. "Who would want to hurt you?"

She thanked him, then said, "I have no idea. I don't have any close neighbors, no recent involvements." Her gaze flashed to his. "Well, except for you."

"That was months ago and we weren't all that involved."

She looked ready to toss the coffee in his face. "If I go to the hospital, someone will recognize my name and tell my brother."

"Your brother?"

"He works in the ER. Nevar isn't exactly a common last name, so he'll know I'm there, and then he's going to ask a lot of questions I can't answer, and probably try to insist I should sell the house."

Every word out of her mouth told him something new about her. Her definition of "chaos" was starting to make sense. "Maxi—"

"I'm feeling better."

She wanted to avoid her brother that badly? Or maybe none of it was true and she didn't want it proved.

Trying to be the voice of reason, Miles lifted her wrist to show her how her hands still trembled. "Better," he agreed, because she was no longer curled in on herself, "but still pretty shaken. You haven't regained all your color, and your eyes aren't completely clear. You have to get checked."

Sahara spoke up. "Miles is right, but I can offer an alternative. Body Armor has a private physician available to clients with special circumstances. I believe you qualify. You'd see her at a very secure, nearby location. Does that suit you?"

Nodding, Maxi said, "That would be so much better, thank you."

Miles stared at Sahara. "You're just full of surprises."

"You'll learn everything as we go along." She strode around her desk to her seat, saying, "I assume you're happy to take the case?"

"Happy?" He snorted. "No."

She arched her brows. "But you'll do it?"

Pretending to think about it, he gave Maxi a long look. "That depends."

Exasperated, Maxi stood.

Since he didn't move, she ended up very close to him, his face aligned with her hips.

As he slowly stood, too, he said, "You've probably figured out that we have a history together?"

"Yes," Sahara said, her tone dry. "I did pick up on that."

"An intimate history," he unnecessarily stated.

Maxi stiffened. "This has nothing to do with that."

"No?" Miles wouldn't let her rile him. After two months of missing her, he'd finally resigned himself to never seeing her again. Yet here she was, not only seeking him out, but in trouble.

Sahara rolled her eyes. "I understand this situation is unique, so please, Miles, there's no need to explain further."

"Well, let *me* explain," Maxi said. "I came here to hire him, not just to get him back in my bed."

Not just *to get him in bed?* Bemused, Miles stared down at her. She said that as if she hoped to accomplish both. "Since you're the one who kicked me out of it, I didn't think you had."

Her back went so straight she looked ready to crack. With a rush of heat flushing her face, she plunked the coffee cup down on the desk. "I didn't kick you out," she stated, her hands fisted. "We were casual at best—"

"By your insistence." To Sahara, who had paused with a finger over the intercom button to listen to their byplay, he said, "I didn't know she had a doctor for a brother, or lived in a farmhouse, or that she had property. Hell, I barely knew her name."

Maxi gasped.

He continued anyway. "No personal questions were allowed."

"I never heard you complain!"

He'd complained plenty...in his own head. From the beginning, Maxi had struck a chord. The sex was unparalleled, yet after having her only three times, she'd cut ties.

He'd wanted more.

Apparently she hadn't.

On only one night had he managed to break down a few of her walls…and that was the last he'd heard from her. He'd awakened the next morning to an empty bed.

"If I'd wanted to see her again," Miles said, keeping Maxi's gaze trapped in his, "I had no way of getting hold of her. That was her plan, of course."

Sahara smiled. "She's here now. I imagine you'll get to know her quite well during this assignment." She pressed the button and said to Enoch, "Get hold of Dr. Brummel and tell her we need an appointment immediately. Let me know as soon as you have a time arranged." With that done, she took her seat, steepled her fingers and looked at each of them. "As Miles put it, he already knows you intimately, and because this will be a job that requires him to stick close to you, that's bound to be a benefit. Who'd want a complete stranger underfoot?"

Maxi looked away without replying.

"While it's true I like to offer sexier agents, actual intimacy with the client is generally taboo—"

Miles snorted. "The horse is out of the barn on that one."

"—but I'm feeling so much animosity that I'm not sure if it'd even be an issue."

Still Maxi stayed silent, not issuing a single objection. So did she want him back in her bed?

Did he want to be there?

Damn straight. Knowing that this time it'd be on his terms only made the idea hotter.

Unaware of his mental ramblings, Sahara asked, "Is there going to be a problem with the two of you getting along?"

Now that he had the bare bones of a plan, Miles said with confidence, "Not for me," as if he could be totally impartial.

Ha! He could deny it all he liked, but in his gut, he knew he'd already staked a claim to Maxi. Even though it appeared she'd gotten into trouble with another man, he still wanted her.

The chemistry was as strong as ever. He knew it. He *felt* it.

Given that she'd noted small changes in his physique, he suspected she felt it, too.

He hadn't been good enough to continue seeing, but now she wanted him working for her, and possibly more. He was definitely the safer bet for her, since he'd never coerced a woman in his life, and he sure as hell wouldn't drug anyone.

Not liking the idea of her with another man, he cut off that thought.

"I realize this is a horrible imposition," Maxi said, staring up at him. "The thing is, I came to you specifically because I know you and I trust you—"

"There's more about me that you *don't* know," he corrected. "But you're right to trust me."

She looked ready to argue that point, but instead she rested against him, her forehead on his sternum, her small body leaning into his.

CHAPTER TWO

Surprised by the sudden affection—or was it simple need for comfort?—Miles put his arms around her. She felt soft and warm, and damn, he couldn't help but react. The stirring came from deep inside him, along with a need to coddle her. "Hey, you okay, babe?"

Nodding, she whispered, "Honest to God, Miles, I don't have the energy to fight." She moved even closer. "Someone did something to me. I don't know who it was, or why, and it's so blasted scary. All I know for sure is that it wasn't you, because you would never hurt me."

She'd rejected him, so why did her trust make him feel so damn good? "No, I wouldn't." He was glad she understood that, but he was also pissed at himself for upsetting her more after what she'd been through.

Even if she lied about seeing another guy or being at a bar, he couldn't bear seeing her like this.

They'd hash out everything, but not until she was in fighting form. "I'm sorry."

She tipped her face up to his. "That's what I was going to say."

He pulled a leaf from her hair. "I've never seen you messy before." It made her somehow seem more vulnerable.

"Well, get used to it. I mean, I'm not usually *this* messy. But with the farmhouse now, and all those cats, it's tough to stay stylish."

"Farmhouse?" he asked. *And cats?*

"I inherited it from my grandmother."

He wanted to know everything about her, and now he had his chance. It was a shitty situation, but it was all he had, so he'd work with it. "It's a nice place?"

"Shoot no. It's a pit."

So she hadn't wanted him to see it…yet some other guy knew where to find her? Leaning closer to her ear, he said, "You should have come to me privately. Body Armor isn't cheap."

"I know. I can afford it."

"Yes, she can," Sahara said, proving she hadn't missed a thing. "I already discussed all that with her while we were waiting for you to arrive."

With his arms still around Maxi, his hands moving up and down her narrow back, Miles glanced at Sahara. "All what?"

"Ms. Nevar not only inherited from her grandmother, but her mother, also."

In one morning, Sahara had learned more about Maxi than he had after sleeping with her on three separate occasions. "Does that mean your mother passed away, too?"

"Yes."

To lose two people so close together was truly tragic. "When did they die?"

"Not long before I met you." She snuggled in again.

Damn, that felt right, always had, and for now at least, he had the excuse he needed to hold her. Sure, he was still pissed. She'd gotten him interested and then disappeared on him, and apparently had still been playing the field. Since he had, too, he'd feel like a hypocrite. Only, he hadn't been the one to call it quits with her.

Given that she'd suffered the loss of two family members before hooking up with him, Miles wondered if he'd only been a distraction for her. A way to cope with her grief. That would explain why she'd been so withdrawn, why she'd given herself physically while holding back emotionally.

It didn't explain why she'd jumped from his bed to the bed of some nameless asshole who'd doped her.

Sahara asked, "Were your mother and grandmother together when they...?"

Maxi shook her head. "Mom died under anesthesia during a procedure a few weeks before my grandma."

"And your grandmother?" Miles asked.

"She fell down her steps and suffered a severe head injury. No one found her until it was too late."

"Damn." He stroked up and down her back, noticing that he could span her shoulder blades with one hand. The scents of earth, warm skin, shampoo and woman filled his head. "I'm sorry."

She tilted back to look up at him again, her chocolate eyes bruised and worried. "There are reasons I didn't tell you any of this."

Right, because she hadn't planned to stick around. Now that she needed him, would she finally open up? It wasn't the time to press her. "We can talk about all that after we've gotten you settled."

"But that's just it. I'm not going to be *settled* for a while." Stepping away from him, steadier now, she straightened the throw over her shoulders. "I don't know what's going on at the farmhouse, but I don't think it's going to be resolved in a day, or even a week. I've already had the county police out there for other incidents, and they've found nothing. I can't keep pestering them when I have no proof of anything."

Maybe the new house had spooked her. Unfamiliar places could do that. You heard and saw things that you didn't recognize. So far her issues didn't require a bodyguard, but he'd be happy to personally ensure her safety. "You didn't need to go through the agency. I could just take a look around—"

Maxi put her shoulders back again. "I want to hire you to stay with me so that someone else is there when things happen. And something *will* happen. It always does. But I can't ask you to do that unless I'm paying."

Because she didn't want to get personally involved? Too bad. It was his turn to set the tone of their relationship. "What kind of things?"

"I don't even know where to start."

"Do you want to sit back down?" By the second, she looked stronger, but it still worried him. If what she said was true, every minute they waited to see the doctor could be critical.

"Not a bad idea," Sahara said. "It shouldn't be long before Dr. Brummel can see you, but you should rest until then."

Maxi shook her head as she paced. "I need to keep moving."

Staying out of her way, Miles leaned against Sahara's desk and folded his arms. "Okay, then let's start with what happened last night. You said other things had happened, but waking up outside, the loss of memory, that was a first?" God, he hoped so. If she'd gone through that before and hadn't come to him—

"That's the only time it happened or I'd have been here sooner." She hugged her arms around herself. "I was dealing okay with everything else. Sort of, anyway. But last night... I don't ever want to go through that again."

"You won't." He'd see to it.

Sahara got up to refill Maxi's coffee. "What kind of other things?"

She gratefully accepted the coffee. "I know some of it

will sound odd, like I'm imagining things. I swear I'm not. There've been sounds that startled me in the middle of the night and left me spooked. Weird noises, not like the house settling. I know that happens. This was more like...someone was actually in the house, walking around. Only, when I check, I can never find anything, and the doors and windows are always still locked."

He could think of a dozen ways to explain that. "Could be a raccoon in the attic."

Maxi shook her head. "No, I have my fair share of issues with critters, believe me. But I'm pretty sure raccoons can't drive."

Sahara and Miles looked at each other.

Maxi started pacing again. "I woke up one morning and my car was parked in a different spot from where I'd left it. I know because I always park it in the same place."

Houses made noises. He could discount that, especially since even she said she hadn't found anything. But this? "Someone moved your car?"

"It didn't move itself."

"Could you have left it in gear or something?" Sahara asked. "Was it on a hill?"

"It was moved from the driveway facing the house to the side yard turned away from the pond. Not on a hill."

"And you're sure you didn't—"

"What?" she challenged, glaring at Miles. "Stagger in drunk and park in a stupid place that didn't make any sense and then—of course, because I was so drunk—not remember it?"

He'd have to see the area before he could come up with an explanation for that one. "I wasn't accusing you of anything."

"I think you were." She glared a second more, then turned away. "Ever since then I've kept it locked."

"You probably should have been doing that anyway."

Another red-eyed glare. "Sometimes things in the barn are rearranged from how I put them. Equipment and stuff." She paused by the window to look out. "One morning when I got up, I found the water turned on full blast in the kitchen sink. It had overflowed all over the floor."

"That's what you were cleaning?"

"No, that was a week ago. Last night I was doing a bigger job, scrubbing everything, including the oven. But I'm having a hard time getting ahead when a bunch of random, weird things keep happening."

Sahara sat back in her chair. "Well, if I believed in the paranormal, I'd say you have a ghost."

Maxi rubbed one eye tiredly. "I don't believe in ghosts, so I need to find out what's really going on. I didn't know where to go. There's no one else I trust. I didn't want to bother you, Miles, but waking up on the ground, with everything so pitch-black I could barely figure out where I was, well, I don't mind telling you, it scared me half to death." She shuddered. "I haven't been back to the house yet, but I do need to go there because the cats will be waiting to be fed."

Miles slowly nodded. She'd said a lot, but he asked only one question. "Cats?"

After asking Enoch to take Maxi to the waiting area right outside her office, Sahara requested a private word with Miles.

"Business talk," she told Maxi. "I'll only keep him a moment."

Miles waited, arms crossed, as Sahara closed the door, then sat her shapely tush on the edge of her desk, braced her hands flat behind her and crossed her long legs at the ankles.

After a lengthy, assessing look, she asked, "What do you think?"

He didn't bother pretending to misunderstand. "That she's leaving out major chunks of the story."

Sahara nodded. "Not a lot of that makes sense, does it?"

"Almost none of it," Miles agreed. "I think she was drugged, but the scenario she laid out is tough to swallow."

"You don't buy that a stranger came to the house, drugged her for reasons unbeknownst to her, carried her outside, laid her gently in the yard, then left without taking advantage of her vulnerable state?"

He snorted. "Do you?"

She gave it some thought before answering. "I don't know. It's almost too bizarre *not* to be true. She's definitely scared. That's genuine."

Yeah, and he hated it. "I'll figure out what's going on. She'll have to fess up, though." Once she did, he'd take charge.

Of everything.

"You want her to 'fess up' about other men, I presume? She said she hasn't been involved with anyone since you."

Miles wasn't buying it. "Why would a total stranger want to bother her?"

"Now, there's the big question—motive." After a thoughtful moment, Sahara said, "It's hard to believe she kicked you out of bed."

Shit. Stiffening, Miles grumbled, "I probably shouldn't have said that."

"I mean," she continued, "look at you. You're such a specimen."

One thing he'd learned while working at Body Armor: Sahara Silver had a twisted sense of humor, and she didn't mind bludgeoning others with it, even her employees. "You're being ridiculous."

"Not a single blush, huh?" She feigned disappointment. "I suppose you have to realize the impact you have."

Impact? He must not have had much, given that Maxi had walked away. "Knock it off already. This is serious."

"Very serious, if what she's said is true. What I find interesting is that you appear to be jealous of this other man that she may or may not have been involved with, and that shocks me. After all, she came to you."

"To hire me." Not *just* because she wanted him back in her bed.

Not because he'd had a damned *impact*.

"You don't like those dynamics, with her being your employer of sorts? Well, consider this scenario. What if some psycho saw her at...say the grocery store? Or the gas station? She's an attractive woman. Even in her ensemble today, I could see that."

"She's beautiful." And sexy as sin, and hot, and—

"And what if our psycho followed her home and realized she lived all alone, with no close neighbors?"

His heart started beating harder. "You think that's a possibility?"

"You know, my brother practically raised me here at the agency. I've seen so many wicked, unbelievable things that I know anything is possible."

Everyone believed Sahara's brother was dead—except Sahara. She'd taken over running the agency, but Miles didn't think she'd ever give up looking for her brother. "You believe that scenario, even if the supposed psycho didn't do anything more than move Maxi from inside to outside?" How did that make sense?

"Who knows what's in the mind of a lunatic?" Sahara brushed back her long hair. "Perhaps that was just his first salvo. He could be building up to something, gaining courage as he goes along."

"Fuck." He really hated that idea.

"Perhaps," she continued, "he's hoping to weaken her resolve, and then he can swoop in to be her hero."

"Not happening." That'd be his first rule. As long as he was hanging around to play protector, no other dude would be horning in.

Eyeing his clenched hands and aggressive stance, Sahara smiled with approval. "I think you care for her, Miles, or you wouldn't be all grumpy instead of your usual jovial self. More than that, I think she cares for you or she wouldn't have come to you when she needed help. I *think*," she stressed, "that she has a rather fantastical story to tell, one that many people wouldn't believe, but she's trusting you with it and that should count for a lot." She straightened and walked around to her chair in a clear dismissal. "But then, what do I know? I just run this place."

"Private," Miles stated as he steered down the long, bumpy gravel drive lined by concealing trees and shrubs. The woods hid the house until you turned the last curve where the cleared land spread out in all its lacking glory.

He parked where she indicated, his gaze scouring the house, barn and pond. Without comment, he came around to open her door. She'd already stepped out, and of course, the cats knew it.

Miles stared in awe as the animals converged from everywhere. They dropped out of trees, crawled out from under bushes, ran up from the pond. There had to be thirty of them currently fascinated by having a new face around. As she'd told him, she didn't get visitors.

The majority of the cats were black, a few white, a few mixed and a few yellow. Some were huge, others petite. Long and lean, chubby and squat. They were all adorable.

They'd been her grandmother's beloved pets and now they depended on her.

Many were feral, coming only close enough to eat the food put out for them twice a day. Others would twine around her legs, and some insisted on being held.

As Miles gazed around at the property, he drew a deep breath. "The air smells really good here."

"Fresh country air." She enjoyed it, too. But now?

She looked over at the small farmhouse she'd inherited. One and a half stories with a painted deck off the upstairs bedroom that created a cover for the front porch below. Every morning she had her coffee on that porch and listened to the birds singing, watched the deer at the pond, and of course, she petted cats. Despite the work that needed to be done, she could truly love it here.

If it weren't for the menace.

Staring at the house now, she felt dread go up her spine. *No one will drive me away.* Her grandmother had trusted her, and by God, she wouldn't let her down.

Of course, she felt a lot safer now with Miles at her side. She gestured toward the barn. "The cat food is in there in a big barrel. I should take care of that first."

He nodded, his critical gaze going over her as if looking for signs of exhaustion or illness. "You want to wait here?"

"Nope." Determined as she might be to stand her ground, for now she didn't want to be alone.

He looked divided, his gaze going back to the dark barn. "It might be better—"

"I go where you go."

The way he studied her face again, she almost squirmed. "All right." He offered his hand. "Let's go."

She hesitated. Being close to him did crazy things to her. His hands, especially, sparked memories of all the ways he'd touched her, encouraged her, driven her wild. She caught her breath, feeling heat blossom.

She still couldn't believe she'd forced herself on him in the office, making him hold her when he'd been clear that he was angry with her.

But, God, she'd needed his touch. She'd needed to feel safe. So she'd swallowed her pride and, despite his obvious—and justified—annoyance with her, she'd borrowed his strength.

And he'd let her. Even clearly irritated with her, he'd been supportive, going with her to the doctor's, treating her gently.

Much as he'd always treated her before she'd run away.

Hopefully, once she explained to him, he'd understand. Not that she could recapture what she'd lost...

With his hand still outstretched, Miles said, "It's not an invitation to get naked, Maxi. It's just holding hands."

No, for her and her sensitized nerve endings, it was so much more.

Grumbling to herself for being a fool, she slipped her hand into his, and all those amazing contrasts converged on her. She was of average height for a woman, but Miles was such a big guy, so ripped and solid and capable that she felt petite in comparison.

The way his strong fingers curved so warmly around hers seemed so blasted *right*. He shortened his long stride to match hers, considerate without having to think about it.

Being here with him, she could almost convince herself that things would be okay. He was that type of guy, always upbeat with a crooked smile that melted a person's heart.

Until today, she'd never seen him annoyed.

"You're quiet," he said, his thumb brushing over her knuckles. "Holding up okay?"

"Yes." After Dr. Brummel confirmed that she'd been drugged, she'd been badly shaken. She'd known, but still, she'd been hoping for another explanation.

There hadn't been one—and she still didn't know *why*.

"It's okay if you're not, you know. The doc said you could be feeling the effects another twenty-four hours."

"My head's clearer by the minute." They'd driven back to her farm with the windows open and the rush of fresh air entering Miles's SUV had helped to clear out the cobwebs.

Most of her recovery, however, had to do with having Miles at her side. Fear, she'd quickly learned, was debilitating.

"Okay, then," he said. "Cats first, then the house, and then we talk."

She dreaded going back inside, but because she knew she'd have to, she only nodded. *I'm not alone now.*

From the day she'd met Miles, she'd wanted him. It was like a craving. He'd smiled at her across the bar, and she'd been ready to say a resounding "yes!" to a question he hadn't yet asked. In fact, only a few hours after their first hello, she was the one to ask, "Want to go someplace more private?"

Luckily his apartment hadn't been far from the bar.

She didn't blame herself for falling hard at the first sight of him. Late twenties, with dark brown hair, green eyes showcased by thick dark lashes, and that endearing smile... What woman wouldn't go after him?

Even better than his face was his body. Tall, broad in the chest and shoulders, carved with muscle. It boggled her mind that one man could be so incredibly perfect. He used to be a professional athlete and it showed. In the two months since she'd last seen him, he'd bulked up even more. Now he looked downright imposing.

But it was his personality that had really done her in. She'd wanted, *needed*, a physical distraction from her troubles.

Miles had turned out to be so much more.

"What are you thinking?"

That I was a fool for walking away. She couldn't tell him that, though. "Just wondering what you must think, seeing all the cats and dead grass and the repairs that need to be made."

"I'm thinking you have a lot to tell me. But if you need to nap, I can wait until tonight."

"No, I don't want to sleep." She didn't know how she'd ever sleep peacefully again.

Someone drugged me.

It kept popping up in her brain, kick-starting the paralyzing panic all over again. As if he understood, Miles tightened his fingers around hers, and that helped her shake it off. She concentrated on looking around the grounds while leading him to the barn.

The building sat a good distance behind the house, opposite of the pond, still sturdy but in need of paint. "Grandma used to keep a horse, cow and two goats in here. The farm animals were gone before I inherited the property, though."

"And a bunch of cats took their place?"

"Seems like. That's how I got the house, you know. My grandmother knew no one else would stay and take care of them. She left me a letter with her will, saying she was counting on me to do my duty."

"Your duty, huh?"

She didn't want to think about that either. "I've been catching them and getting them fixed. See the cats with notched ears? That means they've either been spayed or neutered, and they get a general checkup at the same time so they get their shots and checked for ear mites and fleas."

"Must be expensive."

"It just takes a lot of time. Dr. Miller, the vet, is giving me a discount, since I have so many cats here. He said my grandma would bring them in every so often, but it was a losing battle. She'd catch three, and at the same time another would have a litter of four."

Miles turned thoughtful. "You take the cats to him, or he comes here?"

"I take them to him. I told you, no one comes here."

"How far away is he?"

"It's a twenty-minute drive. Once you get on the main road, it's not far at all." She pointed in the distance. "Opposite direction of how we came, and it's the nearest civilization."

"Not sure any of this feels all that civilized."

She grinned. "Right. There's a grocery and hardware store, a bank. The vet. Things like that. If you want to go to a movie theater or do any real shopping, it's forty minutes back the way we came."

"The cats are everywhere," Miles noted, but not with disgust, not like he thought she ought to run them all off, or worse, destroy them.

She saw that he, too, was busy looking around for signs of danger. Neither of them saw anything but the beautiful trees and the brown grass in need of rain, the pond and the birds.

It was so beautiful.

And somehow treacherous.

The barn door stood ajar. Before Miles could wonder about it, she explained. "I leave it like that. Some of the cats get in there to sleep." When she reached for the door, Miles held her back.

"Let me." He gave it a good pull. As the heavy door swung out, sunlight poured in, slanting across golden straw, sending the shadows to recede. Dust motes floated in the air and earthy scents escaped. He stepped in cautiously, giving his eyes a moment to adjust to the dimmer interior.

They both jumped when a feral cat leaped from the loft and shot out past them.

Hand to her heart, Maxi said, "Blast, they get me every time."

He laughed but said, "You have reason to be nervous and I'm not used to cats."

"They appear at the darnedest times." Like when she was trying to sneak into her own house.

Maxi sighed. She was tired, frazzled and ravenous. More than anything, she wanted breakfast—even though it was now time for lunch—and then she wanted a shower. Knowing someone had touched her made her feel dirty. She wanted to scrub from head to toes in hot water.

Yet nothing would get done until she'd taken care of the cats. They depended on her, and they looked disappointed that she hadn't yet fed them. "There's the barrel. I have to screw the lid on tight or the raccoons open it and it's a free-for-all. Every bit of the food would be gone in one day."

Grinning, Miles said, "I never pictured you on a farm dealing with a herd of cats and raccoons."

She waved a hand down at her hideous outfit. "Yeah, I never pictured it either."

"Actually, you look cute."

Her incredulous gaze shot to his, but he didn't notice as he wrestled the lid off the barrel. He managed it a whole lot easier than she usually did, but then, he was made of muscle.

Cats had followed them in, and now more gathered as he opened their food source. Meows filled the air. It was tough to move with so many animals twining around their legs.

After he almost tripped, Miles said, "Impatient, aren't they?"

"I'm late."

"What time do you usually feed them?"

"By seven thirty or so at the latest. Generally I feed them, then get my coffee and sit on the porch to enjoy the morning before I get started on chores."

"Somehow, that doesn't sound awful."

"No," she agreed. "It was actually a nice routine." If it weren't for so many different things conspiring against her, she'd be loving life right about now.

Several of the cats were trying to stretch up to the top of the barrel. Smiling, Maxi pointed to the long metal channel against the wall behind the barrel. "I use the large scoop inside to fill that trough."

He laughed. "A trough for cats."

"Hey, it was the only thing I could think of to get them all fed at the same time."

"You're resourceful."

Was that two compliments in a row? Maybe he wasn't as

angry as he'd seemed. More likely, it was his compassionate nature trying to make her more at ease.

But…she couldn't be the only one feeling the sexual tension. Around Miles, it hit her like a tsunami. Even under the awful circumstances, she wasn't immune to his appeal. In fact, because of everything she'd just gone through, she felt even more drawn to him and his strength.

Watching as he loaded the scoop, she said, "It's actually a pig trough, but when you see them eating…well, let's just say it fits."

The cats carried on as if they hadn't eaten in days, instead of just being late for breakfast. By the time Miles filled the trough, the cats had lined up side by side and were devouring their chow.

"That has to be half of a bag right there."

"I buy in bulk," she said. "I have to store the extra bags in the house, though, or the raccoons—"

"Throw a party?" Miles grinned down at her.

"They do!"

He laughed, but slowly, as his gaze roamed her face, the grin faded. He removed a dried weed from her hair, tucked a wayward lock behind her ear, then brushed his thumb over her cheek. He leaned toward her.

Her toes curled in the rubber boots. God, she'd missed his kiss so much, the taste of him, the feel of his firm lips and his clever tongue and—

"Wait." She flattened a hand to his chest.

Expression enigmatic, Miles cleaned a smudge off her cheek. "You're exhausted."

Oh God. She'd freaked out over nothing.

Get a grip, Maxi.

After clearing her throat, she said, "Yes, and it shows."

He flicked the end of her nose. "You still look cute."

He'd said it again! Frazzled from the mixed signals, she

propped her hands on her hips. "You're either super horny or just trying to make me feel better."

"How about a little of both?"

Shivering with awareness, Maxi took a safe step back before she thought too much about that big, hard body of his settling over her. "The thing is, I haven't brushed my teeth yet this morning. In fact, not since yesterday morning. I would have last night before I went to bed, if I'd had a normal night. But normal nights around here are hard to come by."

"I wasn't coming on to you, babe. Your teeth are safe from me, so relax, okay?"

"Trying." *Unsuccessfully.* On top of the dull headache still crowding the back of her skull, too many conflicting emotions bombarded her. "The reason I stopped you—"

"You were clear enough on why I'm here. I won't be pressuring you, so stop worrying about that."

Blast. If she was honest with herself, and she probably should be, the reason she'd thought of Miles the second she realized she needed help was because she wanted the closeness unique to him, not only his overpowering sex appeal, but the sense of security he gave her when he focused on her so intimately.

Sure, she'd sworn off guys. Her track record made that the sensible thing to do. But then she'd gotten to know Miles...

She might have expected him to be antagonistic after the way she'd ended things, but she hadn't figured on him actually caring, had assumed she'd be only one in a line of women he knew. Obviously it *had* bothered him, probably because he wasn't used to any type of rejection, and now this was going wrong fast.

Trying to recover a little ground, she explained, "I wasn't exactly worried." *Hopeful, maybe, but not worried.*

Staring up at the sky, Miles watched a turkey vulture, wings spread wide as it glided overhead with little effort.

"The thing is, we do know each other." This time he took her hand, folding it securely in his, and started them on their way. "Granted it was only those three times, but I can't treat you like a stranger."

No, they definitely weren't strangers. In many ways, Miles knew her body better than she did. "I wouldn't expect you to." She'd specifically gone to him because she *did* know him—and odd as it seemed, she was completely at ease with him.

Always had been.

That first time with him had been nothing short of amazing. She hadn't guessed that sex could be like that, so intense and incredibly hot, yet also tender, too. In comparison, what she'd known before Miles was just rutting.

She'd expected one thing and gotten something entirely different. Something so much better. Lights on. Inhibitions gone. He'd served the purpose of making her forget her worries. But he'd also made her hungry for more.

The second time she'd given in and looked for him had turned out even better, and when she hadn't been able to resist seeing him a third time, she'd known she was getting in too deep.

"How about you show me the house, let me look things over, then we can grab some food before I head home to get supplies?"

Her feet stopped working. So did her heart.

When his arm stretched out—his hand still holding hers—Miles turned back to face her. "What?"

"You're leaving?" Renewed panic clawed through her.

He tugged her up alongside him, then slipped his arm over her shoulders and gave her a comforting squeeze. "Yes, and you're going with me."

He said that as if that had been the plan all along. "I am?" Well, then, she could handle that. Tucked against his lean body with his muscled arm encircling her, the panic eased away as quickly as it had come.

"We came straight here from the doctor's so you could feed the cats and take care of yourself. But I need my things, since I'm going to be staying here, right?"

Of course he did. She nodded.

"I'm guessing we need several security cameras and alarms, too. It's still early enough, so I'd like to get everything done today."

She kept thinking she was dealing okay—until something else set her off, then she went to pieces. Weakness sucked.

Hard as she tried, insults kept coming back to her, all the expectations for failure. She had a lot to prove, all to herself. Miles, hopefully, would help her with that.

He, at least, wasn't weak. "Of course."

"You're safe now, Maxi." His arm tightened in an affectionate hug that brought her into brief contact with his hard, hot body. "You know that, right?"

She knew he still had the power to help her forget everything but her need of him. Like now, with her thoughts all focused on his ripped body.

"Maxi?"

Even though she wasn't convinced, she nodded. "Before we go, I have an unusual favor to ask."

"You're paying me. Ask away."

Hmm. She didn't appreciate how he'd put that, as if he was only here for the money. She didn't buy that. As he'd said, she could have come to him directly and he'd have helped.

If that was how he wanted to play it, though, she wouldn't debate it with him. Not yet.

Tonight would be soon enough.

She looked up at him. "After we eat, do you think you could keep watch while I shower and make myself presentable?"

Surprise lit his eyes before he gave a slow nod. "Yeah, I think I can manage that." This time as they walked, it was without tripping over cats, since they were all still eating. "Maybe now's a good time for you to tell me how you want this to work."

How it should work? If she had her way, he'd be with her 24/7, including in the shower and while she slept.

If she could sleep.

Instead, she lied, saying, "I thought you could use the downstairs bedroom and bath, and I'd use them upstairs."

"Hell."

She jumped on that. "What? That doesn't work for you? You had something else in mind?"

He was silent for a bit, his jaw flexing. "Let's see the house first, then I'll make recommendations."

Recommendations, her butt. Had he hoped for an entirely separate place to stay? An apartment over the barn? She almost snorted. If he wanted to sleep with the cats in a pile of hay, let him.

Fat lot of good that would do her when something else happened.

Dejected, she followed along without saying anything. Before they got too far into this arrangement, she needed to clear the air about why she'd walked away from him, when everything in her had begged her to stay, to push for more.

Perhaps during the drive back to his place. For now, she'd take comfort in the fact he was here with her, and she wouldn't have to face the next catastrophe alone.

Unfortunately, the next catastrophe happened almost as soon as she stepped into the house.

CHAPTER THREE

Miles stepped ahead of Maxi on the back porch and tried the door. It opened. "Not locked?"

"It's how I got back in to get my purse. It wasn't locked then either and you can bet I didn't bother once I had what I needed. I just got away."

"Understandable." He stepped into the area and looked to the left at the small bedroom, then to the right up the stairs. Maxi's room would be up there. He'd check that out in a minute.

Peeking past him, she asked, "You hear anything?"

"No."

"Thank God." She stepped in around him, saying, "The kitchen is this way. Let's go there first and—"

The second she stepped around the wall onto the old-fashioned tiles in the kitchen, her feet came out from under her and she landed flat on her back with a thud. Her bottom half was in the kitchen, her head and shoulders visible from the hall.

With a curse, Miles jogged forward, glanced around for any signs of danger, saw nothing more than a hideous kitchen and knelt beside her. "Stay still," he said, before she could move.

She wheezed, squeezing her eyes shut.

Of course, he saw the puddle of dark oil on the floor beneath her. He twisted around, looking into every corner that he could see, but the house was quiet, and they appeared to be alone. There were no remnants left behind, not even the empty can from where the oil had been poured.

"Hell of a spill." He was so pissed he could have chewed nails, but he tried to sound calm. "You okay?"

Gulping air, her expression pained, she didn't attempt to answer.

"You knocked the wind out of yourself." He pulled her arms straight up and said, "Try to calm down. Breathe slowly."

She caught her breath with a vengeance, hissing, *"Blast."*

"Easy now." He helped her to sit up...in the oil. "I'm guessing that wasn't here when you came in for your purse and boots?"

"No." Disgusted, she lifted her hands, now slick, and curled her lip. "It's soaked into my shorts."

Keeping a hand on her, Miles looked around. "I don't see it anywhere else, and there are no tracks." But good Lord, the house... Now that she was okay, he *really* saw it. "You actually live here?"

She shot him a deadly glare. "Yes." And then, as if a dare, she asked, *"Why?"*

He wasn't touching that. "Just doesn't look like you." Hell, it looked like a grandma's place—from maybe a century ago. "I'm guessing everything is original?"

"Pretty much." She started to stand, slipped to her butt again, and Miles stayed her.

"Wait." He got to his feet first, saw a roll of paper towels on the counter and grabbed them. He ripped off several, giving them to her so she could clean her hands. Then, being sure to keep out of the oil, he caught her under her arms and lifted her upright. "Hold on to my shoulders and I'll help you out of those boots."

Grumbling, she said, "My feet are probably sweaty now. This sucks so badly."

Trying to hide his smile, he promised, "I'll hold my breath."

"I'm going to ruin your shirt."

"It's a black T-shirt. You can't ruin it."

"Suit yourself." Her small hands settled on him—and that put her breasts far too close to his face.

Forcing himself to look down, he tugged off first one boot, waiting as she put that foot to the side of the mess, then he removed the other. Her feet were small and narrow, yes, a little sweaty, and incredibly cute.

He glanced up the length of her long slim legs, pausing at the denim zipper in her soft, worn, body-hugging cutoffs. A drop of oil rolled down the outside of her left leg. "Your shorts are dripping."

Letting out a tiny, shaky breath, she shifted her feet. "Yeah."

Absurd the way lust bit into him. Hell, someone had terrorized her last night, they'd returned to a million hungry cats and another prank in her house, and all he could think about was leaning forward and pressing his face to her belly, going lower, breathing her in, tasting her.

He loved the sounds Maxi made while her climax built.

When he felt her hands tightening on his shoulders, he murmured, "Maybe you should drop them, too?" Somehow, he'd keep it together.

"Yeah." But she didn't move.

Up to him, then. Damn. "Let's see if we can do this without getting the oil anywhere else." He reached for the snap to her shorts.

Maxi drew in her breath and held it.

Trying to remember that he had a plan, he said as he slid down her zipper, "Maybe that shower should come first?" It wasn't deliberate, but his knuckles grazed her.

"First?" she croaked.

He glanced up and got caught in her dark-eyed gaze. "Before we grab something to eat."

"Oh. Eat. Right."

What had she thought? That he meant sex? Hell of an idea, but the timing was all wrong.

And why was she thinking that anyway? He could understand how *he* got distracted, but she was terrified, and that should damn well keep her focused.

It was enough that he had to fight himself; he couldn't fight her, too.

Tamping down natural urges, Miles worked the snug shorts over her hips.

Her fingers dug into his muscles as he bent to help her step out—and then she stood there in her panties.

The lady had a killer body, no doubt about it.

But he'd known other sexy women. There was just something special about Maxi.

Maybe the fact that she'd walked away from him so easily.

With that reminder in mind, Miles straightened back to his feet. "Stay put while I look around. I don't see or hear anyone, but I want to make sure whoever dumped the oil isn't still here."

"No one is." She clutched at his arm. "Every inch of this old house creaks if someone moves, even in the basement."

Miles gently pried her hands away. "I'm going to look anyway." He wouldn't take chances, and it'd give him a minute to get his urges under control. "Don't move."

She swallowed hard and nodded, already glancing back at the front door.

Would she do as he asked, or would he find her in the SUV, in her panties, ready to go?

Staying alert to any other booby traps, Miles went into the kitchen. That room was the biggest time warp, with a white cast-iron sink top, a stove that had to be antique and a small refrigerator...on legs. He'd never seen anything like it.

An old ruffled curtain hung under the sink instead of a door, and the yellow linoleum floor was a bit bright, especially since it ran into yellow tile that came halfway up the wall.

Directly to the left was an equally dated bathroom. A row of open shelving divided the kitchen from the dining room, which opened into a small living room. The front door, locked, led to a trellis-enclosed covered porch.

He briefly went through each room, not surprised to find them very tidy, but shocked all the same that Maxi Nevar now called this place home. Nothing he knew about her fit in the setting. Then again, seeing her with chipped nails, rubber ducky boots and tangled hair didn't fit either.

As he passed back through, he saw a book and wineglass on the end table next to the puffy floral couch. The glass was empty, the book closed.

Well, hell.

He returned to where he'd left her, standing there wearing an oversize flannel shirt, pink panties and a load of uncertainty. More than anything, he wanted to draw her close, hug her, reassure her.

Then do nasty, hot, sweaty things with her.

He shook his head and, indicting the door next to the stairs, asked, "Basement?"

"Yes. But it should be locked."

He tried it. "You're right." There was even a dead bolt on it.

"Cat food is stored down there, but otherwise, I don't use the basement."

"I can see that." She had it locked up tight. Later, he'd explore down there. "I'll look upstairs now."

"Sure, why not." She turned to go.

Much as he'd enjoy trailing behind her, getting a great view of her ass on the stairs, he had to put safety first. "You wait here."

"I hired you for a reason. I go where you go."

He saw she was serious, and probably with good reason, so he nodded. "Stay behind me, then."

"Not a problem."

He had to duck to get under the lowered ceiling at the base of the narrow stairs. He suspected someone had converted the attic to living space years ago. "Are these the stairs where your grandmother fell?"

"Yes."

She said nothing else, so he didn't press her. God knew she'd been through enough for one day.

The stairs turned a sharp corner and then opened into a small study with a desk, chair and file cabinet. The only window in that room was a skylight overhead.

From there he went into a more updated bathroom, which meant it wasn't more than a few decades old, yet no one would call it modern either. Her bedroom was next, a rectangular room barely big enough for a bed and nightstand. The lure would be the double doors that opened to a balcony above the porch below.

"Where do you keep your clothes?"

"In here." She slid back a pocket door to show a big walk-in closet nearly the same size as the bedroom.

"I take it you put this in?"

"First thing."

She'd spared no expense. Bright lights showed off detailed shelving, multiple wardrobes and niches for things like shoes and scarves, with a dressing table in the middle. She'd filled every inch except for a mirrored door in the back of the room that, Miles discovered, opened into yet another room.

Ducking down again, he stepped through to a clichéd attic space. Bare rafters loomed overhead, plywood flooring squeaked under his weight and air whistled through a single skinny window in the center of the back wall. Boxes, trunks and random pieces of old furniture cast long shadows over the cluttered floor. A single bare bulb swung from the ceiling, but when he pulled the long string, it didn't work.

Miles didn't say it, but given everything that had happened, it was creepy as hell.

Soon as they were back in the main room, he asked, "Why do you sleep up here?"

"The bedroom downstairs was my grandmother's. It didn't feel right, taking it over."

But she wanted him to sleep there?

"Don't worry," she said, maybe reading his thoughts. "Everything has been packed away and the bedding is freshly washed."

Great. It was still Granny's. "Should I look under the bed?"

Her smile didn't hide her exhaustion. "If you want, but I've got so many storage bins under there, nothing more than a mouse could fit, and mice aren't brave enough to come around with so many cats."

Unable to help himself, he touched her cheek. Her eyes were heavy and smudged with fatigue. "You need a nap."

"I need a shower." Glancing over her shoulder at her own butt, she wiggled. "That oil soaked through."

A dozen inappropriate comments came to mind, but Miles banked them all. "I can either go down and get food started—" although how he'd find his way around that kitchen, he didn't know "—or I can wait right here while you get cleaned up."

"You won't mind giving me ten minutes?"

"You're the boss." As soon as he said it, he regretted it. He'd meant it to be teasing, but damn it, she looked wounded.

Maxi being Maxi, she rallied and said, "Don't you forget it." She gestured to the bed. "Get comfortable if you want. I'll hurry."

Settle on her bed? Breathe her scent in the pillows? Not a good idea. "You can take your time."

"If you heard my stomach grumbling, you'd know I can't."

He stood in the doorway while she went through the closet

and pulled faded jeans from a shelf, a peachy bra and panties from a drawer, and a white tank top off a hanger.

Crazy that seeing her like this hit him so hard. She kept the flannel pulled down in back to hide her rounded behind, but she had beautiful legs, and her long dark blond hair, even uncombed, looked sexy as hell.

He moved as she stepped out again and started for the bathroom.

At the door, she paused. "If anything happens, I want you to be able to come in, so I won't lock it."

It took him a second to find his voice, then he went for teasing again. "Planning on screaming?"

She held the pile of clothes close to her chest. "Someone was in my house again. How, I don't know. But the oil wasn't there when I left or I would have stepped in it."

He nodded, acknowledging that. "We'll buy new locks today, too." Going one further, he whispered, "I promise it's going to be okay." Somehow, he'd make it so.

She managed a strained smile. "In case I haven't said it yet… thank you for being here with me."

Before he could answer, she closed the door. Seconds later, he heard the creaking of pipes.

With nothing else to do, his gaze went to her bed. In no time at all, his thoughts were out of control, focused on things they shouldn't be—like how much he wanted her.

Again.

Still.

And here he'd started to think that working at Body Armor would be a piece of cake.

"This," Maxi said, licking her lips with a groan, "was a much better idea than food at home."

Miles smiled while sinking his white teeth into a loaded burger. "Quicker, for sure."

They sat in his roomy SUV, him half-turned to face her, one arm loosely draped over the steering wheel, a bag of fast food between them. He'd found a recreation area near the store they were going to and parked beneath a shade tree to keep the sun from reflecting off the black exterior. From their position, they could see kids playing on swings, people walking dogs and couples holding hands. With the windows down, a summer breeze kept it from being too hot.

Maxi felt much better now that she was clean and dressed, her hair braided down her back. Before they'd left the house, she'd cleaned up the mess and put her clothes in the wash, but she didn't have hopes of the oil coming out. The shorts would no doubt join her growing pile of "work" clothes, meaning they'd be appropriate for the farm, but nowhere else.

Miles had been silent as she'd put her book back on the shelf and washed her wineglass. She didn't know if he believed her about what had happened, and she wasn't sure if she even wanted to know. He was with her, and for now, that was more than enough.

When she glanced at him, she found him watching her in that intense, very intimate way of his that made her breath catch in her chest.

It would be nice to know what he was thinking, but instead she asked, "Should we make a list of what we need?"

"I already did."

"When?"

"While you were in the shower. I found a pen and paper in your study."

He hadn't left her. He'd stayed right there, very close, as promised.

It was ridiculous to react, given nothing had happened; she'd finished her shower without a single disturbance.

But knowing that she could trust him not to budge mattered. A lot. "It's too bad we couldn't find what we needed in the little town closer by."

"I had to come this way for my stuff anyway. We'll go to my apartment last, then head back to your house. I should still have time to get a few things set up."

"How extensive is our list? I know you mentioned locks and a security camera."

"I'm thinking several, actually. Someone is sneaking onto your property. I want to know who."

"How do you think they're getting in?"

"No idea. But that reminds me. I called my friend Leese."

"Who?"

"Leese Phelps. He used to be a fighter, too, but he was the first one to move to Body Armor. It seems to be a good fit for him."

"You called him while I was in the shower?"

"Yeah. I explained your situation. Thought it couldn't hurt to get an unbiased perspective on things."

Meaning he considered his own perspective biased—because they'd slept together?

Embarrassment disturbed her peaceful moment. His friend probably thought she was crazy or, like Miles, assumed she'd been drunk and imagined it all. "Aren't you the busy beaver."

After putting the last fry in his mouth, Miles said, "You were only a few feet away, buck naked and wet. It seemed like a good idea to keep busy."

Maxi blinked at him, the embarrassment forgotten. He kept saying things that she didn't know how to take. Was he mad at her or not? Did he want her as much as she wanted him?

Or were comments like that supposed to be jokes?

Since she didn't have any answers, she steered the topic back to his friend. "What did Leese have to say?"

"He took it seriously, if that's what you're asking. You'd have to know Leese. He was made for this shit. Being analytical about danger suits him way better than professional fighting ever did."

"So he made suggestions?"

Miles nodded. "I'll get security lights put up today, enough to light up the barn and down to the pond. Anyone sneaking around will be easily seen. I'll add extra locks to the windows and doors—anywhere someone might be able to get in. Oh, and we'll throw out all your food, especially your wine."

"Throw out all my food?"

"Well, I'm not eating it. Think about it. If what you told me was accurate—"

Accurate? At least he hadn't outright accused her of lying.

"—then someone might've drugged whatever you ate or drank. I assume you don't want to chance it?"

"Of course not." Now she couldn't even trust her food? "How would someone have—"

"No idea how it works. Leese is looking into it for me. By the way, he and Justice might come out tomorrow."

She was just about to take her last bite of hamburger when he said that. "Tomorrow?" She lowered the burger. "To my farmhouse?"

"Yeah. Leese trained me for Body Armor, and Justice is great with security systems. Assuming you can afford a decent one, he'll help with that. I know what to buy, and how to set it up, but again, it's good to have fresh eyes looking over things."

"So I'm going to be paying for three of you?"

Miles snorted. "No, they're friends. I'm the only one on the clock, and only because you went to Sahara."

"Well, I wanted to be fair." Done eating, Maxi put the trash into the bag. "Your Ms. Silver is an impressive lady."

"Yeah, she is, and she knows it. If you looked up *confidence* in the dictionary, you'd find Sahara smiling back at you."

Maxi laughed. "She did give that impression."

"You made an impression on her, too."

"A lousy one." It made her shudder to remember the horrid reflection looking back at her in the mirror right before her shower. And Miles's boss, that classy lady, had seen her.

"Not so. Sahara had only nice things to say about you."

Deciding to test the waters a little, Maxi asked, "Does that mean she, at least, didn't think I was making it up?"

Unfazed, Miles shrugged. "Neither of us is quite sure what to think, to be honest. But I'm telling you right now, this will be easier if you tell me about any guys you've been involved with."

Even though she'd suspected he didn't believe her, his blasé confession still annoyed her. "Sure."

A little more alert, Miles waited.

"Let's see. There was..." She met his gaze. "None."

His slight tension eased into frustration. "Seriously? No one?"

"I can only say it so many ways."

"Okay, forget involvement." He slashed a hand through the air. "Whether you were sleeping with anyone or not—"

"I wasn't."

"—there has to have been a guy. A casual date? Someone you only talked to?"

"Why won't you believe me?"

He leveled a look on her. "Because I can't bend my brain around the idea of you being alone. With the way you look, you must've had a dozen men after you."

Warmed by the compliment, she pretended to think about it again. "Now that you mention it, I have talked to Woody a few times."

His back went straight. "Woody?"

"Woody Barstow. Nice guy. Very laid-back, friendly. Kind to the cats."

Brows coming down, Miles said, "Maybe I need to check up on Woody."

"Sure. He's my nearest neighbor at about eight miles away."

"Why didn't you mention him before?"

"Because I'm not involved with him." She took a final sip of her cola, then added, "Plus, he's almost eighty."

The most comical look came over Miles's face, and she couldn't help but laugh.

"I'm trying to be serious." When she continued to snicker, he muttered, "It's not that funny."

"I'm sorry."

"Don't be." A different expression entered his eyes. "You really haven't been with anyone?"

That sobered her real quick. "I need to explain, don't I?"

"Wouldn't hurt."

That was what he thought. So, where to start? "I sort of have to go…well, way back. Be patient, okay?"

"I'm all ears."

"When I was eighteen, I thought I was in love."

Expression arrested, he repeated, "Eighteen?"

"Yeah." She shrugged. "Seven years ago, but it matters."

"Okay."

"Anyway, I was dating this older guy and I thought I was in love. My family didn't like him. They thought he was trouble."

Miles waited.

"And he was. Big trouble. It's a long, hideous story, but the shortened version is that one night, while we were all on vacation, he and his friends came in uninvited. They robbed us, did a lot of damage to irreplaceable heirlooms, destroyed and vandalized just for the fun of it." She looked down at her hands, now clasped together. Shame closed her throat, but she forced herself to finish. "He'd gotten the entry code from me."

Without censure, Miles asked, "You gave it to him?"

"No. But he watched when I punched it in."

"How do you know it was him?"

"Security cameras. They...did disgusting things on my sister's bed. Even on my mother's bed."

"On your bed?" he asked quietly.

"Yes." But as her family had said, she'd brought that on herself. They, however, hadn't. "You can imagine how my family reacted. They'd told me not to see him, told me he was no good, and I didn't listen. I argued, dramatically claimed we were in love, and then he proved them right and I was so ashamed, I didn't even know what to say."

Miles reached over one long arm to tweak her braid. "You were eighteen, Maxi. No one listens at eighteen. Sometimes we have to learn things the hard way."

"Well, I thought I had learned. I went a long time avoiding guys after that. Romance and guilt didn't mix so great." She drew a deep breath. "And then I met another guy a year ago."

"Wait." Miles shifted. "You went *how* long without getting serious?"

"Five years."

"So only casual dating—"

"You don't understand. My first boyfriend destroyed an antique my mother had inherited from her great-grandmother. My sister, who is fanatical about everything, wouldn't even go back in her room because of what he did in there. She moved out."

"Your dad?"

"He died when I was younger. It was just my mom, sister and me. My brother, who's eight years older, had already gone out on his own."

"Well, maybe your sis was just ready to move on, too."

"No, she rightly blamed me."

"Bullshit. There's nothing right about that."

"They would disagree."

"You were a victim, same as them."

"No, I'd set that fire. Getting burned was my own fault. Unfortunately, they got burned, too, and that's unforgivable."

Miles shook his head. "Let's get back to this new guy you're involved with."

"*Used* to be involved with," she corrected. "It fell apart when I caught him cheating." She gave him a stern frown. "I despise cheaters."

"Any intelligent, moral person would."

Mollified, she explained, "He didn't want it to end and continually made a pest of himself."

"If he didn't want it to end, he should have kept it in his pants."

Maxi snorted. "Yeah, that's basically what I told him. But while I was trying to deal with that, my mother passed away during a procedure."

"You said that once before. What type of procedure?"

Lord, she hated explaining it. "Mom was beautiful. She didn't need cosmetic surgery, but she liked it all the same. Seemed like every six months she was having something else done, always tweaking this and tightening that. She got it in her head that she wanted this extreme makeover, and I guess it was just too much. She died of cardiac arrest under anesthesia."

"Damn. So unnecessary."

She nodded. Very unnecessary. "My mom and I weren't really close, not since...well, since I was eighteen and everything happened."

A disapproving frown creased his brow. "Was she close with your sister?"

"Yes."

The frown darkened more. "That has to be tough."

"Not really. I mean, I'm used to it."

One fingertip brushed her cheek. "No one gets used to that."

That rough whisper teased over her senses. "There's so much you don't know about me." Things she needed to confess. "Even though that's the way I wanted it, at least with you, it wasn't the norm. Usually I'm an open book." She hadn't hidden from her failings. No, like a fool, she flaunted them.

"So flip a few pages for me."

She smiled with his jest. "I'll start with family." He needed to understand the many ways she'd disappointed them. "My sister is a fitness buff. She owns her own boutique gym for trendy people. Very exclusive, and very pricey. Harlow is one of those hard bodies...well, I guess like you." Maxi turned her head to stare out the window at the kids playing. That made it easier than looking at Miles. "I already told you about my brother. He was one of those 'top of the class' guys his whole life. Mom is a dynamo. There was no challenge that seemed too big to her." And then there was Maxi. A disappointment.

Miles waited, occasionally drifting his fingers over her bare shoulder in a way that felt comforting more than seductive.

"You should probably know," she finally said, "I'm the odd duck in my family. I love them and they love me, but we don't really fit together. I'm the underachiever. I was never super motivated about anything." Except the farmhouse, and that had turned into a living nightmare.

"You had a good job," Miles said. "That is, if you were really a personal shopper?"

God, it hurt, knowing he didn't believe anything about her. Not that she blamed him after she'd been deliberately elusive. But now...now she needed him to believe, to trust her as much as she trusted him. "I never lied to you about anything, I promise. I just didn't share much."

"Want to tell me why?"

"Gary—my ex—was all about trying to get back with me, especially after my grandma died and he knew I'd had two inheritances. With my dad already gone, everything came to Harlow, Neil and me. But there wasn't a lot of equity in how it was done and my sister and brother were...*are* furious with me for financial reasons."

She could feel Miles staring at her. She knew he had a lot of questions.

Instead of asking any of them, he cupped her shoulder in his big, warm hand and just waited quietly for her to continue.

This was why Miles had scared her so badly. He seemed *too* blasted perfect. The last two times she'd been drawn to a guy, she'd been horribly wrong. She no longer trusted her own judgment, but she also wasn't a fool. Being around Miles would mean falling hard and fast. If he turned out to be a creep, then what?

And even if he didn't, the last thing she needed was another complication in her life. Deep down to her bones, she knew that this was her chance for redemption.

But to accomplish that, she had to be strong.

Of course, she'd never counted on being harassed, terrorized and assaulted.

CHAPTER FOUR

Getting back to her explanations, Maxi said, "The financial mess happened when my mother mostly cut me out of her will to motivate me." Her mouth twisted with the memory. "I not only screwed up when it came to men, I often failed at life, too."

"I don't believe that."

"If Mom was alive, she'd explain it all to you, believe me. I was her big disappointment in so many ways. She had Neil and Harlow and they excelled at everything." She gave a small, deceptive shrug of acceptance. "And then she had me."

"Everyone is different. It's not fair to compare."

Maxi laughed, but she didn't feel any humor. "Trust me, there was no comparison. Neil and Harlow always strived for perfection. Looking back, I think I strived to be contrary."

"Well," he murmured, "I can confirm the contrary part. But that's not always bad."

"I was a screwup and I know it." She couldn't deny it. "Wrong boyfriend, wrong attitude, wrong focus. I had mediocre grades and didn't care. I blew off college. Took an apartment in a terrible part of town. It drove Mom nuts. She decided the best way to make an impact on me was to leave all her business interests evenly divided between my brother and sister. She didn't cut me out entirely, though. She left me an old patch of rental property that wasn't worth much."

In a carefully neutral tone, Miles said, "That sounds more like punishment than positive motivation."

She shrugged. "I figured it was a small price to pay for how I'd disappointed her. But it all backfired anyway." Guilt always tightened her throat whenever she thought of her mother's thwarted plans. "For as long as I can remember, Mom always bought property. She got started with the rental property she gave to me, but throughout my lifetime, she grew her holdings until she could purchase a posh resort. It was her pride and joy, and by all appearances, it was a thriving, lucrative business."

After a brief pause, Miles said, "By all appearances?"

Maxi still couldn't believe that her mother had kept the business problems private. From her, sure. She and her mother didn't talk business. Often they didn't talk about anything.

But not confiding in Harlow and Neil? Incredible.

"After Mom passed, Harlow discovered that she'd filed bankruptcy. That's bad enough, but from what I understand, she'd also transferred assets through a shell company to Harlow and Neil, which makes it look like she was trying to defraud her creditors." Honestly, none of them could be sure she wasn't. "Now, as the recipients of the transfers, they're being sued. Heaven only knows when it'll all get settled."

Miles whistled. "Wow. Can't say I understand all that either, but it sounds pretty nasty."

"Very." Because it was so ironic, Maxi laughed uneasily. "The property Mom left me? Turns out it was smack-dab in the middle of a big land deal. I made a killing off it."

Eyes flaring, Miles said, "Holy shit. I bet your brother and sister aren't happy about that."

"They'd have been fine if it had gone the way originally intended. But for them to be on the short end? They're livid. And then, of course, it wasn't long after that my grandmother passed away, too. I was heartsick when Harlow and Neil jumped me at the funeral, demanding I do the right thing, which to them means selling the house and giving the profit to them."

"Bad timing," Miles muttered.

"Very bad. I was already hurt and angry, more so after Harlow claimed I could never take care of the farm, that I was in over my head. Neil agreed with her. They wanted me to be happy with a chunk of money and forget my grandmother's wishes."

"To care for her cats?"

She nodded. "I didn't react well. I offered them each twenty grand to leave me alone, which admittedly won't go far."

"Sounds generous to me."

At the time, it had sounded generous to her, too. But she hadn't realized the financial tangle her mother had left behind. "They didn't think so. Neither of them has been to the house, but I get plenty of texts and emails reminding me of my duty, and what I should do for them."

"What about your duty to your grandmother?"

"Neil says they're just a bunch of feral cats and don't really matter, not when compared to my mother's reputation." She pressed a hand to her heart. "But they mattered to my grandma. You've seen the farm. She put her whole focus on those cats. They were her pets, her purpose. I can't just ignore that." One way or another, she was determined to finally do something right.

Miles pondered that for a moment. "Has it occurred to you that it might be your brother or sister causing the problems? If they want you to sell, what better way to convince you than to terrorize you into it? Money," he added, "can be a powerful motivator."

"No, they wouldn't do that. Like I said, deep down they love me." Sometimes she had to look *really* deep, but she knew the love was there.

Sympathy crept into his expression and tone. "That could explain why, after you were drugged, you were only moved outside and not actually hurt."

Her throat tightened at the possibility, and she adamantly shook her head. "They wouldn't scare me like that. This is just one of many battles that we've fought over the years." They butted heads, her family got more fed up with her and she worked harder to hide her hurt. But they would never go this far.

Clearly unconvinced, Miles said, "All right. You know them and I don't. Just keep it in mind, okay?"

Keep in mind that her own family would... No, she couldn't believe it. To appease Miles, she said, "Sure. I'll add it to my growing list of disturbing things to think about."

With regret, he whispered, "I'm sorry you're going through all this."

"On the upside, I've been too busy juggling problems to wallow in grief." She tried for a smile, but it eluded her.

"Grieving is important." Miles slid his hand down her arm until he could twine his fingers with hers. "Maybe while I'm helping out, you could slow down and take the time to *feel*."

Oh, she felt plenty around Miles. Too much. "We'll see how it goes." So far, she hadn't wanted to think too much, not about losing her mom, not about losing her grandma and not about having her life turned upside down.

His thumb brushed over her knuckles. "So now I know everything you have on your plate. Want to tell me what it has to do with avoiding me?"

Even that simple touch from him did crazy things to her

insides. Dropping her head back and closing her eyes, Maxi blew out a breath. "That first night I came to the bar… I just wanted to be me, you know? The person I was before I inherited a chunk of money and a farmhouse that needs a ton of work. I didn't want to think about lost opportunities with my mother, or the new tension with my sister and brother. I didn't want to dwell on how I'd once again completely misjudged a man. I wanted to escape for a while."

"With a one-night stand?"

She opened her eyes to look at him. "That was the original plan, yes."

"I wasn't judging," he promised, picking up on her sudden antagonism. "Just trying to get a handle on things."

"Well…good." She'd been judged enough lately.

His mouth quirked in that crooked grin she loved so much. "I was the beneficiary of your 'escape.' There's nothing about it that I regret."

He sounded so sincere, her hope rose. Twisting to face him, still very relaxed with her head resting back, Maxi whispered, "You mean that?"

"Yeah, I do." He squeezed her hand, then withdrew. "The only thing I regret is how it ended."

It kept coming back to that—not that she could blame him. "It didn't exactly work out the way I'd planned either."

"No?"

"I only wanted something for *me*, you know? My life was upside down, and I had so much to deal with, so many emotions pulling me in a dozen different directions. I wanted pure, hot sex—then I wanted to walk away with no strings attached. I had too many strings already." And too many failures.

"I trust you got the hot sex?"

She grinned hugely. "Boy, that's an understatement. You totally rocked my world."

Her words brought a heated look to his eyes that almost singed her.

Softer now, she admitted, "I'd expected to have sex with a total stranger, and that'd be that. It was going to be my wicked splurge, my departure from reality." As she searched his green-eyed gaze, her voice thickened. "Instead, I came back looking for you again."

With satisfaction, he whispered, "And then a third time."

"I knew if I let myself, I'd start a thing with you. But after striking out twice, it seemed really dumb to chance it, especially when I just plain didn't have time or energy for it."

"By thing, you mean a relationship?"

She nodded. After that third time, she'd felt not only physically hooked, but emotionally and romantically, too. That was dangerous.

"You're assuming that's what I wanted?"

"I wasn't at all sure what you wanted. That last time, you were...well, I don't want to say moody."

Brows flattening, he groused, "Yeah, please don't."

His look of affront amused her. "You asked me so many questions, and you shared more of yourself, telling me that you might leave MMA and go into the bodyguard biz. The sex was just as phenomenal, but I was afraid we were getting too chatty."

"And getting chatty spooked you?" Miles shook his head. "Aw, babe, you're nuts, you know that, right?"

"Maybe." Her family certainly thought so. "But for once, I thought I should be responsible and get my life in order. You saw the farmhouse. It was ten times worse when I first moved in. I've accomplished a lot in the time I've been there. I might've gotten more done if there weren't so many strange things happening." Her gaze moved over him. "Now I'm thankful you did tell me about your plans. Otherwise I'm not sure where I would've turned for help."

"You could have come to me either way."

Probably true. After all, as a professional fighter, Miles had the physical skills to handle most types of trouble. It continued to make her uncomfortable, knowing her departure from his life had angered him, so she did a topic switch. "I'm curious. You told me you were leaving MMA, but not why."

"I had my reasons."

She'd researched him online and knew he'd been a force to be reckoned with, a skilled fighter with a string of wins behind his name, respected by others in the industry, adored by rabid fans. Why would he have left all that?

When he said nothing else, she asked, "The reasons are a secret?"

His enigmatic gaze cut her way. "They have no bearing on me being your bodyguard."

"Whoa," she said, holding up her hands as if in surrender. "I didn't know it was a touchy subject. This is me backing off."

"And that," Miles said, "is our cue to get moving if we want to have time left to get everything done."

But...she'd been leading up to something there...something like an invite to share her bed again!

Soon as they'd started talking about it, she'd recalled all the ways he'd touched her, tasted her, the positions he'd favored, how frantic he'd made her feel—and then how fulfilled.

Blast him, he had her craving him all over again.

Who was she kidding? Soon as she'd laid eyes on him at the Body Armor agency, she'd suffered an explosion of need. Not just sexual, but all those special things Miles made her feel.

Sighing in very real frustration, Maxi gave up her slouched posture and handed him the bag with all their empty containers together. He left the vehicle to throw it away in a curbside trash can, then returned and started the engine.

"Is your new apartment anywhere near the agency?" she asked as she fastened her seat belt.

"Yeah, why?"

"I want to get my car." When they'd left, Miles had been adamant that she not drive, never mind that she'd gotten there on her own. Given the fuzziness of her memory, she hadn't argued too much. Since they'd be nearby again, it only made sense for her to drive it back.

"Leese and Justice will swing by tomorrow and get it before they come out."

"They don't have the keys."

"They can get them from the office."

She narrowed her eyes on him. "When you took them from me, I thought you put them in your pocket."

"I left them with Sahara."

Well, that was high-handed of him. "Don't ever do that again."

He pulled away from the curb, asking, "Do what?" as if he weren't the least bit concerned.

"Make a decision for me." Even though she knew it was mostly sexual frustration making her snippy, Maxi said, "Deliberately mislead me."

His brows shot up and he spared her an incredulous glance before getting his attention back on the road. "That's the pot calling the kettle black."

The accusatory tone only irked her more. "The pot is paying the kettle's salary!"

He snorted. "Do you really think you were in any shape to make decisions this morning?"

"No, but you could have just said that you wanted someone else to bring my car to me."

He rolled one big shoulder. "At the time, I didn't even know if Leese would be free. Since he is, it works out."

Maxi closed her mouth before she made an even bigger fool of herself. She'd blame the overreaction on the strain, but she knew that wasn't it.

She wanted Miles, and so far, he wasn't all that receptive to the idea.

Giving up for the moment, she noted the size of the security store where he pulled up and parked. "This place is immense."

"They're top-of-the-line and should have everything we need." After he stepped out, he walked around to open her door.

Always the gentleman. Maxi left the SUV but didn't go far. She put a hand on his chest—and even that, such a small touch, did crazy things to her. There was no give to his rock-hard body; how could she not react?

Reining in her haywire hormones, she said, "Promise me, Miles. I'm not an idiot. You don't have to do things for my own good. Just tell me the plan, and I can be reasonable."

He looked first at her hand on him, then into her eyes. He was so close, she breathed in the scents of soap and warm male skin.

A sultry expression narrowed his gaze. Voice low and rough, almost hypnotic, he said, "Since I don't know you well enough to make that judgment, I can only promise to try."

CHAPTER FIVE

It took longer than Miles had counted on to get all the supplies they needed, plus groceries. Because he knew Maxi wasn't working on all cylinders yet, he made a point not to rush her.

For the most part, she held it together, but even at his apartment, she'd trailed him into every room, sticking close while he gathered up clothes, his laptop and overnight kit.

Apparently she was afraid to be more than a few feet away from him.

In one respect, he liked that. She wanted a protector? He'd gladly step up.

On the other hand, he didn't like seeing her this way. When he'd first met her, she'd been all bold, up-front honesty. She'd wanted him, she'd said so, and they'd both enjoyed themselves.

Now she tiptoed around it. Sure, he'd caught the subtle hints she'd thrown out, picked up on her vibe.

He wanted more than that.

He wanted her outright admission so that this time they could start with a clean slate.

She claimed to have ended things because of poor choices

in her past, and the mess of her life. Well, he wasn't a poor choice, and her life was no less messy now. Hell, if his suspicions were right, it'd get worse before it got better.

He'd give her a day before he started digging for details. Right now, she was too exhausted.

The proof was on the drive home, when she conked out for the duration.

Not that he minded. With her asleep, he was free to look at her all he wanted. Half-curled in the seat next to him, only her seat belt keeping her upright, she had that boneless, utterly relaxed look about her.

Could be the first good sleep she'd had in a while, all because she knew he'd keep her safe.

He constantly glanced at her. The light tan and sun streaks in her golden hair told him she'd done plenty of work outside. Though still shapely, she'd lost a few pounds. Her nails, once perfectly manicured, were now short and buffed.

The changes didn't detract from her appeal; she was still a nearly irresistible temptation.

But he would resist, because he had a plan, and by God, he'd stick to it, starting with giving her some time.

Miles began prioritizing in his mind. Making the farmhouse secure was top of the list. Soon as possible, he'd also get on his laptop to do some research.

That recent ex she'd mentioned... Miles wanted to know more about him, but he'd have to be careful how he asked.

Maxi couldn't know how much it mattered to him.

Had she been in love? Was she *still* in love?

Didn't seem so, but women could be funny about things like that, especially a woman scorned, as the saying went.

She claimed to want to avoid men now, so Gary, the cheating bastard, must have had some effect.

It'd be better, Miles decided, if he'd only hurt her pride, and not her heart.

Unfortunately, her ex wasn't the only worry. Whether she liked it or not, he had to consider her siblings, too. By the minute, motives piled up, growing the list of suspects.

As the wheels of the SUV went from pavement to gravel, Maxi stirred, sitting up sluggishly and looking out the window as if trying to orient herself.

Stiffening, her gaze shot to him, and then she visibly relaxed. "How do you feel?"

"Mmm, good." Stretching—and looking sinfully sexy in the process—she mumbled, "Sorry about that."

"You needed the sleep."

"I don't usually nap."

"All things considered, you were due."

"I guess." She yawned widely behind her hand, rubbed her eyes and smiled at him.

That smile was so sweet, so innocent and trusting, he felt it clean through to his heart. "I want to get started on the floodlights today, but I think we should take care of the groceries first. Will we have to go into town to dump the old food?"

"No. I have a big locking Dumpster and the garbage gets picked up tomorrow."

"Perfect timing."

Her gaze shifted away. "We'd accomplish a lot more if I put away the food while you worked on the lights."

Miles heard the unspoken *but*, so he held silent.

"But," she whispered, "I'm still not ready to be alone."

He wouldn't mind if that attitude carried over to bedtime. "It's not a problem."

"Right. I'm afraid to be in my own home? It's idiotic."

"Actually, it'd be idiotic if you *weren't* worried."

As if he hadn't spoken, she said, "And it's not your job to play grocery shopper and light installer on top of being a bodyguard."

"How many bodyguards have you hired?"

"I…" Stymied, she frowned. "Only you. Why?"

"My job is to ensure your safety. That involves making the farmhouse more secure and, when necessary, sticking close. Since I'm not the type to stand around idle while you do chores, you can damn well plan on me helping. With whatever. Got it?"

Gratitude curled her mouth and softened her tone. "Doesn't sound like I have a choice."

"It's part of the bodyguard code." The SUV bumped and bounced over potholes in the rough road. While he had her undivided attention, he decided to sneak in a little work. "This ex of yours. Does he know you moved out here?"

"I didn't tell him. If he knows, he found out from someone else."

"Like who?"

"Well, he works with my sister."

Great. He really needed to do some research. Getting details in drips and drabs wasn't working for him.

As neutrally as he could, Miles said, "Yeah? Doing what?"

"He's a receptionist." She made a face and added, "Gary is pretty. He looks good in a boutique joint that caters to other pretty people."

Jealousy subsided. "Pretty, huh?" She said it with enough disdain to make him laugh.

"Yeah. Some would call him handsome—but not as handsome as you."

Miles said nothing to that.

"He's tall, too." Then she quickly added, "But not as tall as you."

Semi-amused, semi-annoyed, Miles said, "He's a cheater, so we can kill the comparisons, okay?"

Chagrined, she nodded. "I'm just wondering what I ever really saw in him."

Yeah, Miles was wondering that, too.

Lower, she added, "I guess I thought he was elegant. Very stylish, trim, impeccable dresser. And far, far different from the first guy I cared about."

"You were younger then."

"And obviously dumber. Gary comes off as sophisticated and..." She shrugged with the truth. "More acceptable to my family."

Miles soaked that in. So she still wanted their approval, did she? Just not enough to disregard her grandma's wishes. "Do you think your sister would tell him where you are?"

"Who knows what Harlow might do? She's annoyed enough with me to want payback."

"So she knows you two split?"

"Yeah. She couldn't believe I'd end a relationship over one 'indiscretion.' She thought I should give him another chance."

"Bullshit."

"My thought exactly. But if she did tell him, he hasn't shown up here."

"Or," Miles said with emphasis, "maybe he's shown up and you just don't know it."

She toyed with her braid while considering it. "Gary isn't the type to be a stalker."

"You never know." Miles flexed his hands on the wheel. "Describe him to me."

Wary now, she said, "You're not going to do anything crazy, are you?"

"If you're asking if I'll demolish him, that's not my plan."

"Doesn't sound like you're ruling it out, though."

Being honest, Miles said, "If I find him lurking around here or doing anything shady to scare you, yeah, you can bet your sweet ass I'll take him apart."

She stared at him in awe, then grinned. "My sweet ass, huh?"

"Your ass is very sweet." He cocked a brow and prompted, "Description?"

Biting her lip to keep the grin at bay, Maxi gave it quick thought. "Hmm, let's see. He's twenty-eight. Close to six feet tall. Light brown hair, blue eyes. Trim." She turned to glance out the window, then did a quick double take. "Wow, the sky's getting dark."

Miles bent to peer up through the windshield. "Well, hell. A storm's rolling in."

"We need the rain, but I'd rather it hold off another day or two."

He parked in the driveway and, hurrying now, went around to the back to open the storage area. He noticed Maxi standing there, staring at the front door.

He didn't see anything amiss but asked anyway. "Something wrong?"

"Just thinking about unlocking it for you."

Yet she didn't move. Miles's heart softened. "Come here, Maxi."

Feet dragging, she headed his way. "What?"

"Carry this." He took the keys from her, then gave her his duffel and overnight bag. They weren't heavy, but they required both her hands. "I can get the door." He wouldn't mention her nervousness; they'd said enough on it. Going forward, he'd try to ensure she didn't have to mention it.

Loading his own arms with grocery bags, he said, "Come on."

Together, they made multiple trips until all the groceries were in the kitchen and all the security supplies were unloaded on the dining room table.

They'd just finished carrying bags of the old food out to the big bin when the sky opened up in a great deluge. The cats must have known it was coming, because Miles didn't see a single one. Grabbing Maxi's hand, he raced for the front porch while the stinging rain pounded onto them.

Maxi laughed as she slipped and almost went down. Barely breaking stride, he scooped her up in his arms and bounded up the steps. Because they were soaked, he stopped outside the door and let her slide down his body. Lightning cut through the bloated black clouds. Thunder shook the foundation.

Steam rose between them.

Miles watched as rain dripped down her body, her top plastered to her breasts.

The chill drew her nipples tight.

Well, hell. If he didn't find a distraction fast, he was a goner and he knew it. He glanced around the yard and found inspiration. "The cats are conspicuously absent."

Blinking at the intrusion of that nonsense comment, she looked down and tugged her top away from her body. "They're probably in the barn."

"Hopefully." Already puddles formed around her yard. "It's going to be muddy."

She nodded. "If this doesn't let up, we're going to get soaked again when we feed them dinner."

We. He liked sharing that responsibility with her. Normally he'd have offered to take care of it while she stayed warm and dry.

Knowing how she'd react to that, he kept the offer to himself.

Lightning crashed again, making her jump. "Wow, that was close."

"It'll probably blow over, but yeah, we should get inside." He opened the door and urged her in. "Towels?"

"I'll grab them." After stepping out of her sandals, she ducked into the main floor bathroom and grabbed two large white towels, handing one to him. They dried off the best they could.

Without thinking about it, Miles pulled off his sodden T-shirt, walked back out to the porch and wrung it out. When he turned to step back in, he found Maxi staring at him, her dark eyes consuming, her body tense in sexual awareness.

God, the things she did to him.

For a few heartbeats, neither of them moved. Slowly Miles came in, closing and locking the door behind him.

She cleared her throat. "I need to change." Again, her gaze flickered to his chest.

"Me, too." Ignoring the sparks, he gestured to the steps. "We can go up and grab your clothes first."

Though she nodded, she didn't yet move, and she didn't take her rapt attention off his abs. Miles could almost see her mental struggle.

Oh, yeah, she wanted him.

He wouldn't have to wait long to get what he wanted in return.

Finally, with a low sound of regret, she rushed past him.

Hiding his grin, Miles followed her up.

In her bedroom, she said, "If you don't mind, I'll just change in the closet."

"Suit yourself." He couldn't sit, not with his jeans wet, so he walked to the window to glance out. The rain hadn't slowed yet. He turned back to see that she'd gone into the closet, but hadn't completely closed the door.

Through the two-inch opening, the shifting shadows he saw kick-started his imagination. He pictured her pulling off her wet, clinging top, removing her bra, stepping out of those minuscule shorts—

"You still there?"

"I haven't budged." Would she break down and ask him to sleep with her tonight? If not, he'd do the asking. He wanted her to sleep, not lie awake listening for trouble.

A second later, she stepped out dressed in a soft, oversize T-shirt and fuzzy pajama pants, her feet bare. Her breasts were loose under that faded shirt, her nipples pressing against the soft material, and he had to look away before he forgot his big plan.

"It's cold in here," she complained.

"Guess that means your air-conditioning works?"

"My grandma had all that replaced a few years ago. Up-graded plumbing, too."

"But she kept the old appliances in the kitchen?" The fridge was so small, they'd barely fit in the cold food they'd bought.

"They were sentimental to her. She'd bought them ages ago with my grandpa." Wrinkling her nose, she added, "There's a newer freezer in the basement, but I don't go down there often." Carrying her wet clothes, Maxi led the way back downstairs. Just as she'd reached the bottom step, lightning cracked, making her jump. She grabbed the handrail with a low grumbling curse.

Moving close behind her, Miles listened, but the thunder didn't come as quickly this time. "I think the storm is moving off."

At the landing, she let out a breath. "I swear I'm not afraid of storms. I'm just…"

"You've been a rock," he said near her ear, giving her shoulders a squeeze. She went still, then leaned back slightly toward him. An offer, he knew, but being that close to her tempted him, so he stepped around her into the bedroom she'd assigned him. "Stop thinking I'm judging when I'm not."

She grumbled something, but he didn't hear what.

Biting back his smile, he did a quick study of the room. White curtains opened over a single window facing the backyard, giving a nice view of the pond and barn. An oval rug covered much of the scuffed hardwood floor. As she'd promised, Maxi had packed up everything except the furniture, leaving the room a mostly clean slate. The antique oak wasn't feminine, but it was ornate. Nightstands, each topped with a glass lamp, flanked a quilt-covered full-size bed with a trunk by the footboard and an armoire with a locking door, a key sticking out of the lock.

"There are extra blankets and pillows in the trunk. Everything is clean and fresh."

Miles went to his duffel bag and dug out a T-shirt, boxers and jeans. Aware of Maxi standing just inside the room with him, he said, "I'm not modest, so let me know if you're wanting the full show."

She plopped down on the side of the bed, her back to him. "I won't peek."

Grinning, Miles decided it was going to be even easier than he'd hoped. As he peeled out of his wet clothes, he asked, "Where's the washer and dryer?"

"There's a small stack set in the kitchen."

"I didn't see them."

"In the pantry."

"Gotcha." Did her voice sound more strained? He pulled on the dry boxers and T-shirt. "I like the quilt on the bed."

"The bedding is all freshly washed, but since my grandmother made the quilt, I didn't pack it away. It belongs in here, you know?"

"Works for me."

Maxi smoothed a hand over the patchwork quilt that, surprisingly, wasn't done in floral patterns but rather various stripes and checks in blended tones of blue, yellow and gray. It wasn't masculine, really, but neither was it too frilly. "She made all the curtains, too. She did a lot of sewing over the years."

"She sounds like the quintessential grandma." Cats and all.

"In many ways, she was. She worked hard from sunup to sundown, didn't complain much and always had cookies for me when I visited."

"Nice."

Maxi nodded. "In most ways, I was closer to her than my mother. Maybe because my grandmother didn't equate motivation with gaining wealth. She was happy here and didn't want for more."

Glad that she'd had the woman in her life, Miles said, "You miss her."

She stroked the quilt again. "I do, but being here in her

house, surrounded by her choices, makes it easier. In so many ways, it's like she's still here with me."

Miles would ensure that she never had to leave, and that would start with ending the trouble. "I'll get the locks changed first thing."

"Thank you. I'll feel better once that's done."

"While I do that," he said, stepping into his jeans, "you can give me more info."

She half turned to face him, saw him zipping up, and her eyes widened. After a cough, she squeaked, "Info on what?"

"Your family, your ex." As he snapped the jeans closed, he came around in front of her. Seeing her on a bed, especially a bed assigned to him, ramped up the edgy need to have her again.

It didn't help that her gaze stayed below his navel.

With a finger under her chin, Miles lifted her face, redirecting her attention without words. "I assume you want to come with me while I look around at everything?"

"You already did."

"My first look around was too quick to make note of important things. I want to check out the windows and doors, and I want to see the basement. You can talk to me while I do that." And that'd keep her from being alone. "First, though, let's go check out that kitchen and get our soaked clothes in the washer."

He took her hand and hauled her off the bed. Yes, the rain had cooled everything, but her chilled fingers surprised him. It would be so easy to share his warmth.

Better to save that for tonight, though.

He grabbed his clothes, then picked up hers in the hall, where she'd left them. She decided the house was too quiet and detoured into the living room to turn on music before opening the folding pantry door and showing him the small washer with a dryer atop it.

The sounds of hard rock filled the air as he watched her set the washer, paying attention so he'd know how to use it.

"Next time, I'll do the laundry."

"I don't mind. I do a load almost every day because the washer is so small. Your clothes and mine make it a full load."

Miles walked over to the refrigerator. "I can't get over how small this thing is. I bet it's an antique."

"Probably. The cabinets, too, and even the dinner table."

He glanced at the small wooden table she'd mentioned. It looked more like a toddler table to him, and he wouldn't trust those little chairs with his weight.

Altogether, though, the room had a certain warmth to it. He could imagine Maxi as a kid sitting at the table with cookies and milk while her grandma, wearing a ruffled apron, fussed around her.

It was a nice image.

"I scrubbed everything in here," she said. "The floors, appliances, walls. Remember, I told you that."

"I remember." He'd thought she'd exaggerated, but looking around now, he saw every surface shining.

"When she was younger, my grandmother was meticulous in her daily chores. But as she got older, she couldn't clean the baseboards or under the furniture." Hands on hips, she, too, looked around. "I had hoped it would help, but you can't scrub away age. I need a new floor bad, and the walls are in desperate need of paint. But both those updates require moving the appliances, and I'm afraid if I move them, they'll quit working."

"You don't want to replace them?"

She shook her head. "Not yet. This old kitchen wouldn't be the same without them."

Miles understood that she wanted to hang on to her grandma a little longer, so he said, "It's growing on me."

She laughed. "Fibber."

Slipping his arm around her, Miles said, "For now, let's do the updates we can and worry about remodeling later."

CHAPTER SIX

Together they went over every egress in the house. The locks on the windows were surprisingly strong, so he didn't think he needed to mess with those.

He'd expected the basement to be eerie, but instead long fluorescent bulbs in the ceiling lit every corner of the room. Spotlessly clean—more evidence of Maxi's cleaning fits—with a concrete floor and dust-free rafters. Additional shelving for canned goods, a massive box freezer, new furnace and air unit, and a water heater made it seem more modern than the rest of the house.

In the center of the floor, situated on a pallet, Maxi had piled ten large bags of cat food.

Eyeing the bags, each weighing sixteen pounds, he wondered aloud, "How'd you get those down the steps?"

"One bag at a time."

He frowned over that. There had to be an easier place for her to store the food. While he considered it, he checked the two casement windows and found them secure. "Overall, the house is in great shape. It just needs some sprucing up."

"Will we need to throw out the food in the freezer?"

He opened the freezer, saw the frozen vegetables and meat, and figured they'd be okay. For one thing, no one could break in through the windows, and how would you taint frozen food? "Let me think about it."

He'd ask Leese, get his opinion and maybe do a little research on his own.

They locked the basement again, then Maxi sat on the porch with him while he changed out the front lock and added a dead bolt.

"Where'd you learn to do that?"

"Do what?" he asked, leaning in to tighten a screw.

"The handyman stuff. And don't tell me all guys are born knowing how, because I know it's not true. Gary told me plenty of times that he wasn't great with a hammer."

Under his breath, Miles said, "Got to have a hammer first, before you can get good with it."

"What?"

He shook his head. Bashing her ex wouldn't get him anywhere. "My dad taught me. He always had me with him when he worked on stuff. Not just repairs, but yard work or cleaning gutters—anything that came up. He was big on me learning everything I could, and I liked dogging his heels, so we both enjoyed it." Smiling with a memory, he added, "My mom felt the same. She taught me to do my own laundry and load the dishwasher when I was around ten or so."

"So now you're entirely self-sufficient?"

"Pretty much." With the lock done, he stood, then sent a meaningful glance at Maxi. "But not everything is fun to do alone."

Her face turned up to him, she asked, "Like sleeping?"

"Sleeping with a warm body is nice." Teasing her, he said, "Unless someone snores." Keeping his smile banked, he picked up his tools and headed to the back door.

Predictably, Maxi scrambled up to trail behind him. "I don't snore!"

"I wouldn't know." Yet. She'd always dodged out too quick.

"We slept together," she protested.

"I slept—you snuck off."

Grumbling, she demanded, "Are we back to that?"

"No. You explained. That's good enough." He turned to stare down at her. "But next time we sleep together, I expect to find you in the bed next to me when I wake."

She opened her mouth—and her cell phone rang. Pulling it from her pocket, she checked the caller ID, scowled, hit a button and put it away again.

Trying for a casual vibe, Miles went to work on the last lock. "You want to tell me who that was?"

She sat on the deck facing him, her back to the yard, her legs folded yoga-style. Ready to hand him any tools he might need, she fiddled with a screwdriver. "I told you Gary calls sometimes."

"That was him?" Pretending it didn't matter, he accepted the screwdriver from her.

"Yeah." She twisted her mouth, her expression peeved. "I ignore most of his calls. I swear, he acts like he wants me more now than he did when we were together. I've told him I won't change my mind, but he doesn't seem to believe me."

"Maybe he thinks a sincere apology will cut it."

"He'd be wrong. I could never forgive him for cheating. Never."

Glad to hear it, Miles asked, "How'd that go down anyway? Someone ratted him out, or did you catch him in the act?"

"Neither." She accepted the old lock from him and put it in the bag with the rest of the trash. "It's really dumb."

"Yeah?" Dumb he could work with. "Tell me."

After blowing out a breath, she said, "He texted me. I mean, he thought he was texting *her*, but it was me. The things he said, the stuff he mentioned, I knew right away." Her mouth tightened and she looked out at the side yard. "But then he finished it off with a photo. Of his..." She gestured at her lap.

Incredulous, Miles straightened. "His junk?"

Color filled her cheeks, but he didn't know if it was embarrassment or renewed anger. "Yes. Then he made a few references to what he wanted her to do with it. Again."

He choked. Laughing was a real possibility, except that he didn't want her to think he was making light of something that had obviously hurt her. "What an asshole."

She nodded. "When I didn't reply, he finally caught on and realized where he'd sent those damning texts. He tried calling, but I didn't answer. I couldn't." She picked at the hem to her shirt. "I thought we were forever, you know?"

Not liking that idea at all, Miles asked, "You still love him?"

"God no." She actually shuddered. "I'm embarrassed and disappointed and..." Lifting her head, she looked beyond him to the yard. "Finally."

"What?"

"The rain has completely stopped."

Miles turned, and sure enough, the hot sun pressed through the dark clouds as they blew away. Steam wafted off the sodden ground. With the air now so damp, it'd be a scorcher in no time.

Thinking she'd deliberately changed subjects, he said, "I'll finish up here and get started on the security lights."

The minutes ticked by in silence.

Determined not to pressure her, Miles had nearly finished before she spoke again.

"After my grandma died and I moved in here, I realized I was glad not to have to deal with Gary. He'd have hated this place and all the cats. He'd have been right there with my brother and sister insisting that I sell."

Miles pointed out, "You don't have to do anything you don't want to do."

"True." Shaking off her melancholy, she gave him a brilliant smile. "Now that you're here to help me figure out the threat."

Liking that smile a lot, he waited while she got to her feet, then leaned in to kiss the bridge of her nose. "Grab your rubber boots. We have more work to do."

Maxi enjoyed playing the part of Miles's right-hand man… or woman, rather. He didn't do any actual electrical; in a house that old, they both agreed it'd be better to have an electrician handle any wiring, just in case. Instead, he added bright solar lights to the barn on all four sides. Since there was already electricity in the barn, he ran some thick outdoor extension cords to motion-activated security lights that he mounted on the tallest peaks of the barn. The beams extended all the way down to the pond, to the yard behind the house and to the driveway.

The last thing he did was change out the lock on the basement door. After creating two sets of keys, one for him and one for her, he advised that she not leave them on the key hook in the kitchen anymore. If someone was coming in, why make it easy to copy keys?

Made sense to her.

In her silly rubber boots, they fed the cats. It warmed her heart when Miles bent to pet several of them. The same black cat that had led her back to the house the night before now twined around his legs.

"This one is friendly."

"More so every day."

"Have you named any of them?"

Pointing, she said, "That's Baby, Handsome and Smudge. Let me see, Sweetness, Sugar—"

Miles laughed. "Not that you're getting attached or any-thing."

"I am attached," she admitted softly. "They're very sweet."

Looking around in satisfaction, Miles said, "Now that we've got all that done, I need to unpack and set up my laptop."

She still trailed him, but not so closely now.

Little by little she felt more at ease. She folded the laundry while he fetched a table from the attic to use as a desk in his bedroom. She listened for him but didn't feel the need to stick so close.

He wasn't going anywhere, not for a while anyway, and that fact alone renewed her confidence that she'd be able to make it work by keeping the house and honoring her grandmother's wishes.

When Miles brought down a small card table, she saw that it was layered in dust. Grabbing up his clean clothes, as well as a dusting cloth, she followed him into the bedroom—and pulled up short seeing a gun on the dresser.

Miles glanced up, followed her gaze and said, "Don't worry about it."

"I wasn't worried." But a gun!

Well, it made sense that he had one, but it still shocked her. Having never seen a gun "in person," she set the clothes on the bed and eased closer. A holster was next to the gun, piquing her curiosity.

Miles suddenly stepped in front of her. "No," he chastised.

"No?"

"You don't touch a man's gun."

Where did that rule come from? "I wasn't *touching* it. I was looking at it."

"You were thinking about touching it."

Why the hell did this suddenly sound so sexual? Fighting a blush, she muttered, "Was not," even though she had been.

Miles slowly grinned. "You knew I'd be armed, right?"

"I hadn't really thought about it."

"I won't carry the gun on me when I'm here in the house, but I'm not putting it away either. I want to be able to get to it easily if the need comes up."

Narrowing her eyes, Maxi said, "You're not threatening to shoot Gary, are you?"

He countered with "Do you expect him to show up here?"

"No, but if he did—"

Miles stroked her cheek with one finger. "I already told you I wouldn't do anything to him unless he oversteps. And if he does, I guarantee I won't need a gun to show him the error of his ways."

She wasn't the violent type—so why did that give her the good kind of shivers? Because he was being protective? Yes, probably.

Annoyed with herself, she asked, "What kind of gun is it?"

"A Glock. I also have a small revolver in the nightstand. It fits in an ankle holster—and no, you can't touch it either."

She closed her mouth, swallowing the words she'd almost let free. "Apparently all I can touch is a dusting cloth."

No sooner did she say it than Miles grinned at her. "Oh, I don't know about that."

Images rushed into her brain, and along with them came a load of sexual heat. Yes, she'd like to touch him...in numerous places.

She was thinking delicious things when Miles plucked the dusting cloth out of her hand. "Hey."

"I can do my own cleaning, honey. And next time I'll do my own laundry, too." He gazed down at her. "You don't need to wait on me."

He'd moved the table into an empty corner. It actually looked good there, matching the bedroom furniture and appearing sturdier than the small kitchen table. It made a believable desk. "Did you see a chair, too?"

"Saw several, but none that I want to use. I'll call Leese and ask him to grab an office chair for me when he comes out tomorrow. Until then, I'll use the laptop in the dining room."

"While you do that, I'm going to open a can of soup and make a couple of sandwiches. For both of us. And don't you dare tell me I can't after you've done so much today."

Expression far too serious, he tossed the cloth on the table, looked down at her a moment, then looped his arms around her waist. "Food sounds good. Thank you."

Oh my. Seeing Miles, being near him, was enticing enough. But when he touched her? She wanted to drag him to the bed beside them. "Can we agree to share the load?"

"I suppose so. As long as you don't feel obligated."

Promising, she said, "I won't."

"All right. Then thank you. Afterward, if the rain holds off and there's still enough sun to see, you can put on those crazy boots again and walk me down to the pond. I want to see where you woke up. With the storms today, it's doubtful I'll see anything important, but I want some perspective on it."

A heavy weight settled on her heart. She didn't want to relive it, yet it made sense for him to see just how far she'd been from the house. She nodded, then turned to go.

Miles didn't let her go. "I'll be in here a few more minutes."

"I'm okay now." She realized it was true. "Not saying I want to be here alone, but I think I can unglue from your side enough to get the food ready while you finish setting up."

He studied her face as if searching for the truth and must have been satisfied, because his hands dropped away. "Just so you know, I like having you close." He stole a kiss, pulling away before she could really assimilate what had happened, and even turned his back to her as he got to work cleaning the table.

The smile came slowly. Yes, she could do this.

And tonight? Somehow she'd figure out a way to keep them both on the same floor at least, if not in the same bed.

Who knew Miles could be so stubborn about that? He seemed to want her still. God knew, she wanted him. But he hadn't made any obvious moves.

She pondered that while she prepared their food. From the kitchen she could hear Miles on the phone, talking with his friend. Minutes later, he came and went from the room, putting his laptop on the table, then bringing the dust rag back to the laundry basket in the pantry. He went into the downstairs bathroom with his shaving kit, detoured into the kitchen once to sniff the air and steal a piece of cheese.

He finished up just about the same time as she put the food on the table, using her grandma's beautiful vintage milk glass dishes and linen napkins.

"Fancy," he said, holding out a chair for her. As she sat, his hand briefly caressed the nape of her neck.

After that casual but somehow intimate touch, it took her a second to find her voice. "My grandmother used to keep the napkins ironed, but I didn't go quite that far." Ironing would be a luxury after she got everything else in shape.

Miles sat across from her, his laptop beside him. He put his napkin on his lap and picked up his spoon. "This looks good."

It was such a simple meal that the compliment flustered her. "Just canned vegetable soup. And hot ham and cheese sandwiches."

"It's perfect."

In something of a daze, she watched him dig in. The humidity of the day left waves in his dark hair. His shoulders stretched tight the soft T-shirt he wore. His hands fascinated her, always had. He was so strong, so thick with muscle, that he should have been clumsy, but he was too limber, too smooth. She supposed that was the athlete in him. Strong, but also agile and fast.

And of course, that put her brain right back on sex. It was a miracle she could go a whole minute without thinking about it, given how combustible they'd been together.

Catching her stare, Miles asked, "What?"

She shook her head. "It tastes okay?"

"It's perfect."

"I'm actually a decent cook, but I rarely bother, since it's just me." Now it was Miles, too, though, so maybe she'd put in the effort. "What do you like to eat?"

He cocked a brow. "You have a grill?"

"No." Blast, she should have thought of that.

"We'll pick one up, some steaks, too. This time of year, grilling is a necessity, and then we won't be straining that ancient kitchen."

She wasn't sure what to say to that. The visual was nice, though, the two of them outside on a summer day, sharing a meal beneath the shade of the tall trees. Would the cats be a bother? Probably. "Maybe I'll invest in a patio table, too."

"Great idea. Both a grill and some outdoor seating would be perfect off the back deck with the pond as scenery."

The pond...where she'd been carried, unconscious, by an unknown person. That heaviness filled her chest again, making her struggle for a breath...

"Maxi."

Strangely desperate, she looked up.

In a very matter-of-fact way, Miles said, "You plan to stay here, right? This will be your home?"

Come hell or high water, she'd find a way to make it all work. "Yes."

"Then you need to face your demons." His eyes looked very green, and very sexy, as they encouraged her. "I'll be with you. Tonight, and tomorrow, and the day after. However long it takes, okay? You don't have to do it alone."

Tears burned her eyes. God, it had been so long since anyone completely, totally backed her. Blinking away the emotion, she nodded. "Thank you."

This time he didn't make a joke about her paying his wages. He just nodded and, after another long look, went back to eating.

That was nice, too, sharing a meal with him. She hadn't used the dining room much. Usually she ate on the couch with either her music playing or the TV on, just to help fill the silence. Now, with Miles, she actually enjoyed her music again, so much so that she found herself tapping a foot.

It was more than an hour later, after they'd done the dishes together, that they walked down to the pond hand in hand.

"I feel like the Pied Piper," Miles said, constantly looking back at the trail of cats following them.

He'd locked up the house, insisting that she should always do the same. "When you're down here, you're far enough away that someone could go in. Always lock it and keep your keys on you."

She'd agreed, especially since the key ring he'd used attached to a springy cuff that fit over her wrist, but could also be hooked to a belt or purse strap.

At the edge of the pond, Miles watched a large frog leap in and dive under. "Do you have any fish in there?"

"Sure. I see them sometimes, especially in the morning when everything is calm." Doing her best to fight off the unease, she said, "I've seen big turtles, too, and there's probably snakes."

"Ever swim in it?"

Eyes wide, she asked, "Are you nuts? Did you miss what I just said? Fish, turtles and snakes!"

He shrugged one big shoulder. "They're more afraid of you than you are of them." When he turned, he almost stumbled over the cats sitting around him, staring up with their yellow eyes.

"They're really good at tripping me."

"I bet." He pulled his hand from hers, but only to wrap his arm around her shoulders. "Wanna show me where you woke up?"

Not really, but she'd been wimpy enough. Pointing without actually looking, she said, "Over there, on the other side."

He glanced back at the house, which was now a good distance away. Then up at the sky. "All these trees probably blocked out any light from the moon."

"Mostly." It'd be so easy to lean on him. He'd invited her to; that was what the arm around her meant. He was strong enough and solid enough to take some of her worries. But he was right about her having to face up to things. If she gave in to the fear, that meant some faceless, nameless bastard won.

Though it made her a little sick, she started around the pond.

Miles kept up with her, his pace slow and easy—to give her time, she knew. The cats followed, occasionally one racing past, or climbing a tree, occasionally distracted with a bird.

"Do they ever catch any?"

"Birds? Unfortunately, yes. They don't eat them, though. They leave the bloody carcasses on the porch for me. Like a morbid gift."

He laughed. "You'd think the birds would learn."

"You know what I'd like? A few of those super tall poles with birdhouses on top. Cats can't climb poles, right?"

"We'll make it happen."

She stopped under the tree where she'd awakened. The raw ground was spongy now, more rocks washed to the surface, weeds tangled. She choked down the strangling memory and whispered, "Here," with her eyes fixated on the spot.

Miles turned her toward him, for a hug, she thought, but then his hand curved around her neck, his thumb under her chin, tilting up her face…and his mouth settled on hers.

A wash of sensual heat clashed with the cloud of memory—and won. The fear disappeared in the wonder of finally kissing him again. Opening her hands against his chest, feeling the heat and hardness of him, she gave a soft moan.

He turned his head, his lips moving over hers, coaxing

them to open. The second she followed his lead, his tongue slowly sank in.

Maxi clung to him, lost, confused, in need. She got closer, as close as she could.

His hand moved down her back, fingers spread, until he ended just above her bottom. He eased his mouth away with soft nibbles, making her sigh.

Of course she knew what he'd done, and she appreciated it. "Nice distraction."

"Yeah," he said, his voice low and rough. "That was as much for me as for you." His arms crushed her tight. "I'm sorry I doubted you at first."

"It's a bizarre story." She tilted back to see his eyes. "Thank you for believing me now."

After one quick nod, he gave her another kiss, this one quick and firm, then released her so he could study the area. "I think we can rule out a woman, unless she's a beast. Only a man, a strong man, could carry you this far from the house. Deadweight..." He flashed her a look of apology.

"I know what you mean."

Face tight, he ran a hand through his dark hair. "Unless someone used a wagon or something, right? The ground was dry and solid that night, so tracks wouldn't show." He crouched down, picking at a few rocks.

"That's the first thing I felt," she said. "Those blasted rocks digging in. I didn't understand, you know?"

"The drugs were still in your system, too. Rohypnol has an amnesiac effect." He twisted to examine the trees. "Let's put some lights down here, too. There are solar spotlights that work great without electricity. We can place them around the pond and on a few trees beneath the branches."

"We've got time to walk the whole property if you want."

"How many acres do you have?"

"Twenty-five, but only about ten that are cleared."

Standing, he gently touched her face. "Let's save that for tomorrow. It's been a long day and you need a good night's sleep."

She didn't want to think about that yet. Sleeping meant her going upstairs alone and she just knew she wouldn't be able to close her eyes.

After that kiss, she'd hoped he'd take things a few steps further, but he hadn't yet made that move. Her jitters were returning big-time, and the idea of the dark really did her in.

As they made their way back to the house, she said nothing, but she noticed the lights, some of them already flickering on as dusk fell.

Miles had accomplished so much in such a short time.

No matter what else happened, she owed him an enormous debt—one that went well beyond his salary as a hired bodyguard.

Through the binoculars, hunkered in the woods a good distance away, he watched Maxi and the man stroll back toward the house. He couldn't see the man's features well, but he looked big. Was he a boyfriend? He'd meet him soon and draw his own conclusions.

Not that it mattered. Whoever he was, his presence complicated things. He'd have to adjust his plans...and ramp up the pressure.

He thought about them kissing. Odd that Maxi had chosen that particular spot, right where he'd put her. He'd thought drugging her would be enough, that she'd finally give up and move out.

Instead, she'd brought reinforcement.

Damn, but he almost admired her gumption. She was a tough lady. But not tough enough—because he *couldn't* lose this particular game of wills.

One way or another, she had to go. There was no other option.

CHAPTER SEVEN

Maxi sat on the couch staring blindly at the small television, not really seeing the sitcom that played. She'd already gotten ready for bed in her usual soft shorts and T-shirts. Usually she lost the shorts to sleep, but she wasn't sure she could be that blatant with Miles so reserved.

He'd kissed her but stopped short.

Honestly, she had no problem telling him what she wanted, except that he'd been angry with her over their last time together and she wasn't sure it'd be fair to get pushy now. He had a right to set the parameters of their relationship. It would be wrong to come on too strong, knowing he'd take her fear into account, and might do something he'd rather *not* do.

Besides, if he wanted her, wouldn't he say so? Like her, Miles wasn't exactly the shy type.

Hearing the shower shut off, she licked her lips. Tension, both sexual and the kind tinged with fear, thrummed through her bloodstream. She kept her gaze glued to the TV, but that didn't calm her rioting thoughts.

As she'd told him, every step he took squeaked so that she could almost track his movements in her mind…and imagine him breathtakingly naked. She went stiff and still when he stepped out of the bedroom. In her periphery she saw him coming toward her.

Freshly showered, wearing flannel pants and nothing else, he stopped in front of her.

Good God, those loose-waisted pants hung low. Her heartbeat quickened at the sight of ripped abs dusted with dark hair, at those cut muscles over his hips angling down as if pointing to the prize and at that happy trail of downy hair that traveled from his navel to beneath the waistband.

"I already brushed my teeth. You?"

She nodded.

"Ready for bed, then?"

It was only ten, but after the day they'd had, of course he would assume she was tired. She stood and came eye level with his chest. How could he be so wide in the shoulders, but so trim in the waist and hips?

And how could he smell so sinfully good?

Before she grabbed him, Maxi turned on leaden feet and went to the base of the stairs. Right behind her was the room Miles would use. No, she wouldn't look. If she did, she'd end up in there.

She put one foot on the step.

Miles took her arm. "Maxi."

"Hmm?"

He dropped his head in clear frustration. She waited, and finally he turned her to face him. "Why don't you just ask?"

"What?"

He smoothed her hair, now loose from the braid. "You don't want to sleep alone. We both know it. Just ask if you can sleep with me."

Had she been noble for no reason? To be sure, she asked, "That's what this is? You were waiting for me to ask?"

He cupped her face. "That's right. You're going to ask,

and I'm going to say yes—but this time it's going to be on my terms."

Relief that she wouldn't have to sleep alone outshone everything else. "Okay." And then out of curiosity, she added, "But what exactly are your terms?"

"Let's get in the bed, then I'll tell you."

"The pillows are new," Maxi said as she crawled in. "And I washed all the bedding."

"You told me that." Knowing she was nervous, Miles felt like an ass for not reassuring her earlier. While riding on his anger and wounded ego over the assumption that he'd been dumped, the plans had made sense. He'd wanted the upper hand, and what better way to get it than to hold out?

Now? Now he wanted her confident and relaxed. He wanted her trust. He just plain wanted her.

Leaving on the stupid sleep pants, he crawled into bed next to her, turned out the light and made an attempt to get comfortable.

Maxi immediately turned toward him, one hand sliding across his abs. "Miles…"

"Shh." He caught her hand, raising it up to hold against his chest. Safer territory—but still he burned with need. "We should get some sleep."

Her silence felt palpable, until she whispered, "You don't want me anymore?"

Damn, how could he be immune to that wounded tone? "You know better." If her hand had wandered a little lower, she'd have the proof of how much he wanted her. "But the doc said you could be feeling the effects of that drug for up to twelve hours."

She snatched her hand away from him. "You *know* that I'm not."

Quietly, reminding her of their past, he said, "I know you were there one minute, gone the next, and now you're back—"

"We're in *my* house now, not yours."

"And that makes all the difference? Why, Maxi? Because you *can't* leave, or because you're scared and want to keep me close to feel safer?"

Her indrawn breath made him feel even worse. He didn't want to accuse her, but the facts were there, a solid wall between them.

"You say you're interested again, but how are either of us to know if that's truth, or circumstances? I'd rather wait and get things figured out."

Temper gathered as conspicuous tension in her slim body culminated with a stated "Fine." She jerked around, her back to him. A fist landed on her pillow, once, twice, then she curled up tight.

Away from him.

But she didn't leave, which proved his point. Right?

Even pissed, she wanted to be with another human being. Not him specifically, but anyone who could be a shield from her terror.

Pretending he'd missed the anger, Miles spooned her, one arm sliding under the pillow to cradle her head, the other wrapped around her waist. He aligned his legs with hers so that he surrounded her. And protected her from her demons.

It'd be a tough way to sleep, but for Maxi, he'd suffer in silence.

An hour later, neither of them was asleep when the soft flash of lightning penetrated the curtains. He felt Maxi go alert. He, too, opened his eyes to stare toward the window.

The storm started quiet, a slow strobe that gradually built until thunder rattled the windowpanes. One crack of lightning came so close it lit up the bedroom like a beacon.

In the next second, the house went utterly quiet. No light, no sound.

Maxi came up to an elbow.

He tightened his hold on her. "Electricity is out."

In a whisper, she said, "I know."

"Another example of why solar lights are great." He said, "Stay put and I'll check it out."

"No." Her hands clutched at him.

"I just want to make sure, that's all."

"How?" she demanded. "The circuit breaker box is in the basement, and it's locked up. This is a small town and the lights go out in storms."

"It's happened before?"

"Yes."

And she'd been alone. Was it before or after the trouble started? Miles's eyes had adjusted enough that he could see her in the dark. "Okay, then. I'll just make sure we're locked up." That would help her to rest easy, he figured. "And maybe find a flashlight?"

"I'll come with you."

She crawled over him before he could stop her. For one heart-stopping moment, her hips straddled his, then she slid off the side of the bed and tugged on his hand. "Come on."

Using his cell phone for light, Miles went with her into the kitchen, where she pulled a hefty utility flashlight from beneath the sink. Together, they checked each door and window. Finding it all secure, he let her lead him to the living room, where she chose a fat candle in a holder, then located matches on the open shelves.

In the bedroom, she put the candle on the dresser and lit it. The mellow glow stretched out to the bed but didn't quite reach the shadowy corners of the room.

With that done, she crawled back into the bed, propping up

against the headboard to wait for him. "Storms don't bother me," she said. "Not usually."

"I like them." He put his cell back on the nightstand and got in next to her.

Nodding, she agreed, "They're sexy." Then with a narrow-eyed glare, she added, "Usually."

"You're still angry with me?" She should have lost that edge by now.

"Not really, no." Under the sheet, she pulled up her knees and crossed her arms over them. "I'm mad at myself, actually. You don't believe me about anything, and I have no one but myself to blame."

"I believe you," he protested.

She shook her head. "No, you don't. You think I stopped wanting you, when that's absurd." Her gaze moved over his body and she said again, "Absurd."

Appreciating her admiration, Miles smiled.

"You think I only want you now because I'm spooked, but if that was true, believe me, Gary would have been happy to play big bad protector. It's not a natural fit for him, being the selfish, cheating bastard that he is, but he'd have been here in a heartbeat if I'd asked."

Now Miles scowled. He didn't want her thinking that way.

"I never stopped wanting you. I thought I was being noble by leaving you alone. I mean, who'd want to get dragged into my dicked-up life? For once, I was trying to prioritize the right way instead of just winging it and hurting people along the way."

"I'm a big boy, honey. I can take care of myself. You should have trusted me to make that decision on my own."

Her gaze, dark and sharp in the candlelight, cut to him. "The way you should trust me to know what I want?"

Ah, hell. He was only a man. He'd always gone after what he wanted, and he wanted Maxi.

A small voice in his head reminded him that he'd wanted an MMA career, too, but he'd accepted the reality of altered opportunity.

He couldn't change the facts on his fight career, so he shook off those misgivings. This was totally different. Maxi was here, alert, clearheaded and stating her case.

She wanted him.

While he mulled all that over in his head, she held very still. Not until his gaze met hers and he said, "Come here," in a rough growl did she let out her breath in a long rush.

He reached for her at the same time that she threw herself against him. It was as if they'd both been fighting the inevitable.

Their mouths meshed, not with slow seduction, but desperate hunger. He took her to her back, one leg locking over hers to keep her still. Her fingers tunneled into his hair, her grip tight, almost desperate.

Kissing a path over her jaw to her throat, Miles fumbled to raise her shirt. She released him to help and the second his naked chest met hers, she groaned, her body arching into him.

He'd thought about this moment a lot, but plans disappeared under the force of overwhelming lust. Not just lust, because that he could handle. It was the gentler emotions that stole his breath, the fact that this was Maxi, that she was both vulnerable and demanding, sweet and scorching hot. She set him off like no other woman could, and he loved it, craved the wildness and the ultimate satisfaction.

Rearing up over her, he tugged the shirt off and tossed it to the floor. He shifted to the side of her to strip away the soft shorts and tiny panties. Helping, Maxi lifted her hips, and the second she was naked, she reached for him.

But not just yet. He caught her hands while he looked at her body bathed in candlelight. "God, you're beautiful."

"Right now, Miles," she insisted. "Take off your pants."

He shook his head. "Let me look at you first."

A little desperately, she said, "You've seen me before."

"And I've missed looking at you." Now, with her completely naked, he saw that she was slimmer, her hip bones more noticeable, her stomach concave. She'd had so much on her plate and stubbornly hadn't asked him for help as soon as she should have.

He didn't question wanting to make her life easier. Hell, he'd been hooked before she disappeared on him. Having her back, understanding, at least in part, her reasons for not sticking around, only ripened everything he'd felt.

Her breasts, still full and firm, drew him first, and he bent to take one nipple into his mouth.

Moaning, she tried to tug her hands free.

"Stop fighting me." He caught her nipple in his teeth for a careful tug that made her whole body stiffen, then moved to the other breast.

"This was my idea," she protested.

"Great idea." After circling with his tongue, he sucked hard, heard her keening cry of excitement and lifted up to kiss her. "But it was never your idea alone. I haven't stopped wanting you. Not for a single second."

Understanding caused a smile. *"Good."* She breathed hard, her eyes dark and determined. "I want to touch you, too."

"Soon." He looked down her body again. "I've missed the taste of you so fucking much."

"Miles," she groaned.

He should have given her more time, but he couldn't wait. "Open your legs, Maxi."

With a small whimper, she bent one knee out to the side.

Still holding her hands in one of his, Miles stroked her, over her soft breasts, down her ribs and flat belly, over each silky thigh—and then between them.

She lifted into his touch.

He didn't mind that. Her urgency was yet another turn-on. This time, though, he'd keep control. She needed relief? He'd give it to her, and devastate her in the process.

Cupping his palm over her mound, he felt her heat. She immediately moved against him, showing him what she needed. One of the things he'd enjoyed most about Maxi was her uninhibited response.

Letting his fingers explore, he watched her face. Her eyes were closed, her head tipped back. When he stroked a finger into her, she groaned low and bit her bottom lip.

So damned sexy.

Since she was already wet, he added a second finger, stroking deep.

She almost came.

He hadn't realized she was so close to the edge, and now that he did, he couldn't hold back. Scooting down in the bed, he adjusted them both so he could rest between her legs, lift her hips and bring her to his mouth.

"Oh God," she gasped, her thighs closing against his jaw at the same time her fingers clenched in his hair.

While breathing in the rich scent of her, tasting her sweetness, he ate her with stabbing strokes of his tongue, rhythmic flicks and gentle suction.

All too soon, a rising climax twisted her body. Fast breaths matched her frantic movements. Reaching up, he covered her breasts with his hands, his fingertips lightly playing with her nipples.

Lightning flashed and thunder boomed, but they barely noticed.

When she groaned out her climax, long and raw and real, he held her steady, making sure she got every drop of pleasure he could give.

The second she eased, he left the bed to grab his wallet and find a condom.

"Hurry," she breathed, her breaths still labored.

Settling over her, he said, "I'm here." He hooked her legs with his arms, lifting them high, and sank into her silky heat.

Her tender inner muscles, still convulsing with pleasure, squeezed him tight.

"So perfect," he whispered, rearing back to drive in deep again and again. "So damned perfect."

He'd planned to treat her gently, but his good intentions went off the rails. Not that she minded. He took her hard and fast and she matched him, crying out a second time right before his own release slammed through him.

With Miles's body heavy on hers, her muscles deliciously free of tension, Maxi teased her fingers over his damp skin. She loved the feel of him. And his potent scent…she inhaled slowly, filling herself with him.

Speaking of filling—he remained inside her, just not so much now after that numbing orgasm.

Unable to resist, she pressed a kiss to his shoulder, hugged him to her and sighed. Thoughts of tomorrow, of the remaining trouble, tried to intrude, but she didn't let it.

When Miles started to move, she held him tight. "No. Not yet."

Lifting up anyway, he moved his mouth over hers in a warm, thorough kiss that was both stirring and emotional. Matching his tone to hers, he said softly, "I have to get rid of the condom, honey, or we're taking chances."

She knew he was right. The last thing she needed in her life was a baby. Irrationally, the thought of having a baby with Miles sent a little thrill down her spine.

And *that* scared her enough that she released him, making her tone teasing when she said, "Then by all means, but try to hurry. I need to cuddle."

He kissed her again. "No more than a minute."

When he stepped out to the hall, he didn't take the candle or flashlight with him. No doubt, Miles had great night vision to go with all his other sterling qualities.

Coming up to her elbow, she watched for him, listening as water ran in the bathroom next door. She didn't hear his footsteps, but when he appeared in the doorway, she smiled. The candlelight played over his magnificent body, showcasing his height and muscles, the long flat planes, emphasizing dips and bulges. She loved the light covering of hair on his chest, that sexy trail that bisected his body and expanded again around his sex. He had mouthwatering abs, long muscular thighs, hairy calves... So incredibly perfect.

He paused by the candle but left the decision to her.

"I don't need it now."

Without a word, he bent to blow out the flame, and then she felt the mattress dip. He reached for her, but she was already curling against him.

"It's gotten warmer," she said, "now that the air is off. Will I smother you?"

For an answer, he went to his back and used his arm around her to tuck her to his side. "You can sleep?"

"Mmm." Yes, now she could sleep. "Thank you, Miles."

He laughed softly into the darkness. "Anytime, honey."

Oh, she liked the sound of that.

Miles didn't remember much after listening to Maxi's breathing go deep and slow in slumber. He hadn't lasted long beyond that. Knowing she was relaxed, finally getting the rest she needed, allowed him to do the same.

Then suddenly he heard the sound of a car door closing. Eyes opening, he found dreary sunshine creeping through the windows. Without electricity, the air felt muggy and thick. Maxi's slender body was glued to his side.

Smiling slightly in satisfaction, he kissed her temple, then lifted his head and listened, wondering if he'd imagined that sound or not.

It took only a second before he heard footsteps coming up the porch and muttered, "Damn."

"Mmm-mmm," Maxi mumbled, snuggling in closer.

"Wake up, honey. We have company."

Her eyes shot wide. She half sat up, giving him a beautiful view of her breasts. "Company?"

"Probably Leese, but he's earlier than I expected. Stay put."

She latched on to him before he could move. "I go where you go."

Damn. He'd hoped she would awake today feeling more secure, but he wasn't surprised that she'd still need more time. "Then pull on some clothes," he said, already reaching for his jeans. "The guys will like you a little too much if you meet them like that."

She glanced down at her body, grinned and slid off the side of the bed. "I'm only immodest with you, so no worries on that."

Wondering if that somehow made him special, he said, "Good to know."

Wearing only the shorts and T-shirt, both now wrinkled from a night on the floor, and her hair a little wild, Maxi headed for the door.

Hell, he thought, already annoyed. She probably thought she only looked a mess, when in fact she looked like a woman who'd just spent an active night in bed with a man. Not that he needed to hide his relationship from his friends, but he'd as soon not hit them with it first thing either.

He caught her before she got the door open. "Allow me to do my job, please."

With another cheeky grin, she gestured for him to go ahead.

Sex had certainly lightened her mood. Or maybe it was the solid sleep. Hard to tell.

Miles opened the door with a smile that blanched when he saw it wasn't Leese standing there, but a township cop. Dressed in a tan uniform shirt and pants, the guy was probably five-eleven or so, toned, maybe late twenties or early thirties. Brown hair, blue eyes and an exaggerated look of surprise that Maxi wasn't alone.

"Can I help you?" Miles asked.

The cop said, "Who are you?" at almost the same time.

Maxi squeezed in next to him. "Good morning, Fletcher."

The man's gaze went from Miles to Maxi and back again with a lot of speculation. Brows tightening, he remarked with loads of suspicion, "I noticed a different car in your driveway."

"The SUV is mine," Miles said, without explaining where they'd left her car.

The cop wasn't appeased. "Everything okay here?"

"You mean because of the storm?" Maxi pretended to be oblivious to the real question. "Yes. Power is still out, but that happens, right?" Squinting against the glare that penetrated the gray clouds, she looked up at the overcast sky. "It's still so stormy, I don't guess it'll be back on anytime soon?"

Fletcher pulled off his hat, slapped it against his leg with impatient curiosity while weighing his words. "Probably not." Giving Miles a probing stare, he asked, "Do I know you?"

"We've never met."

"Still…" Suddenly his eyes widened. "Wait. Aren't you…?"

Maxi put a hand on Miles's arm. "This is Miles Dartman. Miles, meet Officer Fletcher Bowman."

"You're The Legend."

Well, shit. Seeing no way out, Miles gave a slight nod. "Used to be, anyway. I've left MMA."

With new fascination, Maxi asked, "You recognize him?"

"Sure." Fletcher shifted uneasily. "If you don't mind me asking, why'd you retire?"

"I mind you asking."

That statement sent palpable tension thrumming in the air. Fletcher stared even harder. In turn, Miles kept his expression inscrutable.

Filling the silence, Maxi chimed in with "Miles, do you remember I told you there'd been a few other issues here? Fletcher was nice enough to check them out for me."

Fletcher finally drew his gaze away from Miles. "I hadn't realized that you had company."

"So you were checking on me? That's so nice of you. Thank you."

Fletcher said, "I'm just sorry I never did find anything."

"Maybe you didn't know where to look." Miles gave a semblance of a smile. "No worries, though. I'll take care of it going forward."

Fletcher didn't like that at all. "I wanted to stay in touch to see—"

"If we actually need anything, we'll call you."

The dismissal was clear—something he'd learned from Sahara—but old Fletch didn't take the bait.

Deciding to ignore Miles, he turned back to Maxi. "Could I have a word?"

She opened her mouth, but Miles said, "We haven't had coffee yet, but we can give you two minutes."

Maxi stared at him like he was nuts. To counter that, Miles put his arm around her shoulders.

When she didn't pull away, Fletcher slowly nodded in understanding. He didn't like it, but he accepted the evidence in front of him.

That's right, asshole. She's no longer alone.

"All right." He nodded to her. "That's how you want it?"

Confusion dimmed her attempt at a bright smile. "Yes, of course."

"I thought you were still out here all alone, and I wanted to make sure you were okay, since you'd been worried."

"Worries you dismissed," Miles reminded him.

Fletcher ran a hand over his head before addressing Miles again. "I never dismissed anything. But there wasn't any evidence."

"Other than her word."

"Miles," she protested, appalled.

Fletcher locked his jaw, but after a breath he visibly relaxed. "When I pulled up, I noticed the extra lighting on the barn. That's your doing?"

"I put in the lights, yes, because Maxi asked me to."

"Has there been more trouble, then?"

Maxi started to reply, and Miles gave her a squeeze. For whatever reason, gut instinct maybe, he didn't trust Officer Fletcher Bowman. He wasn't about to give the man any more details. For damn sure, he didn't want Maxi to mention that she'd been drugged.

"Nothing I can't handle," Miles said.

"I'd like to know—"

"I'd like coffee," he interrupted. "And since it looks like we'll need to head into town for it, we'll let you get on your way."

That dismissal was more blatant. Fletcher stewed for several moments before regaining his voice. "Power is restored in town, so you're in luck. It's just the outlying farms that are still being worked on."

"Thank you," Maxi said, trying to make up for Miles's slights.

Fletcher turned to her again, this time with a sheepish smile. "I should have thought to bring you a cup."

"That's so considerate, but I'll survive."

Not liking the way the cop looked at Maxi, or the friendly way she replied, Miles asked, "You live around here, Officer?"

"Born and raised."

"Keeping your own family here, too, then?"

He shook his head. "It's just me." He eyed Maxi and added, "Maybe someday I'll settle down." He hesitated a second more, put his hat back on his head and turned to go. "Y'all take care and let me know if you need anything."

Miles watched him walk back across the yard, his black combat-style boots leaving muddy tracks in the sodden ground. He got into his marked Suburban with the township police logo on the side.

Maxi stood frozen beside him, not moving, not speaking, no doubt flummoxed by his reception to the cop.

And he couldn't even explain. Jealousy could sum up his immediate distrust and suspicion. But was that it? *Only* jealousy? He wasn't sure.

As soon as the officer disappeared down the long drive, Miles preempted her questions by saying, "An important part to being a bodyguard is trusting instincts." And with that, he turned and headed to the bathroom.

"But what does that mean?" Maxi raced after him.

"It means I don't trust him."

"Why?"

He glanced over his shoulder at her. "I don't like the way he looks at you."

Stopping, she propped her hands on her rounded hips. "You were obnoxious to him because he was *nice?*"

"There's nice, and then there's interested-nice. He's interested-nice." Miles closed the bathroom door on her. He needed a minute, damn it. It wasn't every day that jealousy flattened him. In fact, he thought this might be a first.

Maxi hit the door once. "I had to go, too, you know!"

Yeah, waking and then greeting guests wasn't the usual course of things. "It was your boyfriend that interrupted the morning," he growled. "If you can't wait, go upstairs." As he flushed the toilet and stepped to the sink, he saw a hickey on his shoulder. Slowly smiling, he said, "Or wait thirty seconds more."

Through the closed door, he clearly heard her say, "Blast," then listened to the faded sound of her footsteps going up the creaky stairs.

Either she *really* had to go, or she was feeling a little more secure today. He hoped for the latter. A good night's sleep, he knew, could work wonders on a person's perspective.

With Maxi otherwise occupied, he washed up and brushed his teeth, finger-combed his hair, then went back to the bedroom for fresh clothes. Hearing the shower upstairs and knowing she'd be a minute, he dug two condoms out of his shaving kit and put them in his pocket.

Tempted as he was to join her right now, he stepped back out on the porch with his cell phone.

The air smelled amazingly fresh, like summer rain, wet grass and electricity in a blender. Noticing the muddy footprints left on the porch, he walked around them and, barefoot, sat on the top step to call Leese.

The cell reception was sketchy at best, so as soon as his friend answered, he said, "If I lose you, it's the storm."

"No problem," Leese said. "I should be to you within the half hour."

"Great. Justice has her car?"

"He's right behind me, probably still bitching." Without waiting for Miles to ask, he explained, "Justice barely fits in it, and he definitely looks out of place in a small lemon yellow hatchback."

Picturing it, Miles grinned. "Power is out here, so how about bringing coffee and breakfast?"

"Bacon and eggs, or donuts?"

"Donuts work for me."

Leese chuckled. "Sahara has us all addicted to pastry."

Yes, his boss did like her morning sugar highs. "I don't

know Maxi's preferences yet, so maybe a bagel or something, too?"

"Sure, no problem."

After thanking him, Miles went back inside and rummaged in the kitchen for a way to clean the porch before the mud dried. He found a long-handled scrub brush and a bucket that he filled with soapy water. He was just finishing up, rinsing the porch with clear water, when Maxi appeared in the doorway.

A subtle amount of makeup emphasized her dark eyes, creating a stark contrast to the blond hair that fell soft and loose around her shoulders. Wearing a peach camisole and white shorts, she took his breath away.

He recalled, in scorching detail, everything they'd done the night before. He wanted to do it again, right now, in fact.

Thirty minutes, though, wouldn't be near enough time for him to get his fill. Bare minimum, he needed an hour. Preferably longer.

So he'd wait, and let the anticipation build for both of them. Yet he couldn't resist saying, "Damn, you're beautiful."

Her slow smile only made her more appealing. "Don't try to sideline me with compliments, *Legend*. I want to know what that whole macho-man conflict was about."

"No conflict," Miles denied, ignoring her use of his fight name.

"Baloney." She sauntered toward him on small bare feet. "I half expected you guys to whip out your dicks and compare sizes."

He choked, but the strangled surprise turned into a laugh. "I bet I would have won." After a quick, firm kiss to her teasing mouth, he promised, "But I don't whip it out for dudes, so rest easy on that." Gesturing at the porch, he added, "Your boyfriend tromped mud everywhere. We need to add some welcome mats to the list—or in his case, just a good-manners mat."

She frowned at the porch, then picked up on what he'd said. "He's not interested in me personally and you know it. He was just being a good public servant, not flirting."

Miles gave her a long, pointed look. "He wants in your panties. Make no mistake." Going back into the house, he stored the bucket and scrub brush in the pantry and tried to shake off his new, territorial mood.

Maxi stopped in the kitchen doorway, her expression perplexed. "Thanks for cleaning that up."

"Not a problem." He pulled out a chair at the small table for her. "Let's talk."

"You're being ridiculous. Fletcher isn't—"

"He *is*, but there are other things to discuss."

"All right." She dropped into the chair with a huff. "Let's hear it."

"First, we're not updating good old Fletch on anything. Unless I say otherwise, whatever happens here, stays here."

She stared at him in awe. "You're serious? You meet the man for two minutes and suddenly agree with me that I shouldn't tell the police about being drugged and taken from my own home?"

"We'll tell the police. Just not him."

She sat back. "But…he's the police around here."

"He's township police."

"Exactly. He knows everyone in the area."

"And could be biased because of it." Adamant, Miles shook his head, and now, finally, he felt like he had his feet planted on solid ground. He had good, sound reasoning behind his dislike. "Small towns build alliances. You begin to think of people only as you see them. He might know someone who's totally psycho, but to him the guy is just the awkward kid from high school who tortured bugs."

Maxi blinked. "That's…"

"Or if he does know the truth, he could be covering for someone because of a long history together."

Frowning, Maxi said, "I just didn't want to bother him again."

That attitude alone made Miles want to take the cop apart. Bother him? For doing his damned job? "If it comes to that, we'll get hold of the county police, but I don't think we need to do that yet. Calling them in would just tip your hand, and maybe whoever is doing this will go to ground. If you want me to catch the bastard, I need him to make another move."

Suspicious now, she asked, "We're not still talking about Fletcher, are we?"

"No." At least, not completely. But he couldn't shake his distrust of the guy.

"Well…okay, then." She tapped her fingertips on the tabletop. "God, I need coffee."

In the design wreck of the kitchen, Miles wasn't sure he could get the coffee down, but he told her, "My friends will be here soon. They're bringing coffee with them."

"Bless them." She turned her face up to his and got caught in his intense scrutiny.

With a sigh, she asked, "Now what?"

CHAPTER EIGHT

Maxi had slept so soundly that she'd awakened refreshed. After her shower, even without coffee, she'd been in a great mood. After all, Miles had made her night so much better than her day.

She knew she'd convinced him last night, even though he'd been resistant to having sex. Did that account for his edgy attitude this morning?

Planting his hands on the table in front of her, his arms straight as he leaned in, he said, "You told me no one else had been around here."

"No one has."

His gaze sharpened in accusation. "What about the cop?"

She barely resisted an eye roll. "He was never here to visit, and I'd already told you I'd talked to the cops."

"You didn't tell me the cop was young and good-looking."

So it *was* jealousy riding him this morning and making him so surly? She almost laughed. "Really, *Legend*?" It blew her away that Fletcher had recognized him. Was Miles a bigger deal than she'd realized? Sure, she understood that he was an MMA star, and she assumed people who followed the sport might know of him. But he was even recognized in this Podunk town? Amazing.

To think she'd been worried about him wanting a relationship with her. A guy nicknamed Legend? Not likely.

With her mood quickly souring, she needled him. "He's not really my type, so I hadn't noticed. But you think he's good-looking, huh? I'll have to take a second look, won't I?"

Muscles in his shoulders bunched. "You know what I'm saying."

If he hoped to intimidate her, he could keep on hoping. Shoot, all his flexing did was ramp up her interest.

She scowled. "No, I don't, so why don't you explain it to me?"

His attention dropped to her mouth. "You know, babe, all that attitude is wasted when you look like that."

"Like what?"

"Good enough to eat for breakfast."

She swayed toward him...and he straightened.

Well, *that* blew whatever shred had remained of her good mood. Now she was all hot and bothered and he, the jerk, stood several feet away, arms crossed and his own attitude on display.

Pointing at him, Maxi said, "You're a miserable tease! Don't say it if you aren't going to back it up."

His gaze brightened. "Are you asking me to—"

"No!" Color bloomed in her cheeks. "Blast it, Miles, you know what I meant."

A knock sounded on the door, interrupting her attempts to explain. This time she didn't stand but instead gestured for him to go. "That's your cue, right? Have at it."

"You're learning," he said, and as he passed her, he bent to her ear, his warm breath giving her gooseflesh when he whispered, "Sorry for the tease. I'll make it up to you later, I promise." He continued on and she heard the front door open.

His apology hadn't helped, not when his nearness was so

potent, and the way his lips had barely touched the shell of her ear…

Conversation preceded him back into the kitchen, and she looked up in time to see two more extreme specimens entering the room.

Holy smokes.

They both wore jeans, and both were shredded. But that was where the similarities ended.

The biggest—damn near a giant, he seemed, at six and a half feet tall—wore old, comfortable clothes…which matched his slightly crazy hair and unkempt goatee.

The other guy, in jeans that fit perfectly and a nice polo shirt, was as tall as Miles, but leaner.

The enormous guy gave her a goofy grin, then asked Miles, "Damn, dude. What were you up to before we got here?"

The man with the air of a *GQ* model smiled knowingly. "Did we interrupt something?"

Miles sighed. "Not what either of you are thinking, so knock it off."

The behemoth came farther into the room. "But it was a little prelude, right? You only have to look at her to see it."

To see what? Good Lord, was it obvious that she'd been sexually primed? Scowling, which she hoped took care of any soft effects, Maxi said, "Well, Miles? You want to explain?"

Miles grinned, held up his hands and said, "Apparently I'm a tease."

Once she got over her embarrassment, Maxi decided she liked Miles's friends. Justice, the gargantuan guy, was a real sweetheart with a sense of humor and a knack for easy banter. Leese, however, was more serious. Currently he and Miles were hovered over the laptop looking up God-knew-what while she drank a third cup of coffee and ate a second donut.

One of *them*, she'd told the men, could eat the tasteless bagel.

Justice, leaning against the kitchen counter, said, "There's a cat in the window."

She glanced up and saw a small whiskered black face staring in with wide green eyes. Before she could remark on it, two more cats joined him, making her smile.

"It's time for their breakfast."

From the dining room table, Miles said, "I'll go."

She flapped a hand toward him. "I can do it."

"Not by yourself."

"I managed for quite a while before you got here."

"But there are reasons I'm here, so forget it."

Forget it? How dare he use that tone with her, especially in front of his friends.

Temper rising, she slowly stood—and Justice held out his arms.

"Not sure why it's a big deal, but I'll go." He stepped forward and slipped an arm around her waist. "You can come along and direct me."

Miles held her gaze, waiting.

Finally, she nodded. "Fine. But you and I are going to have a talk, *Legend.* Count on it."

Shaking his head, Miles leaned over the back of Leese's chair to see the laptop screen again.

Maxi grumbled under her breath while heading for the back door and her boots. As she stepped into them, she noticed Justice peering into the room she and Miles had shared. He glanced at her and tried not to grin.

"Your shoes are going to get ruined. It's really muddy out there."

"Where exactly are we going?"

"To the barn." She opened the back door and more than a dozen cats started meowing, twining around her legs, anticipating her trip to the barn—until they spotted Justice.

Then they scattered.

Justice stood there agog. "Man, they're fast. Where did they go?"

"You scared them, so they're hiding."

"I didn't do anything!"

"They don't know you." She stepped out, calling, "Kitty, kitty, kitty," while heading to the barn.

Justice hurried after her, taking care to avoid the worst of the mud puddles. "How many cats do you have anyway?"

She briefly explained, and as they walked, the cats timidly returned but now kept their distance.

To her surprise, Justice totally got into it, feeding them first and then doing his best to win them over. A few of the cats allowed his touch, even arched into his hand as he stroked them. Others kept a wary eye on him, ready to bolt at any second.

"Were they this skittish with Miles?"

It struck her when she said, "No, actually, they seemed to like him right off." Odd that she hadn't realized it at the time.

"Must be females, then." He grinned and stood.

Crossing her arms, Maxi looked way up at him and asked, "Meaning?"

"The females always purr for Legend."

"That's a stupid joke."

"Stupid, maybe," he agreed. "But not really a joke. Miles has always had an easy time collecting ladies."

Annoyance rising, she repeated with a touch of menace, "Collecting?"

Justice just laughed at her. "Personally I don't see it. I mean, I guess he looks okay."

She snorted. "He's *gorgeous*."

"And he stays in decent shape."

"He completely chiseled!"

Trying unsuccessfully to quell his grin, Justice said, "And you know, the bastard is nice, too. Everyone likes him. So naturally women—"

Realizing she'd been had, Maxi growled, "Oh, just...shush it!"

Letting out a laugh, Justice looked around at the property. "Damn, it's nice here." He walked to the side of the barn, peering down at the pond, then toward the woods that bordered the property. "Fallon would like it here."

"Fallon?"

"Yeah." He nodded. "I'd say girlfriend, but she's more than that. She's just not yet my wife. Will be, next May. She wanted some time to just enjoy me, you know, before she has to start all the wedding prep." He made a face.

Now that she was grinning, too, Maxi teased, "You don't want a big wedding?"

"I want whatever Fallon wants. If that means waiting, I'll wait."

Liking this particular friend of Miles more and more, she asked, "Do you miss her?"

"Sure."

"When will you see her again?"

He gave her an odd frown. "Soon as I get home tonight. Why?"

She almost laughed. "So you live together?"

"Sure." And then with a grumble, "But it's not the same as making it legal." Almost to himself, he added, "May can't get here soon enough for me."

In nine months, but she didn't say it aloud. She knew that time was subjective. Hopefully in nine months she'd have the property together, and the house in better shape. "What about Leese? Is he with anyone?"

"He's married to Catalina. She keeps him on his toes. You'd like her. You'd like Fallon, too." He glanced around again. "We should have a party or something."

Maxi almost choked. "Soon as I get the place together, I'd love that." Maybe. The guys seemed so awesome, they had to have amazing women.

And she had a million cats.

"I overstepped, didn't I? Fallon tells me I do that all the time. She doesn't mind. Says my bluntness is one of the things she likes most about me. But I didn't mean to put you on the spot."

Wondering if she'd measure up, Maxi admitted, "I like your bluntness, too." And while she had him talkative, she asked, "Why is Miles called The Legend."

"Aw, well, you know most of those names have two meanings, right? There's the name that goes in the cage, like he's a legend in his own time. Demolished guys left and right, climbed right up the ladder and all that."

"And the other meaning?"

Justice tugged on his ear, then said in a low voice, as if they weren't the only two around, or like maybe the cats would overhear, "It's sexual. Probably better if you ask him."

Ha! Maxi could almost guess the attributes to the nickname, since she'd been the recipient of them. "Sounds like bragging to me."

"Miles didn't pick the name," he said, aghast at the suggestion, which made her laugh.

They'd just rounded the barn, ambling slowly while Justice explored the views, when suddenly she heard a whizzing sound. Thinking it was a bug, she turned to look—and Justice landed against her, knocking her to the ground and covering her with his body. She felt mud seep through her shirt and shorts, and squish against the back of her head.

Justice's body, all six and a half feet of solid muscle, completely covered her.

Not understanding, she screamed. Loudly.

She didn't hear Miles running toward them, but she definitely heard Justice's *"Gunshot,"* which slowed the others to a bent-low rush.

Everything seemed to go into slow motion, her thoughts, the words being said around her. Somehow, with only one arm, Justice scooped her up against his chest and, mostly crawling, dragged her to the front of the barn.

Leese was gone, she didn't know where.

Miles appeared in front of her, his words urgent. "You okay?"

She couldn't think. Someone had shot at them? She tried to nod, but it ended up more of a wobble, sort of a cross between a yes and a no and a what-the-hell-happened?

His arm around her, keeping her low, he ducked inside the barn with her and urged her to a corner. "Stay put."

That roused her. "Wait! Where are you going?"

"Stay put," he reiterated and then dashed back outside.

Hand to her heart, throat tight, Maxi listened to...silence. Oh God, why was it so silent?

Well, there were birds singing. She heard that after the sound of her frantic heartbeat stopped rushing in her ears. A few cats came to investigate her, rustling the hay on the floor of the barn, purring softly.

But she didn't hear the men, or any more shots. *Was Miles okay?* When he got back, she'd tell him off! How dare he leave her alone like this, worried sick for him with no idea what he was doing, or how long she should wait.

Five minutes felt like an hour before all three of them walked back in, talking quietly to each other. Miles crouched down beside her where she sat with her back against the rough wood wall.

She really did mean to yell at him, but instead she launched herself at him and, despite her mud-covered body, got held tightly in his arms.

Leese, who stood nearby, turned his back to give them a modicum of privacy.

Justice went to a ladder and climbed up into the loft. He was such a big man, he had to duck down to walk around, looking for...something.

"Found it."

Miles levered her back. "Sit tight. Just a few more minutes."

Now that she could see him, she nodded.

Leese had moved over to stand below Justice. "Stuck in the wood?"

"Yeah. Should I pry it loose or leave it be?"

"Leave it," Miles said. Then he turned to Maxi. "Remember what I said about not calling your boyfriend?"

If there'd been a rock nearby, she'd have thrown it at him. "If you mean Fletcher," she gritted out, "yes, I remember."

"I've changed my mind." He handed her his phone. "Call him."

Miles couldn't remember ever being so enraged. *Someone had shot at her.* Both he and Maxi had followed Fletcher up into the loft, waiting while the officer looked at the slug half-buried in the wood.

"You say it passed through?"

It took all Miles's control not to throw the other man down to the hay-strewn floor. He kept his tone calm by a sheer act of will. "I showed you the hole in the outside barn wall." Only four feet above Maxi's head.

"Looks like a rifle slug."

Down below, Justice said, "You think?" as if speaking to a dumbass.

Miles agreed with that assessment.

Fletcher rubbed the back of his neck. "I hate to say it, and I'm sure it's not going to sit right with you, but just about everyone in this county from fifteen to eighty-five likes to hunt. My best guess is that someone missed a deer."

"Is that what they pay you to do? Guess?"

After giving Miles a frown, Fletcher went back to the ladder to climb down. "Let's call it an educated guess for now."

Standing next to Justice, Leese said, "Hell of a shot for a

miss. We scanned the line of trees in front of the house, and even the woods behind it, but didn't find anyone."

"No reason a hunter would hang around once a deer ran off." Then the bastard waited at the bottom of the ladder, as if he planned to assist Maxi. *Not happening.*

Holding her arm so she'd wait, Miles said, "Leese?"

And Leese promptly elbowed the guy aside. "Come on down, Maxi."

"You guys act like I can't climb a ladder," she grumbled, her feet already on the top rung. "When I first came here, I found a litter of kittens in the loft and climbed up almost every day until they were old enough to be spayed and neutered."

Leese didn't touch her, but he ensured Fletcher couldn't either. "That was before someone shot at you."

"I doubt it was *at* her," Fletcher said. "Still, I'll ask around and see who was hunting today. If I find out someone was being this reckless, there'll be hell to pay."

Miles dropped to the ground halfway down. "I'm not buying that it was a hunter, but if it was, the son of a bitch needs to lose his license." And more. Much more.

"Agreed." Fletcher turned his focus on Maxi. "I'm sorry your clothes got ruined."

It was the back of her clothes that were muddy, and Miles just knew the cop had stared at her ass as she descended.

Maxi said only, "Couldn't be helped," as if none of it really mattered, when he knew it mattered a lot.

Then again, she probably thought landing in mud was better than waking on gravel. Miles clenched his jaw and pulled her into his side.

"None of you saw anyone?"

Maxi shook her head. "I heard a noise that I thought was a bug, then Justice tackled me."

Eyeing Justice, Fletcher said, "It's a wonder you weren't squashed."

"He was actually very careful." Apparently irked by what she took as a slight to Justice, she insisted, "Didn't hurt me at all."

Justice winked at her. "I didn't see anyone either, but I did hear a motor off in the distance."

"Probably an ATV."

"That's what it sounded like to me," Leese said. "But even with the ground so soggy, I didn't see any tracks on her property. Just mud on the road."

Miles folded his arms. "I suppose everyone around here has one of those, too?"

"Afraid so. They use them to hunt, or just to play." He said to Maxi, "I'll let you know what I find out."

"Thank you."

Her tone remained clipped. Miles didn't know if it was residual fear after another incident or lingering annoyance because she felt Justice had been insulted. It didn't make any sense to Miles. Justice was a hulk and they all knew it.

After Fletcher reluctantly took his leave, Miles went into the house with her while Leese and Justice discussed key places to put security cameras.

"I'm okay," she told him for the tenth time. "I know you'd rather be out there plotting and planning with them."

"You're wrong." He smoothed back her hair, now with dried mud in it. "You want a shower?"

She looked at the stairs with dread. "I do, but—"

"Come on. I'll go up with you and wait."

"No." She stopped him. "Your friends will think I'm a wimp."

"Wrong again." He leaned in and kissed her softly. "They're already impressed."

"You can't know that."

"Sure I can. I know them well." He teased his fingers over her cheek. Seeing the shadows in her eyes, he decided she needed a distraction, and he had the perfect idea in mind. "I think I'll shower with you."

Eyes widening, she said, "But your friends—"

"Will understand, believe me." This time when he took her small hand in his and headed for the stairs, she didn't argue.

It felt odd to be so passive as Miles adjusted the water temperature and then undressed her. Odd, but exciting.

He kept his touch almost impassive, as if he undressed her every day with no thought to sex.

Shoot, she couldn't think of anything else.

When he knelt to pull down her shorts, she sank her fingers into his thick dark hair. It felt cool and silky and her heart beat a little harder.

"Step out."

She did, and he dropped her shorts and panties to the side, then turned her, his hands moving over her hips and backside. The brush of his mouth over her cheek made her breath catch.

"Justice would be upset to know he bruised you."

"What do you mean?" she asked, surprised that she could get her voice to work.

"You have a bruise starting here." He kissed her bottom again. "And here." His lips teased over her side. "Must be from where he took you down to get you out of the line of fire."

That reminder almost squelched her growing desire. "You don't believe it was a hunter?"

"No, I don't." Turning her back to face him, his heated gaze drifted over her body. With a small groan he folded her close, his face pressed to her belly.

"Miles?"

In a rush, he took a nibbling, kissing path up her body, pausing at her breasts to suck leisurely at one nipple before switching to the other.

He fired her up so quickly, she forgot about the rifle shot, forgot his friends were downstairs and almost forgot about her shower.

Miles didn't. He ripped off his own clothes, tossing them aside, then stepped into the shower with her. With his mouth moving heavily over hers, he sudded his hands with her scented soap, then showed her a new torment, his fingers slick as he played over every inch of her, rinsed her and started again.

Braced against the tile wall, Maxi clutched at him. "Miles..." she groaned. *"Now."*

"Shh." He washed her hair, his fingers massaging her scalp, while he kissed her throat and shoulder.

Trembling with need, Maxi reached for him, but he caught her hands in his and maneuvered her under the spray. "Close your eyes."

With her whole body aching for him, she accused hotly, "You're being a tease again," then couldn't say more, not with the water washing over her head.

That didn't stop Miles from teasing her, though. When she raised her hands to her hair, using her fingers to hurriedly rinse out the shampoo, he gave his attention to her breasts.

God, the man was diabolical.

After hefting her breasts in his palms, gently squeezing, he tugged on each nipple, rolled and flicked. Voice low and gruff, he asked, "You like that, don't you?"

"I do," she had to admit. She liked it *too* much. A little desperately, she added, "But I don't think I can take much more."

As he turned her away from him and stroked conditioner through her hair, he countered, "I think you can."

She always used conditioner, but *not* with a naked hunk's erection nudging her bottom. Trying to encourage him, she pressed back and heard his hissed breath.

"Behave."

Her eyes flared wide. Behave? What did he think she'd been doing?

There wasn't enough room in the shower for her to tackle him. If they were going to do this, she'd need his cooperation. In fact, it'd probably be easier if they got out of the shower.

With that idea in mind, she stepped away and quickly rinsed off again.

Smiling, Miles reached past her and turned off the shower.

He stood before her, glistening droplets trailing over his broad shoulders, down his chest and abs, and over his straining erection. The water made his hair darker, on his head, chest and groin, and spiked his eyelashes so that his eyes appeared even greener.

She stroked a hand over his tight abs, then wrapped her fingers around him. "You are temptation personified."

His eyes closed, his body tensed.

The knock on the bathroom door made them both jump. Leese said, "Sorry to interrupt, but Maxi has company."

"Who?" Miles demanded.

"Claims he's her fiancé," Leese said with a hint of humor.

His gaze pinned her, one brow raised. "Fiancé?"

"Not anymore." Horrified by being caught, but equally appalled by the idea of stopping, she licked her bottom lip. "Maybe your friend can just tell him to go away?"

Suspicion slowly faded from Miles's expression. "Keep him out of the house, Leese. We'll be down in ten minutes."

"Will do."

When the sound of retreating footsteps faded, Maxi nearly wailed, "Only ten minutes?"

He looked pained, but he managed a grin.

Then she felt his hand between her legs, his fingers probing hotly. She was already wet, of course, her body in frantic need. "Are we...?"

"Just you for now." He hooked an arm around her for support, then bent to her ear. "I'll get mine later."

She would have protested, but he stroked two thick fingers into her, pressing them deep while his thumb settled on her clitoris, moving in small circles. His mouth found hers, swallowing her frantic cries as he took her higher and higher.

She sucked on his tongue, heard his raw groan and held him tighter, lifting one leg up along his hip. The kiss was deep, voracious, matching her mood. Her body clenched.

So close. So very close...

The climax hit her hard and she freed her mouth on a ragged moan. Her eyes squeezed shut and her head fell back.

Vaguely she heard Miles growling, "That's it. Let me hear you."

Like she had a choice? The pleasure tearing through her was too much for her to try to be silent. Gradually, though, it ebbed—along with her strength.

Miles held her upright, pressing small kisses to her temple. Slowly he withdrew his fingers. He touched them first to her mouth, making her go still until he bent to lick her lips.

She'd gotten her release, but tension still rippled through him.

Trying to get her faculties working, Maxi whispered, "I could—"

"No. We've kept everyone waiting long enough."

That reminder hit her like a douse of cold water. "Oh my God. What will they think?"

"Justice and Leese won't have to think about it—they'll know exactly what we were doing. No idea what your *fiancé* will make of it, though."

She managed a light punch to his stomach. "Gary isn't my fiancé anymore and you know it."

He lifted her hand, kissed her knuckles and said, "Get dressed so we can explain it to him, too."

CHAPTER NINE

Miles expected to find all three guys outside when he came down the stairs ahead of Maxi, but both Justice and Leese were sitting at the dining room table, opening security cameras in preparation of setting them up.

Maxi frowned. "You said Gary was here?"

Justice shrugged. "Don't know his name, but he's out front."

"You left him out there alone?"

"The sun broke through the clouds," Leese said. "It's broiling out there, and since your electricity came back on—"

"Oh." She listened. "It is back on. I hadn't noticed."

Grinning, Justice said, "Wonder why."

Miles saw her face go hot.

"I was muddy—"

"Yeah," he said. "Sorry about that. I didn't hurt you, did I?"

"No, of course not."

"You weren't just saying that for the shady cop?"

She shook her head. "I'm relieved you reacted so quickly."

Justice looked at her a second longer, then asked Miles, "Did I bruise her?"

"Only a little."

"Miles!"

"There's no reason to fib to him, honey. He's got eyes, he knows you're soft and he knows he took you down hard and fast."

"It wasn't bad at all," she assured Justice. "I wouldn't even have noticed if Miles…hadn't…" She shut her mouth and tried not to blush again.

Justice laughed. "You'll have to get over those blushes if you plan to hang around Legend."

"I didn't embarrass her," Miles said.

"No," Leese agreed. "But your friends—" he gave a pointed look at Justice "—will take every opportunity to turn her pink."

"He's right," Miles said, then gestured toward the door. "With any luck, your guest has melted by now. But just in case, we should probably check on him."

Apparently glad for an escape, she spun around and marched for the door. Following her, Miles watched the swish of that delectable ass, now in denim shorts. She had beautiful legs, and her breasts were a major turn-on for him. For her, too, given the sensitivity of her nipples. He wouldn't mind spending an hour there, sucking on her, listening to her breath catch, watching her squirm.

He was in a bad way, but so far, things were going according to plan—though honestly, it was getting tougher to remember the plan. He sure as hell hadn't thought of it in the shower. If Leese hadn't knocked, he'd have been buried inside her and he might not even have recalled that he had condoms in his jeans pocket.

At the door, she hesitated, either unsure about seeing her ex, or perhaps remembering Miles's preference for leading the way.

Miles tipped up her chin. "We don't want to tell him too much, okay?"

"How am I supposed to know what's too much?"

"Just take your cues from me."

"All right." She stayed him with a hand on his forearm. "But don't *you* tell him too much either. I want Gary out of my life, not inadvertently drawn back into it."

"We're agreed." Miles stepped out and found her ex pacing the yard, dodging the cats that tried to get too close.

He heard the man say, "Get away!" and knew that attitude alone would ensure Maxi didn't have any second thoughts.

"Damn," Miles said. "It's cooking out here."

Gary looked up, then his eyes shot wide. He tried to smooth his light brown hair, but the breeze just mussed it again. He wore an immaculately trimmed goatee, designer sunglasses, a short-sleeve button-down shirt and black slacks with dress shoes.

To a farm. On a hot, humid late August day.

Gary looked away from Miles to Maxi and started forward. "Oh God, honey, I've been worried sick about you! Why the hell didn't you reply to any of my calls or texts?"

Before he could reach Maxi, Miles held out his arm like a blockade.

Gary came to a halt. "What's this? Who are you and what are you doing here with my fiancée?"

Miles raised a brow at Maxi.

She put her shoulders back. "Where I go and what I do is no concern of yours, and we are *not* engaged, not anymore."

Gary opened his mouth, but she wasn't done.

"How did you find me? And how dare you show up here uninvited."

Gary struck his own militant stance. "I came because I love you. No, don't say it! No way is it over. It can't be. I won't accept that."

Incredulous, Maxi said, her voice suddenly lower and meaner than Miles had ever heard it, "You have no choice in the matter."

"Bullshit! We belong together and no fucking way am I giving up on you!"

Startled by that impassioned speech, Maxi stared at him as if she'd never seen him before. Then she laughed. "What's wrong with you?"

"I've missed you, damn it. I fucking *love* you. So I made a mistake. It won't happen again, I've told you that." He pressed closer. "One fucking indiscretion can't change our futures."

"This is…" A burst of hilarity escaped her. "It's absurd."

Miles looked down at her, curious at that reaction. "You okay?"

She nodded, looked at Gary and fell into a fit of nearly hysterical giggles.

Leese and Justice stepped out, and that helped her to get it together—though given the twitching of her lips, she looked capable of losing it again at any moment.

Without looking at Gary, Leese said, "We need a few more things, so I'm running back to town. You need anything else while we're out?"

"Yeah." Miles pointed at Gary, said, "Back up," and then ensured he did so by walking toward him, crowding his space.

Gary backpedaled so fast, he almost fell. "What are you doing?" he demanded in alarm.

"Right there is far enough." He turned back to Maxi. "Just a sec, okay?"

Still fighting that grin, she waved a hand. "Take your time." She sat down on the top step.

Gary looked from her to Miles. "I don't—"

"Stay put." Miles moved away from him to speak privately with Leese and Justice, but he did so quickly. He didn't want to chance that Gary might find his balls and move back in on Maxi.

She was in an odd mood, laughing like that, and he didn't understand it. He hoped it didn't mean she still cared for the putz, but he just wasn't sure.

Either way, he didn't want to hurt the guy. Hell, he sort of felt sorry for him, given her reaction to his bizarre declarations of love.

After telling Leese the other items he wanted, he came back to Gary. Arms folded, he said, "She's laughing at you, man."

"I know." Gary pulled off his sunglasses and rubbed his brow, his expression puzzled. "Her sister told me to be more assertive, but I don't think she expected hilarity to ensue."

"Probably not." Wondering where this tactic would take old Gary, Miles asked, "Want to give it another try?"

Gary started to nod, then caught himself. "Who *are* you?"

"I'm her bodyguard."

"What?" And then with disbelief, he said, "No."

From the porch, Maxi said, "He really is." Then she snickered again.

Gary charged forward. "I don't understand why you're laughing."

"Because it's hilarious," she insisted on a snicker that grew into a roar of laughter.

Seeing her like this spurred Miles's humor, too, but he only quirked his mouth.

Gary got enraged. "What the fuck is so funny?"

"Oh God, *stop!*" She wrapped her arms around her stomach and almost toppled sideways on the step.

Miles said, "Honestly, honey, I think we're both missing the joke."

"It's him cursing..." Gasping for breath, she explained to Miles, "He doesn't use language like that. I've never heard him swear!"

"Never?"

"Not even once!" She took three gulping breaths while Gary stood there, red-faced and humiliated. She wiped tears from her eyes and tried to calm herself. "Do you believe that he used to lecture me on my language when I'd say *damn* or *hell*?"

Miles shook his head.

She nodded and spoke around her chortles. "One time, I said *cock*, and he was mad at me *for a whole day*!"

Her explanation ended on a high note and more gales of amusement. Miles couldn't help it. He chuckled, too.

Gary growled, "Your sister is a stupid bitch! I knew this was a bad idea."

Maxi's humor died. "A bitch?" She swiped away the tears, no longer at risk of laughing. Her eyes narrowed. "I'll tell her you said so."

Aghast, Gary cried, "Don't you dare!" And then, more earnestly, he pleaded, "Isn't it enough that I lost you? Do you want me to lose my job, too?"

Letting out a long sigh, Maxi shook her head. "Honestly, Gary, I don't really care what you lose. But I do care that you're here, because you shouldn't be. Now, tell me what my sister has to do with anything."

Gary gave it up without a whimper. He looked around as he explained, "You're living out here in this dump. It's not you, Maxi. You're a city girl at heart."

"No, I'm not."

"Harlow wants you to sell."

"I'm aware. I've told her many times that I won't."

Undeterred, Gary continued, "But she said if I manned-up and was more assertive, you'd know I was really sorry—because, Maxi, I really, *really* am—and that you'd forgive me."

"She's wrong."

Before Miles could stop him, Gary ducked down to sit beside her. "We could sell this place and buy a real home. That's what you always wanted, isn't it?"

Leaning away from him, Maxi gave him a pitying look. "I owe you, Gary."

He brightened. "You do?"

"Yes. If you hadn't so blatantly cheated, I might have married you." She shuddered, Miles assumed for effect. "Of course, I know now that I would have been miserable with you. But you showed that you're a liar and cheater, so instead I'm here on the farm and I'm so happy, it's almost surreal."

Gary didn't seem to get it. "You actually *like* it here?"

A cat poked its head out from behind her, purred and crawled into her lap. She smiled as she cuddled it. "Yes. I love it here."

Gary inched away from the animal. "You're afraid."

Tipping her head to the side, Maxi asked, "Why do you say that?"

He frowned back at Miles. "Why else would you need a bodyguard?"

Rather than answer, Maxi deferred to Miles. "Why, indeed?"

More cats ventured close, most of them black. One with a bent tail brushed against Miles's leg, so he leaned down to stroke along its back. Doing so gave him some time to decide what to say.

When he straightened, he looked down at the ex, who, in his opinion, sat far too close to Maxi. "The thing is, Gary, nothing about her is your concern anymore."

"I love her."

"No," he said. "Men who love women don't cheat on them."

Gary flushed. "It was just that one time."

"That's the thing, though. Once is enough to prove you can't be trusted. It's over. You should accept that."

Gary turned back to Maxi. "I won't give up."

"Wrong answer," Miles said, his patience waning. "As her bodyguard, I'm telling you to hit the road."

Cautiously, Gary stood. He picked a cat hair off his shirt, dusted off his pants and again tried to smooth his hair. "I'd like to speak to Maxi alone."

Maxi snorted. "My ribs already hurt from laughing. Don't get me started again."

The insult brought him closer again. "You never took me seriously. Harlow said that was part of the problem."

Tsking, Maxi stood, a cat held in her arms. "Sounds like my sister was oh-so-helpful. I'm sure with the best of intentions, but she obviously doesn't get it any more than you do." Solemn now, she stared at Gary. "I was going to marry you. I would have been faithful and I would have put everything I had into our marriage."

Jumping on that, Gary implored, "It's not too late—"

"It is. Because whatever I felt for you is completely dead. I'm not hurt, not disappointed. I'm not even mad anymore. Actually, I'm relieved. So get on with your life. Go back to what's-her-name."

"She meant nothing to me!"

"Then find someone else. But it's not going to be me."

Gary fisted his hands. "I'll go. But this is *not* over." He nodded to Miles, then marched toward his car, veering off course only when it was necessary to step around a cat.

They'd come out in force, lounging in the sun, rolling in the grass, digging in the dirt. One had even climbed up onto the hood of Gary's bright blue Corvette.

He shooed the cat away before getting in and revving the engine.

Shielding his eyes from the sun, Miles watched him go, aware that his tension faded at the same time. "Nice car."

"Gary's really into his rides." She sounded more tired now than anything else. "He leases something new every year."

Switching his gaze to Maxi's car, Miles smiled. "Did it bug him that you drove a little yellow hatchback?"

"Hey, I love my car!"

"I like it, too. Somehow, it suits you. And you've been in my ride, so you already know I'm not car crazy." His three-year-old SUV was comfortable for a man of his size, with nothing showy about it. "So Gary disliked your car?"

"*Sooo* much," she said with a grin. "I can't tell you how often he tried to talk me into leasing. One time when his car had a ding and was getting repaired, he refused to ride in mine. He insisted on getting a loaner instead."

After seeing them together, Miles wondered how the relationship had lasted as long as it had. "And you had still planned to marry him?"

She brushed her cheek against the top of the cat's head. "I told you, I'm a terrible judge of men."

Miles didn't take offense at that backhanded insult; odds were, Maxi didn't yet realize that she'd judged him just fine. "At least he makes you laugh."

She didn't look up. "I'd had so many plans. The wedding, the honeymoon. We'd even talked about where we'd buy a house, and yes, he'd convinced me a new car would be in my future. Strange how one decision can change all the others."

The poignant way she said that put him on edge. Did she regret losing Gary? If so, he didn't know why. "You deserve a whole lot better than him."

"I do, don't I?"

"Absolutely. When a guy makes you laugh, it shouldn't be because you're laughing at him."

The grin took the melancholy out of her expression. "Gary cursing was the oddest thing I've ever witnessed. I'd love to know exactly what Harlow said to him, and what she actually hoped to accomplish."

"Ask her."

Wrinkling her nose, she said, "We're not exactly chatty right now."

Yet the woman felt entitled to interfere in Maxi's life? Miles kept the criticism to himself, especially when he saw Maxi yawn behind her hand.

"One thing's for certain. Gary never would have fit in here."

She hugged the cat. "I know. It's almost fate that he kept me from having to choose between him and the farm."

Softly, Miles said, "I think the farm would have won."

"I like to think so. I want to believe that I'd have been smart enough to see through him before changing my whole life."

Yeah, she was smart, all right. Smart enough to know what was important, and smart enough to admit when she needed help.

Miles drifted his fingers over her hair. "It's dry now."

"No wonder." She pulled her T-shirt away from her skin. "It feels like it's ninety out here."

Taking the cat from her, Miles set it on the porch, then drew her up to her feet. "Let's go in."

"At least the air is on now."

Already the small house had cooled, a nice contrast to the humid day. Miles led her to the couch, then sat with her. "You've had a busy day. Why don't you chill for a bit while I do some computer work?"

"There isn't anything you need me to do?"

"Not right now." He kissed her forehead, urged her to lean back, then went to the dining table and his laptop. "Do you mind if I have this out here right now? I haven't gotten the chair yet from Leese, and there's more room here for us."

Eyes closed, she said, "You should make yourself at home. Be comfortable. That's what matters."

Already her voice had thinned to a sleepy whisper, so Miles didn't say anything else to her. A few minutes later, he heard her breathing deepen. When he looked at her, she was utterly boneless.

An hour later when the guys got back, she was still sound asleep.

★ ★ ★

Maxi woke slowly to the sound of muted conversation. At some time during her nap, she'd stretched out on the couch. A throw covered her, her bare feet poking out the other end.

Her body felt heavy from such a sound sleep.

Someone had turned on the TV, maybe for background noise, but it was the low, masculine voices that she focused on.

She was so utterly, peacefully relaxed, she didn't want to get up yet, but she did tune in to the conversation.

Justice said, "She's after Brand hot and heavy. I've seen him up in her office for three meetings now."

"She can court him all she wants, but I don't think he'll leave MMA," Miles insisted.

"He turned down a fight." That voice she recognized as Leese.

"Why?" Miles asked.

A snort, and then the reply, "I don't yet know why *you* left, so how would I know what's going through Brand's head?"

"You feel like sharing?" Justice asked. "You were on a winning streak, man, and then suddenly you joined the agency."

After a slight hesitation, Miles said, "Just felt like a change."

"Bullshit."

Leese spoke up again. "It's his own private business, Justice. Let it go."

"Thank you."

Justice grumbled. "Doesn't seem right, that's all. Hell, I switched because I knew I'd never be champion."

"Same here," Leese agreed.

"You were both top-tier fighters."

"Maybe, but I had no interest in staying in the second or third spot. The Body Armor agency gives me plenty of room to continue using my skills. Just not in the cage."

"I miss the cage," Justice complained. "But if I hadn't switched gears, I'd never have met Fallon. So it's worth it."

"I don't understand why you two are waiting to tie the knot."

That was Miles again, and Maxi had the thought that he'd wanted to change the subject. Why had he left MMA? If, as the others said, he'd been doing so well, why give it up?

"I'm still courting her," Justice said with thick sexual innuendo that made the other two laugh softly. "But we're working out the details now."

"Speaking of details…" Leese let that hang for a moment. "Care to share what's going on with Maxi?"

"Actually, I'd like to get you in on everything. But let me talk to her first, okay? I'm not sure how much she wants shared."

None of it, Maxi silently stated. It had been difficult enough admitting to Sahara and Miles what had happened. She felt… violated. Vulnerable. Anytime she thought of waking outside, her stomach twisted.

But she knew that wasn't realistic. Not only were they Miles's friends, they were also bodyguards. If they could help him in some way, well, that'd be helping her, too, while also cutting back on the risk to Miles.

"I like her," Justice announced. "She's gutsy."

Apparently agreeing, Leese said, "Most women would have fallen apart after being shot at. But she held it together."

"She's got backbone," Miles agreed, and he sounded so admiring, she suddenly felt bad for playing possum.

"I remember her hanging around Rowdy's a bit, when you two were hooking up. But that ended, right?"

Justice laughed. "They're still hooking up, if you ask me."

Miles didn't reply to that, asking instead, "What do we have left?"

Leese let it go. "I think this is it. Once we have this camera in place, there shouldn't be anywhere around the house, barn and pond that you can't see what's happening. Problem will be all those woods, and anytime it's dark. She has so much land, it's impossible to light it all at night."

"Until this is resolved," Miles said, "she won't be out alone at night anyway."

"How long you going to live here with her?" Justice asked.

"Long as it takes."

Mmm, Maxi liked the sound of that. Maybe Miles didn't mind the job so much after all.

After a yawn and a stretch—which immediately made the men all go quiet—she sat up and looked toward them.

Whoa.

Because they'd apparently been working outside while she slept, they were all shirtless. Lord help her, what a way to get alert. Her mouth went dry as she looked from one naked, chiseled chest to another, then naturally moved down to those impressively cut abs.

Even Justice, gargantuan man that he was, lacked any body fat. The men were all lean, honed strength, body hair and testosterone.

Miles laughed. "You're embarrassing Justice, honey."

She snapped around to face forward. "I'm sorry. I didn't realize…"

Justice said, "He's kidding. I don't get embarrassed." Then he walked around to the front of the couch, where she couldn't help but see him all up close and personal. "You sleep well?"

She nodded and tried not to look at that expanse of bared skin. There was just so much of it, from the low waistband of his jeans to those broad shoulders. She groaned, "I'm not awake enough for this."

Leese made a noise. "Leave her alone, Justice."

Justice winked at her. "You're in luck, because we're heading out now to install the last camera."

"How many are there?" she managed to ask without croaking.

"Miles can tell you all about it."

A few seconds later, the front door closed and Miles sat down beside her. The couch cushion dipped and their hips touched.

He was still shirtless, and in her opinion, he was by far the most handsome of the three. Even better, his skin smelled of sunshine, and clean sweat, and, oh my God, it was delicious.

He handed her a glass of tea, his gaze tender. "Feel better?"

"I didn't feel bad." She sipped the tea and hoped it would help to cool her down even though Miles had shifted and his thigh now pressed firmly to hers.

"You were exhausted. Nothing wrong in admitting that, you know. You've been through a lot."

She still felt like a wimp. "What time is it?"

"Almost dinnertime. We're throwing steaks on the grill in a minute."

"Steaks?" Then the rest of it registered and she asked, "Grill?"

"Yeah. Leese brought me a chair, so my makeshift office is in the bedroom now. After the incident this morning, we decided more cameras were needed, and while they were out buying those, they also stopped and got a grill and propane."

"That's a lot of stuff."

"If you don't like the grill, I'll keep it, no problem."

"It's not that." The idea of all they'd accomplished while she snoozed unsettled her. "How long was I asleep?"

He touched her cheek, his fingertips gently caressing. "Don't worry about it. You needed the rest."

How could she not worry when it seemed she'd missed the entire day?

Looking far too serious, Miles said, "You weren't alone. One of us was always in here with you."

The blush rushed to her face. She hadn't even considered that, but of course, *now* she did. Good grief, what if she'd snored? Had Justice or Leese seen her looking ridiculous?

Smiling, Miles tipped up her chin and kissed her mouth. "You looked soft and sweet, and if those two weren't already in committed relationships, I wouldn't have let them anywhere near you."

That got her face even hotter. "I wasn't suggesting that they'd be interested."

"They're not blind, honey."

Hopefully that meant she hadn't drooled on herself or squished her face too much on the armrest.

Moving on, Miles asked, "What would you think about a party? The guys want to come back every so often to check on things, and Justice is convinced that this would be a terrific setting for everyone to get together."

A party sounded wonderful to her. She hadn't gotten together with other people her own age for quite a while. "Who's everyone?"

He shrugged one hard shoulder. "Friends of mine, their wives or girlfriends. We could do a bonfire and a cookout, if you're up for it."

She loved the idea of using the house and property to entertain. It'd give a whole new facet to her ownership of it, something more lighthearted and fun to contrast with the sadness and the threats. "I'd like to meet your friends. And maybe if enough people started showing up here, whoever is harassing me would be convinced that I'm not a woman alone."

"We came up with the same idea."

It wasn't easy to talk after just waking to the sight of all that masculine beauty, especially when the hunkiest part of the display was right there next to her, bringing not only a close-up of the visual, but his scent, as well.

After working outside, heat and humidity had put a few waves into Miles's dark hair. He hadn't shaved yet today, and the shadow of whiskers only made him more appealing, somehow contrasting with the lightness of his green eyes.

He'd gotten a little too much sun on his shoulders, cheek-bones and nose. Unlike Leese's and Justice's jeans, Miles wore dark shorts and old running shoes.

Seeing the way she looked him over, he grinned, showing off beautiful white teeth. "You okay?" he asked.

"Yes." Unable to resist, Maxi rested her hand against his chest, relishing the heat of his body, the sleek male skin, the soft chest hair.

Crazy, the things he did to her without even trying. It had been like that from the moment she'd met him. If she could bottle his unique appeal, somehow capture his effect on women, she'd make a fortune. But it was an elusive thing, hard to peg. Yes, he was gorgeous. God yes, he had a terrific physique. Those green eyes, that crooked smile, the intense focus and cocksure attitude. Yet it was even more than those things, too, somehow a collective of traits, both corporal and expressive.

"You still with me?"

She shook off the preoccupation with a sigh. By now she should be used to him, but she was beginning to think fifty years wouldn't be long enough for that. "Yes, sorry."

Miles covered her hand with his own. "Let's get dinner going, okay? I'm sure Leese and Justice are hungry by now."

Because they, at least, had been working instead of sawing logs. "I can't believe they stayed all day to help."

"It's how we do things."

"At the agency?" Their time spent with her should go on her bill. "I want to make sure they get compensated."

"No need. It's how we do things *as friends.* I've pitched in plenty of times when they needed something done, so don't worry about it."

"But…" The heat of his body against her palm made her fingers curl a bit. *Focus, Maxi!* "This wasn't a favor for you."

"Yeah," he whispered, "it was." He lifted her hand away, kissed her knuckle and stood, bringing her up with him.

Maxi wondered what he meant by that, but he walked her outside to show her everything they'd done, and she decided to let it go.

Additional lights had been added, along with security cameras, in several key places. "I thought we had to wait on an electrician."

Justice, up on a ladder at the front of the barn, glanced down at her. "I did it. I'm good with this stuff."

She figured "this stuff" must be the wiring of surveillance. "Then thank you."

"No problem. A lot of the wiring and the electrical box all looked new. Did you do that?"

She shook her head. "My grandmother updated a lot of things recently."

"Just not the kitchen."

She grinned with Miles.

Leese, standing inside the barn, said through the doorway, "We decided it was better not to bring in a local electrician. No idea who's involved in a town this small, and it could take a week or two to get an electrician out of the area."

"I didn't want to wait," Miles explained.

With every step Leese took, he had a cat trying to trip him, yet he didn't lose his patience. At least Justice, up on the ladder, didn't have to deal with that.

Miles walked her over to show her the grill. "What do you think? It's a beauty, right?"

She whistled at the modern stainless steel appliance. "Fancy."

"Lots of prep area, a wide cooking surface and these little storage cabinets will be good for your grill brush and stuff, so they don't get cat hair all over them."

He sounded so much like a salesman, she laughed. Only a guy would get that pumped up over a grill. "I think I'll shop tomorrow for outdoor furniture. Bummer that we don't have anything to use tonight."

"We'll manage." He tipped his head. "What time did you want to do that tomorrow?"

"Early afternoon, maybe? I have to use the morning to catch up on work. I'm still a personal shopper, you know. I just don't personally meet clients anymore. Instead, I handle everything online."

"I didn't realize."

"I lost a few clients went I went cyber-only, but not most. And with being online, I picked up a few more." She shrugged. "It's working out, and it gives me time to set my own schedule, since I still have so much that needs to be done around here."

"If you make it before one o'clock, we could go by the office, too."

"Or," she offered, giving him an alternative, "you could go by the office while I shop." She really needed to get back to her original idea of independence and responsibility. "I don't think I need a bodyguard when I'm away from here."

"I'll go with you."

"But surely you have other things to do. I never meant to monopolize your every moment."

His eyes narrowed, making the green oddly brighter. "I go where you go."

Those had been her words to him. Was he throwing them back at her, or just reminding her of his purpose? "Yes, when we're here. But away from here—"

"Hey, Miles!"

Justice's call gave him the excuse he needed to end the conversation. With her hand held in his, they walked together back to the front of the barn.

Justice was now completely on the roof, standing as comfortably and sure-footed as he did on the ground, his hands on his hips as he stared at something.

Miles shaded his eyes. "What is it?"

"The storm did some damage up here. I don't think it's too bad, but it needs to be fixed."

Maxi groaned. "Just what I don't need, another repair."

"I'll go up and take a look."

Realizing she'd just inadvertently put Miles on the spot, she stepped in front of him. "Shouldn't I do that? It's my barn, after all." And he'd already done enough, far more than she'd ever intended.

Looking merely curious, he asked, "Do you know anything about roofing?"

"Well...no. But I didn't know much about cats either, until I inherited them." Just as she'd inherited all the crazy, irrational threats. "Besides, I can call someone in roofing, right?"

Miles nixed that with a shake of his head. "I'd rather no one else come around, at least not until we can sort friend from foe, okay?"

What could she say? He was the bodyguard. "It wouldn't make much sense for me to object, given that's your area of expertise."

One side of his mouth lifted. "Appreciate your restraint."

"Okay, so while you do—" she flapped a hand "—whatever it is you'll do, I'll start meal prep."

His brows lifted. "You know how to grill?"

Did he think she was completely helpless? Given what he'd seen so far, probably. "I'll have you know I'm a good cook whether I'm using the stove or a grill—charcoal or propane."

He continued to scrutinize her. "You don't mind being in the house alone?"

With all honesty, she replied, "Nope, not anymore, I promise." Having three hunks nearby went a long way toward reassuring her, especially with one of them on the roof. There was no way he wouldn't see trouble coming.

She must have convinced Miles, because after the briefest
hesitation, his gaze went back to the roof. "Give a yell if you
need anything."

She watched him walk away, admiring the long line of his
back and how the breadth of his shoulders tapered to a narrow waist and tight butt. Mmm, she couldn't wait to get her
hands on him again.

But food first.

Maxi hurriedly washed potatoes, then made a salad that
she covered and put back in the fridge. Heading back outside,
she got the meat and potatoes on the grill.

While those cooked, she went back inside for her grandma's
big platter. Without thinking too much about it, she made
multiple trips in and out of the house, cooking, setting the
table, getting drinks.

Having other people around really did make the farm feel
less isolated. It didn't matter that at first she had enjoyed the
peace and quiet. She worried that now, when she was back
to being alone again, she'd forever think of what had happened and she'd be afraid.

Would she ever again be comfortable living here?

Maxi gave herself a mental shake. She wasn't a weak
woman, despite recent evidence. She would do what was
right and honor her grandmother's wishes. Somehow. Time
would do the trick, and luckily, she had plenty of that.

With Miles.

No doubt about it; he made the adjustment a whole lot
easier.

When the guys smothered her in compliments over the
food, she forgot about all the tomorrows so she could focus on
tonight. Luckily they'd put on their shirts before joining her
at the table. The conversation was relaxed, the mood mellow.
It felt like she had new friends in her life, so when questions

came up, she freely answered. Talking about everything now was easier than it had been.

It'd be nice if the shock of it was finally wearing off. She desperately wanted to get back to being herself.

Justice and Leese had a few more security ideas to share with Miles, so while they talked shop, she busied herself with the dishes. They offered to help, but after everything else they'd done, she wasn't about to let them in her kitchen.

It was night before they left, and she had a wonderful time. Tomorrow she'd shop for outdoor furniture so that the next time they visited, they could all sit outside under the stars. She already had some pieces in mind, and she knew right where to put them, including a few rockers for the front and back porches. Nothing padded, not with cats all too willing to laze on every surface in sight. She'd spend all her time cleaning up cat hair if she got anything with cushions.

Once they were alone, Miles showed her how to check each of the cameras on his laptop, and on her computer, where he'd loaded the appropriate software. She now had alarms on each door and every window, too.

Despite the rifle shot that morning, the rest of the day had been so relaxing, she felt more secure by the minute. Maybe because she could believe Fletcher's explanation of a hunter with lousy aim. Actually, she could believe a lot things to be mishaps.

But not waking up outside before dawn.

It kept coming back to that.

That night she slept with Miles again, and after the teasing all day long, he was a little rough in his urgency, taking her fast and hard—which she loved, since he ensured she was right there with him.

God, he was an amazing lover.

An amazing bodyguard.

An amazing *man*.

How would she ever let him go?

CHAPTER TEN

Maxi's nap three days ago was the last time Miles saw her actually relax. She worked sunup to sundown, slept seven hours a night—usually after exhausting sex—and never seemed tired.

She was back to being the dynamo he remembered, both in bed and out.

The following week went by without a single threat, but that didn't mean it was problem free. The damage to the roof of her barn exposed wood rot, meaning they needed to rebuild part of the roof. A bigger job than expected.

He could do it, but she'd complain.

Hell, the more she got back to herself, the more she wanted him to kick back and watch her work. Miles wasn't sure how to break through that stubborn wall of independence. What did she expect him to do? Sit on the porch drinking iced tea in the shade while she seeded the lawn and dug in the flower beds? Even when she'd put together the lawn furniture she'd bought, she'd tried to refuse his help.

Like hell.

Now, with him on the roof again, tearing away the damaged section, she stood below the ladder fretting.

He wore jeans to protect his knees, but no shirt, and he had to admit, he liked the lustful way Maxi stared at him.

"What's the verdict?" she asked.

"A lot of damage." He dug his fingers into a spongy section of wood, then crumbled it over the side to show her.

They both heard an ATV approaching. Maxi shaded her eyes and stared toward the long driveway.

Miles, alert to the visitor, since she hadn't had any, hurriedly came down the ladder. The last person to call was the cop, Fletcher, and he'd had the good sense not to return, not even with a report about the rifle shot.

But the guy now arriving wasn't Fletcher, was at least fifty years his senior.

Wearing a straw hat, a gray T-shirt and jeans, the guy smiled and waved as he pulled up on a dusty ATV and stopped right in front of them. He pulled off his hat, swiped his forearm over his brow and gingerly swung a leg over the side of the vehicle to dismount, his movements slow and methodical to match the limits of his age.

Once he had both feet on the ground, he brushed off his hand on his jeans and extended it to Miles. "How do? I'm Woody Barstow, Maxi's nearest neighbor."

Miles felt the strong grip, despite the man's age. "Mr. Barstow. Nice to meet you. I'm Maxi's friend Miles."

"Call me Woody. Everyone in these parts does." He grinned, putting creases into aged cheeks. "I'm glad to see she has some company out here."

Maxi was all smiles. "It's good to see you again, Woody. How've you been?"

"Oh, I'm all right. But that storm gave me some trouble and I've been doin' repairs or I'd have been over to check on you sooner."

She pointed up at the barn roof. "Us, too."

"What's this?" Woody went past them to the ladder. "Lost some shingles?"

Miles answered, "A few, but that's not the problem. It's the wood rot that's the bigger issue."

"You don't say." He scratched at his chin. "I built this barn for Meryl 'bout fifteen years ago."

"You?" Maxi said, "I didn't know that."

"Oh, yeah. Your grandma and I were real friendly. Good woman. Liked her a lot." Troubled, he glanced at Miles. "If there's wood rot, that means I didn't seal something properly."

"No," Miles said, wanting to reassure him. "I think another storm took shingles off a few years back. They weren't replaced, and that probably let the water in."

"I should'a been checkin' for Meryl. Just never thought of it." He gazed out at the rest of the property. "She was an independent sort, always wanting to do for herself, but usually I could talk her into lettin' me help on upkeep. I trimmed back big branches from these trees so they wouldn't fall on the house, replaced a window for her once and helped her pick out the new furnace and air-conditioning."

"Did you do the electricity?" Miles asked.

"Nah, that was a friend of mine. He put in the new breaker box and such at cost as a favor to me. I worried she'd burn the whole place down without it, everything was so overloaded." His graying brows pinched together. "Will's gone now, though. Passed a year ago."

"I'm sorry," Maxi said.

"It was his time. He'd had a good life." Woody drew a breath and again looked around the land. "I kept all this mowed for your grandma, you know. That's why I'm here. Figured I'd offer to come up with my tractor and take care of it."

"Oh," Maxi said, surprised by the offer. "That's so sweet of you, but I can take care of it."

"Why would you wanna do that when I already have the equipment?"

Miles didn't say it aloud, but he was thinking about Woody's friend Will who'd just passed away. He didn't think it'd be a good idea for Woody to be out in this heat for any length of time.

"I'll be around," Miles said instead. "I can take care of it."

"No," Maxi stated. "It's my property and I'll do it."

Woody looked between them before cackling a laugh. "Damn, she reminds me of Meryl."

Miles smiled with him. "I actually saw a riding mower in the barn. If it works, it should do the trick."

"It works," Maxi assured him. "I started it up one day."

"You look mighty happy about that," Woody noted aloud.

"Thinking about my grandma. A few times when I came to visit her, I caught her on the riding mower. For some reason it always embarrassed her."

"The woman hated to sweat," Woody stated. He leaned in to whisper, "I know cuz I caught her on it once, too."

Miles would be willing to bet there'd been a romance brewing between Meryl and Woody. "I'm sure she valued you as a good friend."

"That she did." His expression sobered. "I'm the one who found her, you know. Came to tell her I was heading into town and wanted to see if she'd go along. She sometimes did. We'd do our grocery shopping together, stop at the diner, just...chat."

Two elderly people alone, finding companionship together. Miles felt extra bad for the guy. Did he have any other friends around? Maybe he and Maxi could extend an invite or two.

Maxi, probably thinking the same thing, put her hand on his shoulder in sympathy. "I'm so sorry, Woody."

"It was the awfulest thing." He patted her hand. "Just the awfulest."

After a comforting squeeze, Maxi asked softly, "Woody, would you mind giving me some advice?"

He swallowed hard, shifted and finally nodded, his friendly expression back in place. "Be glad to. About what, exactly?"

"Well, I'm going to cut the grass soon. With all this rain, it's really greened up."

"Yeah, it's real pretty, ain't it?"

"But I was thinking about another way to keep it trimmed. First, though, I thought I'd add an extension to the barn."

That was news to Miles. "An extension?"

She nodded. "For goats."

Together, Woody and Miles repeated, "Goats?"

"I've been researching it, and goats could keep that property cleared for me. They're friendly and smart and, from what I've read, they eat a lot."

What the hell? Miles stared at her, but she didn't meet his gaze.

Woody looked as startled as Miles felt. "Well, now, goats ain't a bad idea. It's a good idea, actually. But you don't need to add on to the barn. Why, I could build you another shelter farther out—"

"No, I want all the animals right here, closer to the house. In fact, I'm considering a chicken coop on the other side. So what do you think? How hard would it be to add on to the side of the barn over there?" She pointed to where she, apparently, wanted the first addition.

Woody scratched his chin again, then looked at Miles. "It'd really be easier to build a different shelter."

Miles agreed, but it wasn't his decision. He shrugged. "She's the boss."

Woody gave him an assessing look. "I figured maybe you two were sweethearts."

He didn't deny or confirm that when he said, "Wouldn't matter. It's still Maxi's property to do with as she pleases."

Maxi beamed at him for that reply. "Here's what I'm thinking." Assuming both men would follow, she headed for the far side of the barn. "The rotted wood is up there, and I understand that part of the roof will have to be torn out to repair it with fresh lumber. Well, why not extend the roofline down a little farther? We could cut a door into this wall, to connect it to the main body of the barn. I could close it when I want to keep the goats outside, but open it when I wanted to let them in. I figured a smaller enclosure could be built out here." She swept her hand to show what she wanted.

Miles could see it. "You'd need to fence in the property, too."

"Luckily the rain has softened the ground." She wrinkled her nose. "Lots of postholes to dig."

Startled by that, Woody rubbed the back of his neck. "Goats, huh?"

She nodded. "Goats."

"And chickens, too?"

"That'll be the project after the goats."

He nodded in distraction, then jumped subjects. "You know how I met your grandma? I wanted to buy this property from her. She wouldn't sell, though."

Guessing where that was headed, Maxi said gently, "I won't sell either."

"Oh, I know that. Knew it soon as I met ya." Then his eyes twinkled. "But if you ever change your mind..."

She smiled with him. "You're the first person I'll call."

"Then if you're sure I can't cut the grass for you—"

"I'm sure."

"—I'll be on my way."

As he headed back to his ATV, Miles followed. "I like your ride."

"This old thing? She gets me around to the neighbors. On these old gravel roads, damn near everyone drives their four-wheelers—even though we're not supposed to. Gotta take the truck when I go into town, though."

"You know any hunters who use them?"

"Yeah, 'course I do. Bastards, er, excuse me, Maxi."

"That's all right."

"Anyway, damned hunters drove through my property and tore up my garden. If I'd seen them, they'd have felt the sting of buckshot. But it was early morning, and by the time I got outside, they were gone." His gaze sharpened on Maxi. "You had trouble?"

She glanced at Miles, clearly remembering his warning. He smiled to let her know he appreciated it.

Answering for her, he said, "Someone took a wide shot or something. Rifle slug hit the barn, passed through and got embedded in the rafter."

Eyes wide, Woody whistled. "Someone could have been hurt!"

"That's how I saw it. Anyway, if you hear of anyone hunting around here, let me know, okay? I'd like to have a word or two."

Woody grinned again. "I bet you would, a big guy like yourself."

"You're not exactly small," he pointed out. Woody Barstow was probably five-ten at least, and while he looked thin, he didn't appear frail. He stood straight, shoulders relaxed but back.

"Aw," he groused. "These old bones damn near rattle when I walk. But I can't complain. No, I can't." He climbed onto his seat with as much care as he'd used getting off the ATV. "Maxi, you have my number. You need anything, especially with that barn addition, you just let me know, okay?"

"Thank you, Woody. And the same to you."

He smiled. "Yes, ma'am. You're a good neighbor. Appreciate that." He started the engine, did a slow, wide turn and puttered cautiously down the long driveway to the gravel road.

Miles turned to her, his brows up and his curiosity ripe. *"Goats?"*

The surprise in his voice made her laugh, and damn, he liked that, seeing her so relaxed and excited about a project.

"I've been thinking about it, mostly because my grandma thought about it before me. I saw her a few weeks before she passed and she was talking about it."

"Just hadn't gotten around to it?"

"I think it was more that she read up on them." Mischief twinkled in her dark eyes. "She told me the term *horny goat* suddenly made sense, and that goat sex definitely didn't sound sexy."

Miles grinned. "No?"

"Actually, it's pretty gross."

Ready to tease her back, he asked in feigned innocence, "How so?"

In a scandalized whisper, she confided, "Apparently male goats stay ready, if you get my drift. And it's...visible. Plus, they pee on everything, including themselves."

"Glad I'm not a goat."

Her mouth twitched. "I'm glad you're not, too."

This was the first time he'd seen her so animated, and like every other facet of her personality, it turned him on. "So you really do want to extend the barn?"

"Even though it's what my grandma had wanted, I'd been putting it off, since I had so many other repairs already on my plate. But since we have to redo part of the roof anyway, now seems like a good time."

"That's a lot more involved than just a roof repair."

She stepped up to him, her small, soft hands pressing on his bare chest, her head tipped back so she could smile up at him. "I know." She took a breath. "Don't blow a gasket, but I'm going to hire someone."

Blow a gasket? Yeah, he just might. Irritation gathered, making him frown, but he attempted to keep his voice even. "Are you forgetting that you hired me to protect you?"

"Not for a minute." She stepped closer still, until her plump breasts pressed to his ribs. "But I can't stop living my life, right? And what better way to move on than to stay busy."

Was that what she was doing, making her life so busy that she couldn't think about the existing danger?

Was he part of that plan, a means to keep the bad things at bay...but nothing more? "No one is asking you to stop living, but you do need to run things by me, at least until we've solved the mystery of who's bothering you." Such a mild way to remind her she could have been killed, yet even in his annoyance he was reluctant to disturb her current upbeat attitude.

"You said it yourself, having more activity here will get rid of the illusion that I'm all alone."

If Miles could help it, she'd never be alone again. *And just where the hell had that idea come from?* Sidestepping his appalling inclination to make more out of what they currently had, he said, "I suppose I could get the guys out here to help—"

"No."

That adamant denial gave him pause and ratcheted up his annoyance. "No?"

Uncertainty shifted her gaze away from his. "I don't want you doing more than what you were hired for."

There it was, her insistence that he sit around twiddling his thumbs—a stark reminder that while she might have employed him, and she sure as hell enjoyed the physical part of their relationship, she still hadn't let him in. He was no closer to her now than he'd been before her visit to the Body Armor agency and, damn it, it infuriated him.

Because she didn't want him close.

Stung by that truth, Miles considered how to react. Yeah, he wanted to tell her what he really thought, that he didn't appreciate being used, but would that get him the desired effect? Probably not. After weighing his words for a few seconds—while trying to ignore the touch of her fingers against his bare skin—he finally said, "Maybe now's a good time for you to tell me the exact parameters of my job."

Those teasing fingers curled against his skin. "You already know."

"No, I don't think I do." He caught both wrists and, to help him focus on his grievance, gently moved her hands away. "Enlighten me."

Going stiff, she stepped back. "You're supposed to protect me."

"Yeah." So far, so good. "And?"

Her frown deepened. "Setting up the surveillance stuff was good. You did such a great job with it, Woody didn't even notice. Everything blends in."

He nodded, accepting the accolade. "Thanks. And?"

Taking a stand, she said, "That's it. Protection. Not roof repair or grass cutting or—"

Her repeated efforts to cut him out irked enough that he asked, "Sex?"

She sucked in a breath, her expression suddenly hurt. "I figured that was freely given."

"Oh, hell yeah, it is."

She relaxed the tiniest bit.

Until he added, "Just as my help with other things is freely given."

She went right back to bristling...times ten. "That's different and you know it."

"Yeah. At least you don't mind using me in bed."

Heat rushed to her face. For a second, she looked like she might cry, and it devastated him. Then she fisted her hands and snarled, "We use each other."

He wanted so much more than that. Laughing at his own stupidity, he bit out, "Jesus, I'd almost forgotten. Sex doesn't mean much to you, does it? It's less personal than me hammering in a nail on the roof."

The embarrassed color washed from her face. "I'm not paying you to hammer nails."

"Not paying me to fuck either."

As if he'd slapped her, she dropped back a step. Before Miles could apologize, she stiffened her shoulders. "I misunderstood your interest."

He did his own stiffening. "That's not what I said, so don't do that whole female BS of twisting my words around."

"Female BS?" Charging forward two steps, she poked a finger at him. "Listen up, *Legend*."

Shit. He was back to his fight name again?

She breathed hard but said nothing else. Finally, she twisted around, her back to him, arms crossed tightly and one hip cocked out.

Miles waited. He knew a pissed-off woman when he saw one, not that her anger wasn't deserved. Yeah, his comment about paid fucking was over the line.

Hell, he didn't want to fight with her. He wanted her to open up, accept him.

He wanted her to want him, in all ways, as much as he did her. He just didn't know how to make it happen. But insulting her sure as hell wouldn't do it. "Maxi—"

"I was unfair."

Miles wasn't entirely sure what she meant by that, so he didn't yet say anything. Sometimes silence was a safer bet than another verbal fumble.

Her proud shoulders slumped. In a small voice, she whispered, "You made it clear you didn't want to get sexually involved again." With a humorless laugh, she added, "Obviously I did. But knowing how you felt, I shouldn't have…insisted."

Wondering where she was going with this, wishing he could better understand, Miles said, "Pretty sure I was willing."

She shook her head. "No, you weren't, but I teased you and even got annoyed when that didn't work. You finally gave in, but it wasn't your idea." She used the toe of her shoe to nudge at a weed in the yard. "I didn't take 'no' for an answer. I forced the issue and that was wrong of me."

He would have laughed if he didn't know for certain how she'd react to that. Force? Not even close. Yes, she'd worked against his plan, but so what? The end result had sure been memorable.

He couldn't bear seeing her look so guilty and dejected. "Truth is, Maxi, that's one of the things I enjoy most about you."

She went still, then peeked back at him. "What do you mean?"

"How up-front and honest you are about sex. How much you enjoy it." *With me.* He stared into her startled eyes. "You don't play games about what you want, and that's a huge turn-on."

Biting her bottom lip, she faced forward again. After a second, she gave a shrug. "I want you. Did from the moment I first saw you. And you were even better than I'd anticipated." Again scuffing the toe of her shoe in the dirt, she complained, "It's so blasted complicated. It's like I know what I need to do, but you're here now and I can't be expected to resist that." Another glance. "Unless you don't want the same. And if you don't, I swear I won't pressure you again."

He couldn't help smiling. "You know better."

"Do I?"

Slowly Miles closed the space between them, then cautiously rested his hands on her rigid shoulders. She didn't jerk away, so he considered that a good sign. "I was trying to make a point."

That had her turning away again with bitterness. "Yeah, that I'm needy enough to take sex even though it's not in the job description?"

"No." Well…yeah. Sort of. "You're not needy, so forget that. After everything you've been through, I do think you enjoy the closeness, though. And so do I."

She said nothing.

"The point is more that this situation isn't the usual job. We're both adapting, right?" He rushed to clarify, "I don't mean the sex. If you'll recall, I wasn't the one who called quits on that the first time around."

Her head dropped forward and she heaved another breath. "I know."

Rubbing his thumbs into her shoulders in a brief massage, he reiterated, "I want you, Maxi, no matter what else is going on. Remember that, okay?"

Beneath his hands, the tensed muscles in her shoulders loosened. This time her head tipped back. "I can't help but feel the same."

So she might fight herself, but the chemistry was too strong for her to resist? Relief hit him like a wave of…lust?

He gave it quick analysis and concluded, *definitely lust.*

Any acceptance from her fired his blood, and damn it, that wouldn't do. He'd been ridiculously obvious in wanting her, and yet she still held him at an emotional distance.

She'd said it plain out, that she didn't *want* to want him, and that made all the difference to things. It was the reason he'd been reluctant to get involved again in the first place.

He'd completely lost sight of his plan, but it was past time he got back to it. If sex was the big draw, then by God, he'd use it to his advantage—and hopefully make other, more concrete and lasting, progress along the way.

"Usually a bodyguard is there to ensure things go smoothly in a designated time frame, rather than an open-ended deal."

Showing some interest, she asked, "What kind of time frame?"

It didn't take him long to come up with an example. "Like an MMA fighter who doesn't want to get mobbed by fans. The bodyguard can run interference on that during a promo stint for one evening."

Interest growing, she looked back at him again. "Did that ever happen to you?"

"Few times."

She twisted to face him fully, her umbrage possibly forgotten. "Really?"

As she'd turned, he'd adjusted his hands so that they now framed her neck, his thumbs caressing her jawline. It'd be so easy to slide them under her chin and tilt her face up for a kiss that led to a whole lot more.

Uncommitted sex, that was what she wanted.

He wanted the sex, too. Well, that and more.

But they needed this talk.

"I was doing a promotion gig once and there were some fans that'd had too much to drink. Even though I was behind a table, one of them kept trying to crawl over to get into my lap."

Her expression of fascination flashed to irritation. "You're talking about women?"

Miles hid his grin. "The sport does have its fair share of female fans."

"I didn't realize."

He noted her acerbic tone. Jealousy? He'd like to think so. "There were four of them being outrageous, three of them egging on the fourth to steal a kiss."

Her lip curled. "Oh, and I just bet you were all kinds of unwilling."

"Actually, I was. They were completely smashed, and I was working. Hell, the line of fans was long, and people were taking pics left and right. I knew then that I needed a bodyguard, someone other than me who could play the heavy and tell them to get lost. Luckily Cannon and Armie were there, and they lent a hand."

She blinked. "Cannon and Armie?"

"Friends of mine. Both champion fighters."

"What did they do? Drag the women away?"

Miles couldn't help but laugh at that image. "Hardly. If either of them had been noticed, they'd have been mobbed more than I was. No, they sent over a guard from the event and that guy corralled them. It wasn't a dangerous situation, but it was awkward as hell."

"Did you ever hire a bodyguard?"

He shook his head. No, instead of needing a bodyguard, he'd quit the sport he loved. Thinking about it twisted his guts.

Talking about it was out of the question. Not yet. Definitely not while she stayed so uninvolved.

He forced a smile. "I became one instead."

"But—"

Choosing to finish that particular battle on another day, he said, "Let's check on that mower you mentioned, see what kind of shape it's in."

"Miles!"

He turned, relieved that she was no longer using his fight name. "I didn't quite bring that full circle, did I?"

"No, you didn't."

"Okay, so I'm going for plain speaking and I hope you'll try to hear what I mean, even if I say it wrong."

Impatient now, she said, "I'll try."

"I'm not an idle guy. No way am I going to sit around day in and day out doing nothing, especially not when you're working. It's not how I'm made. I can keep an eye on things, which is all I'm really doing right now, while also getting some of the things done that you mentioned—things I *enjoy* doing."

She gave that some thought and offered an olive branch. "You really do enjoy it?"

"Don't you?" He could almost swear that she did. Dirt under her nails, sweat on her brow, cat hair everywhere—she looked to be in her element. But she seemed just as at ease in the kitchen, or shopping, or, better still, in bed.

With him.

"Yes," she confirmed, and then logically, "but it's my place."

"Doesn't matter. I like using my hands. I like the sunshine and fresh air. Hell, I like sweating." *And he liked spending time with her.* No, better not go into that right now. "I want you to stop worrying that you're taking advantage. If I don't want to do something, I won't offer."

"But you're working so hard."

He laughed. "I work harder at exercise."

"When you were in MMA?"

"And at the agency." He explained, "Body Armor has a gym and an even better indoor gun range so we can all stay at the top of our game."

"That's part of your job, then," she decided. "But this is just...labor."

"Do I look like I can't handle it?"

With a soft sigh, she said, "You look amazing."

Damn, he did love the way this one particular woman looked at him, as if she could devour him with that dark, velvety gaze. "Keep that up," he warned, "and we'll be doing the nasty here in the dirt."

The crude comment made her grin, lightening the earlier antagonistic mood. "With a bunch of cats watching?"

"Probably." He held out a hand. "Will you trust that I'm enjoying myself?"

She waffled, but in the end she stepped up to him, took his hand and said, "Thank you." With her head on his shoulder, she asked, "Will you kindly remember that it's my property and I'm not an idle person either?"

"Sounds like a deal." They'd both work all day, and burn up the sheets at night. Yeah, a very sweet deal.

And somewhere along the way, maybe he'd win her over.

A guy could hope.

CHAPTER ELEVEN

Fresh from a shower, Maxi stood at the kitchen counter watching the setting sun through the window. The brilliant shades of pink and purple over the horizon never failed to take her breath away. The power of nature, the beauty of it and the peace it gave her left her awed.

Somewhere out there, danger remained. Nothing that insane would just disappear. Eventually it would return, but presently it couldn't intrude on her contentment.

She had wonderful plans in the works. Little by little the farmhouse was coming together. And best of all, she and Miles had ironed out a few conflicts…at least, she hoped they had.

Midweek they'd gone shopping and she'd bought a patio table and chairs that fit on the small deck off the back of the house, along with a larger set now in the yard near the grill. She'd also bought rockers, a glider and a few random lawn chairs.

The cats loved it all, as she'd known they would. They draped themselves over every surface. Anytime she or Miles wanted to sit outside, they had to first move a cat or two.

He never once complained about the cat hairs on the seat of his jeans. Instead, Miles put in an effort to win over some of the more feral animals, convincing them with patience—and food—to come close enough for him to pet.

It never failed to soften her heart, and that worried her more than any external threat.

It would be so easy for her to lose sight of the endgame: independence, responsibility and honoring her grandmother's wishes. This could be her last opportunity to do things right, to make amends for a thoughtless past.

To prove to herself that she had what it took to make it.

Playing house with Miles, because that was how it felt, could so easily make her forget her goals. She continually had to remind herself that he was a gorgeous, successful MMA star, now working for an elite, expensive agency. He could have his pick of women.

Why would he choose her?

Just because he enjoyed playing on the farm for a bit didn't mean he'd want to settle down here for good.

Yet that was exactly what she planned to do. This place would be her home forever. She'd grow old here, while Miles had a whole exciting life ahead of him.

He was here because she'd hired him.

He was in her bed because she'd been pushy. Oh, he enjoyed it now, she wasn't worried about that. But if she hadn't come on so strong, would he have been content sticking to the letter of the job—protecting her, and nothing more?

Was it the sex, she wondered, that made him feel obligated to do so many other chores?

She hadn't yet hired anyone, and he hadn't mentioned the idea of bringing his friends around to help. In fact, she wasn't quite sure where they stood with things and she wasn't keen on rocking the boat.

Since their small argument, he'd been insatiable, always reaching for her morning, noon and night. The man was tireless, and he left her in a fog of satisfaction. But was it more than the amazing sex? She couldn't help wondering.

Twice burned, you'd think she could keep things straight in her head instead of grabbing for a romance that didn't exist.

Didn't mean she couldn't have fun, just that she had to keep reality uppermost in her mind.

She was thinking about Miles in her life while watching a black cat make his way to the barn, his sleek body silhouetted by the bright hues of the sunset, when she felt Miles nuzzle the back of her neck.

Tingles ran over her body. He melted her so easily that now she felt addicted, always wanting more and more. When the job ended and he left her, his absence would be crushing. She'd miss his presence, his touch, the taste and feel of him. Talking with him, laughing, discussing plans…it was like a fairy tale that would end far too soon.

What she needed to do was store up memories to carry her for a good long while afterward.

Determined to do just that, she turned within the cage of his muscular arms where he'd braced his hands on the counter at either side of her hips. He wore only shorts again, leaving the rest of his incredible body bare.

Without a word, she leaned up to taste his mouth. He accommodated her, turning his head a bit, parting his lips when she teased her tongue over them.

He gave his tongue in return, and she sucked on it, earning a soft growl from him.

She loved his heady taste, the delicious scent of his body.

Touching him was a unique joy, feeling the light covering of hair over his firm chest, the rock-hard shoulders, the tensing of his biceps, down to his hair-covered forearms.

Leaving his mouth, she put a nipping kiss on his chin, lazily licked his throat and rubbed her nose against his sternum. "Mmm. You are such a treat."

"There we go again," he murmured against her temple, "with the pot calling the kettle black."

Maxi knew she wasn't a hag. She had more than enough style sense to know she usually presented a nice appearance. Her blond hair was thick, her lashes dark, her figure trim. Her B-cup boobs satisfied her, and her legs were nicely shaped. But was she on a par with Miles? That was asking for a lot, so she doubted it. Even on her best days, when she'd been dressed her finest, manicured and polished, she didn't think she'd compare to him.

Now that she spent her days in bedraggled comfort? Not even close.

Proving he didn't mind her lack of style, he stepped against her so that she felt his erection against her belly. "What are you thinking, babe?"

Too many things to explain. "How perfect you are."

The smile came slowly. "Perfect, huh?"

She ran a hand over a sculpted pec muscle. He wasn't over-blown like a bodybuilder, but she doubted he had an ounce of fat on him anywhere. "You know it's true."

"It's not, but I'm horny, so I'm not about to talk you out of that attitude."

She laughed. That was another thing to adore about Miles. He lightened her mood and effortlessly made her happy so that it was hard to remember the misery of only a few days ago. "Are you ever not horny?"

"Around you? Afraid not."

Oh, she liked the sound of that. Hopefully he felt the attraction as strongly as she did.

Staring into his eyes, she lowered her hand down his body until she cupped his testicles through the soft nylon of his shorts. His lids grew heavy and his jaw flexed.

She loved touching Miles, watching his muscles clench, hearing the harshness of his breathing. She stroked her palm up his pulsing shaft, then wrapped her fingers around him. "Maybe I can help you with that."

His eyes closed on a low breath. "Counting on it."

When she nudged him back a step, they opened again in question. She smiled before slowly sinking to her knees in front of him.

"Damn." One hand cupped the back of her head, the other braced against the counter as if he needed help staying upright.

"Let's get these shorts out of the way." She tugged them down, not surprised to discover that he'd skipped boxers. Miles often went commando when he was in the mood.

He kicked the shorts away in haste and planted his big feet apart.

"You're so cooperative," she teased, running her hands up and down the front of his strong thighs while leaning forward to kiss his stomach. The already defined muscles drew tighter.

Making a rough sound, he used the hand at the back of her head to direct her where he most wanted to feel her mouth.

Since she wanted that, too, she didn't deny him. She wrapped the fingers of one hand around the base of his erection, then brushed her lips up along the underside...to the sensitive head. His fingers tangled in her hair.

Enjoying the rush of his labored breathing, she licked back down to the base, taking a moment to inhale his scent before licking back up—and drawing him in.

His legs locked and he tipped his head back. But not for long.

He looked down at her again, his gaze burning hot while the fingers in her hair massaged, guided, urged her to take him deeper. Miles wasn't a small man, but she loved the taste and feel of him, and his reaction to what she did to him turned her on as much as the act itself.

His big hand slid to the side of her face, and she felt the rough pad of his thumb brushing over the hollow of her cheek as she sucked him in.

Maxi took her time enjoying him, opening both hands over his firm butt, trailing them around to his abs, cuddling his balls again. She swirled her tongue as she withdrew, flattened it against him when she swallowed him down once more.

"Enough," he groaned.

No, it wasn't even close to enough. She wasn't sure a lifetime would be enough.

"Maxi."

She sucked as she pulled back, got rewarded with his groan, but instead of releasing him, she came down again, taking even more of him this time.

"God."

She tasted his pre-cum and knew he was close. It was a heady thing, pushing Miles Dartman, *The Legend*, to lose his control.

He tried one more time to warn her. "I'm going to come."

In answer, she increased her efforts, and after the briefest of hesitations, both his hands fisted in her hair. She felt the tension spiraling through him, felt his legs stiffening, then he groaned harshly, his body shuddering as he took his release.

She still didn't want to let him go, and only when he flinched away, his hand smoothing back her hair, did she look up at him.

My, my, my. He might have come, but he wasn't done. The heat remained in those beautiful green eyes, now bright with intent.

He drew in a deep breath, blew it out slowly, then said, "Up with you, now," and pulled her up to stand before him. She leaned against him, feeling soft and aroused and, damn it, almost desperate.

His arms came around her, the embrace languid. After several warm, soft kisses to her shoulder, her cheek, he whispered, "Let's see to you now."

"I'm okay." She wasn't, but since he'd just come—

"You're better than okay." He nuzzled against her until she lifted her face. "You're fucking amazing. You didn't think once would be enough, did you? Because I'm getting hard again right now."

Dubious, she glanced down, then slowly smiled. "So you are."

"You doubted me?" Catching the hem of her T-shirt, he peeled it up and over her head, then leaned back to gaze at her breasts. "Much better. But the shorts need to go, too."

Liking this game, she leaned back with her elbows on the counter and said, "Feel free."

He stepped up against her, kissing her neck while sliding both hands into her shorts and over her cheeks. He growled against her skin, "I love this ass," and gave her a soft love bite that made her gasp in pleasure.

He pushed the shorts down until they dropped to her feet. "Let's play a little."

Her heart started tripping. "Okay."

His smile teased. "Now who's agreeable?" Without waiting for an answer, he turned her. "Brace your hands on the counter."

Maxi did as told.

"Beautiful." His hand slid down her spine, over her bottom, then under her, stroking until his fingers were wet with her excitement.

Unable to stay still, she squirmed.

"Move your feet back," he said, and then, "A little more." The position had her stretched out, balanced on her straightened arms.

Still touching her, Miles whispered, "Arch your back."

It felt so risqué to be doing this in the kitchen of all places, the overhead light shining down on them. Risqué and wonderful.

She arched, her backside in the air and the recipient of his keen attention.

"Damn," he whispered. "Don't move."

She looked over her shoulder and saw him swipe up his shorts, then draw a condom from the loose pocket.

"A man who comes prepared."

He tore the packet open with his teeth. "Around you, I keep a rubber nearby, always." Sheathing himself, he stepped up behind her, his hands firm on her hips as he slid his shaft against her. "Keep your arms tensed. This is going to be hard and fast and I don't want you bruised against the counter."

That warning made her shiver in anticipation. She was so wet, it should have embarrassed her, but it didn't. Wanting him to hurry, she pressed back against him.

He opened her, looking at her, she knew, but that didn't embarrass her either. Not with Miles.

She felt the head of his cock pressed to her, and her eagerness grew. "Miles," she pleaded.

Abruptly he sank in, as fast and hard as he'd promised, going deep even on that first stroke, stretching her, filling her.

Crying out, Maxi gripped the counter as he drove in again and again, rasping against her sensitive, swollen flesh, building up even more heat, more moisture.

She burned for him.

His hands cupped her breasts, his thumbs busy on her painfully tight nipples while he pounded into her.

She did her best to match his rhythm, tightening around him, squeezing greedily.

He groaned, and his right hand left her breast only to dip between her legs, his fingers now strumming over her clit until a bolt of sensation racked her. She went stiff, the scream of pleasure caught in her throat as a powerful climax cut through her, then slowly left her as a soft, vibrating moan.

Vaguely she became aware that Miles now had one arm locked around her middle, giving her support, his other hand flat beside hers. Right after that realization, she heard his hoarse groan as he found his release again.

They stayed like that, slumped over the sink, both of them gasping for breath. Maxi felt sated in body and mind. Give her a pillow and she could have slept right there on the kitchen floor.

She smiled with the thought, especially when she heard Miles moan as he stirred. *Not yet*, she wanted to say. *Please don't leave me yet.* She liked having him draped over her, still a part of her, their heartbeats aligned.

When her legs started to tremble, she gave it up. Once she got him in bed, she'd crawl against him and, she knew, he'd hold her all night long.

With that thought in mind she lifted her head and, through the window, something odd caught her eye.

It was the dark silhouette against the last rays of the pink sunset.

By slow degrees she realized what she was seeing.

There at the far edge of her property was a person...watching them with binoculars.

Damn, but he'd gotten sidetracked there. He'd planned to sneak to the barn and was only checking to make sure he wouldn't get busted, but he hadn't expected his own personal porno.

So the lady was not only bullheaded, she was a wild little thing, too. He'd tried not to notice her looks. It didn't make any difference if she was pretty or a dog. He wasn't a bastard to take advantage of a woman that way either way. But after seeing that show today, it'd be hard to put it out of his mind.

He'd gotten so involved in watching, he'd damn near gotten caught—and he'd never made it to the barn. From now on he'd have to be more careful.

And somehow he'd have to block those sexual images from his brain.

Midway through the next day, Miles continued to stew. Last night, he'd almost charged out buck naked. Only Maxi's panicked grasping on his arm had slowed him enough to pull on his shorts and detour into the bedroom for his gun.

Of course, by then whoever had been spying on them was gone.

Maxi had been understandably shaken. After a thorough search of the grounds, he'd returned to find her redressed and frantic. The second he stepped in she'd grabbed him— almost as if he mattered to her—and held him tight, her face against his chest.

He'd checked the surveillance cameras and found nothing more than a shadowy figure dressed in black. With the bright kitchen light on, they'd probably been easy to spot.

He'd done what he could to reassure her, but what could he say? The fucker plaguing her might not have seen her body, or at least not more than her upper torso, but there would have been no mistaking what they'd been doing.

On a gut level, it disturbed him to know he'd been watched—and it had to be far worse for her.

Now, on the way to town, it bothered him that Maxi remained so quiet. He reached across the seat and took her hand.

Flashing a quick, barely there smile, she squeezed his fingers. "I can't help worrying. What if someone comes in while we're gone?"

"We'll see it on the cameras." But her reasoning was why he'd insisted on going early. He wanted to be back by the afternoon.

When she suddenly looked around, finally paying attention to their direction, she frowned. "I thought we were going to shop."

"We are." He brushed his thumb over her knuckles. "We're sticking to the area, though." He'd deliberately decided to use the small store in town rather than making the trip out of the area. "They have a Walmart or something, right? We can get some blinds there." That would be their number one purchase—privacy blinds for all the windows.

"My grandmother rarely bothered to close the curtains."

"I'm glad she didn't have to."

She thought about that, then nodded. "You're right. Now, do you want to tell me why we're using the limited options in this Podunk town instead of going where there's more shopping?"

"Information."

"Meaning?"

Last night, while he'd held her close to him and listened to her slow breathing, he'd known she couldn't sleep any more than he could. That was when he'd made up his mind.

Waiting to catch the bastard in the act wasn't working. He needed to go after him instead.

"In a small town, everyone knows everyone. If we visit a few shops, someone might tell us something we don't already know."

"Heck, no one even knows I'm here."

"That cop knew. Mr. Barstow knows. Maybe they've talked to others, maybe not."

"What in the world could they have said that would make any difference?"

"No idea." He knew not to make assumptions about anything. After all, he had assumed he'd still be a fighter. He'd assumed he'd have a title fight coming up. Making assumptions just set you up for surprises—and disappointment. "But the best way to find out is to visit town and introduce ourselves."

She rolled in her lips. "You know people are going to think we're living together."

"We *are* living together."

"Not like that we aren't." Clearly trying not to offend him, she said, "I hired you."

"I'm glad you did." He grinned to let her know she didn't have to tiptoe around him.

She started to smile, too, when the roar of engines caught them both by surprise. Seconds later an ATV raced out of a field directly in front of them, followed by two more.

Miles damn near collided with them. He braked, holding the wheel tight when his tires skidded across the gravel road, almost putting him in a ditch.

The lead ATV driver spun around on the other side of the road and came to a stop. His two cohorts did the same.

Furious, Miles turned to Maxi. "Are you okay?"

She nodded. "Good Lord, that was close."

He jammed the gear shift into Park and reached for the door handle.

"Miles." She placed her hand on his arm. "They're boys."

He looked up to see that the lead driver was off his vehicle and, expression stunned, was walking toward them.

"So they are." He patted her thigh. "Stay put." He was out of the SUV before she could say anything more.

Miles stepped toward the boys. "Everyone okay?"

The kid in front, probably fifteen or so, ran a hand over messy brown hair. "Yeah, you?"

Miles nodded.

"I'm sorry. No one is ever on this road."

"Hard to believe there's a road for no reason."

The boy flushed. "I meant that we ride here all the time and there's never anyone around." He looked beyond Miles to see Maxi. "She okay?"

"Thankfully, yes. You boys should be more careful."

"Yes, sir."

That sign of respect went a long way. Miles asked, "What's your name?"

"I'm Lee. That's Hull and Billy."

He glanced at the helmet Lee held under one arm. "You three old enough to be driving those things?"

Hedging now, the boy said, "You gotta be sixteen unless you have an adult supervising."

"Are any of you adults?"

Guilt flooded his face. "No, sir. But no one around here really cares."

Miles managed a smile. "Guess it's a little different here in the country."

Jumping on that, Lee said, "Right. There's no harm." His eyes widened. "I mean, usually."

"So you boys are out here often?"

He nodded fast. "Mrs. Nevar never minded. She'd let us ride through her property near the woods."

"Is that right? Any of you boys hunt?"

"Yeah, but that's something we only do when one of our dads is with us."

Insane. Miles kept his smile in place. "You hunt around here?"

"Sometimes. Mrs. Nevar said having hunters prowl through the woods out back of her house helped to keep the coyotes away from her cats."

"That makes sense. But you know Mrs. Nevar passed away, right?"

Lee nodded, his gaze back on Maxi. "Is she the grand-daughter who moved in?"

Miles lifted a brow. "Where'd you hear that?"

"Everyone knows it. Most people figured she'd put it up for sale. Some had already been talking about buying it. But she moved in instead. It was a surprise."

"I bet. You boys been hunting around here lately?"

"No."

The other two finally worked up the nerve to join their

buddy instead of hanging back. Hull, a taller, blond-haired kid, said, "I did a few weeks back but haven't been here since."

"Who'd you hunt with?"

"My brother." In a hurry, he added, "He's twenty-two. But there are so many cats now, we were afraid we'd spook them." He rubbed his ear. "Everyone liked Mrs. Nevar. No one wants to bother her cats. Donny and me even went by there a few times to give them food."

"That was nice of you, thanks." Miles wondered how many other people felt comfortable just showing up on the property. "And I agree, shots would probably spook them." Eyeing the boys, Miles said, "The cats were important to Mrs. Nevar just as they're important to her granddaughter."

From behind him, Miles heard Maxi say, "They're like my pets now."

All three boys gawked at her. You'd think they'd never seen a woman before. Granted, she looked extra fine today in tan shorts that showed off her beautiful legs and a white tank that hugged her torso. Her fair hair hung in loose waves and her smile was damn near enough to level him, so he could imagine what it'd do to boys.

"We'd appreciate it if you guys didn't hunt around the property anymore," Miles said, attempting—and failing—to draw their attention back to him.

"Actually," Maxi said, "the loud ATVs could scare the cats, too. I hate to be a stick in the mud—"

They all three tried to reassure her at the same time, making Miles almost roll his eyes.

"—but do you think you could ride the vehicles away from my property?"

"Sure thing."

"Not a problem."

"Wouldn't want to scare the cats."

That last one made Miles laugh. "You boys ever do any

yard work? Ms. Nevar has plenty of grass to cut, weeds to clear out from around the pond, stuff like that."

Maxi smiled. "That's a wonderful idea, Miles. If you boys are interested, why don't you come by in the morning and we can work out an hourly wage."

Billy elbowed Hull hard, prompting him to ask, "Are you Miles Dartman?"

"I am."

"The fighter?" Lee asked for clarification.

"MMA, yeah. Or used to be. I'm retired now."

The three looked at each other, and Lee said, "Shoot, I'd work for you for free!"

A few minutes later, back in the SUV, Miles said, "That went well."

She looked a little stunned. "Does *everyone* recognize you?"

"Not usually, no. But you heard the kid. Your buddy Fletcher is telling everyone who'll listen that you're living at the property now, and that you have an MMA fighter staying with you."

"Those boys seemed to think it's your property."

"I explained. You heard me."

"Not that they believed you." She fussed with the hem of her shorts. "They think we're a couple."

"Might not be a bad thing to let people assume." If he got his way, it could turn true. Every day, in a dozen different ways, he liked Maxi more. He'd wanted an opportunity to let that relationship grow without her putting limits on it, and without the threat encouraging her to a false closeness.

Always, in the back of his mind, he couldn't help but wonder if she'd have ever come back to him if she hadn't needed his help.

As to that, if things were miraculously resolved, would she send him packing again?

"You know," she said, "I was already thinking about asking them if they wanted to do some work."

"So I didn't overstep too badly?" Because she might not give him the answer he wanted, he continued smoothly with "They seemed more than eager to chat. I figured it couldn't hurt to have them around. We could get in some subtle questions and maybe find out more about the town than we'll accomplish with this visit."

"And," she added, "I really could use some help."

Since she didn't plan to let him do her tasks? He'd disabuse her of that—soon. But he saw no reason to start a fuss right before they reached their destination.

The town, if you could call it that, came into view with an antiques shop...next to a used car dealership, a printing store and a post office.

Each business practically sat on the road, separated only by the width of a sidewalk, proof that the two-lane road didn't start out that way. It was probably widened as the town grew.

"Every building is different," he marveled. "And look at all those details." Typical of older architecture, the facades had intricate scalloping, carved porch posts, eave brackets and bay windows, each trimmed in a complementary color so that on one house there might be three or four colors, not counting the slate shingles.

Maxi, having been to the town before, enjoyed watching his amazement. "It's like a step back in time, isn't it? Wait until you see the funeral home. It's amazing."

The only semi-modern buildings were a gas station/quick mart and a liquor store that shared the same roof as an accountant.

They passed a general store, but no Walmart. The town ended abruptly on one side with a bar, and on the other with residential houses.

"Huh."

"Told you it was tiny."

No exaggeration there. "Where's the vet?"

"Farther down, with homes on either side of it. You wouldn't know it was the location of the veterinarian's office if it wasn't for the Dr. Miller's shingle hanging out front."

"So the general store is it, I guess."

"I've been in there once before. They have just about everything, and anything they don't have in stock they can order."

"Then we'll head there first." Miles parked in a small lot opposite of the building along with six other cars. Together they crossed the street, and damned if people didn't come to gawk, some staring out of a quaint pharmacy window, others through a beauty salon window and some from a small grocery. He waved with a smile and kept walking.

Maxi snickered.

"They're bizarrely curious about outsiders."

"Right." She gave him a look. "I'm betting they know who you are and that's why you're drawing so much attention. You'll be like a local celebrity or something."

Snorting at that, he opened the chiming door for her and waited until she'd entered. They didn't have far to go before a petite, trim woman in her sixties greeted them. Given her name badge, she worked there. "Hello. Beautiful day, isn't it?"

Maxi said, "Hot, but I love the sunshine." Holding out her hand, she read the name badge. "Joan? I don't think I met you last time I was in. I'm Maxi Nevar. I moved into my grandmother's farm."

Joan clasped her hand in both of hers. "It's a pleasure, Maxi. What a pretty name! Very unusual."

"Thank you."

"You probably met my husband if you were in once before. We take turns running the place."

Miles stepped forward. "So you own the general store?"

"Yes, and my parents before me." She looked him over, smiled and held out her hand. "I'm Joan."

Miles took the small, thin hand in his. "Miles Dartman. I'm a friend of Maxi's."

"Helping her to get the place in shape, I bet."

Relieved that she didn't ask him about MMA—or worse, about being a bodyguard—he smiled and said, "Exactly."

She turned back to Maxi. "Meryl had her hands full, that's for sure." As if sharing a confidence, she lowered her voice and leaned in. "We all figured she and Woody were sweet on each other. Nothing ever did come of that, though. Guess they were just friends after all."

"Woody is very kind," Maxi said in a noncommittal way.

"He'd have done just about anything for Meryl." She shook her head in apparent sympathy, then perked up and asked, "What can I help you with?"

"I wanted some blinds for my windows."

"Right over here."

Amazingly enough, Joan had exactly what they needed for four of the five windows. Nothing fashionable, but the functional white mini blinds would do the job. For the fifth, bigger window in the kitchen, they chose a roll blind.

And by God, Miles would ensure the house was sealed up before dark.

They purchased other supplies while they were there, taking the time to meet and visit with various locals.

They'd just finished grocery shopping and were heading across the hot blacktop parking lot when Fletcher Bowman, his head down as he spoke on his cell phone, left his patrol car. Dark sunglasses in place, he headed toward them, still involved in a heated discussion.

"I haven't seen her, so how the hell should I know? No, I can't do that. Because he made it clear—"

Not until he almost collided with Miles did Fletcher realize they were waiting on him.

When he did, he pulled up short, started to automatically apologize, then realized who stood before him. He went still, saying into the phone, "I'll call you back."

Beneath the broiling afternoon sun, heat wafted off the blacktop in suffocating waves.

"Fletcher," Miles said and, indicating the phone he held, asked, "Problem?"

"What? No." He shoved the phone in his pocket and turned to Maxi. "Here, let me help you with that." Without giving her a chance to deny him, Fletcher took the bag she carried.

Miles resisted the urge to roll his eyes.

Maxi, nonplussed, fashioned a smile and said, "We're right here." She headed toward the SUV.

Fletcher, the bastard, watched her. The sunglasses hid his eyes, but Miles knew damn good and well that the officer was eyeing her ass.

He rudely pressed past Fletcher, bumping him hard on the wall.

Maxi had the back of the SUV open and waiting on them. They'd bought so much that not a lot of room remained. Shifting everything into one arm, Miles pushed the new boxed blinds into a pile and set down his groceries.

Fletcher took in their haul. "Looks like you hit up the town."

"Close," Maxi said. "Most of that is from the general store, but I also needed some new tools from the hardware store."

"And groceries," Miles said, taking the bag from Fletcher and squeezing it in with everything else.

Pulling off his sunglasses, Fletcher took in the posthole digger and post driver, both long, heavy tools that took up a lot of space in the cargo area. His gaze shifted to Maxi. "You putting in some fencing?"

Miles noticed how Maxi judiciously avoided eye contact with him while explaining about her plan for goats.

When he'd steered Maxi to the hardware store to pick out the tools, he'd known that he might be ending their truce over the distribution of work. So far, though, she hadn't mentioned that a hired contractor would already have those tools to use.

Whether or not that meant she'd go along with *him* doing the work, he didn't know yet.

"Goats, huh?" Fletcher gave her a fond smile. "No cows or horses?"

She wrinkled her nose. "Let me start with goats, and then I'll see."

"Think they'll get along with the cats?"

"I don't see why not."

He cast a glance at Miles, before giving her a longer look. "If you need help maintaining the property—"

"She doesn't." *How dare the dick flirt with her right in front of me?*

Maxi said quickly, "No, I don't. I'll have the goats, right?"

"But if you'd rather not get goats—"

"Now, Fletcher," she teased, "don't you start, too. I'm looking forward to the goats. Cows and horses are a bit much, but I might get some chickens, too."

Fletcher laughed. "Next time I see you, you might be growing corn."

With a slanted glance, she confessed, "Well, I *was* thinking of a garden in the spring."

Picturing that, Miles smiled at her. She kept taking on more work with enthusiasm. As a personal stylist, Maxi was amazing, but here, in this small-town setting, she was in her element.

Fletcher finally gave all his attention to Miles. "Don't know how much experience you have, but woven wire fencing is best for goats. If the wire squares are too large, they get their heads in there, then get their horns stuck."

"We don't want that," Maxi said.

"Denton Lumber is your best bet. They have the posts and the wire and they deliver to the job site. They're about a mile south of here, past the vet's, over the railroad tracks and then to the right."

Miles nodded. "Thanks. Any idea how long they take to deliver?"

"In a hurry to get started, huh?"

While Maxi was agreeable? Yeah. But he only shrugged.

"Odds are if you called Larry Denton now, he'd deliver by tomorrow morning."

Nice. Holding out his hand, Miles said, "Appreciate it."

Fletcher accepted without any attempts at one-upmanship, just a friendly handshake and a fare-thee-well as he went on his way.

Miles watched him go, wondering what the officer was up to.

"He was *nice*, Miles, so why are you looking so suspicious?"

"Because he was nice." Putting his arm around her and leading her to the passenger side, he asked, "How do you feel about one more trip? It's still early enough that we could be back to your place before dinner."

She fastened her seat belt. "The lumberyard?"

Leaning one arm over the open door, the other on the roof of the SUV, Miles nodded. "Might as well."

"Do you mean 'might as well, since she's not fighting me,' or 'might as well because we're nearby'?"

Knowing he'd already won, he grinned. "Both?"

"You're incorrigible."

Miles laughed. "That's a new one." Bending down to steal a quick kiss, he said against her lips, "Thanks, honey."

Maxi was still shaking her head when he got behind the wheel. "Only you would be thanking me for letting you put in a fence on my property."

Only me. Yeah, he liked the sound of that.

CHAPTER TWELVE

Maxi could honestly say it was the best week of her entire life. Justice came out one day with his fiancée, Fallon, who fell in love with the cats. She and Maxi spent most of their time in the barn, playing with the animals, while Justice helped Miles hang a heavy bag from one of the beams.

That fascinated Maxi, especially when Miles did some hits and kicks to ensure the bag was secure. He moved so fluidly, with seeming little effort that caused incredible impact. It further boggled her when Justice, despite his great size, moved with equal speed and ease.

Fallon had leaned toward her to say, "Isn't it amazing?"

Maxi nodded, unwilling to take her gaze off the men.

"Justice stays in that amazing shape, although he tells me he's not as 'shredded' now as he used to be. How that's possible, I don't know, because he's definitely solid."

"Miles is, too, even though he eats three times what I do."

"He's three times your size," Fallon said with a smile. "And they're always busy doing something. I'm convinced that fighters have incredible metabolisms."

Maxi watched as Fallon tucked back her silky dark hair.

She, too, had brown eyes, but on Fallon, her eyes were probably her best feature, fringed by long black lashes. She was a very pretty woman with a gentle nature that naturally drew the cats to her.

"Miles does." Feeling like she had a new friend, Maxi said, "He gets irate when I don't want him to work."

Fallon laughed, then nudged her with her shoulder. "So let the guy have fun. I'm sure he relaxes when he wants to."

Probably good advice. Besides, it took too much effort maintaining a distance from Miles. She'd end up with some heartache, no doubt about it. But the payoff in the meantime would be more than worth it.

Before they left that day, Fallon promised to return for the upcoming weekend when Justice and Miles would start on the fencing.

It still amazed her that Justice was just as willing to work as Miles was. In fact, he didn't consider it work, saying, "A day in the country? Maybe a dip in the pond? Sounds like fun to me."

Two days later, Leese came out with Catalina. Together, the four of them walked down to the bank of the pond, each carrying a handful of cat food. Naturally, several cats followed them.

Catalina, a pretty brunette with blue eyes, looked around in awe, taking in the tall trees, the way a breeze carried a leaf over the water, how fluffy clouds reflected on the surface of the pond. "Such beautiful scenery," she whispered. "If I lived here, you'd find me down here every morning to paint."

"She's a talented artist," Leese explained. Then he sat down and pulled Catalina onto his lap.

Catfish, carp, bluegill crested the surface of the pond, causing circular ripples that expanded until they faded away. At the far end, a frog croaked, leaped in and disappeared. The scents were different down here, richer, muskier. It felt hotter, too, maybe because of the sun's reflection off the water.

Maxi wondered if she could commission Catalina to do a painting, then she could hang the artwork in her house. The idea made her smile.

It was odd, but in such a short time the bad memories connected to the pond had left and now only the good remained. With Miles she'd made new memories, feeding the fish, skipping rocks, picking wildflowers. Walking and talking, usually hand in hand. Yes, she'd been violated, nothing would ever make that go away. But it wasn't the predominant feeling anymore.

She owed Miles for that.

As Miles dropped in the food, more and more fish gathered.

"They're huge," Leese said. "Do you ever swim with them?"

"Good God, no." Maxi quelled at the thought. "You said it yourself, they're enormous."

"They'd swim away from you," Catalina said, then added with worry, "But are there any snakes?"

"Yes." Maxi peered at the green water. "I assume there are turtles and frogs, too."

"Let's see," Miles said, already peeling off his shirt. "Come in with me."

Horrified by that idea, Maxi backstepped. "Nope. Not on your life."

"Chicken."

As he waded in along the rough bank, her eyes widened more. "You're going to cut your foot on a rock!"

"Actually, my toes are sinking into mud." He slipped but caught his balance.

The fish didn't swim away. In fact, they converged on him, no doubt looking for another bite.

Laughing, Leese tossed food behind Miles to draw the fish away.

When Miles suddenly dropped, going completely under, Maxi screamed, thinking something had grabbed him.

Before she knew what she was doing, she was hip-deep in the water and reaching for him. "Miles!"

Sputtering with laughter, Miles resurfaced with his hair slicked back, his body glistening in the sunlight. When he saw her, he lifted a brow.

"You're okay?" She touched his shoulders, his chest, her gaze searching his.

His smile came slowly. "Careful. It drops off suddenly."

Realizing that she'd overreacted, she slapped the water, splashing him. "You scared me half to death!"

"Half to death, huh?" His gentle, amused tone infuriated her more.

With a growl, she spun around to leave, but he caught her waist—and good thing, since she slipped and would have gone under, too.

Against her struggles, he gathered her to him until her feet were off the bottom and her breasts pressed to his chest. He kept her there with his hands opened wide over her bottom. In a low, sexy rumble, he asked, "Were you saving me, honey?"

Now feeling like a fool, especially since she could hear Catalina and Leese chuckling, Maxi grumbled, "I thought something got you."

"And you came in anyway?" He nuzzled her face up until he could treat her to a kiss that took away the chill of the water. "Thank you."

He sounded sincere, which probably meant she'd just given herself away. Why else would she act against her own fears unless she already cared too much for him? Luckily he didn't pin her down. In fact, as she stared into those intense green eyes, she decided he looked arrogantly pleased.

Huh. She'd have to think about—

She screeched when a fish nibbled on her toes, startling Miles. Before he could ask, she thrashed her way out of his arms and back up onto the shore.

"What?" Miles asked, looking around as if he expected to see Nessie in the pond with him.

"Something bit me!" Her ignominious exit from the pond was bad enough, but worse, the second her feet were on dry land, she did the crazy "panic dance," bouncing around with her arms flailing wildly.

Miles laughed. "It was probably just a water reed."

She saw the others watching her in amazement but didn't care. Pointing at Miles, she said, "Water reeds don't bite! And don't you ever do that again."

All innocence, he asked, "Do what?"

"Scare me and then distract me." She shuddered.

The arrival of Woody Barstow on his ATV, which he rode right down to the pond, drew attention away from her humiliating hysterics. Soaked from the waist down, splashed from the waist up, the ends of her hair sticking wetly to her skin, Maxi made a face as she walked over to greet him.

Trying to sound normal instead of still frazzled, she said, "Hey, Woody."

With his gaze glued to Miles, his tone appalled, Woody asked, *"What are you doing?"*

Not understanding, she glanced back at Miles, who was now climbing onto the bank. "Swimming?"

"In the *pond?*"

So odd. "Well, I know *I'm* afraid, but there's probably no reason, right?" Unless…maybe Woody was a kindred spirit? Not everyone was adventurous enough to swim with fish as big as her thigh in water so dark you couldn't see the bottom. Noting Woody's pale face and the sweat beads at his

temples, Maxi touched his arm. "I take it you're not a swim-
mer either?"

A flash of some strong emotion narrowed his eyes, but it
was there and gone before she could identify it. A bad experience in his past? She wouldn't make him more uncomfortable by asking.

He swallowed, pulled a bandanna from his pocket and
mopped his brow before managing a weak smile. "I think
the heat is getting to me."

He did look far too pale beneath the broiling sun. "Why
don't we go up to the house, where it's cooler? I'll get you
some tea."

"No, no, I'm fine." He flapped a hand, irritated at his own
weakness, then changed the subject. "I see you have more
friends visiting."

A hint to be introduced? She felt sorry for him, knowing
he must be lonely since her grandmother's passing.

Miles had already left the pond and was approaching. Leese
stood up with Catalina held in his arms, but he set her on her
own feet before joining them.

She must not have been the only one to note Woody's pal-
lor, because Miles steered everyone into the shade and Leese
watched him with concern.

Once the greetings ended, Miles asked him, "You okay,
Woody?"

The sickly smile reappeared, and he looked at the pond
again. "Guess I'll have to confess that your pond spooks me.
I've seen water turtles in there as big as tires."

"Tires?" Maxi gulped, feeling a little sickly now, too. She
glanced at the pond. "Seriously?"

He nodded. Sheepish, he said, "Fished one out for Meryl
once. She had no idea my knees were shaking. Couldn't tell
her I was afraid, now could I? But she was worried that turtle
would eat one of the cats, it was so damn big."

Miles smiled. "How'd you get it out?"

"Used a sturdy net with a real long handle. The thing was on the bank sunning itself, so it was easy to sneak up on it. I got it snagged in the net easy enough, too, but hauling it up the land and to my truck was a job. It kept snappin' at the air." He shook his head as if reliving the horror.

"What did you do with it?" Catalina asked, and her tone made it clear that she hoped it hadn't been hurt.

"Lots of folks around here like turtle soup, but Meryl wouldn't hear of it. That big soft spot in her heart covered all critters, not just the cats. So I took it to the river and turned it loose."

"Without getting bit?" Leese asked.

"Just barely. I pulled back the net, then ran like hell for my truck. Lucky for me, the turtle went into the river. Don't mind telling you, I was pretty shook up, but it was worth it to be Meryl's hero." He gave a genuine grin and boasted, "She fed me homemade cookies for a week."

When the laughter died down, Miles said, "Worth the payoff, huh?"

"Definitely." He nodded back up by the house. "Make up your mind on the addition to the barn?"

"The posts were delivered yesterday." Miles looped his arm around Maxi. "Got them from Denton Lumber."

Woody nodded. "Was gonna suggest them."

"We're all set." Leaning against Miles, Maxi added, "I'm thinking since I already have the tools, and such a willing worker, it might be a nice idea to add a dock to the pond, too. That way I won't have to worry about running into any turtles on the bank when I come down here to feed the fish."

Miles looked down at her with surprise. "Seriously?"

"Unless you'd rather not—"

"Are you kidding? I love the idea."

Of course he did. She had to laugh and then explained to

Woody, "He's a one-man construction crew. Claims he's happiest when he's working."

"I reckon that's most men," Woody said with a smile. "Keepin' busy also keeps you young." He winked as if that was his own secret to staying strong and capable.

Was Woody angling to help? She just didn't know, so she compromised by inviting him back over the weekend so he could check out the progress. He happily agreed.

For another hour or so, Woody stuck around asking questions about her various plans, offering suggestions and reminiscing about her grandma. Being able to share with someone else who'd known her gave Maxi a lot of peace.

Not long after Woody left with the promise to see her that weekend, so did Leese and Catalina. Like Justice, they promised to be back to help with the work. And Miles planned to ask the boys, Lee, Hull and Billy, to help out, too.

With a lightened heart and a serene smile, Maxi realized they'd be having a party after all.

Saturday morning brought a slight breeze and overcast skies, which Miles considered perfect for working outdoors. He didn't think it would rain, but the clouds cut down on the heat of the sun.

Beyond frazzled, Maxi ran around, doing her utmost to make sure everything was perfect. It amused him, this domestic side of her. The woman he'd first met had been more of a fashion plate, sexy in her boldness and direct approach. She'd fascinated him so much.

But seeing her like this, her thick hair in a ponytail, feet bare as she repeatedly went from the house to the yard setting up seats and tables—with burning candles on them to keep the cats from sprawling everywhere—affected him in a different, yet no less powerful, way.

As she hustled past, she asked, "Will you get out the coolers and fill them with ice?"

"Sure." He admired her lightly tanned limbs beneath cut-off shorts and a halter that did more to heat his blood than the sun ever could. No matter what she wore, or didn't wear, it spiked his interest.

While he got the large coolers set up at either end of the back deck near the table, she raced out again, this time with flowers.

Miles felt the smile tugging at his mouth.

When she rushed past on her return to the house, he caught her. "Slow down, babe. Take a breath."

She fretted, her bottom lip caught in her teeth. "I want everything to be perfect."

"You know my friends don't expect anything special. Feeding them is good enough. Paper plates, burgers off the grill, a few beers and colas and they're good."

She dropped her forehead to his chest. "I've never really had a party before."

He laughed. "It's not a party, so relax."

Exasperated, she said, "Of course it is! It's a 'work for free' party—and that's the most stressful kind." She looked up at him, her eyes dark with worry. "I don't want them to feel unappreciated."

Smoothing a finger over her downy cheekbone, down to her mouth, over that plump bottom lip, Miles said, "They'll have fun."

Her expression told him he was nuts.

He'd like to think that once she got to know them better she'd realize the truth of it. But he still didn't know the long-term plan, if she wanted the same things he wanted—or if he was just her "bodyguard with benefits" until the issues got resolved.

"They will," he insisted. "The ladies like the cats, right? And the guys will swim for sure."

"So a gazillion feral cats and a pond infested with killer turtles is the lure? I should have realized."

That dry tone made him laugh. And made him want her. More.

How that was possible, he didn't know, since he wanted her all the damn time.

While they still had a little privacy, he kissed her, slowly at first to ease her past her need to race off again.

As usual, though, she nestled against him, her lips parting at the touch of his tongue, her hands sliding up and over his bare shoulders.

With a groan, Miles scooped his hands under her ass and lifted her so that her body fit tight to his. Her arms went around his neck and she tilted her head, drawing on his tongue, making him crazy.

The sound of an approaching car brought him reluctantly back to his senses. Maxi must not have heard it yet, because when he lifted his head, she stared at his mouth and whispered softly, "Do we have time?"

He groaned again. "God, I wish we did." He never should have started what he couldn't finish, especially with her so anxious about everything. "Company will be here in another thirty seconds."

The sultry haze gradually left her eyes, and when it did, she pushed out of his arms with haste. "Blast, busted again!"

"Again?"

"First time I met your friends? You don't recall them teasing me?"

Grinning, he gave her another quick kiss. "That's right." She did have a sultry, aroused look in her dark eyes. Maxi expressed her feelings so openly, it'd be hard for her to hide it.

"It's not funny," she grumbled.

"I wasn't laughing."

"Baloney."

"Actually," he said, "I was thinking how damned lucky I am." While confusion pinched her brows, he turned to see who was coming up the long drive. "Wow, it's a damn parade."

She held up a hand to shade her eyes. "But who...?"

"Looks like the whole gang came. I recognize Cannon's truck and that's probably Armie riding shotgun. Behind him is Denver."

Her reaction was hilarious. She blurted, "I don't have enough food!"

Miles planted an arm around her to keep her from running off in a panic. "So we'll order a pizza or something. Don't sweat it."

"Don't sweat it?" she repeated. *"Don't sweat it!"*

Distracting her from her panic, he said, "Damn, I can't believe it, but that's Sahara's car, too."

That distracted her, all right. She gave a despondent groan.

Hoping to reassure her, Miles tipped up her chin. "Honest to God, honey, it's fine, I swear."

As the cars parked, Maxi straightened and pasted on a smile, but in an aside to Miles she said, "I was going to change into something nicer."

"You look great."

The smile never slipped when she said, "I do not look appropriate for your boss."

He snorted. "Sahara doesn't judge. Remember, she liked your rubber boots? But it wouldn't matter if she didn't, because I think you're beautiful."

She blinked fast, and to his pleasure, her smile turned more genuine and the tension eased out of her posture. Leaning into him, she said, "Thank you. Guess we'll just roll with it, huh?"

"Yeah," he said, knowing in that moment that he was a

goner. He'd fallen in love with Maxi Nevar, a chameleon who kept changing, but never bored him. "We'll roll." Arm around her waist, he led her forward to meet most of the people important to him.

Fallon was with Justice, Catalina with Leese. Cannon and Armie had ridden together, Stack with Denver. Their wives, it seemed, had already planned a day together but said they'd meet Maxi next time.

If Maxi caught the implications in that, namely that the guys assumed they were a couple with plenty of opportunities to mingle, she didn't show it.

She was too busy gaping. And no wonder. The guys had come prepared to work, meaning they wore tattered jeans or shorts with T-shirts. Seeing them from her vantage point, he realized they made an imposing picture.

Armie, the most outrageous of the group, grinned at her. "I don't mind you staring, honey, but Miles probably doesn't like it."

Cannon gave him a shove, then said politely to Maxi, "I hope we're not intruding."

She finally got it together. "No, of course not." Red-cheeked, she cleared her throat. "Wow, I just... Miles is impressive, you know?"

Barely keeping a straight face, Armie nodded. "That's why they call him The Legend."

That earned a few snickers.

Maxi didn't seem to notice. "I mean, he's one man. Then I met Justice and Leese and that was astounding. Now the rest of you..."

Everyone else grinned, too.

From behind them, Sahara said, "It's like an assortment of delicious man candy, isn't it? One at a time is shocking, but all together, they steal a girl's breath away."

Miles shook his head at Sahara, amused at her idea of dress-

ing down. The sleeveless white sundress with a splashy floral print had a blouse-like bodice, a formfitting waist and a
soft, full skirt that hit just below her knees. It looked cool and
comfortable, but still expensive and stylish.

No spiked heels this time, but her white flip-flops showed
off her hot-pink toenails. She wore white sunglasses to shield
her eyes and had her long brown hair in a loose topknot.

A million bucks, that was what she looked like. No surprise there.

The surprise was that she held on to Brand's arm.

Miles wasn't the only one wondering about it either, given
the way his buddies all watched the pair.

Brand wore his own sunglasses along with a blasé expression.

When Armie opened his mouth, no doubt to say something
shocking, Brand beat him to it with a succinct "Shut up."

Of course, that just got everyone harassing him that much
sooner.

Interesting, Miles thought. Sahara had made no secret of
chasing Brand...for the agency. She'd chased him and Justice, too, yet it always felt like more than that where Brand
was concerned.

Not once had she ever looked at Miles with that same type
of personal interest.

Wondering how Brand felt about it, he smiled. "I'm glad
you found some free time, Sahara."

"Surprised you, didn't I? I hope that's okay. I needed a distraction." She waved back at her car. "And I brought goodies."
She handed her keys to Brand and, with sugary sweetness,
asked, "Would you mind?"

He took the keys without comment and headed for the car.

Sahara tsked. "He was very gallant to come to my rescue,
but he's still far too moody." In stern warning, she mentioned,
"It'd be shameful of any of you to tease him."

"He's still saying no?" Justice asked.

"He is, but I haven't given up."

Denver, who was as big as Justice, shook his head. "He's at the top of his game. I can't see him leaving MMA."

Sahara pinched her lips together...almost as if she knew something that the rest of them didn't.

Seeing that expression, Leese folded his arms and glanced at Miles.

Miles shrugged. He didn't know any more than the rest of them.

Leese turned back to their boss. "Why did you need rescuing?"

She glanced away, released a long breath and took off her sunglasses.

Everyone went still at the sight of her puffy eyes.

Crying? *Sahara?*

"I heard from my PI." Looking nothing like her usual indomitable self, she whispered, "Last week he thought..." Emotion choked her and she had to clear her throat. "He thought he'd found a trace on my brother, but today that turned out to be a dead end."

Damn. Miles said softly, "I'm sorry."

Maxi didn't understand the issue, but she was such a compassionate woman that she looked just as concerned.

Justice gathered Sahara up for a gentle hug. Leese patted her shoulder. Cannon, Armie, Denver and Stack gave their own versions of understanding and concern.

They all liked and respected Sahara a lot. As employees, Miles, Leese and Justice knew firsthand that she was a confident, strong, bona fide badass of a boss who ruled with a tiny iron fist. The rest of the guys knew her in a more peripheral but no less admiring way.

None of them wanted to see her hurt.

"Thank you." Uncomfortable with sympathy, she slipped

the sunglasses onto the top of her head and looked around. "This is beautiful. Who'd like to give me a tour?"

Maxi volunteered, but before they left, Brand returned with an overflowing bag of chips, pretzels, nachos and dip in one arm, beer in the other. He said to Miles as he passed, "There's more in the trunk."

The "more" turned out to be food aplenty, drinks, a watermelon and, because Sahara had a sweet tooth, an assortment of cupcakes.

"My goodness," Maxi said, overwhelmed by the generous gesture. "You brought so much."

Sahara smiled. "I'm not so gauche as to crash a party emptyhanded."

And to that, Maxi turned on Miles. "See, I *told* you it was a party!"

After a quick trip around the property to let the newcomers see it all, Maxi poured cold drinks.

Seated in a lawn chair and her sunglasses back in place, Sahara said, "Your idea for goats is perfect. They'll definitely keep the back pasture cleared."

"That's what I decided, too!" Finding a kindred spirit in the goat argument thrilled Maxi. Even better, Catalina and Fallon backed her up.

"Women sticking together," Leese explained with a grin.

Catalina tried to protest, but she didn't know anything about goats. She did offer to draw one, though, which Fallon found hilarious. Actually, so did Maxi.

She liked the women a lot and had already relaxed about being underdressed, especially since Catalina and Fallon were dressed similarly in shorts but with cute tops instead of a halter.

Miles said to Sahara, "So you're a goat expert now, too?"

Too? Maxi wondered. But then Sahara did seem to be competent on almost any subject. Luckily her mood had improved during their walk.

Maxi didn't remember much about her first meeting with Sahara. Shoot, she'd been drugged, upset, frightened and a little unsure how her reunion with Miles would go. But now, in a much better frame of mind, she found that Miles's boss was quick-witted, and she dished it out to the guys so rapidly that they almost couldn't keep up.

"I'll have you know that I was madly in love with a farmer when I was twenty-one." Sahara looked struck. "My God, that was nine years ago." Smiling, she said, "I still remember him fondly."

Brand narrowed his eyes on her. "So what happened to him?"

"My brother didn't like him, so that was that."

Justice said with surprise, "You needed your brother's approval?"

"I value his opinion a great deal."

Everyone turned to stare at Brand, but he held silent.

Sahara looked down at her iced tea, saw it was empty and stood. "If you don't mind, I'll go refill this."

Maxi started to offer to do it for her, but Miles laid his hand over her arm. She frowned in concern. "Something awful happened with her brother?"

"Yeah." Miles stared after Sahara, too, watching until she disappeared into the house. "I don't know all the details, and I'll have to keep it short. Sahara doesn't need to hear us talking."

The last thing she'd want to do was add to Sahara's obvious distress. "I didn't mean to be nosy."

Brand said, "It's okay. She'd tell you herself if today hadn't been such a disappointment."

As if trying to convince himself, Justice said, "She just needs a little time to get used to the news. Coming here will cheer her up."

Miles took Maxi's hand and gave it a gentle squeeze. "Sahara's brother, Scott, was out on his yacht with his girlfriend, but something happened to them. They found the yacht floating at sea, but they never found any bodies."

"Oh my God." Maxi turned her hand over in his, now gripping him tightly. "I can't imagine anything that awful."

"Without a body for proof, Sahara won't accept his death. She's had a PI on retainer ever since it happened."

"What makes it even worse," Leese said, "is that her parents died when she was younger and her brother practically raised her. He was all the family she had."

"She's a strong woman, though," Justice said with admiration. "She was already familiar with the agency, since Scott had taken her there a lot, so she stepped in to run things."

"After he was declared dead," Miles said, "Sahara officially inherited the business."

"That was about a year before I signed on." Leese gave a small smile. "She's putting her own stamp on it, that's for sure."

"A sexier image," Miles said, quoting his boss with a crooked grin. "She's good at what she does, and God knows she loves it, but she'd hand it back over in a heartbeat if she found Scott alive."

"It's tragic," Fallon said. "My heart breaks for her."

Justice pulled Fallon over onto his lap, cradling her close. She looked very petite wrapped in his arms. "Since you lost your sister, you know how hard it must be for her."

There was a lot about her new friends that she didn't know, Maxi realized, but she wouldn't press. When they wanted to share, they would.

Sahara returned from the kitchen, a thoughtful look on her face. Everyone clammed up, and Maxi felt guilty for inadvertently bringing up her past.

Then Sahara reached them and turned brisk and businesslike. "Your kitchen is charming."

"That's one word for it," Miles said.

Pretending insult, Maxi huffed at him. "I certainly like it."

"Because of all the wonderful memories," Sahara guessed. "But I'm sure it's also difficult. The appliances can't be efficient or convenient. Since they belonged to your grandmother, and must be very special to you, you wouldn't want to simply replace them, but have you ever considered contacting a local museum?"

"A museum?" Maxi asked, surprised.

"Yes. I know several curators I could contact for you if you're interested in donating to them. If there's a museum specific to this area, I'm sure they'd be thrilled to reenact that exact kitchen."

"Wow. I'd never thought of that."

"It'd be really cool," Catalina said, "to see it all set up in a museum, wouldn't it?"

"Very cool," she agreed, and then to Sahara, she added, "But I don't want to put you to any trouble."

Brand said softly, "Might as well let her do her thing. Once Sahara gets started, she's like a runaway train. There's no stopping her."

Rather than be insulted, Sahara smiled at him. "Yes, I'm very effective."

"I'm sure that's exactly what he meant," Miles said.

Knowing the kitchen was badly in need of an update, but hesitant to lose that link to her grandmother, Maxi considered the idea—and decided she loved it. "Yes, please."

CHAPTER THIRTEEN

As soon as Lee, Hull and Billy showed up, Miles got everyone organized. Maxi found it comical, seeing the worshipful
way the boys stared from one fighter to another. They could
barely concentrate on the instructions Miles gave.

Armie, especially, drew their adoration, which worked
out, since he seemed more than willing to joke with them.

"He's really good with kids," Catalina said as the guys
started to work. "Actually, they all are. But Armie relates really well to them. He's a terrific dad."

"You might not know this," Fallon added, "but Cannon's
gym is also a rec center for at-risk youth. The men pitch in
teaching MMA and working with different age groups."

"They each fit in nights at the rec center around their own
training schedules." Catalina smiled. "It's one of the things
Leese misses most."

"Justice misses it, too, but he mostly misses competing.
We attend events to watch his friends whenever they're local
enough."

Sahara nudged Maxi. "I think you and I need to get in on
that action."

"Watching a live fight?" She'd love it, but it seemed to be something reserved for significant others—and that, she wasn't. It almost ruined her good mood, wondering what would happen once Miles deemed her house safe again.

Would he leave her?

Yes, she already knew he would. Small-town life was not for him...no matter how much he seemed to enjoy it.

"It would be fascinating, don't you think?"

Catalina leaned forward to confide, "Unfortunately, not all fighters look as hot as our guys."

"Some are more average-looking," Fallon agreed. "Not that they aren't dedicated, because I think they are."

"They just don't have the necessary genes to rock the ripped bod." Catalina bobbed her eyebrows.

Laughing at her expression, Maxi glanced toward the men and... Oh good Lord.

Her stare drew the attention of the others.

"If it wasn't for the boys," Sahara murmured, "I could take a photo and use that to hard sell the agency."

"What woman wouldn't want to hire one of them?" Fallon asked.

Catalina groused, "I, for one, prefer that men hire Leese."

Sahara lifted her tea glass in a toast. "And yet he's so popular with my female clients." Before Catalina could say anything to that, she added, "Not that he's veered from business since he met you."

"Still," Catalina grumbled.

Fallon teased her, saying, "You, better than most, know how good he is at protecting a woman."

"There's protecting, and then there's *protecting*."

Fallon grinned. "Amen to that."

Maxi had already learned a little about Leese and Catalina's romance. It had been strictly taboo, of course, not that rules had dissuaded Catalina. She'd wanted Leese, so she'd gone after him.

Maxi couldn't blame her for pushing. Her situation had been so dire that it made sense to grab any happiness she could. In the process of dodging evil, they'd fallen in love.

Fallon, however, had let Justice do the chasing—and he had, up to and including quitting as her bodyguard while still insisting he'd protect her. He'd figured if the client/bodyguard dynamic made a romance unacceptable, he'd stop being a bodyguard. Luckily it had worked out in the end so that he got to keep the job and the woman.

Maxi hadn't understood it at the time, but she recalled now the exchange in Sahara's office, when Miles had wanted Sahara to understand up front that they shared an "intimate history."

Sahara, no dummy, had stated that she knew their situation was unique and assured him he didn't need to explain further.

So from the beginning, Miles had wanted more than a business relationship with her...and his boss had agreed.

It should have embarrassed her, but instead it gave her hope. Miles might never want to live with her, but that didn't mean things would have to end completely once the assignment was over.

They could...what? Date? She'd take whatever she could get.

Glancing toward where the men worked, she heard laughter mixed with the sounds of a pickax hitting the ground and rocks tossed aside. Sunlight glistened on Miles's shoulders and reflected off his dark hair. She saw him say something to one of the boys, point down the line of posts and laugh at whatever the boy said. Miles gave him a pat on the back and sent him on his way with a shovel.

Such an amazing, gorgeous, capable, caring man.

Love was an elusive thing, she knew, there and gone before you could fully appreciate it. She was twice burned and that made her extra cautious. Yet…she had to admit, Miles was unlike any other man she'd known.

"Funny, isn't it?" Fallon, too, watched the men. "They have all those muscles and enjoy using them but act as if it's no big deal."

"They take their strength for granted," Catalina said with a sigh.

"And use it to advantage." Fallon smiled. "There's something very sexy about a strong but gentle and protective guy."

Oh, yes, *very* sexy…and maybe that was what had first drawn her to Miles. She'd gone into that bar looking for a distraction, and the second she'd spotted him, he'd been so casual, smiling back at her as if he didn't realize he was better-looking, taller, more ripped than other men. He'd been relaxed, interested, and that crooked smile…

"I plan to live here until, like my grandma, I pass away." Since no one else knew her thoughts, Maxi realized her comment came entirely out of context.

Sahara blinked at her. "Well, of course you'll stay here. It's not only beautiful, but peaceful, too. Or at least it will be once the threat is resolved. Plus, it's obvious that you loved your grandmother." She toyed with her glass, touching one fingertip through the condensation left on the table. "When I inherited the agency, it was like a lifeline, a way to remain attached to Scott even after he'd gone. This is your lifeline to your grandmother."

The fact that Sahara got it was both comforting and incredibly sad. "I'm so sorry for your loss."

"That's the thing," Sahara said. "I'm not convinced that he's gone. I think I'd know. I'd *feel* it. But in my heart, I believe Scott is still alive." Her mouth twisted in a crooked smile. "I can't say that to the men. I don't want their pity, and I won't allow them to think I'm suffering some fanciful female emotion." With a shrug, she added, "I know what I know."

"And you know Scott is still alive?" Maxi asked.

"Instincts are an amazing thing." She gestured toward the pasture where muscle flexed and power worked. "They'd all back me up on that. Instincts are the number one quality for a bodyguard, but they refuse to equate instinct with emotion. I, however, think the two are closely related."

"That makes sense to me." Fallon brushed back her inky dark hair. "Caring for someone would hone that instinct, right? So emotions enhance instinct."

"Exactly!"

Cat propped her chin on her fist. "It amazes me that you took over the agency without a hitch, especially considering what you were going through."

"It was a good fit," Sahara said. "Scott was sixteen years older than me. Often when our parents traveled the world, he let me stay behind with him. I loved being at the agency, listening in on all the shoptalk, hearing the different cases and learning about the various contacts. He let me observe and learn and…it was wonderful."

Maxi slowly nodded. "It sounds wonderful."

Sahara's usual shark smile softened with the memories. "He's alive." She pressed a fist to her chest, near her heart. "I'd know it if he was gone."

After giving her a long look, Maxi said, "I believe you."

Catalina nodded. "Me, too."

"And me," Fallon said.

That was when it really hit Maxi. When she lost Miles, she'd be losing these people, too, and God help her, she didn't want to let any of them go.

Shirtless, sweat dripping from his temples, Brand held a deeply embedded post in place while Miles tamped down the dirt around it. He could tell something was bothering Brand, but he didn't know what. Farther down the fence line, evenly spaced, the men worked in twos placing in the posts.

He heard a soft laugh and looked up to see the women wandering out of the barn, a trail of cats following them. He liked seeing Maxi so happy and carefree.

He liked it that she fit in. Hell, even Sahara, who was her polar opposite, was drawn to her.

That reminded him... "How is it you became Sahara's ride?"

Brand shrugged. "She's always coming to me for the odd favor. Maybe because she's not my boss, she's more comfortable with me."

More likely, she was hitting on Brand and he was being deliberately obtuse about it. "She looked like she'd been crying."

Brand drew a wrist across his forehead. "She was. Not real obvious-like or anything. I can't imagine her really cutting loose sobbing or anything."

No, Miles couldn't imagine that either.

"But the tears were there, sort of hanging on her lashes." Brand shook his head. "She keeps building up her hopes that her brother isn't dead."

Thoughts aching in tandem with his shoulders, Miles straightened to stretch. "Doesn't matter what evidence they found. Without a body, she won't believe it."

"Must suck bad to lose someone like that."

The maudlin way Brand spoke sharpened Miles's attention. "They were close." He swiped up a water bottle and chugged down half while studying his friend. Brand had always been a little more distant than the rest of them. Not unfriendly, but not quite as open. If you needed him, he was there. Today was evidence of that. But he didn't intrude, and he didn't invite intrusion either.

Miles glanced to where Cannon and Armie worked, then to Denver and Stack. Justice chose the job of digging a trench between the posts where the fence would fit into the ground to keep the goats from going under it. Lee helped with that. Billy and Hull took turns pushing the wheelbarrow to the far side of the pond to empty it. The ground there could use some leveling, so it'd work out.

Goats. Miles shook his head, still having a hard time bending his brain around that one. Maxi had truly set down roots here, and he understood why. Somewhere deep inside himself, he envied her. She'd inherited the type of place that instantly felt more like home than most houses could after a decade.

Maybe it was the fresh air, or the camaraderie with his friends. Or maybe it was the unending turmoil over Maxi, but Miles heard himself confessing, "I didn't have a choice but to leave MMA."

Brand glanced up, his gaze penetrating.

Like Maxi, Brand had brown eyes, but that was where the similarities ended. Maxi's eyes were velvety soft, like melted chocolate. Sometimes nervous, sometimes content. Always a focal point in her face.

Brand's were darker, almost black. Often cynical, and currently filled with sharp surprise. It was an uncommon expression for Brand, one that almost made Miles laugh.

"What do you mean, you didn't have a choice?"

It was the first time Miles had brought it up, but now seemed like a good time to talk about it.

Tapping his head, Miles explained, "One too many concussions. The doctors said I was playing with fire."

"Damn, man, I didn't realize. Hell, I didn't even know you'd been concussed."

He smirked. "Right. What fighter hasn't?"

"Yeah, but usually it's not a big deal."

No, it was always a big deal, apparently. Fighters just chose to think otherwise. "I was private about it." As if it made sense when he knew it didn't, Miles said, "I wanted to keep fighting."

Dropping down to sit, wrists draped over his knees, Brand stared thoughtfully toward the pond. "You're okay?"

"Yeah, I'm fine." He sat, too. "But it took me a while to get used to the idea of giving up MMA. I had plans, you know?"

Brand nodded in understanding. "The title."

"Right." He hesitated, but why not? So he asked, "You?"

Brand picked a weed, briefly examined it, then crushed it in his fist and tossed it aside. "What fighter doesn't have that plan?"

Shrugging one shoulder, Miles said, "Apparently Leese and Justice."

"True." Brand fought a smile. "I always admired Leese for recognizing his limitations."

"And for refusing to be second best. He's a hell of a fighter..."

"But not championship material," Brand said. "It was never going to happen and he accepted that."

"This job suits him better." Miles didn't mind admitting, "I might've been a better fighter, but Leese is a better bodyguard. More analytical. He's in his element."

Brand thought about that, then asked, "You like it?"

"I do." Miles had to laugh. "What I've seen of it, anyway. I'd only had a handful of assignments before Maxi hired me. The others sure as hell weren't like this."

"Dull in comparison?"

"Definitely." And they hadn't had the side benefits of amazing sex.

"Seems like you two are all cozy here."

"Something like that—at least most of the time." He updated Brand on everything that had happened so far with Maxi, even about her being drugged. Yes, it was a breach of her privacy, but she'd accepted Leese and Justice knowing, so what was one more perspective. He'd take all the help and input he could get.

Even now, he kept scanning the outlying areas and wondering if someone was there, spying on them, on *her.*

"It's been one giant puzzle, and it pisses me off every time I think of it. But unless I can catch the prick, there's not much else I can do except keep her safe."

They again heard laughter and looked up to see the women coming toward them with canned drinks in hand.

Brand studied them. "Maxi doesn't act like a woman who's been through all that."

"She gets shook sometimes, but she's so damned determined, and so strong, it's unreal." He thought about that, then had to add, "Strong, but also really sweet. And...comfortable. To be around, I mean." He shook his head at that rambling nonsense.

"She's sexy, too."

"Yeah, there's that."

Brand grinned. "I knew you were serious about her. Hell, we all did."

It sucked to have to say it out loud, but he'd already gotten far into it, so... "I'm as serious as she'll let me be."

"Bullshit. If you want her, she's yours."

If only that were true. "She'd already ditched me once before stuff went off the rails here. If it hadn't, I probably would have never heard from her again. I only did because she wanted to hire a bodyguard and already knew and trusted me." That required more explanations, so Miles shared the details. It was humiliating to admit he hadn't known how to get hold of her. "Hell, she's still resisting, but I'm working on her."

"Trust is a good start."

He nodded. The sex was smokin' hot, too, but Miles kept that gem to himself.

Brand said, "Not that I think you need it given how she looks at you, but good luck."

How did Maxi look at him? He glanced at her again. Still a good distance away, they'd stopped to talk to a couple of cats following them.

Deciding it was time for a different topic, Miles said, "I think you're wrong about Sahara. I think she singles you out for another reason."

"True, but it's not what all of you are thinking."

Miles lifted a brow, waiting. It took a little getting used to, the idea of his hard-nosed, controlling, business-savvy boss going sweet on one of his friends. But hey, he wasn't one to judge.

Brand shook his head. "You can stop thinking that right now. Sahara might act interested in me personally, but that's because I don't work for her. She likes it that she's not my boss and can't tell me what to do."

Skeptical, Miles lifted a brow. "You think she actually likes that? I'm pretty sure she enjoys being the boss—always."

"Not with me." He plucked at another weed. "She leans on me a lot, too, but I know that's just her latest shtick to rope me in."

"You think?"

"Sure. She's not a woman who takes 'no' lightly, so I can see her doing just about anything to get her way. And truthfully, she just might."

Miles gave him a look. "Are we talking sex, or you as a bodyguard?"

Brand snorted and, ignoring the comment about sex, said, "I have to leave MMA."

Have to?

One minute remained, maybe less, before the women reached them. Miles wasn't sure what to say, so he pulled off his sunglasses and asked, "Anything I can do?"

"No." Brand got back to his feet. Hands on his hips, he stared out at the land, his shoulders taut, his jaw locked. Right before they lost the privacy, he said quietly, "My mother had a heart attack and it's...bad. I don't want to go into it, not now anyway, but I can't see me leaving the country to fight anytime soon."

Miles's throat went tight. "Jesus, Brand. I'm sorry—"

"Don't." He shook his head. "I feel enough like a prick."

That didn't make any sense. "Why?"

"We weren't close. Ever. My aunt raised me like her own after my mother bailed. She only came back into my life because she needs me and I fucking well resent it."

Because he seriously had no clue how to respond to that, Miles was almost grateful for the lack of privacy. Yeah, he'd known Brand wasn't close with either parent, but he'd never realized...

It struck him that Maxi had come back into his life only because she needed it, but the two scenarios were light-years away from each other. To have his mother do that, and be gone throughout his entire life, would bring resentment to anyone.

"I shouldn't have brought it up," Brand said. "You already have your hands full."

"Wrong. I'd be happy to talk about it with you, you know that. Maybe when we have more time?"

"Maybe." Brand picked up a rock and, taking a pitcher's stance, zipped it through the air toward the pond. He missed it by only a few feet. In contrast to the heavy news he'd just unloaded, he said, "This was nice today. I like it here."

"Come back anytime."

"Yeah, I just might."

The ladies reached them then. They were a funny mix, with Maxi wearing that boner-inspiring halter that cradled her breasts, Fallon and Catalina in casual shorts and T-shirts,

and Sahara still soft and fresh, despite the heat, in her sum-
mery dress.

Different, yet each of them was special in her own way.

Maxi edged closer. "I'd hug you," she said, "if you weren't
covered in sweat."

That was just the sort of nonsense he needed to hear to
shake off his dark mood. Grinning, Miles warned, "A little
sweat won't hurt you," and he reached for her.

She squealed, backing up fast. "Don't you dare!"

"A challenge?"

And the chase was on.

The guys swam in the pond while the women grilled and
prepared the food. The boys especially got into it, running
fast along the bank and leaping in with big splashes that they
called cannonballs. Stack swam to the bottom and brought
up some freshwater mussel shells.

Armie, doing a funny flip, almost lost his loose shorts,
which caused the women, watching from up the hill, to hoot
and holler.

Maxi had just called them up, the food now on the tables,
when she heard a car pull up. Shading her eyes with a hand,
she looked but didn't recognize the white Mercedes-Benz
sedan. Still, something inside her froze.

She heard Miles shout something to her, felt Fallon come
to stand beside her, then Catalina and Sahara. But she couldn't
acknowledge them and she couldn't look away.

The car parked behind the others, temporarily out of her
view. She heard the car door slam, the crunching of shoes
on the gravel drive.

Of course she knew who it'd be. She even recognized the
sound of that confident gait.

Miles reached her, his arm, still wet, dampening her shoulders when he slipped it around her.

And then her sister, Harlow, stood there, her disdain more withering than the heat.

Maxi forced air into her lungs, but she couldn't bring up a smile. "Harlow. I didn't expect—"

"Obviously," Harlow said in her moderate, even tone. Her short, tousled blond hair was chic, her nude heels stylish and her powder blue dress fit to perfection. A designer purse hung over her arm. One brow arched above the lens of her sunglasses. "A party, Maxi? Really?"

No, it didn't feel like a party any longer. She stiffened her resolve. "Just some friends helping me with repairs."

Harlow's gaze scanned everyone, stuck on Sahara, and her smile turned mean. "Yes, the work outfits are adorable."

Sahara laughed. "Oh, honey, when I dress for work, it's far from adorable." She leaned forward, the shark smile in place, and said, "It would put you to shame."

Harlow had no idea what to say to that. Suddenly Miles stepped forward. "I'm going to guess that you're Maxi's sister, Harlow?" He held out his hand. "Miles Dartman."

Harlow quipped, "Her latest mistake?"

Maxi's eyes widened over that insult. She stared at Miles, sending him a silent message: *don't say it, don't say it*—

"Actually, I'm her bodyguard."

Maxi almost groaned. Aware of the small crowd now surrounding her, she separated, joining Miles and finally finding that smile, sickly though it might be. "I can explain that, Harlow, if you want to step inside?"

Harlow crossed her toned arms, her stance provoking. "No. I think I'd like to hear him explain it."

"Miles—" she tried again.

He put his arm back around her, belying the idea that he was *only* a bodyguard. "Someone has tried to hurt her. Repeatedly."

"Hurt her?" Mildly alarmed, Harlow asked, "How?"

"Let's just say it's a very dangerous situation."

Harlow snatched off her sunglasses. "I'd like details."

"No," Miles denied her. "I'm not comfortable with your relationship to her—"

"I'm her sister!"

Sahara laughed, doing her own provoking.

"I know that," Miles said. "But I also know a lot more, and since I'm not sure where the threat originates, I'm not taking any chances."

Blast! *Why would he say something like that?* Maxi knew the second her sister's temper ignited.

Her eyes narrowed, her mouth tightened and then Harlow jabbed a finger toward the house. "Inside, Maxi." And off she stalked.

Resigned to another confrontation, Maxi started to follow... Only, everyone suddenly stood in her way, blocking her.

It surprised her so much that she just stood there, mute.

"You don't have to jump to do her bidding." Miles squeezed her shoulder and drew her around to speak to her. "Let her wait a minute."

That made her scowl. "I wasn't *jumping.*" *No, you were just following orders.* Exasperated, as much with herself as anyone else, she explained, "If I leave her to stew, she'll only get more furious."

"So?"

So...she didn't enjoy the conflicts with her family. Never had and never would. Too often she felt like an outsider, and too often she was the one to blame for it.

Miles didn't understand what it was like with her family, how they felt about her and the choices she'd made—

When he bent down and pressed his mouth to hers, she snapped out of the fog of uncertainty. "Miles!"

"Maxi." He smiled. "Don't let her bully you."

"It's not like that."

Armie snorted.

She glanced back in time to see Sahara roll her eyes. The others wore varying degrees of reaction, from annoyance to understanding to pity. She hated it.

Turning back to Miles, she glared. "It's complicated."

"No, it's not. She came here spoiling for a fight. Disappoint her, but do it on your own terms, not hers." When she didn't exactly look convinced, Miles cupped her face. "It took little more than a split second for me to get it. You deserve better, okay?"

Maxi bit her lip. That was the crux of it, the reason for her uncertainty. "And what if I don't?"

"I'll convince you that you do." He took her hand. "Ready?"

"You should wait out here." Maxi already knew the accusations would be flying, and it'd get ugly quick.

"I'm your bodyguard. I go where you go."

"Don't be ridiculous. I know what she wants." Just as she knew she couldn't give it to her. "It won't be dangerous, but it's definitely going to be uncomfortable."

"I can handle it."

Blast him, why did he have to look so jovial about it? Arguing with him in front of everyone wouldn't solve anything, though. "Fine, but don't say I didn't warn you."

He smiled. "Duly noted."

"Maxi!" Harlow snapped from the doorway.

Sahara gave an exaggerated wince. "Please, if I ever screech like that, force me to resign."

Maxi fought the urge to defend her sister…but then, Harlow really had screeched, so instead she smiled and said, "Please, everyone, enjoy the food." She glanced at the pond to see Hull, Billy and Lee still swimming. "And someone get those boys out of there before they're eaten by turtles."

Without waiting for Miles, she marched ahead, yet he still reached the door before her and held it open like a gentleman.

Luckily Harlow had disappeared back inside.

Maxi headed for the kitchen and found her sister pacing around the small table and chairs. "What—" Harlow started but abruptly cut that off when Miles came in behind Maxi. Annoyance stiffened her posture. "I assumed we'd talk privately."

Yeah, Maxi had assumed that, too. "Would you like something to drink?"

"Scotch?"

That took her off guard. Her sister, the health nut, usually drank only as a precursor to a real blowup. A little alcohol might've soothed her temper, but she'd thrown out all the liquor after being drugged. "The best I have is a beer, but I made fresh iced tea or—"

"No," Harlow said with derision, "thank you."

Maxi gestured to the dining room. "Let's sit at the bigger table to talk." Making it clear that he wouldn't budge, she added, "Miles is more comfortable in those chairs." This time *she* was the one to walk away from her sister.

Harlow joined her quickly enough, with Miles trailing her…almost as if he didn't trust her at his back.

He really needed to stop thinking the worst of her family.

Apparently Harlow felt the same. "What did you tell him to make him think *I'd* be the one to try to hurt you?"

Blast. Not a great start to their confrontation. "Nothing. In fact, I've insisted that it definitely wasn't you or Neil."

Harlow slanted her gaze at Miles. "But you didn't believe her?"

He shrugged. "I have a few reasons to consider you suspect."

Copping an attitude, she said, "Let's hear them."

Miles's smile wasn't friendly. "You came here pissed off."

Eyes sparking with challenge, Harlow asked, "Did she tell you *why*?"

"Yup, she did."

As if he hadn't spoken, she continued, "We need the money this place would bring, but she selfishly refuses to think of her family."

"Our grandmother *is* family." It didn't surprise Maxi that Harlow ignored her.

"Lack of funds," Miles said, "didn't keep you from a new car, did it?"

Startled, Maxi realized that Harlow *was* in a new car. She stared at her sister and saw her flush.

"Because of my elite clientele, I have to keep up appearances. It's an important business expense."

Miles nodded as if he bought into that but then said, "You knew her ex cheated on her, yet you sent him here to be aggressive with her anyway."

Harlow gasped. "That's a lie!" She stormed up to Miles. "Yes, I sent him here, but I did not tell him to be aggressive."

"Forceful, then?"

She snapped her mouth shut, glared at Maxi, then pivoted to pace. "I told him if he really wanted her, he had to go after her."

Maxi fought back the hurt. "And what I want doesn't matter?"

Harlow flapped a dismissive hand. "You said you wanted back in the good graces of your family."

The careless comment cut deep. She imagined what Miles was thinking and that, more than the cruel way Harlow had stated things, crushed her. "So I'm supposed to buy my way back in?"

"Don't be dramatic," Harlow snapped. "You were happy enough with Gary before you decided to play Suzy Homemaker." Her eyes narrowed. "Or is it your *bodyguard* who swayed you away from Gary?"

Her own temper started a slow boil. "I was done with Gary before I ever met Miles." Expression impassive, she said, "I feel like I deserve better than a cheater, whether you do or not."

"Oh, as usual, you're the victim? Please." Harlow pointed at Miles. "Do you deny you're sleeping with him?"

"Not that it's any of your business, but no, I don't deny it. I met Miles right after I found out…everything. I already had a relationship with him—" a relationship she all but ruined "—before I realized I needed protection."

"Protection from *what?*"

Maxi pulled out a chair. "It's a long story, so you may as well sit down."

Frowning, Harlow joined her at the table. Her shoulders were straight, her posture impeccable, but Maxi knew her well enough to recognize the belated worry.

Her sister loved her, damn it. She was sure of it.

Maxi sat at the head of the table, Harlow to her left, Miles to her right. She didn't wait for Miles's permission, or for him to guide the conversation. With as little emotion as possible, she shared everything that had happened.

Harlow was suitably horrified, and she looked at Miles with new eyes. "Dear God."

"She softened it for you," Miles said. "I guess because you're her sister and she cares about you."

"Well, it's settled, then."

Maxi had no idea what Harlow meant. "What is?"

"You have to move." Discounting all the reasons Maxi had previously given for why she wouldn't leave, Harlow slapped both hands on the table, half stood and insisted, "This ridiculous lark is over. Never mind the financial reasons, you have to sell this place for the sake of your own safety. And I, for one, am relieved."

That did it. Maxi pushed to her feet in a rush and faced off with Harlow. "I am *not* moving! *Accept it.*"

"My God," Harlow breathed. "Your stubbornness is absurd! Whatever you're trying to prove, forget it. It's too late—"

Sudden loud blasts shocked the air. They all three jumped, staring toward the door and the continuing noise outside.

Miles barked, "Stay inside," and then disappeared into the bedroom, but only for a second. He came past them, gun in hand, and rushed outside.

Maxi looked at Harlow, who'd gone pale.

Hand to her throat, Harlow whispered, "Is that gunfire?"

"I don't know," Maxi replied honestly. It almost sounded like cannon blasts to her, it was so loud.

Suddenly Justice was there with Catalina and Fallon. He deposited the women inside, saying, "Please don't budge."

"Sahara!" Fallon reminded him.

"She ran off."

"I did not," Sahara gasped, as if he'd offered a terrible insult. She had all three protesting boys corralled, more or less forcing them into the house. They must've come straight from the lake, because they dripped a puddle on her floor.

Maxi darted into the bathroom to grab towels, and through the window, she saw the men spreading out, one behind a tree, another at the side of the house, one at the barn... Her heart tried to thunder right out of her chest.

The touch on her arm squeezed a startled yelp out of her. Harlow whispered, "Sorry."

"Don't do that!"

"Come back in here with us where I can see you."

Again, she saw the worry in her sister's eyes. Nodding, Maxi led the way back to the room and gave the towels to the boys.

Looking worried, Lee said, "It's fireworks, right?"

"Of course," Sahara said, as if she really believed it. "But someone is playing a prank, and I don't like it."

She sounded so mean, Hull blinked at her. "You don't?"

"Someone will pay," she murmured with a small smile, "because this just got personal."

Maxi thought of those big strong men outside…and realized that the bigger threat was Sahara, at least to anyone who crossed her.

For a big man, he could move fast when he needed to. Shooting the fireworks at them was genius. Some landed on the roof of the barn, others exploded in the field. He hadn't used any with a big flash; that would defeat the purpose of causing confusion. He wanted loud, not bright.

The disorienting noise forced everyone to take cover while deciding if it was gunshots or something else. That gave him time to set the trap…and get out of the area. Once they reached the woods, they'd have a surprise waiting.

It was not that he wanted anyone hurt, but she gave him no choice.

Why wouldn't she leave?

She'd been to town, gabbing it up with everyone, planning a fence, and now she was having a damned party, as if she hadn't a care in the world. Strange girl, but she shouldn't push him.

He'd already proved himself. He'd taken care of things in the past. He could, and would, do what needed doing now.

CHAPTER FOURTEEN

Miles realized what was happening at about the same time as the others. He didn't relax. He was too enraged.

"Fucking fireworks?" Armie crouched next to him at the side of the house.

Stack was there, too. "What the hell is going on?"

"I told you," Miles said, his gun in his hand. "Someone is menacing her and I'm about done with it." He stepped out cautiously, inhaling the acrid scent of smoke.

"Shit," Justice said. "The barn roof!"

Backing up enough to see the roof, he realized small flames were beginning to lick upward. That wasn't from a firecracker, damn it. Had the bastard somehow launched a Molotov cocktail at them?

Leese pointed toward the back property. "They were shot from back there. Loud blasts."

Miles waffled. *Chase after the fucker, or put out the fire?*

Armie gave him a push. "Go on. We've got this."

Already Denver had found the garden hose, Stack was leading it forward and Justice was halfway up the ladder. Miles glanced back at the house.

Brand said, "I'll go in with the women. They'll be fine."

With all that taken care of, Miles took off in a full-out run. Leese was right behind him. They ran past smoldering blotches on the ground. Thank God for the recent storm. There was so much dry brush, they might have been putting out fires everywhere.

As they reached the edge of the woods, Miles slowed, his gun out and ready…and his instincts screaming.

Leese said, "I feel like he's gone."

"Same." Miles scanned the woods. "But something feels off." He put out an arm to stop Leese from going any farther.

They both breathed evenly, alert, listening, looking…

And finally Miles saw it. "Shit!" He pushed Leese back and down with the momentum of his own dive, landing half over his friend just as an explosion shook the ground. Thank God it wasn't as powerful as it sounded, but the pile of exploding debris sent a shard of something into his left forearm, the burn searing.

Leese must have heard his grunt, because he immediately rolled Miles to the side and rose up over him. The way he winced told Miles he'd been hit, but he confirmed it with a glance—then cursed a blue streak.

The others were starting toward them. Miles sat up and shouted, "Don't!" He struggled to his feet, telling Leese, "We have to move. There could be more traps set."

Leese asked, "Do you need help?"

He shook his head. The chunk of glass that had sliced into his arm hurt like hell, but it didn't affect his legs. As they walked, Leese tucked his gun into a pocket, then pulled off his shirt to catch the steady trickle of red blood.

Leese had to wrap it gingerly because jagged pieces of glass protruded. "I wonder what they have in the way of an emergency room around here."

Already his hand went numb. "No idea." He knew Maxi

would be upset, but he didn't know what he could do about it. Before he reached the house, the others were there with him. Smoke still trailed off the roof, but no flames.

Justice whistled. "Damn, man."

Stack said, "This is looking less and less like paradise."

"I'm thinking you need around-the-clock guards," Cannon said.

Armie, the one handiest with injuries, took over without thinking about it. He wrapped the shirt loosely around Miles's arm. "No telling how deep that's in there. We have to get you to a hospital."

Cannon said, "I'll check on the women and let Brand know what's going on."

"And get some ice," Armie said. "As much as you can."

Before they reached the front of the house, Fletcher pulled up. When he saw them all together, he parked short and was out of his car in a rush. "What the hell happened?"

If it wouldn't make him bleed more, Miles knew he'd flatten him. "Just happened by, Fletcher?"

"Hull's brother said he might be here. He's looking for him. Since I was driving by..." Fletcher's gaze strayed from Miles's injury to the gun in his right hand. "Is that loaded?"

"Someone," Miles said, still walking, "shot fireworks at us, and I'm not talking sparklers. It caught the roof on fire. Since it came from the woods, I went to check it out and ran into a homemade bomb. So yeah, you bet your ass it's fucking loaded."

They all ignored him as they continued on.

Suddenly the back door burst open and Maxi came running out, her expression stricken. When she reached him, she slowed. As if no one else existed, she stopped to look at his arm—and then surprised him with her calm. "We need to get you to the hospital."

"That's the plan," Miles told her. He handed his gun to

Armie, who, after an odd look, handed it to Justice. Now that he had a free hand, Miles smoothed her hair and drew her close. "I'm okay, but I do need stitches."

She nodded. "I'm going with you."

"Okay." Hell, he wanted her with him where he could see her and know she was okay. "Someone can drive my car."

"You can follow me," Fletcher said. "I'd offer to drive, but I need to head right back here."

Miles ground his teeth together. "Planning to investigate?"

"Yes, but I'd rather get you to a hospital first. Then I'll come back here." He scanned the faces of Miles's friends. "Don't anyone touch anything, and please don't anyone leave."

"That include the boys?" Leese asked. "You did say Hull's brother was looking for him."

"I'll call Donny on the way." Lifting a brow, he asked Miles, "You riding with me or—"

Leese said, "I'll drive."

"No." Stack stepped forward. "This is your gig, so you'd do better to stay. I'll drive."

Leaving them to sort it out, Miles—with Maxi's unnecessary assistance—got into the back seat.

Just then Cannon trotted out with multiple crushed ice packs, plenty of clean cloths and a Coke. Lifting the drink in salute, Cannon explained, "Sahara insisted you needed some sugar."

He actually laughed. "Yeah, sugar is her cure for everything."

"Thank her for us." Maxi took everything from Cannon and got into the back seat with him. She fastened his seat belt, smoothed his hair, then told Stack, who'd won the driving debate, "Let's get going, please."

Stack smiled into the rearview mirror. "Yes, ma'am."

Fletcher drove fast, Miles would give him credit for that.

It took very little time to reach the hospital, and along the way Maxi pampered him.

He didn't need pampering, of course, but she seemed so intent on it, so focused, he let her do as she pleased. Hell, he was impressed with how well she kept it together. She'd unwrapped Leese's shirt from around his arm, saw the gruesome damage, and although she gasped, she otherwise didn't react. Carefully she put clean cloths around him, then the ice at either side of the injury.

The pain in his arm was nothing compared to the rage inside him. What if Maxi had been up there by the woods? What if they'd all still been there working? Someone could have lost an eye, or worse, been killed. Pieces of the explosive device were deadly—chunks of metal, glass, wood.

As if she knew the tingling in his hand, Maxi touched each finger, gently flexing. "Not much longer."

That slight tremble in her voice devastated him. The way she leaned over him, her head bent as she continually examined the wound, the closest he could get was to kiss the bridge of her nose. It wasn't enough, but for now it'd have to do.

When she looked up at him, he said, "I really am okay, babe."

"I know." She kissed his shoulder, his sternum, his chin. "Do you realize you're still shirtless? It's going to shut down the hospital."

"Leese gave me his shirt," Miles told her, so if he'd driven, he'd be shirtless, too.

"I thought to grab mine," Stack said with a grin.

"Thank goodness." Maxi tried to smile, but it was a strained effort at best. "Two of you semi-naked would cause a riot."

Stack said, "I'm impressed, Maxi."

She lifted her brows. "About what?"

"Your lack of hysterics."

That brought her brows back down. "Because I'm female?"

Stack snorted. "No. Male or female, most people would be freaking out right about now. But you're not." He never took his eyes off the road. "I hope that's not because you've been through so much, you're getting immune."

"It's not," she assured him. "It's just that hysterics wouldn't help anything. Once I get Miles back home and in bed, I'll probably fall apart."

Stack grinned. He, at least, knew Miles had no intention of going to bed over a hurt arm.

"I left my gun behind," Miles said, "but if anything happens, I have another in the glove box. I don't think it should come into the hospital with me, but I wanted you to know where it is."

"Sure, Calamity Jane," he replied. "Though you realize guns aren't my thing, right?" He lifted a fist. "These are the weapons I usually use."

"And your feet and knees and elbows," Miles added. To Maxi, he explained, "Stack is brutal in the cage, but MMA fighters rarely need guns."

Wide-eyed, she repeated, "You have another gun in the glove box?"

So that was the only part she'd heard? "Of course I do." He leaned forward for another kiss, this one on her slightly parted lips. "I'm not taking any chances with protecting you."

Maxi hugged herself up to his side, her face in his neck, and whispered, "Please just worry about being okay."

He didn't bother telling her again that he was absolutely fine. She'd find that out soon enough now that they were in the hospital parking lot.

It did cause some chaos, walking in shirtless, but Maxi didn't put up with any gawking. They lucked out that it was a slow night, according to the doctor, because Miles was seen right away.

Fletcher came in with them to explain what had happened,

but he didn't stick around. He said he was heading back to check out the scene—not that Miles trusted him to actually do his damned job. He felt more confident that Leese and Justice would get the details needed, and that they'd follow any trail that might remain.

Maybe it was time to call in the city cops.

He was still stewing on that when less than three hours later, with a tetanus shot and twenty-five stitches, they were on their way back home. As he'd told Maxi, he was fine. No arteries hit—which he knew, or there'd have been a lot more bleeding. And no bones chipped—which he also knew because he'd had broken bones. He'd have a scar, but fighters, or retired fighters, didn't worry about things like that.

Maxi, leaning against his good side, was far too quiet.

When she looked up at him, he saw it in her eyes and knew what she would say, so he beat her to it. "No."

She blinked as if surprised. "No what?"

"No, I'm not leaving." She, on the other hand, needed to go until he could make it safe.

Her gaze shifted away from his, and her fingertips stroked his shoulder. "It's getting too dangerous."

From the front seat, Stack said, "Someone is getting desperate. If the house is suddenly empty, the threats will stop, and you'll never know who was doing it."

She frowned. "I don't want that." And then, in a lower voice, she added, "Someone has to pay."

"Exactly." Miles tipped up her chin. "It can't be empty, but, honey, you can't stay."

A dozen emotions flitted over her face until she settled on pacifying him. "We'll talk about it later, okay?" She went back to leaning on his shoulder and petting him.

Disgusted, Miles said to Stack, "That's her way of telling me she doesn't plan to budge."

With a sigh, Maxi said, "My house, my problems. And no,

Miles, don't act like I'm an idiot who doesn't see logic. I'll be extra careful. Shoot, I'll put a privacy fence along the woods, even. But I'm not going to let some nut drive me away." She absently trailed a hand over his bare abs. "Besides, Fletcher might have some news for us when we get home."

"Don't hold your breath." Somehow he'd convince her to leave the house for a while. He wasn't sure how, but something would come to him.

They arrived home to find the crowd even bigger, and Fletcher nowhere to be seen.

It was a subdued party for sure, but among their ranks, Maxi saw that Gary had shown up and was talking quietly with Harlow. The urge to have him booted out burned like a volcano ready to erupt, but with so many people around she didn't want to cause yet another scene. The day had been insane enough.

Forcing her attention away from Gary, she spotted Woody. The young man he spoke with looked enough like Hull for her to assume he was Hull's brother.

Sahara served drinks and food to everyone, basically playing hostess in Maxi's absence. Even as she envied Sahara the ease with which she took over, Maxi appreciated the effort.

The other fighters were spread out, Armie, Cannon and Denver talking to the boys, Justice and Leese with Fallon and Catalina. Now that they'd returned, though, some of them headed over to talk to Miles.

With no thought of usurping Sahara's current reign, Maxi tried to usher him inside before his friends reached them.

Resisting her efforts easily, he gave her a long look. "When I go to bed, it'll be tonight with you, not before, so save your energy."

Hoping no one had overheard him, Maxi crossed her arms. She should be annoyed with him for his stubbornness—after all, he'd lost a lot of blood, and despite his stoic manner, he had to be in pain. Bruising had formed on his arm from above his knuckles to his elbow.

Unfortunately, she understood that for a take-charge man like Miles, it wouldn't be easy to leave questions unanswered. Getting annoyed would serve no purpose, so she let it go with a long sigh.

Leese joined them, saying right away, "There wasn't a trail to follow, but Fletcher said he has some ideas."

Disbelieving, Miles asked, "Where is Fletcher?"

Cannon nodded his head toward the back of the property. "Still up there poking around."

"Great," Miles muttered. "So even if I wanted to call in the city police, he's probably fucked the scene."

Leese shrugged. "Probably. I took my own photos and did some poking around, too."

"And?" Miles asked.

"There really wasn't much to see except the remains of the makeshift bomb. Basically just a bunch of garbage jammed into a can with fuel. Rocks under one side of the can aimed it toward Maxi's field. It was so amateurish that it could've been made by a kid."

Maxi knew without asking that Miles wasn't looking at this as a juvenile prank gone wrong. On its own, maybe, but not as part of the ongoing harassment and threats.

Woody came over to see them, his hands shoved deep into his pockets, consternation pulling his gray brows in a frown of worry. "You okay, Miles? Your friends told me what happened."

Miles lifted his bandaged arm. "Fine, just a few stitches. Nothing to worry about."

The casual attitude didn't reassure Woody. "I keep thinking about Meryl, how she might've been here all alone when this happened. It's usually so quiet out here, fireworks like that would've scared her half to death, but she'd have been worried about her cats and would have gone right out of the house to check on them." He shook his head. "Damned scary."

That was the very moment that it struck Maxi: What if her grandmother hadn't fallen? What if, God forbid, *she'd been murdered*?

Dazed with the idea, she swayed on her feet. Miles, always so attuned to her, pulled her into his side. Even one-armed, he was such a rock that she gladly leaned against him while tumultuous thoughts blasted through her brain.

Near her ear, he asked softly, "Hey, you okay?"

She needed to talk to him alone as soon as possible. "Yes, but—"

Misunderstanding her upset, Woody said fast, "We checked on the cats. Most of them hunkered down in the barn, so don't you worry none. The smoke was all on the outside. I'm sure they're fine."

The cats were okay—but Miles could have been killed.

Like my grandma?

The new possibility made everything different—because now she was doubly determined to find the person responsible. She wanted him to pay dearly for all the heartache he'd caused.

Mean-spirited pranks probably designed to run her off, scare tactics that caused an injury, an invasion of her privacy— those were bad enough. *Scary* enough. But murder?

Maxi didn't realize how tense she'd gotten until Miles stroked his hand up and down her arm. The last thing he needed right now was her having a meltdown, so she pulled it together. She would have silently plotted, too, but the man Woody had been talking to, younger and new to the group, joined them.

Hand out, he greeted Maxi first. "I'm Donny, Hull's brother."

"Maxi Nevar. I inherited my grandmother's property." Accepting the handshake, she said, "I'm so sorry about this, Donny. It's not what we expected to happen when we invited the boys here." What a terrible way for her to meet others in the community, by dragging boys into danger.

"Not your fault." His curious gaze went to Miles, who had to let her go so he could shake hands, as well.

"Nice to meet you, Donny."

"Same." He cleared his throat. "So you're Miles Dartman, huh? I mean, I know you are because Armie told me." He wiped his hands on his jeans in a nervous gesture. "Never expected to find a bunch of SBC fighters hanging around here."

"You follow the sport?"

"Well, yeah," he said, with a "duh" inflection. "Can't believe Hull didn't tell me."

Miles smiled. "I imagine since I'll be here, my friends will be here often, too."

Maxi froze as those words sank in. *Since I'll be here.* When had that been decided? Or maybe he meant just in the present, not the future—

"About Hull..." Donny glanced toward his brother, who showed signs of hero worship as he spoke with Armie and Denver. "He had a great time and I appreciate you including him."

"He worked hard," Miles said.

"Yeah." Almost pained, Donny ran a hand over his head. "We haven't had problems like this for a long time. It's a mostly quiet area. Hull's kicking up a fit about it, but I know our parents won't want him around again until you get things under control."

Maxi could see how it grieved the young man to have to say that, likely because *he* wanted to hang around, too. "I agree." She turned to Woody, who stood there in his own silent misery. "The same goes for you, too. I'd feel terrible if any of you got hurt in any way."

Donny put a hand on Woody's shoulder. "Fletcher watches out for him now. Payback, you know? I don't doubt he's already grounded Woody away from here."

Woody glared at him but then softened his expression for Miles and Maxi. "I should get going, too, I guess."

His smile staying fixed in place, Miles stopped him before he'd taken a single step. "Why would Fletcher warn you away?"

Donny, still being helpful, said, "Woody might not feel like he needs someone looking out for him, but his grandson disagrees." He winked, then called to Hull.

Grandson? Maxi tried to get that to click into place, but her brain felt sluggish.

Miles was a little quicker. "Fletcher is your grandson?"

Hull had just reached them. "You didn't know that? Woody raised them both."

"Both?" Maxi asked, even more confused.

"Fletcher and his sis, Anna," Donny said.

"But… Woody's and Fletcher's last names are different."

"My daughter's kids," Woody explained. "She and her husband died in a car accident."

"Anna's only a year or two younger than Fletcher," Donny explained. "Woody raised them like they were his own."

Woody scowled. "It's not a big deal to take in your kin."

Donny grinned. "Taking in two kids was enough, but Fletcher was a real hell-raiser to boot, always has been, always will be. It helps that he's an officer now. Gives him a license to be bossy, you know?"

Miles narrowed his eyes, and that worried Maxi. "He seems like a very calm, controlled person to me."

Donny laughed. "It was only five or six years ago that he

got in his last scuffle. Caused such a spectacle, the whole town knew about it."

"In a town this size," Maxi said, "I imagine everyone knows everything about everyone else."

"True." Donny leaned closer in a conspiratorial way. "This was huge, though. Fletcher went after a couple of bad-news dudes with a baseball bat. Put them both in the hospital, too."

Miles lifted his brows. "Was there a reason?"

"Young and dumb," Woody grumbled. "That was the reason."

Twenty-five or -six wasn't all that young, Maxi thought, curious about this other side to Fletcher.

"C'mon, Woody," Donny said, "you know Fletcher always liked to hit first and ask questions later."

Gruff in his defense, Woody said, "The boy has a temper, that's all. He went through a lot, losing his folks the way he did. But he turned it around." Woody glanced at Miles. "I'm real proud of him for being county police."

"And actually," Donny added, "the guys were hassling Anna about something. Fletcher doesn't tolerate anyone giving his sister grief. The two of them are real close."

Miles didn't look impressed with any of it. "If he assaulted two people, what came of it?"

"The guys threatened to file charges. They yelled it all over town." Donny shrugged. "But then they split and no one ever heard from them again."

Maxi tried not to look as surprised as she felt at the disclosures. "I don't think I've met Anna."

"Um…she's not around here anymore." Donny sent a furtive glance at Woody, then quickly focused on his brother. "We're late as it is. Tell Fletcher if he needs to talk more to Hull, he'll have to come to our house, with our folks there."

"Tell him yourself," Woody said. "I'm heading out with you."

"I'll tell him," Maxi offered, just to keep the peace.

Miles watched them go, his expression probing.

So many things bombarded Maxi that she wasn't sure where to start. The indecision ended quickly when she spotted Sahara going into the house with an empty pitcher of tea.

She turned to Miles. "Will you please sit down?"

"What for? My legs weren't injured. Besides, I want to take a look—"

She threw up her hands. "Fine. Suit yourself." Arguing with him had never done her any good, and if she didn't hurry, Sahara would be right back outside again. Sahara was not a woman to dawdle. "If you get hurt again, I'm going to..." While she tried to think of something dire, Miles grinned.

Gently, he brushed the backs of his fingers over her cheek. "What?"

Blast, but it was so easy for him to distract her. "I'll think of something."

He stopped her from running off. "You sure you're okay?"

Impatient now, she nodded. "I'm going in to get a drink. Do you need anything? Aspirin maybe?"

Unconvinced, he studied her. "No, I'm fine."

That made her roll her eyes. The man was wounded, not fine, but she didn't want to lose her opportunity to speak to Sahara alone. She turned to Leese. "Watch him, okay?"

Leese said, "Uh...yeah, sure."

With no more assurance than that, she walked quickly into the house. Sahara was just on her way out, but Maxi relieved her of the pitcher, saying, "Can I ask you something?" as she hooked her arm and led her back into the kitchen.

Sahara never faltered, switching direction and going along without a single objection.

In the kitchen, Maxi put the pitcher back on the counter and asked without preamble, "How can I get a gun?"

Without a single show of surprise, Sahara said, "It's not difficult as long as you can pass a background check."

"I'm sure I can." If she ever found the person who had hurt
Miles, it might become a problem, since he was the one she
wanted to shoot.

"Then I can help you. What type gun would you like?"

She knew nothing about guns, but she understood her own
limitations. "Something easy to load, and easy to use."

"A revolver, then. Small?"

Thinking that she might have to hide it from Miles, she
nodded. "Please."

"Have you ever shot a gun?"

"Does laser tag count?"

Sahara gave her a look. "Unfortunately, no. But I can get
you a gun with a laser on it so you'll know if your aim is
true." Leaning back on the counter, arms crossed, she asked,
"Why do you want it?"

"For protection, of course."

"Miles is your protection."

Yes, he had been…and now he had a giant gash on his arm.
"I'm going to let him go."

Sahara shot forward, her relaxed posture blown. "You're
firing one of my bodyguards?"

"Shh," Maxi cautioned. "I'm not firing him. I'm just calling it quits."

"No, absolutely not." Sahara turned and started out of the
kitchen with a determined, militant stride.

"Where are you going?" Maxi rushed to keep up with her.

"I will not have the agency's rep damaged." Finger thrust
in the air, she stated, "Body Armor finishes what it starts!"

"But this isn't ending," Maxi explained in a panic. She got
ahead of Sahara and, arms spread, barred the door. "You saw
what happened. You know how long it's been."

"Pfft." Sahara lifted her nose. "Hardly any time at all has

passed, and clearly the danger has amplified. If you fire Miles now, it's not only going to infuriate him, but it's going to reflect badly on the entire agency."

"I'll give a sterling recommendation."

"And say what? That we failed? Unthinkable. I'll help you get a gun. You can even come to the agency to practice shooting if you'd like. But you can't dismiss a bodyguard in the middle of a case."

From behind Maxi, Miles said, "No one is dismissing me."

Eyes widening, Maxi bit back her groan and instead, in a harsh whisper, complained to Sahara, "You could have told me he was there."

"When I was going out to explain all this to him? You just saved me the trouble." She reached for the door handle, paused to say, "The tea. I almost forgot," then pivoted back for the kitchen.

Maxi huffed out a breath, girded herself and turned around to face Miles.

Holding the door open, he stepped into her space, crowding her back, his eyes piecing in their directness. "We are *not* done."

She'd never seen Miles volatile like this. Furious, yes. Sarcastic, sure. But now he looked ready to implode.

She stiffened her resolve. "Sahara is going to help me get a gun."

He said, "No."

Her eyes flared. Of all the… "You don't tell me what to do!"

Moving closer until her shoulders touched the wall, he leaned in to brace his uninjured forearm beside her head. "Let me rephrase that. You don't need a gun. *I'm* your protection."

"You," she emphasized, "got hurt."

His mouth tightened. "So what? You know I got hurt as a fighter, too. Far as injuries go, this was nothing."

Incredulous at his attitude, she dropped her head back to the wall with a thunk. "You could have been killed."

His forehead touched hers. "And if you'd been here alone, Maxi? You think you'd have fared better?"

As she passed with the tea pitcher, Sahara said, "I'm going to help her get a gun and teach her to shoot."

Miles closed his eyes, then straightened to say to his boss, "No you're not."

Unperturbed, Sahara kept going.

"If you weren't injured," Maxi growled, "I'd sock you."

His gaze bored into hers. "I have guns. If you want to learn to shoot, *I'll* teach you."

She opened her mouth…but rethought blasting him when she realized what he'd said. "You will?"

"Yes."

"When?"

His eyes narrowed more. "In a hurry?"

Given everything she'd realized today, all her new suspicions? "Definitely." If need be, she'd protect him.

"Then we can start tonight if you want, after our company leaves."

Anticipating her first lesson, she asked, "Any idea when that might be?"

"You want to boot out my friends, too?"

Ignoring the growled tone, and the implication that she didn't like their guests, she said, "No, of course not. It's just that—"

"They already started stringing the wire fencing, so it might be late."

Maxi weighed her need to tell Miles of her suspicions with the need to have that area fenced. Everyone was already here, and the day had been crazy enough without adding her suspicions—suspicions that could be totally ungrounded.

She'd still tell Miles, of course, but she made the decision to wait until they were alone.

"Well, *excuse me.*"

At that intrusive voice, Miles and Maxi stared at each other. He lifted a sardonic brow. "Want me to handle this so it's over once and for all?"

Since she'd just been thinking about murder, it was no wonder his acerbic tone had her whispering, "What are you suggesting?"

"This." He stepped away, putting himself in Gary's path. "You're going to leave, and not come back."

"But—"

Muscles flexed in his biceps and shoulders. "And you won't call her anymore."

"But I—"

"And," Miles said, his quiet tone somehow extra threatening, "if you bother her again, you'll answer to me. Understand, Gary, I'm not nearly as patient as she's been."

Silence pulsed around them.

Miles took a step closer. *"Go."*

"This is bullshit!" Even as he said it, Gary turned to run out, almost knocking over her sister.

Harlow, insulted, glared at Gary's retreating back. "He is such a disappointment."

"But I'm not," Miles said, drawing her startled attention. "So knock it off, okay? I don't know about Maxi, but I've had more than enough ridiculous drama." He shouldered his way around her and went back out to the yard.

Maxi grinned at the way he'd shut down her domineering sister. "He's amazing, isn't he?"

Nodding, Harlow said, "In many ways." She looked Maxi over with concern. "You're okay?"

"Yup."

Harlow sighed. "You're not going to leave, are you?"

Feeling absurdly cheerful, Maxi said, "Nope."

Looking away, Harlow whispered, "When I realized what could have happened today, God, what you've already been through... I don't mind telling you, Maxi, it made me feel like crap."

"I never wanted that."

"I know." She rubbed her brow. "You're my sister, and although we've had our differences, I hope you know—"

"You love me," Maxi said for her. "Back atcha."

"We're family, through thick and thin. I lost Mom. I don't want to lose you, too."

That statement was so full of acceptance that Maxi hugged her. "You won't," she promised.

With a touch of desperation, Harlow squeezed her tight, then thrust her back the length of her arms. "Since you rarely listen, I'm only going to tell you this once—your bodyguard is a keeper. Do your best not to screw it up."

And there, Maxi thought with errant humor, was her bossy, judgmental sister. She didn't mind the warning; at her age, she was well used to her sister's general attitude on things. This time, however, it was probably out of her hands. After all, she and Miles had hit it off from the start, but she was afraid she'd already burned that bridge by walking away.

Now only time would tell.

CHAPTER FIFTEEN

He tried to hide it, but Miles was so furious he couldn't see straight. He'd walked away from Maxi and her annoying sister before he said too much.

Maybe he shouldn't have given Gary the option of leaving. Punching someone, especially that asshole, would have alleviated some of his rage. Problem was, Gary wouldn't even come close to being a match for him. He had friends here who'd offer a real challenge, but he didn't want to pound on them.

Maxi had ended things with him once—*and now she wanted to end them again.*

Would he ever understand her? At times she seemed so content, as if her world were near perfect despite the ever-present danger. She'd included him in that contentment, he knew it, had felt it. So why start pulling away again?

He liked her. Hell, he *more* than liked her. The longer he spent with her, the deeper his feelings became.

Fuck it.

It was time, past time, that he settled their relationship. And damn it, it *was* a relationship, whether she wanted to think that or not. Even if she fired him—*ha, let her try*—he wasn't going anywhere. He'd sleep in the barn if he had to, but he would ensure that no one hurt her.

He wanted to join the others working. Physical labor was the next best thing to pounding a heavy bag to alleviate rage. But then he caught sight of Fletcher just as he was about to leave.

A target. Not that he could rip Fletcher apart without a really good reason. But at least he could vent some of his anger.

Before the officer could leave, Miles jogged over to his car and tapped on the window.

Startled, Fletcher lowered it, and cool air-conditioning blasting from the console hit Miles.

Nodding at his arm, Fletcher asked, "You're okay?"

Miles stared a moment at the passenger seat...and a pair of long-range binoculars. Did the good officer own a rifle, too? Likely.

"Yeah," Miles said, pulling back before he gave himself away. "I'm fine. Just a few stitches."

"A few dozen?"

"Something like that."

After following Miles's gaze, Fletcher put up the window and got out. "No need to cool the area." He closed the door behind him and leaned against it, arms crossed—which blocked Miles's view of the inside.

He acknowledged that with a snide grin. "It's a nice ride."

"It gets me around these old country roads."

So they were both going to hedge? Fuck that. "Did you find anything?"

"I'm going to check on some of the materials that were around or part of that idiotic 'bomb.'"

"Like?"

"Brick, pipe, glass from a beer bottle. They could be from anywhere, even the junkyard, but it's a starting point." He stared at Miles, unblinking. "Also saw some boot prints in the dirt."

"Yeah?" Miles lowered his gaze to Fletcher's boots. "Like yours?"

"A lot like mine."

Was that a taunt, or defiance at the indirect accusation? Miles didn't know, didn't care and didn't ask. He'd make all the accusations he wanted. "I don't suppose you have a rifle and an ATV?"

Fletcher gave a mock bow.

"Both, huh?"

"It's the country, son. Everyone has a rifle and an ATV." He straightened away from the vehicle. "Whatever you're thinking, feel free. I don't give a shit. But don't get in my way while I do my job."

"Actually," Miles said, "I'm thinking of calling in the city police. Township police isn't cutting it."

"You do that. 'Course, they usually defer back to us, so the best you might get is another officer. There are four to choose from. But hey, knock yourself out." After glancing behind Miles, he said, "Tell Maxi I'll be in touch." He got back in the Suburban and slammed the door.

No, he wouldn't be telling her shit, because Miles wasn't going to let Fletcher around her again. He didn't trust Fletcher, never would.

But he wasn't convinced of his guilt either.

Yeah, the guy was cocky and abrasive, but if that made him guilty, then he had a yard full of guilt, because no one did attitude like an MMA fighter.

Frustration rode him hard, made his neck sweat and his vision burn.

Would they continue with the work, or had he done enough damage to dissuade them? He wasn't sure, and it made him testy.

He'd almost said too much today.

Not a good thing. He had to remember that they weren't his friends, would never be his friends. When it came down to it, they were nothing. He needed to keep his edge.

It should have been so easy, but instead it got more complicated. Lately, nothing had gone as planned. Every day he got closer to blowing it—and every day Maxi came closer to discovering his secrets.

Secrets that should have been buried for good.

What would it take to make her go?

How far was she going to push him?

The sun was setting by the time everyone left, but the fence was mostly complete. Miles would be able to finish up on his own in the morning. He wanted more solar spotlights attached to the posts.

Maxi's goats would be protected.

He was still a little pissed at her, and she was definitely pissed at him when he locked the front door and went into his bedroom.

She followed.

That didn't surprise him. She'd been dogging his heels and fretting over him ever since Fletcher had left. His friends, Armie especially, would never stop razzing him about her coddling instincts.

Didn't matter that Cannon told her he was fine.

Didn't matter that Denver promised not to let him lift anything heavy.

Didn't matter that he got irate over all that mothering—she hadn't quit.

Stack thought it was some sort of warped female guilt—though he hadn't called it that exactly. He'd said that Maxi felt guilty because Miles had gotten hurt while working for her.

The others had backed up that probability. Hell, Armie had suggested he take advantage of all that sweet concern. But then, he didn't know that Maxi had tried to fire him. Only Sahara knew, and thankfully, she kept it to herself.

Neither of them had spoken yet. Maxi stood there, arms hugged around herself, watching while he peeled off his sweaty T-shirt and grabbed fresh clothes out of the drawer.

"What are you doing?"

She sounded so suspicious, he cast her a look. "I'm going to shower."

That got her away from the door and into the room. "You can't. You have stitches."

"So?"

"The doctor said not to get them wet."

He shrugged. No way was he going to bed in his own sweat. "I'll be quick."

"No."

He was as incredulous with her refusal as she'd been with his about the guns. "Excuse me?"

"You can't take a shower. I'll run a bath for you and then help you wash so you don't—"

His laugh interrupted her. "Sorry, babe, but you're not giving me a bath."

"Am, too." Nose in the air, she walked out.

Bemused, Miles heard the bathwater start a few seconds later. Huh. Well, this ought to be interesting.

With the blinds drawn, he stripped off the rest of his clothes and dropped them into his laundry basket. Naked, clean clothes under his arm, he stepped out and found Maxi standing there, waiting for him.

Holding his arm, she led him along, saying, "Come feel the water. Make sure it's not too hot."

She'd run him a hot bath instead of the cool shower he'd wanted? He'd have laughed again except that she looked so serious. He decided to go along, curious to see what she would do.

At least if she was helping him in the bathtub, she wasn't mad.

Maxi took the clothes from him and set them on the sink. Luckily the water wasn't all that hot, more like room temperature, which suited him okay. When he stepped in, she held his uninjured arm as if he might…what? Slip and fall?

"I'm a big boy, honey. I think I can get into the tub on my own steam."

Chagrined, she let him go but warned, "Be careful."

Miles shook his head and eased down into the water. It surprised him that it felt so good. "It's been ages since I took a bath instead of a shower." When she didn't reply, he glanced over and found her staring fixedly at his body.

Specifically, his lower body.

Maybe he liked this more than he realized.

Watching her, he said softly but with steel demand, "Take off your halter."

Her gaze shot to his. "What?"

"You'll get it wet if you don't." *And he'd get her shorts wet if she did.*

After another lingering look at his body, she reached back and untied the strings behind her neck. The halter dropped forward, showing her breasts.

Smooth, plump and pale, her breasts were a perfect fit for his hands, making his palms tingle. Her nipples had already drawn into peaks, and he wanted her in his mouth.

Staring at him, she reached behind her back and untied the lower string. The halter fell to the floor, leaving her in hip-hugging cutoff shorts.

Maxi had always looked great, no matter what she wore. But he really loved her in the casual country clothes, like frayed shorts and body-baring halters.

Those shorts she had on now…nice decoration, that was all they were, but he'd like to see them gone, as well. Maxi naked was a unique pleasure for him.

Miles shifted. He loved her body, every sexy, curvy, creamy little inch of it. Heavy with suggestion, he asked, "Wanna lose the shorts, too?"

"You want me to?"

"Yeah," he said, his voice rougher, almost hoarse.

With a note of teasing, she whispered, "All right."

He watched those slim fingers as they opened the snap, slowly dragged down the zipper, as she hooked her thumbs along the waistband. Already his heart pumped faster and he went semi-hard.

When she bent to push down the shorts, her breasts swayed. She took off her panties at the same time and straightened, completely naked.

"I will never tire of looking at you."

Her gaze shot to his. After a moment, she said, "Never is a long time."

He couldn't imagine a day where he wouldn't thrill at the sight of her. "Time passes quicker than you think." He sat up higher in the tub and bent his legs, making room for her. As she stepped in, beautifully bare, he asked, "Was this your plan all along?"

"No." She lowered herself to her knees and, bracing one hand on his shoulder, the other on the tub shelf, leaned forward to take his mouth in a kiss that burned.

It surprised him for about two seconds—then he tangled a hand in her hair, keeping her close when she would have withdrawn, parting his legs so she could settle against him. He kissed her harder, deeper, his tongue exploring.

Her belly pressed against his rising boner. If she'd told him what type of bath she'd planned, he wouldn't have been resistant. He was just considering how sex in the narrow tub would work when she suddenly protested.

"Wait." Breathing heavily, she stiffened her arms to push away. "I wanted to talk to you."

Miles tried to draw her back. "We'll talk after."

"We both need to wash first. And your arm—"

"It's not my arm that's aching right now."

Her small smile teased him. "I'm a little achy myself."

He thought he'd gotten his way until she went back to her knees and reached for the washrag and soap. "You like to torture me, don't you?"

"No, but I don't mind teasing a bit. I won't make it so hard—"

"Too late."

"—that you suffer." The smile widened into a grin. "I promise we'll both survive." Now with a soapy cloth, she sat back on her heels and started washing him, knees first, then calves and each foot. "I should have gotten behind you."

"Then I wouldn't be able to look at you." Already soap bubbles dribbled down her breasts, dripped from her nipples and trailed along her flat belly. Little tendrils of blond hair clung to her cheeks and neck. He looked at her lips, swollen from their kiss.

He wanted her. Nothing new in that. So yeah, maybe they should take this time to talk, then after the bath he'd be free to indulge.

She beat him to it, saying, "That was weird about Fletcher and Woody, wasn't it?"

"Being related, you mean?" He closed his eyes as she massaged the soapy cloth over his throat, his chest and shoulders.

"Yeah. I had no idea." She dipped the cloth down his body, over his abs, lower still until she was stroking him under the guise of cleanliness.

It took him a second to find his voice. "Apparently it's not a secret. Hull and Donny were surprised we didn't know."

"What happened today..." She paused to rinse his body, her hands lingering over his chest, her fingertips slicking over a nipple.

He opened his eyes. Much more of that and the talking would be over. "Today?"

Sitting back, she looked into his eyes and whispered, "Do you think it's possible my grandmother was murdered?"

Damn. He'd hoped she wouldn't make that possible connection, but he should have known better. Maxi was not an obtuse person.

He sat up, too, and, preparing for a more serious conversation, took her hands in his.

"Your arm!"

"Is out of the water." He held on when she would have pulled away. "Quit fussing."

Mulish now, she frowned. "I'll fuss if I want to."

"You already did. *All* day. I'm never going to hear the end of it." He gave her a quick kiss to let her know he wasn't all that annoyed by it. Not anymore anyway. "About your grandmother...who contacted you about her death?"

"Fletcher."

He should have known. Every time he turned around, Fletcher was there, on the very edges of being involved.

So that he wouldn't upset her, he tamped down his reaction and spoke in a calm, almost detached way. "Do you recall what he said?"

"He was kind, I remember that. And he asked me to come to Burlwood so we could talk. I knew it was about my grandma, of course. On the drive here, I kept telling myself that maybe she'd just been hurt...but I knew."

Miles cupped a hand to her face. "He met you here, at the house?"

"Yes." Tears welled in her eyes, but she quickly blinked them away.

Maxi was all about actions.

"She'd already been taken away, but he assumed I'd want to see her, and I did."

Seeing her hide her emotions almost hurt him worse than the tears. "Shh… I shouldn't have asked."

Angrily she swiped at her eyes. "Crying is so dumb."

"Crying is natural when you're talking about someone you loved." He kissed the bridge of her nose. This, he knew, was one of the special things about Maxi. He couldn't imagine sitting naked in a tub with any other woman while discussing something so heartbreakingly serious. But with Maxi, whatever they did always felt right.

With her emotions now in control, Maxi sighed. "Why did you ask?"

He'd wondered about the scene, but he changed his mind. She didn't need to relive that, so he shook his head.

"Miles?" Trying to guess, she said, "No one was here except Fletcher, but he drove me to see her, then brought me back."

Jesus, she'd been alone with him a lot when she'd been most vulnerable.

"I stayed at the house that night. I just… I wanted to be close to her, you know? And I didn't have the energy to drive back to my apartment. Once I stayed, I didn't want to leave. I only came back to Cinci to get more of my things."

"That's when I met you?"

She nodded. "Yes."

What if she hadn't come to the bar that night?

What if she'd focused on a man other than him? He might have never met her.

And if someone hadn't intruded into her peace, he might never have had a second chance with her.

His thoughts were so disturbing, he shoved them aside.

"Each time after that when we…got together," she said, "it was because I had to be in town, but I hadn't yet learned that the house was mine until right before the funeral."

Where her sister and brother had given her grief. With his

thoughts headed in a new direction, he accepted that if there'd been any signs of violence, she would have mentioned it. So probably no blood on the stairs, no weapons left around, no sign of a struggle. Of course, that didn't mean her grandmother had only fallen—

Maxi leaned into his palm. "Miles, what if someone pushed her?"

He cradled her cheek gently, his fingers curving around her skull. "I don't know, babe." He wanted to say that he'd find out for her, but where would he even start? He was a bodyguard, not a PI. "How soon after you moved in did the trouble begin?"

She went still, thinking, then straightened as she shook her head. "I'm not sure. I was here a week, I think, when I first noticed things missing or moved. But I assumed it was just me, that I was forgetful because of all the new changes, or that I was confused because it was a new place. Then it got more obvious, to the point I thought someone was in my house." She drew a deep breath. "And of course, someone was."

If Fletcher had responded to the call the day Meryl died, he could have grabbed keys then. "Do your brother or sister have keys to this place?"

"Not since you replaced the locks."

"But before that?"

"I don't know. My grandma gave me a key because I was always visiting, but I don't think Neil or Harlow came out here nearly as often." Suddenly she stood. "I need to get behind you so I can wash your hair."

Getting behind him meant sidling past, very closely. Miles put a hand to her hip to stop her, then turned his face and breathed in the scents of outdoors and sunshine and damp woman. He kissed one thigh, then the other, before pressing his face close and really tasting her.

She groaned—and quickly slid behind him. "Behave or you won't get clean."

Like she thought getting his hair washed was still a priority for him?

Slipping down into the water, Maxi now had her thighs open around him, and when she said, "Lean back," he didn't argue.

He rested between her open legs, his head on her breasts. She kissed the back of his neck, making his dick twitch, then got to work on his hair.

"Relax."

He laughed, but as her fingers massaged his scalp, his tensed muscles loosened.

Who knew baths could be so nice?

But that was how it was with Maxi; everything was sharper, deeper, hotter.

"I'm worried, Miles."

He half turned his head. "Please don't be. I'm not going to let anyone hurt you."

She gave him a small smile, then began rinsing his hair.

Never in his life had he spent this much time on his head. Usually he finished a shower in under five minutes—

"You misunderstand," she said softly, after she finally deemed his hair clear of shampoo. "I'm worried about *you*."

He sat up so fast, twisting to face her, that water sloshed out of the tub. "Me?"

"Yes, you. You're the one who got hurt."

When he completely turned, more water spilled over the side.

"Your arm!"

"Is fine, damn it." Fed up, he pulled the drain on the tub and stood.

"What are you doing?"

"Drying off. I can't think with you like—" he looked at her naked body "—that."

She started to rise. "I'll dry you—"

"Forget that. Finish your own bath before the water is gone. I have a few important things to say to you and it's better said out of the tub."

After a long look, she quickly washed her face and body, finishing just as the last of the water drained out.

Now with the sweat off and a temporary hold on his lust, Miles felt more in control. It wouldn't last; around Maxi it never did. They had things to settle, and by God, he'd settle them tonight before she threw him for another loop.

He was still drying the floor when Maxi stood, and she damn near took his breath away. Pink from the bath, her skin glistening and her shoulders back in irritation, she was almost too beautiful to resist.

He wrapped a fresh towel around her, kissed her forehead and stepped back to pull on his boxers.

She seemed pensive as she dried, her gaze repeatedly darting to his. Just as he figured out what to say, she asked, "Are you leaving?"

"What?" Damn it, he hadn't even finished dressing yet!

She wrapped the towel tight around herself. "I know what I said earlier. And I really do hate it that you got hurt." She nibbled on her bottom lip, her eyes big and troubled. "I don't want you to go, though."

That admission damn near took out his knees. "Ah, babe." Miles gathered her close and, despite her gasping concern for his arm, hugged her close. "I'm not going anywhere."

She took a long, slow breath. "Good." With her cheek to his chest, she asked, "You'll still teach me to shoot?"

"Yes." He tipped up her chin. "But not because you *need* to know, not when I'm going to keep you safe."

She nodded. "Okay."

Satisfied with that, he promised, "I'll teach you because you want to know."

"Thank you."

Miles almost smiled. Maxi ran him through so many emotions, sometimes in a single minute, that he could barely keep up. He smoothed a damp lock of hair away from her cheek. "I left MMA because I had a few too many concussions."

She reared back in shock. *"What?"*

Miles tapped his forehead. "My last fight, I took a knee to the head that left me spinning. I still won." He felt compelled to mention that little fact. "But I was out on my feet."

"Oh my God."

"It's not oh-my-God worthy, honey. I had worse injuries. Torn muscles, dislocations, breaks. It comes with the territory. My plan had been to stick with it until I got the belt, then semi-retire. But it didn't work out the way I planned, so here I am."

Pale, she slowly lowered until she sat on the side of the tub, staring at him in accusation. "When that blasted bomb went off, I kept thinking that you could have been killed."

"And all I got was a little cut."

"It's not little, damn it! And what if you'd hit your head?"

Hell, he'd hit *everything* when he'd landed on the ground with Leese. No reason to mention that, though. "My point is that in comparison, a few stitches are nothing."

"You're insane, aren't you?" She shoved to her feet and tried to get around him.

It was a small bathroom, so he easily contained her, turning her around and, despite her huffy resistance, gently pinning her to the wall.

In the struggle, she lost her towel.

He tried not to notice. *Yet.* "I'm a fighter at heart, Maxi, regardless of what job I do. If you freak out over a few stitches, then we're going to have a problem."

She breathed hard and muttered defiantly, "I'm not freaking out."

"What would you call it?"

Very lightly, she touched his bandaged arm. "Concern for someone I care about?"

It was the first time she'd ever admitted caring, and it obliterated his touted control. Wanting her, needing her, right this very second, he took her mouth hard.

It didn't surprise him that she matched his lust just as fiercely. From day one, he and Maxi had been sexually explosive. She seemed to forget about his arm as she clutched at him, pressing her naked breasts to his chest, groaning softly.

Even when he rushed her into the bedroom, she never mentioned his arm.

In fact, she teased him, saying, "And here I thought we were about to make use of the bathroom wall."

"Next time." He pulled her down to the bed with him, his kiss possessive, his tongue twining with hers while his hands covered her soft breasts.

She lifted against him in a sultry rhythm, her need already escalating. Miles freed her mouth, but just so he could latch on to one taut nipple.

Crying out at the strong suction, she tangled a hand in his hair. Her movements grew frantic. To help her along, he wedged his free hand between her thighs, his fingers searching. She arched, her body straining.

Miles slowed enough to look up at her, seeing her at the peak of release. God, he loved it.

Hell, he loved her.

No other woman could make him feel like this. He knew it, accepted it.

Now he just had to get her on board.

More gently, he kissed his way over to her other nipple, licking it lazily.

Maxi groaned.

Still at a leisurely pace, he pressed a finger into her and felt

LORI FOSTER 265

her muscles clamp down. *So wet.* He drew in her nipple, sucking softly while fingering her—and her whole body went taut, straining. As she came, she gave a sharp, undulating cry that little by little diminished into faint, hoarse moans.

Miles gave one last lick to her nipple, removed his fingers from her and hurriedly donned a condom.

She was still sprawled out, boneless, her legs lax and her breathing ragged, when he thrust into her.

She purred his name, wrapping her legs around him and locking her ankles at the small of his back. Her nails stung his shoulders, her hot little mouth opened against his chest, the sharp edge of her teeth teased—and he stiffened with a rush of release. It went on and on, always with Maxi.

Only with Maxi.

As he caught his breath, he felt her limbs slipping away from his body. Just that easily, she dozed off to sleep. Miles lifted up, a tender smile already in place. Guess he'd have to have that longer talk with her tomorrow.

At least now he felt confident there would be a tomorrow—and a day after that.

She'd quit trying to end things and instead admitted that she cared, that she wanted him to stay.

He called that progress.

After he disposed of the condom, he got back in bed and pulled her naked body against him. In her sleep, she curled close, her head against his shoulder, one leg over his hip.

Yeah, he wanted to sleep like this, with her, for the rest of his life. Whatever it took, he'd make it happen.

CHAPTER SIXTEEN

"Keep your finger straight along the barrel, not on the trigger, until you're ready to shoot."

Maxi flushed. He'd already told her that a few times, but she kept forgetting. Luckily Miles made sure to stay behind her when she held his small revolver, which he often strapped to his ankle and she found easier to use than his Glock.

Actually, he stayed behind her with his hands on her—her waist, her hip...she was starting to think this whole exercise was just so he could fondle her.

Not that she would have denied him. No way. When Miles touched her, she could almost forget the rest of the world existed.

"Now," he said near her ear. "See the can? No, don't close an eye. Both eyes open, babe."

The instructions went on and on, and after several tries she did finally hit the can. It excited her so much, she started to turn to Miles, but he caught her quickly and relieved her of the gun.

Another blush. But then she saw him smiling at her, his

arms open, and she threw herself against him. "Who knew target shooting could be so much fun?"

"With you?" he said, pressing a kiss to her mouth. "Everything is fun."

"Ha, right." With the sun behind him, she squinted to see his face. "Not getting stitches."

"Let's just say I'd rather do that with you than without you."

He kept confusing her with the things he said. Was it no more than the usual banter between a man and a woman, or was he telling her that she was somehow special? God, if only she hadn't walked out on him the first time, she wouldn't hesitate now to ask him how he felt about her.

But the history was there. She *had* walked away, and she didn't know if that had forever altered his trust. Plus, he was now her bodyguard, so he was basically forced into close proximity to keep her safe. Being sexually compatible might just be a convenient perk for him.

She realized he was watching her intently, waiting for her reply.

Joking seemed like a good cover for her ridiculous insecurity, so she said, "Well, if I had to get stitches, I'd rather get them with you, too."

"No stitches for you." Miles touched her mouth. "Promise me."

It couldn't be her imagination. He was definitely warmer toward her, more demonstrative now in ways that didn't lead them straight to bed. It was almost as if he'd made a decision that she knew nothing about.

Whatever his reasons, she liked the way he was with her now, so she smiled. "I promise."

For once, the cats weren't around them. The loud gun blasts had sent most of them scattering, but not far. They sat up the hill around the house, observing from a safe distance.

Only one cat remained close and Maxi bent to stroke along his back.

"He's a brave one," Miles said. "Hope he's not watching and learning. That's all we need is an armed cat."

She grinned, scooping up the black cat and cradling him to her chest. A gentle breeze drifted over the pond. Somewhere in the distance, a frog croaked. The humidity felt lower today, and the recent rains had left the landscape a vibrant green.

Miles tilted his head. "You amaze me, did you know that?"

Surprised by that sudden disclosure, she said, "But my aim wasn't all that great."

"I don't mean shooting. You'll get better at that with more practice." He, too, pet the cat. "I'm amazed because even with what happened, you don't feel uncomfortable down here anymore."

He didn't have to clarify; she knew exactly what he meant. They were very near the spot where someone had put her unconscious body in the dead of night.

At first, she'd feared that she'd never be able to visit the pond again.

It was thanks to him that she'd conquered that fear. He'd been casual about walking with her around the pond, always sticking close, there if she needed him.

Such an amazing guy, in so many ways.

She managed a smile. "I used to be, but not so much anymore." Her gaze sought his. "Not when you're with me."

Looking far too serious, his hand curved around her cheek, his thumb brushing the corner of her mouth. "I'm glad."

They kept dancing around declarations and it made her nuts. In her heart, she wanted him to stay, but being rational, she knew he couldn't. The Body Armor agency was a good forty-five minutes away. His friends, his family, his life...they all existed in a world separate from hers.

That he treated her so affectionately was probably because

of the phenomenal sex, a carryover to that intimacy. She, better than anyone, knew that sex didn't necessarily equate commitment. After all, she was the one who'd insisted that it *not* be anything more than sex. Since he'd become her bodyguard, she hadn't requested a change in those parameters. He was only abiding by her rules—how could she change those rules now, when he was still obliged to stay with her?

Obviously she couldn't, and damn it, she would not get emotional about it.

Everything was currently too nice to dampen it with what-ifs and worries for a future of their convoluted relationship.

"This sweet baby," she said, hugging the cat and effectively diverting her thoughts, "stayed with me. When I finally woke up enough to realize what had happened, he was there, watching me. He even came closer and sat by me." At the time, the familiar cat had felt like a lifeline in the middle of the unknown.

Miles, always attuned to her moods, scratched beneath the cat's chin. "Don't take offense, buddy. She doesn't mean to insult you."

Mouth twitching, Maxi asked, "How did I insult him?"

"You called him a sweet baby. He's actually a total badass. I've seen him stalk birds, a rabbit and a fish in the pond."

"Ah, well, then, I'm sorry."

"Are you set on the name Baby?"

She nodded. "At first I was calling him Shadow, mostly because when he sits in one, the only thing you can see is his eyes. But then he was such a cuddler, I started calling him Baby and it stuck. Now I'm starting to think that name isn't nearly grand enough."

The cat stretched toward Miles, his purr rumbling, his big yellow eyes closing in pleasure as he got attention from both humans.

Mesmerized, she watched the gentle way Miles handled

the cat, taking him from her and holding him close. "So as a hero, he needs a grander name?"

An idea dawned on her. "What do you think of calling him Hero?"

"I think he doesn't care what you call him, as long as you keep loving him."

Again, it felt like he was talking about more than her cat. In truth, Miles was her real hero.

Did he know that?

Just in case, she whispered, "I'll love him forever."

Miles gave her a long look, then, holding the cat against his shoulder, put his other arm around her and started them all toward the house.

It had been only two days since his trip to the ER, but he barely paid any attention to the injury. It definitely hadn't slowed him down—not in bed, and not around the farm.

Before they could do any practice shooting, he'd built a barrier down by the pond that gave her a wide range for missing and would catch any stray bullets. It was more complex than she'd expected, but Miles was good with his hands.

She grinned while thinking that. *Yes, the man was very, very good with his hands.*

Even though they couldn't see anyone beyond her property, they both knew that on occasion someone lurked out there, spying on them.

She didn't want to kill anyone. Catch them, yes. Pulverize them, sure. But she didn't want an accidental death on her hands, so she'd waited for him to build the barrier.

Now that it was done she wanted to get in as much practice as she could before the farmer delivered her goats. She'd purchased five of them, and after they were in the pasture, she wanted them to get used to their new home before possibly startling them with gunfire.

Yesterday, Brand had visited again and he and Miles, with

her help, had put solar lights on every third fence post. They'd also installed two very tall birdhouses on poles—so that the cats couldn't disturb them—and each one had a powerful solar light attached that would shine into the woods.

Brand was different from the others, more intense. Still friendly with an easy smile, but she had the feeling his thoughts were troubled. Because of that, she'd tried to give him time alone with Miles, but neither man wanted to let her out of his sight.

As she and Miles reached the house, his cell phone rang. He set down the cat and, after glancing at the screen, told her, "I'll just be a minute."

Meaning it was a private call?

Not liking the way he'd just excluded her, she nodded and continued to the barn to feed the cats. They appeared out of everywhere, already knowing it was dinnertime.

The cats, at least, loved her.

She filled the trough to the brim, then folded her arms on the top of the closed barrel to watch as the cats ate. Her heart warmed. Yes, there were too many to call them pets, but she cared about them all the same. She even loved the barn, which still needed some repairs to the roof.

Miles's plan was to get to that tomorrow. When he'd claimed to dislike idle time, he hadn't exaggerated. He truly seemed happiest while staying busy. But then, so did she, and every addition, every improvement to the farm, filled her with contentment.

Could she give it all up for Miles?

Immediately she shook off that thought. In no way had he asked for a commitment, so why was she even considering it?

This was home.

But would it still feel that way after Miles left? She had the disturbing feeling that her love of the place was closely tied to Miles being there with her.

When his arms came around her, she jumped. "Blast, you startled me." She would have straightened, but he didn't let her.

"Sorry," he murmured, nudging in close against her bottom to keep her in place.

She felt his smile when he pressed a kiss to the back of her neck. Miles's kisses never failed to make her shiver. She relaxed again.

To her surprise, his hot mouth moved down her neck to the sensitive spot where it joined her shoulder while his hands scooped over her breasts, gently kneading.

"Miles?"

"I love it when you go braless."

Given the way he now touched her, she loved it, too. "It was way too hot today for a bra, and since we're the only ones here—"

"You don't need to convince me." He pressed his hips against her backside again, and she felt the rise of an erection.

Would they have sex here, in the barn? With the cats aware? No, she couldn't do that. "Um, Miles..."

"Let's go into town for dinner."

Startled again. "I thought we were going to grill."

"I changed my mind."

It wasn't what he said that did it, just a feeling she got, but she pushed away from the barrel, forcing him to back up. The second he did, she turned to face him—and got arrested by the heat in his eyes. Oh, that was a very real interest, so he hadn't faked wanting her. But why all of a sudden, and why did it feel like he was keeping something from her?

Ripe with suspicion, she asked, "What's going on?"

His crooked smile told her she'd hit the nail on the head, but he answered her question with one of his own. "What makes you think something is?"

"I don't know. Just a feeling. But I'm right, aren't I?"

His hands settled on her hips and he bent to kiss the tip of her nose. "Partially. I always want you, so don't doubt that. And actually, I came in here to explain, but you were bent over that barrel, which was an invitation if I ever saw one, and I got a little distracted."

"You're not distracted now."

He pulled her forward so that she felt a full erection now. "Wanna bet?"

His need fired her own, but she held on to that suspicion. "Does this have anything to do with your phone call?"

With an abrupt laugh, he said, "The call was from Leese, and no, he doesn't give me a boner."

She choked back her laugh. "I meant the mystery of why you want to go out for dinner."

"Actually…yes." He kissed her again and stepped back. When cats began circling his legs, he knelt down to pet them. "Leese did some checking on Fletcher for me."

What? That was news to her. She sat in the hay across from him, and immediately three cats crawled over her legs. "When did you ask Leese to check on him?"

"After the bomb. But if I hadn't asked him, he probably would have on his own. We all got an uneasy vibe from Fletcher. At first I wasn't sure if it was just jealousy, but—"

"Whoa, wait." Did he really just say that? To be sure, she repeated, "Jealousy?"

"Yes." His gaze traveled slowly all over her, ending at her eyes. "Fletcher wants you. You might not see it, but every guy here knew it, including his grandpa."

"Woody said something?"

Miles shrugged. "Armie heard him warn Fletcher away, telling him that you and I were a thing and he shouldn't cause any trouble."

Were they a thing? Sexually compatible, sure, but more

than that? "I don't think Fletcher would have anyway." The idea of Miles being jealous both thrilled and worried her.

"Now that we know Fletcher has a dangerous temper, I wish Woody hadn't butted in." He smiled with menace. "I'd love for Fletcher to give me a reason."

A reason to *what*? She was afraid she knew, and it made her scowl. "You're aware that I'm not into Fletcher, right?"

"Doesn't change how he feels, does it?" A small female cat crawled up his chest and licked his chin. Miles laughed and readjusted her to his lap.

"I don't happen to think he feels anything but friendly toward me. But no matter what, I don't want you hurting him."

Miles stiffened. "And why the hell not?"

"He hasn't done anything!"

Miles looked down at the cat, his hands gentle but his words hard when he said, "Or maybe he's done a lot."

All the breath squeezed out of her. "You think Fletcher...?"

"I think it's possible." His gaze cut up to hers. "More and more, it's looking that way."

"So we're going to town to do...what?"

"Get information. If he fought with those guys, I want to know exactly what happened, and if they really did disappear."

"Donny said they were bad news."

"And yet they didn't stick around to get even."

God, that did sound bad. "If Fletcher is behind all this..." Her stomach pitched and she shot to her feet. "I was alone with him. He was in my house—was in it after my grandma died! He could have gotten copies of the keys easy enough."

"Since we changed the locks, no one else has gotten in." Miles set the cat aside and slowly came to his own feet. "There are other things to consider."

Arms wrapped around herself, Maxi tried to fight off the hot waves of dread. It all came back to her, the mishaps, the terror—finding herself outside in the dirt. She shuddered.

Miles reached for her, but she stepped away. She had to get it together and she knew she couldn't, not if she leaned on him.

Then suddenly she found herself spun around and against him anyway.

Glaring down at her, Miles growled, *"Don't do that."*

Her jaw loosened at his aggressive tone. "Do what?"

"Shut me out." Hands on her shoulders, he lightly shook her. "You're not alone, damn it."

"I know." His fury had just wiped away every bit of nauseating fear as if it had never been there. She even grinned. "I wasn't exactly doing that anyway."

"Bullshit. You're still keeping me at a distance."

For a minute there...yeah, she had. But she had a good reason for it. "Desperation isn't pretty. In fact, it's awful. No one wants to be around a desperate person."

His scowl lifted. "More bullshit." Then with more exasperation than anger, he blew out a breath. "One, you're not desperate. Stubborn, sure. Sensibly frightened when things are out of your control, yes. But never desperate. And two, even if you were, I've already told you that I want to be there for you."

"But—"

"No buts, damn it. You can cry, Maxi. You can get a little desperate. You can have a hundred cats and call a friendly gathering a party. Doesn't matter."

Unsure where he was going with this, she muttered, "It was a party."

Miles *almost* smiled. "What you can't do is shut me out."

More and more, the things he said screamed of commitment. She dropped her forehead to his chest and nodded.

Apparently he wanted a verbal confirmation. "Okay?"

"Yes." She wrapped her arms around his waist, and damned if she didn't feel tears burn the back of her throat. "Okay."

"Good." He hugged her off her feet, turned her toward the house and gave her a swat on the ass. "Then grab your purse and let's get going."

She jerked around to gasp, "I can't leave yet! I have to change and fix my hair and—"

Now Miles laughed.

As her eyes narrowed, he managed to quell the humor long enough to ask, "How much time are we talking?"

"Ten minutes."

"Is that all?" He came forward, scooping his arm around her and getting her walking toward the house. "You're damn near perfect, do you know that?"

"Don't be ridiculous."

"Actually finish in ten minutes, and I'll swear it's true."

It took her fifteen, but only because Miles insisted on changing in the same room with her. And then helping her.

With his hands on her.

And his body pressed to hers...

They left the house an hour later and got to a small diner in town just as the dinner crowd exited. That worked for Maxi in her new mellow mood.

Amazing how Miles could take her through so many emotions, and always left her content in the end.

"Don't correct me on anything, okay?" He watched her sip her iced tea and waited for the questions.

They didn't come.

Every time he looked at her, he thought of how quickly he'd taken her, how hard she'd wanted it and how fast she'd come apart. Damn, but it kept getting better and better.

Lambent sensuality remained in her dark eyes, and it turned him on, even though he should have been satisfied for at least a few hours.

Her lips still looked rosy and swollen, too.

When the waitress brought their food, Miles smiled at her. "It smells good." He'd ordered the fried chicken and Maxi had gotten a club sandwich.

"The mashed potatoes are real," she said with a wink. "And the gravy is so good you'll want extra, so I brought it along."

"Thank you. I take it you're a good judge of your customers?"

"Worked here since I was fifteen, so yeah. I can usually pick a meat eater from a salad fanatic—or a man who likes his gravy."

"Guilty," Miles said, although as an athlete, he tended to avoid things like excess gravy. "Since you were fifteen, huh? So you've been here five years?"

She laughed and swatted at him. "I'm thirty-three, but thanks for the compliment."

Just what he'd judged her to be—close to the same as Fletcher.

With his ridiculous flirting, Maxi finally tuned in, but out of curiosity, not jealousy. "That's a long time to keep the same job. Guess you love your work?"

She propped a hip on the booth top and smiled. "I do, but it's a family business. You're both new here, so I guess you didn't know that."

"You grew up around here?" Maxi asked.

"Born and raised."

Miles said, "So you know everyone, huh?"

"I do." She held out her hand. "Jenny Williams."

Maxi introduced herself and then Miles. "I inherited my grandmother's property."

"I knew your grandma. She was a nice lady, real kind to everyone. I'm sorry for your loss."

"Thank you."

Maxi looked at him, then picked up her sandwich, leaving it to him to do his questioning.

He tried to ease into it. "Have you heard about the trouble Maxi's been having?"

"Who hasn't? Did Fletcher catch anyone yet?"

"Unfortunately, no." Miles was formulating a way to further discuss Fletcher when Jenny continued.

"Well, don't you worry. Fletcher won't put up with that nonsense. He has a real mean streak when it's called for. He'll find the guy and make him sorry."

He couldn't have asked for a more perfect setup. "A mean streak?"

Jenny grinned. "Mean and hot-tempered. You don't want to be on his bad side."

"No," he lied, "I don't. In fact, I heard something about him going after a few punks with a ball bat."

Jenny sobered. "Yeah, but that was for Anna." She shook her head. "Poor girl."

Maxi paused, staring at her. "What happened to her?"

Jenny, a world-class gossip, slid into the seat beside Maxi and lowered her voice. "She got mixed up with some bad people." Even lower, she added, "Drugs."

"How terrible." With honest sympathy, Maxi said, "Poor Woody."

"It was bad on him. Here he was raising them like his own—you know his daughter died right, and Fletcher and Annie came to him?"

"Yes, Woody told us," Miles said.

"He did? That's a surprise. Usually Woody won't discuss it."

"Someone else brought it up first," Maxi said.

Jenny accepted that. "Well, Woody did everything he could to keep those boys away from Annie. He knew she was getting her drugs from them. Then one night it got really bad. Fletcher found her, totally out of it, at a party and he flipped. He took her home but then went back with that bat. It wasn't just two boys he laid low that night. It was everyone at that party—until he found out who'd given her the drugs. Those two got the worst of it."

"I heard he put them in the hospital."

"They're lucky he didn't kill them."

"Telling tales, Jenny?"

Jenny and Maxi jumped in guilt. Miles slowly straightened in satisfaction.

Fletcher stood there, his expression masked, until Jenny made her excuses and hurried away.

The officer turned to watch her go, then smiled down at Maxi. "We used to date a few years back. She's a gossip, but a sweet one. You'll like her, just don't ever tell her your secrets."

Seeing Fletcher flirt with Maxi right in front of him infuriated Miles. "What secrets of yours did she tell?"

Fletcher turned a steely gaze on him. "I know better than to tell her any." He gave a curt nod and walked away.

Soon as Fletcher was far enough away, Maxi melted across the table with a groaned "Oh my God, that was awkward."

He almost laughed. Picking up a long lock of her hair, he teased, "You're not cut out for this, are you?"

"Subterfuge?" She lifted her head to glare at him. "Veiled threats? No, absolutely not."

"I learned more than I expected to." He wound the silky strands around his finger. "Jenny is apparently an endless well of info. Wonder if I can lure her back by ordering chocolate cake."

"You're kidding, right?" Maxi freed her hair and straightened, then pushed her half-eaten sandwich away. "I lost my appetite."

"I didn't." He dug into the fried chicken and mashed potatoes, and he had to admit, the gravy was incredible.

He did order the chocolate cake, but with Fletcher sitting a few booths away, Jenny tried not to linger.

Miles had to ask, "Are you afraid of him?"

\The surprise on Jenny's face, along with her laugh, was answer enough, but she added, "Afraid of Fletcher? No, of course not. But he's a friend and I don't want him to know I talked about him. What he did back then, defending his sister, he sees it different than most. While the town cheered him, he was disgusted with the whole thing. He'd worked hard to turn himself around, even became a cop. These days when he loses his temper, he just gets quiet. Real intense."

"So you haven't seen a repeat of the violence?"

She glanced at Fletcher, then away. "He's a nice guy. You should ask him about this stuff."

After she left, Miles asked Maxi, "What do you think?"

She took her time answering, even stole a bite of his cake. "I honestly don't know. Fletcher has been nothing but nice since I came here."

"Nice because you haven't seen his temper yet."

"Maybe. But if that's all in his past, should we really hold it against him? I don't want to be a hypocrite. God knows I've made too many mistakes myself."

"Any mistakes you made didn't include a ball bat."

Regret shifted her gaze away and lowered her voice. "No, it involved destruction of my family's home."

Miles reached across the table, taking her small hand in his. She was a delicate woman, small-boned but with a backbone of steel. He looked at her hand, running his thumb over the edge of her short nails. The manicure was gone, but to him she was even more beautiful in her ability to stand firm against all odds. "You trusted the wrong person, babe, that's all. Let's not do that again, okay?"

"You're saying not to trust Fletcher?"

Rather than answer that, because he wasn't quite sure what he felt about it, Miles said, "I feel like we're onto something here. Don't you?"

"Actually... I do." She sighed. "But I hate it. He's so well respected. If we're right and he's behind all the trouble, and *if* we can prove it, how will I ever get accepted here?"

He hadn't thought about that. True, he didn't want to do anything to upset her ultimate goal: settling in Burlwood, Ohio, for the long haul. She wanted to live in her grandmother's home—now very much *her* home—where she could care for the cats and the land and her soon-to-be-acquired goats. The atmosphere, the openness, suited her. It was like she was always meant to be there.

But then, it often felt like *he* was meant to be there, too.

"It's early yet. Let's do some more asking around before we tackle problems that might not be there."

Relieved, she nodded and started to stand.

He said, "Don't freak out, but I have a few questions for Fletcher first."

Her behind dropped right back in the seat. "But—"

Already on his feet, Miles put money on the table, enough to cover a nice tip—because Jenny had surely earned it—and then drew her up beside him. "It'll be fine."

In a low whisper she begged, "No fighting, not in here."

"Hadn't planned to throw any punches, and Fletcher doesn't have a ball bat, so no reason to worry." She couldn't say more because they'd already reached the officer's side.

Fletcher paused in eating a meat loaf dinner, his gaze on only Maxi. "Did you enjoy your meal?"

"I did, thank you."

"Everything is home-cooked here."

Miles asked, "Mind if we join you for just a minute?" He didn't wait for Fletcher to deny him, already urging Maxi into the seat.

Fletcher laughed. "Using her for bait? You know I won't refuse her, but you now...you could take a hike."

"I'm not going anywhere." Miles sat beside her. "I'm curious about the police department here. So far all we've seen is you, but there have to be other officers, right?"

Fletcher shrugged while shoveling in another bite of his meal. He took his time chewing, wiping his mouth with his napkin, taking a drink.

Miles had to admit, the guy was gutsy. He wouldn't bow easily to pressure—of any kind.

Finally, Fletcher gave his attention to the question. "Besides the chief, there are nine of us full-time and a handful of part-timers. You don't see anyone else because Maxi lives in the area I cover."

"24/7, huh?"

"Pretty much." He crossed his arms on the table. "There's not a lot of crime around here, so middle-of-the-night calls are few and far between. Since I'm already familiar with the history and what's happened, it wouldn't make sense for someone else to have to play catch-up."

"If there's so little crime, why the hell do you have nine full-time cops?"

"Being in the country means a lot of ground to cover. You're talking more than forty square miles. When something happens, the citizens don't want to wait an hour for someone to show up."

"That makes sense," Miles allowed. "What kind of crime have you had?"

"Mostly vandalism, domestic violence and sometimes reckless driving, especially during the summer during school break."

"No robbery?" He watched Fletcher. "No drugs?"

The other man didn't even blink. "Occasionally both, but it's not a big problem here."

"Not since you ran off the guys bothering your sister?"

That got a reaction. Fletcher's eyes narrowed and his mouth curved in warning. "So you did your homework? Big fucking deal. It's old news."

Miles didn't back down. "What happened to those men—after you laid them up?"

"Don't know, don't care, so if you're thinking to get a confession out of me, well, here's one for you—if they were still around, I'd do it again, and this time I'd make sure they couldn't crawl away." He abruptly stood, threw a twenty on the table and stalked out.

Jenny, seeing that, ran after him, her expression full of angst.

Much of the diners stared at them with disapproval. Had everyone overheard? Probably. Fletcher hadn't exactly been quiet in his replies.

"I feel terrible," Maxi whispered.

Yeah, he didn't feel so great himself. He'd wanted to ask Fletcher where his sister was now, but given his reaction, he was glad he hadn't. "Let's go."

Maxi smiled at all the gawkers, then stood to join him yet again. In no way did she look cowed by their censure. Instead, she kept her head up, that placid smile in place.

Miles took her hand, saying, "Have I told you lately how proud I am of you?"

Surprise replaced the smile. "Proud?"

"Very. Never forget that, okay?"

She still looked flummoxed when they got outside and found Fletcher waiting for them.

CHAPTER SEVENTEEN

The second Fletcher noticed them, he pushed away from his car and walked over. Again, he spoke only to Maxi when he said, "I apologize for being rude. Since she moved away, any talk of Anna sets me off."

Possessiveness prodding him, Miles kept his arm around Maxi but said nothing. If Fletcher would confide in her, he could handle that. Maybe.

"I'm sorry," Maxi said. "We didn't mean to upset you."

"I didn't think *you* had." Other than that barb, he ignored Miles. "Believe it or not, Maxi, I don't want to see you hurt. And no, you don't have to say anything. I get it, I really do. So if it's what you want, I'll arrange for another officer to take over."

Hell no, Miles wouldn't let him put her on the spot like that, not when he could shoulder the blame for the decision. "It's what she wants."

Finally, he looked at Miles. "I don't like it, but in your position I'd probably do the same." Seconds ticked by while Fletcher's jaw flexed and his gaze hardened. "I guess you're going to be around awhile?"

Miles answered with his own hard, anticipatory smile. "You guessed right."

"Now wait a minute!" Maxi tried to step in front of him, but Miles held her back, so she aimed her cannon at Fletcher. "Whether he's here or not, I'm the one making the decisions."

Her misunderstanding earned her a squeeze. "He wasn't questioning your independence."

Standing her ground, she said, "Sure sounded like it to me."

Miles actually laughed. "He's just hopeful that my time here is coming to an end."

"Oh." Embarrassment burned her cheeks, and she studiously kept her gaze on Fletcher. "Miles is here to help me until—"

Miles snorted. "Your first assumption was right." Hell, Maxi might not want to go there yet, but he wouldn't hesitate, not with Fletcher all but salivating over the idea of having a chance.

"She doesn't seem convinced."

No, she didn't. "It's true all the same."

Maxi threw up her hands. "This is ridiculous. I don't even know what you guys are talking about." Still with heat in her cheeks, she turned and stalked away.

Fletcher hadn't moved, but his gaze tracked Maxi's every step. More precisely, it followed the angry swish of her ass.

Miles saw red. He took a step closer and warned, "Don't."

Slowly, reluctantly, Fletcher gave up the view and instead raised a brow at Miles. "One way or another I'm going to have to deal with you, aren't I?"

"That's right."

Fletcher smirked, turned his back on Miles and went to his car.

Miles didn't move until Fletcher was in his Suburban and driving away. Then his gaze located Maxi, already seated in the SUV, seat belt on, arms folded, mouth tight.

He sighed.

It would have been easier if she'd accepted that they had a relationship, a *real* relationship, based on more than compatibility in the sack.

He'd given her an opening—but she hadn't taken it.

Carrying his own irritation now, Miles got in the SUV and closed the door without a word. He fastened his seat belt, started the car and pulled away.

After two minutes of silence, she asked, "We're heading home now?"

He was just pissed enough to specify, "Your house, yeah." Then he felt like an ass. It wasn't like he wanted to take her house from her. Nothing like that.

But he did want to be included.

She turned to look at him, a question in her eyes, but her cell rang before she could ask anything. She glanced at the screen and groaned.

"Who is it?"

Long suffering, she confessed, "Gary."

Damn it, how many men did he have to put up with? Holding the steering wheel with one hand, he thrust out the other and demanded, "Let me talk to him."

"Ha, no." She held the phone closer. "You've done enough talking, thank-you-very-much." With a press of a button, she put the phone to her ear. At least she made it clear that she didn't want to talk to him with her snapped "What is it, Gary?"

Miles kept his gaze on the road, but he was so attuned to Maxi, he sensed her frown without seeing it.

She listened, then said, "Do whatever you want... No, it truly doesn't matter to me... Yes, it does sound like a terrific opportunity." She paused, nodded. "Harlow must have a lot of faith in you... Of course... All right, and, Gary? No more calls. Ever. There's no reason."

Satisfaction settled into his bones, but Miles resisted the smile that came with it. Maxi was too bristly right now and he didn't want her thinking he was amused by her surly attitude.

When she disconnected the call, she started to shove the phone into her purse, and a text message dinged. Grumbling, she held the phone up again and laughed.

"Can I get in on the joke?"

"Sure." She half turned in the seat to face him. "Gary called to let me know that Harlow has offered him a manager's position in a second location that's brand-new, opening in about a month."

"Where?" Hopefully in Timbuktu.

The smile twitched on her lips. "Indianapolis. He was concerned because, given the distance, it'll truly mean the end of us." With an eye roll, she added, "As if that wasn't already a done deal."

"He's an idiot. Good riddance."

"An idiot who apparently called me in front of Harlow, wanting my blessing before he accepted her job offer." She turned the phone so he could see the screen. "The text was from Harlow."

It said only: You're welcome.

Miles laughed. "I have to admit, I wasn't a fan at first, but your sister is growing on me."

"That's good." She fussed with putting her phone away, then stored her purse on the floor before saying, "Because she sort of endorsed you."

Better and better. "Yeah?" he asked, still being cautious with her prickly mood.

"Says you're a keeper."

He grinned. "Smart woman." *Would Maxi want to keep him?*

"She told me not to screw it up."

Miles nodded in understanding. "That's good advice."

Laughing, relaxing a little, Maxi swatted his shoulder. More mellow now, less on edge, she asked, "Did you mean what you said to Fletcher?"

"Every word—but which part are you talking about?"

Her gaze searched his face. "That you'd be around?"

Deep satisfaction settled into his bones. "Definitely that part." He spared her a glance. "Does that work for you?"

"Yes," she whispered. "Very much so."

Tonight, Miles decided, he'd tell her that he wanted a chance to make things work, to see where the relationship took them. And he wouldn't let her distract him. Not this time.

After he told her how things would be, then he'd show her...and that'd help to win her over.

Just as they were pulling down the long, wooded drive to her house, dark clouds rolled in, obliterating the usual vivid sunset. They didn't see Sahara's car until they pulled into the clearing.

She had her phone in her hand but smiled and put it back in the pocket of a flared pink skirt with a bold flower print.

As both Miles and Maxi got out of the SUV, Sahara said, "I was just about to call you."

She approached, pressing forward a small man in a business suit that had to be sweltering in the summer heat.

Miles had no idea who the guy might be, but he looked nothing like a bodyguard.

As usual, Sahara's sense of style didn't entirely mesh with farm life, though he realized she'd "dressed down" for the visit. Or as down as she could be.

She'd paired the feminine skirt with a silk tank top and black sandals. Her brown hair was up in a loose knot on top of her head, sexy little tendrils floating along her face. She wore no jewelry, but then, she didn't need any.

The poor fellow she dragged along appeared to be smitten, given the way he kept gazing at her in worshipful awe.

She didn't bring him to Miles but steered him to Maxi instead, saying, "This is Mr. Delacroix. He's from the local historical museum and he'd like to obtain your grandmother's kitchen. They'll reenact it as is, even down to the tiles on the floor and wall. Not all of the tiles will survive, of course, but they'll salvage what they can and replicate the rest. They want all the appliances and some of the dishes, and—"

"Ahem." Finally finding his voice, Mr. Delacroix held out a hand. "Ms. Nevar, thank you for meeting with me."

Maxi, who'd been momentarily shocked into silence, took his hand and said, "You haven't even seen the kitchen yet!"

"We peeked through the windows," Sahara confided. Lower to Miles, she said, "No doubt you'll see us on your surveillance cameras."

"It's a wonderful room," Mr. Delacroix gushed. "Quaint and homey, and so original. I can almost picture your grandmother standing in front of the cast-iron sink, wearing an apron, listening to an old radio—"

"She has an old radio in the basement."

Mr. Delacroix looked ready to swoon. "Oh, but I must see it, as well."

He appeared so hopeful that Maxi grinned. "I've got all kinds of things to show you. Some stowed in the attic, most in the basement. A lot of the furniture I'm actually using, but you're welcome to any that I'm not."

"You don't plan to sell it?"

"To a stranger? No."

Pleasure showed in his grateful smile. "We would truly cherish each piece if you can find your way to part with such sentimental mementos."

She glanced at Miles. "What do you think?"

Knowing what that kitchen meant to Maxi, hell, what the radio probably meant to her, too, he rubbed the back of his neck. "Since you're living here, I think you'll be happier with a fully functioning kitchen, especially if you know the pieces are appreciated. But it's up to you, honey. If you can't bear to let them go, I understand."

The very idea left Delacroix stricken—until Maxi nodded.

"I think it's an excellent compromise. I would like to update the kitchen, I just couldn't bear the thought of disposing of her things." She smiled at Sahara. "Thank you for thinking of such a great alternative."

Sahara put her hands together. "I just love being instrumental to a happy ending." And with that, she gave Miles a long look.

Maxi and the curator started for the house, their heads together in conversation, so Miles felt safe saying to Sahara, "I can handle my own happy ending, thank you."

"Of course you can. But let me remind you that I knew right off there was real danger, *and* that the two of you were meant to be."

"Meant to be, huh?" Sure felt that way to him. "I don't recall you using those exact words."

She waved that off. "Admit I'm excellent at what I do."

"At whatever you do," he agreed, gesturing for her to precede him. "It's going to start raining any second now. Let's get inside."

And hopefully her prediction would come true.

Even in his coat and wide-brimmed hat, the rain soaked him through to the skin, running in icy rivulets down the back of his neck. It stung his face and made visibility even more difficult. He didn't dare use a flashlight, not with all those damned cameras around.

They thought he was a fool, that he'd blunder into view and they'd catch him. They were the fools, and when they were dead, they'd know it.

He frowned over that warped logic; how could they know

anything as corpses? Shaking his head, he continued picking his way forward. It was a miserable night, perfect for what he had to do.

But do I really have to do it?

Yes, she's left you no choice.

Aloud, he agreed, "No, she hasn't." *Neither has he.*

He could have handled her on her own, but Miles was like a guard dog, keeping him from getting too close with all his suspicions.

And all the damned renovations. *Why wouldn't she leave well enough alone?*

He had to kill them both. Everything else had failed. Not even a bomb had chased her away. *This is on her. She forced you to it.*

"But to kill her?" he asked of the silent woods. "Isn't that a little much?" *No choice, damn it.*

A great bolt of lightning split the sky, followed by a crack of thunder. With his heart in his throat, he lurched back, banging his elbow against a gnarled tree.

After he finished cursing, he drew a deep, calming breath. Here beneath a canopy of trees, the worst of the rain couldn't reach him. "Maybe I've gone off the deep end." His heavy boots slipped in a muddy patch of wet moss and he almost fell. *The deep end?* He snorted.

He was as clearheaded as he'd always been, doing what needed to be done.

The binoculars hung around his neck, his rifle sling over one shoulder and the strap to his utility lamp over the other. The lamp, with its multiple functions, would be critical to his success, as were the police-issue metal handcuffs in his pocket.

He'd come prepared. Tonight was the night.

You've done it before, you can do it again.

This is different. She's a nice girl.

"Not nice enough to leave!"

His own voice, so loud in the darkness, startled him again, so he clamped his lips together.

The last of their guests had finally left and the house was quiet now. Who knew she'd be a damned partyer, constantly keeping people around? It made his job a lot harder—but not impossible.

While he waited, he peered through the binoculars, wondering if he'd catch another show. There was too much rain to see clearly, and they'd pulled down their new blinds, too, like they thought he was a pervert.

Like they thought he wanted to see them going at it.

He locked his jaw.

I'm not a pervert.

I know it.

Just do what you have to do.

"Damn it all." If he waited any longer, he'd lose the advantage with the rain.

He stuck as much to the shadows as he could. When he had to step out in the clearing, he kept his head down so the cameras wouldn't be able to make out his features. Unlike the other times, his heart beat too fast now that he knew they were watching for him.

Cats scattered as he stepped inside the dim interior of the barn. They didn't know him well—but they knew not to trust him.

It had been a hot day and now the rain sealed all that heat inside, turning the barn into a sticky sauna. He pulled off his hat, slapping it against his leg to remove some of the rain.

His boots had left muddy prints behind. *So what? By the time it's noticed, it'll be too late.*

Familiar with the barn, he set the rifle in a corner next to a sharp pickax where it wouldn't be noticed, and then put the binoculars on top of the food barrel.

Finally, he would end this.

So what are you waiting for?

For you to shut up.

"Go to hell."

The cats stared at him with wide glowing eyes, suspicious of his presence. A wonderful idea occurred to him, the perfect excuse needed to get Miles to the barn. He looked from the cats to the pickax and back again.

Smiling, he knelt down and said, "Here, kitty, kitty, kitty."

The sudden pounding on the front door startled Maxi so badly she almost dropped her bottle of water as she left the kitchen. Miles had settled on the couch after his shower and she was about to join him. He'd said he wanted to talk. Despite common sense, she was hopeful he'd say what she so badly wanted to hear.

But now they had more company.

Scowling, Miles bounded off the couch. "I'll get it."

She nodded but followed closely behind him. "It's probably Fletcher, worrying about the lights going out again because of the storm. Be nice, okay?"

"No." He lifted aside the curtain covering the window in the door. "Damn. Not Fletcher."

"Who is it, then?"

Miles jerked the door open. "Woody, what the hell? What are you doing out in this rain?"

Hands on his knees, breathing hard, Woody said, "I saw someone in the woods headed here. I followed…" His gaze went past Miles to Maxi, then warily back again. He cleared his throat. "You gotta come quick. He went into your barn." Lower still, he said, "I, uh, I think he's doing something to the cats."

Miles's expression turned into a thundercloud. "Stay here."

"Miles!" Maxi held herself tightly. *If that madman hurt a single animal, I'll kill him myself.* Right now, though, her biggest concern was Miles. He couldn't just charge out there without a plan or—

Already shoving his feet into his shoes, Miles said, "Not now, Maxi."

The horrified look on Woody's face scared her half to death, but Miles was so different from her, so confident, that he likely saw this as an opportunity.

Oh God, what if he got hurt?

"At least take your gun." She could tell he didn't think he'd need it. True, he had lethal fighting skills, but they were no match for a weapon. Insisting wouldn't do her any good, so instead she tried a heartfelt *"Please."*

One look at her face—which no doubt showed her upset—and he relented.

He was in and out of the bedroom in five seconds. "Lock the door behind me. If I'm not back in ten minutes, call Sahara. No matter what you hear, you stay inside with the door locked. Understand?"

Maxi nodded. The last thing he needed to do was worry about her. "I promise."

Woody said, "I'm going with you."

"I'd rather you stay with Maxi."

"But you'll need me! You don't know what I saw—"

"Woody." That single word, accompanied with Miles's dark warning expression, silenced him.

Maxi covered her mouth with her hand. *What had he seen?*

"I need you to stay here with Maxi. I don't want her to be alone. Can you do that for me?"

"I can't come in. My boots are too muddy."

Maxi knew exactly what Miles was doing—giving Woody a purpose so he'd feel useful. But what about her?

It was her property, her cats.

Her problem.

No, she knew that wasn't true. Not anymore. Miles had

stepped in and accepted half responsibility for *everything*. It wasn't his job, but he didn't complain.

"Your boots are fine," she promised. "I can clean up later."

Reluctantly, Woody stepped in, staying on a rug in the foyer.

Miles immediately slipped out the door, pulling it silently shut behind him.

It almost killed her to see him walk out there alone. She locked the door and drew a deep breath, but it didn't help.

Nothing would help until Miles was back inside with her, safe. Unharmed.

"It'll be okay." Woody rubbed his palms against the denim of his jeans.

Tears stung the backs of her eyes and she trembled all over. Finally, needing to do *something*, she made a decision. "I have to call Fletcher."

"No," Woody said, catching her arm, full of solemn regret. His face almost crumpled and his voice cracked when he said, "You can't do that."

"It's him, isn't it?" Maxi pulled away, a hand in her hair. "Miles suspected, but I didn't believe it." And now he'd have to face Fletcher alone. One on one, he'd annihilate Fletcher. But Fletcher wasn't a dummy. He wouldn't engage in a physical fight.

She remembered that rifle shot that hit her barn, and she knew without a doubt that he'd be armed. So was Miles, but he wasn't a killer, not like—

"I'm sorry," Woody said, walking farther into the house. "Sorrier than you know."

"It's not your fault."

"Feels like it is." He lifted the collar of his jacket and slammed the hat back on his head. "I'm going out. I have to."

She wanted to argue with him, but Woody looked so set, she nodded. "Please be careful."

"Yes, ma'am. I'll be right back, okay?" This time he headed for the back door. "Don't lock me out."

Hurrying after him, stepping around the muddy footprints, she said, "I'll watch for you." The second he was out the door, she grabbed her cell phone off the table and, standing at the door, divided her time between staring at what she could see of the barn and dialing Sahara.

Please let her be home. Maxi knew she had to do something to help.

And she couldn't wait ten minutes to do it.

Miles approached the barn cautiously. From around the cracks of the closed shutters over the windows and the loosely closed doors, he could see lights flashing.

What the hell? He felt the mud sinking into his athletic shoes but paid it no mind. The rain, softer now, dampened his hair and torso. He moved up next to the barn wall and inched closer to the door.

The screech of a panicked cat made his blood run cold.

Glock held close to his chest, he eased up next to the barn doors and tried stealing a glance inside.

The crazy strobe of bright lights made it impossible to see anything. That was a tactical light, possibly police issue, meant to disorient. He'd need to locate the source of that light and distinguish it first. Using the toe of his shoe, he edged the door wider. A few cats shot out, running like hell.

The screeching came louder.

Muddy footprints went in and out of the barn, reminding him of the time Fletcher had tracked mud up onto the porch.

But in weather like this, Woody's feet had been mud-covered, too. He paused, thinking about that, but the sounds of the cat regained his attention. He had to do something.

He glanced in again, this time with a hand mostly covering his eyes, concentrating on the floor and corners of the barn. He didn't see any feet, and other than the frenzied cat, he heard nothing. Another look, and he realized the light sat on a post.

Gaze averted, he shot in low and fast, arm extended, and knocked it to the ground. It hit with a clatter and died. At the same time Miles swept the room with his gun, searching through the sudden darkness for any movement.

The only thing he saw was Hero, the black cat Maxi had renamed. Fury erupted when he realized why the cat was so upset.

His tail was tied to a post.

"Hang on, baby," he said softly, but the cat was inconsolable. No one had ever mistreated it and it didn't understand.

He searched every corner of the barn, but the muddy prints showed clearly on the dusty, hay-strewn floor. They trailed in, around the floor, then back out again. No one had climbed the ladder to the loft, and the prints didn't lead behind any of the equipment.

Fletcher had already come and gone.

Cautiously, Miles came forward. The cat was pissed, hissing and snarling, ready to lash out, but it calmed as Miles slowly got closer. Rough rope that had hung on a nail in the barn was now tied brutally tight around the cat's tail, then high up on a cross post so that the cat couldn't get all four paws on the floor.

I'll kill the fucker. Trying to disguise his fury, he murmured, "Easy, baby. Easy now. I'm going to help you."

Carefully he lifted the cat to his shoulder to relieve the tension. Wincing from claws that pierced his shirt and dug into his skin, he worked to loosen the knot. When the cat was finally free, Miles stroked his back, whispering reassuring words. The cat panted but was otherwise passive—until suddenly it hissed and launched away.

In the next second pain exploded in the back of Miles's

skull. He fell forward to his knees while the world spun around him, darkened and slowly closed in.

Well, fuck.

He'd been knocked out before during fights, so he recognized it for what it was—and did his best to fight it off.

If he lost consciousness, who would protect Maxi?

Something cold and hard clamped around his right wrist. Years of conditioning, of muscle memory, had him automatically shifting to a defensive position on his back.

His legs could be a deadly weapon.

Still seeing stars, he kicked out but only managed a glancing blow.

"Bastard! Try that again and I'll kill you now, to hell with the consequences."

Woody? It was difficult to think with his head still pounding so painfully.

A chain rattled and yanked his arm tight, wrenching his shoulder and making his throat burn with the need to puke.

Through bleary eyes he saw Woody picking up the Glock that must have fallen from Miles's waistband when he hit the floor. Just as quickly, Woody backed up and out of reach.

If Woody was here, where was Maxi? If he'd hurt her…

He must have spoken aloud, because Woody said, "I'm getting her now. Be right back."

"*No*, wait—" But Woody was already gone. After two slow, deep breaths, Miles forced himself more upright. It relieved a little of the tension on his arm, but not the turmoil in his brain.

Had Maxi already called Sahara? God, he hoped so. He knew Sahara, knew she wouldn't take chances. Backup would be on the scene in minutes.

But did they have minutes?

He hadn't suspected Woody—and neither would Maxi. Like a lamb to the slaughter, she would follow him out.

He had to do something.

Recovering by the second, he ignored the pain in his skull and instead stared in disgust at the metal handcuffs, one tight around his wrist, the other fed through a chain wrapped around the same post that had held the cat.

He had to get free.

Every movement sent pain slicing through his head, but it was nothing compared to the fear for Maxi. Bracing his feet against the post, he pulled as hard as he could. The cuffs were solid, but the chain might give. All he needed was for one of the rusted links to open. The muscles in his arm and shoulder complained, but he didn't let up.

Not until Woody walked in with Maxi. At first, she only looked confused, but then her gaze landed on him and she stopped dead in her tracks.

"*Miles?*" She started toward him in a rush.

With a hand twisted in her shirt, Woody roughly jerked her back, then gave her a shove in the opposite direction.

"Stay away from him," Woody ordered.

"But he's hurt!"

"Yeah, and next time I hit him, I'll cave in his skull."

Shock, confusion and then outrage all flashed over her face. She rounded on the older man in a fury. "Don't you touch him!"

Jesus, Miles thought, the last thing he needed was for her to do something reckless.

"Maxi," he said sharply, to cut through her anger, "I need you to calm down, okay? I'm fine." The link would give. It *had* to. "It's going to be okay."

Woody leveled a rifle on her. "Yeah, listen to him."

It chilled Miles's blood to see the weapon trained on her. "Woody, what are you doing?" *Look at me, you bastard, not her.*

"For now I'm just separating you two," Woody said, and then to Maxi, "Back up there. All the way back to the corner. That's it. Now sit down, legs out. If you try to get up, I'll shoot him first, and then you."

With a threat like that, Maxi sat. "You told me it was all clear, that the cats needed me."

Woody chuckled. "One did, but looks like Miles already freed it."

In a low, mean voice, she asked, "Did you hurt one of my cats, Woody?"

"More worried about that damned rodent than your boyfriend?" All the menace left his expression when he smiled with a memory. Once again he spoke to them like they were his friends, instead of his captives. "Just like your grandma. She loved those critters, too. I remember when she found kittens once. She was so sweet and excited."

Miles stared at him. The obvious insanity made him even more unpredictable. *Why was he doing this?*

Different cats tried creeping in, wanting to get closer to Maxi. Even Hero now peered around the barn door. The cat still looked wary, body arched, fur standing on end, teeth showing.

Miles couldn't blame him, but he hoped Hero didn't give Woody another chance to abuse him. Maxi might well lose it if he did, and she needed to stay calm.

He silently strained against the chain.

"Let me get this out of reach, before you do something stupid." Woody carried his Glock to a ledge on the opposite side of the barn.

Hoping to send Maxi a silent message, Miles glanced at her, but the second their gazes met, she flashed up the hem of her shirt to show the small revolver tucked into the waistband of her shorts.

No. Hell no. Woody was certifiable and Maxi's aim still sucked—a very bad combo. If she tried to shoot Woody, she was as likely to hit Miles...if Woody didn't turn his rifle on her first.

Miles gave a small, stern shake of his head, warning her against any spontaneous action.

But she'd already looked away to Woody, her dark eyes pinning him. Mixed with her obvious fear was pure, red-hot rage. He understood, because he felt the same.

Unfortunately, that emotion could make her impulsive.

However this went down, he had to be ready to act.

He loved her. No way in hell could he lose her now.

God, please don't let Miles be seriously hurt.

It worried Maxi, seeing the blood in his hair and on his shirt, knowing he'd had concussions and that Woody had likely given him another.

To buy herself some time, she asked, "Why are you doing this, Woody?"

From the corner of her eye, she saw Miles straining against the chain. Did he honestly think he could break it?

Yes, she knew he didn't want her to take matters into her own hands, and she wouldn't—if she could avoid it. But Miles was already hurt, and by God, she wouldn't let Woody touch him again.

If she had to, she'd shoot Woody, and this close, surely she'd be accurate.

When Woody glanced at him, Miles went still. Her heartbeat skipped, then blasted into overtime as Woody turned to face him, his gaze suspicious.

She had to draw his attention away, so she demanded, "Did you kill my grandma?"

"What?" Genuinely baffled, Woody glared at her. "I don't kill innocent people!"

Maxi noted the qualification on "innocent." Had he killed *bad* people, then? More to the point, she and Miles were innocent. "Forgive me if I don't believe you. We're here, after all. You've wounded Miles, and with the way you keep aiming that rifle, am I supposed to assume you just want to visit?"

Chagrined, he growled, "I loved that woman. I tried to get her to marry me! If she weren't so cursed stubborn, saying we could just carry on as we had been, she wouldn't have been living alone. I'd have been there with her when she fell."

Relief briefly closed her eyes. "So she *did* fall, like you said?"

Woody's hold on the rifle loosened. "It about killed me, finding Meryl like that. It's true that I wanted to marry her so this place would be mine, but I loved her, too. Her dying not only broke my heart, it ruined everything." Suddenly he brought the rifle back around, now pointed at Maxi. "If your grandma had just given in, it'd all be fine and no one would've ever known. Hell, if *you'd* given in…" In a blast of irritation, he asked, "Why didn't you just sell the place to me? Stubborn, just like your grandma. Now I have no choice but to kill you."

Between worried glances at Miles, Maxi watched Woody closely. He chatted about loving her grandmother in one breath, and murdering her in the next. How should she deal with him?

If he decided to shoot her, she'd charge him first. She'd go down fighting—for herself and for Miles. "I didn't know it was that important to you. Now that I do know, I've changed my mind. We could still work out a deal, right?"

Woody snorted. "It's too late now. You already know."

"Know what?"

The barn door shifted and Woody swung around, the rifle aimed.

Fletcher froze in the doorway.

For the first time it occurred to Maxi how much grandfather and grandson looked alike. They shared the same height, and although Woody had lost some muscle tone, it was clear he'd once been as fit as Fletcher.

Tension held them all silent as Fletcher's steely gaze took in the scene, lingering on Miles for a moment before settling on Woody.

He said calmly, "Granddad."

"Fletch." Slack-jawed, Woody blinked at him. "What're you doing here?"

"I came to help, of course." He gave Maxi a look before his mouth lifted in a strained smile. "I think I know what happened, but it's okay now."

Maxi glared at him. So Fletcher was in on it after all? And to think she'd defended him! "What happened?" she demanded. "What are you talking about?"

"He doesn't know shit," Woody protested, backing to the side so he could keep all three of them in his sights.

Showing a healthy respect for Miles's ability, even when chained to a pole, Fletcher stayed out of his reach as he answered Maxi. "My sister got in with a bad crowd. Drinking, drugs, armed robbery…it almost killed her. My guess is that Granddad did what he always did." He looked at Woody. "You protected her, didn't you?"

Woody straightened with pride. "Damn right I did!"

"But…" Maxi frowned at Fletcher. "I thought it was you who beat up the men—"

"I did," Fletcher confirmed. "But that wouldn't have fixed things. So many times we'd get her turned around, but then the addiction would steal her away again."

Woody's face went red, his eyes bulging. "That miserable dealer and his cronies were to blame!"

Fletcher agreed. Almost as if it didn't matter, he asked Woody, "What happened to them?"

"I killed them."

Silence weighed heavy in the barn.

"I had to! I couldn't let them ruin Anna and you both."
He hitched his chin. "After that beating you gave them, they
were going to press charges against you. And I couldn't defend you without telling the world that Anna was an addict."

Recovered, Fletcher said softly, "I understand." He rubbed
the back of his neck. "What did you do with the bodies?"

Now Woody grinned. "Buried the worst one of the bunch
in the ground—and put a pond on top of him."

Bile rose in Maxi's throat. "My pond?" she choked out.

"I *told* you not to swim in it!"

Her skin crawled. Hull and Armie and...dear God, Miles...
they'd all been in the pond—*with a dead body beneath them.*
"You said there was a *turtle!*"

"There was."

She stared at him, taken aback by his insulted tone. "You
didn't make that up?"

"I'm not a liar."

In his twisted mind, Woody thought a liar was worse than
a murderer? He seemed so volatile she didn't dare move, didn't
even dare breathe.

"What else did you do, Granddad?" Fletcher asked, which
gave her a chance to gasp in air.

Smug now, Woody said, "Buried one of the others to the
side of the barn and just told Meryl I was replacing some of
the wood."

The answer surprised Maxi enough that she almost forgot
her fear. "That's why you didn't want me to add on to the
barn for the goats?"

"You wouldn't leave well enough alone, girl." As if he spoke
only truth, Woody said, "This is your fault," and again he
pointed the rifle at her.

"Anyone else?" Fletcher asked, trying to distract him again.

Woody narrowed his eyes. "What does it matter?"

"How else can I help you unless I know everything?"

Woody shrugged his chin at Maxi. "Why don't you ask her? She was probably ready to build something on it." He muttered, "A dock for the pond, goats, for God's sake. Anything else, girl?"

While Woody looked at her, Maxi saw Fletcher reach into his pocket, then toss something small toward Miles. It landed in the hay near his hip.

To keep Woody looking at her, Maxi said, "That willow tree in the side yard. It blocks my view of the pond, so I—"

"*Goddamn it,*" Woody exploded, stomping in a circle until he could glare at Fletcher. "Didn't I tell you? She'd have dug up the last one!"

The suddenness of Woody's violent fit sent Maxi's heart hammering, but then his words sank in. "You're not joking?"

He raged, "Who would joke about a thing like that?" as if *she* were the lunatic.

She'd only been making conversation, meant to keep him preoccupied, yet she'd blundered into a third site for a victim? "Dear God."

He used the rifle to gesture at her again. "Why the hell can't you leave well enough alone? This place was perfect as is. I'd have loved it here." He swung the barrel toward Miles next. "You helped her to change so much, but I wouldn't have changed a thing."

"Except to add a few more grave sites?" Maxi asked, deliberately provoking him. She'd do anything to keep that rifle off Miles. *Anything.*

And yeah, Woody gave her a killing glare. "Only three... until I add you two."

Miles said in soft command, *"Maxi."*

But the warning came too late. "You are such a little bitch, aren't you? I'd thought you were a nice girl, so I hadn't wanted to hurt you. I tried everything else I could think of to avoid this."

Everything… "You drugged me!"

Petulant now, Woody shrugged. "Didn't do me any good, did it? You're still here."

"You carried me outside." She shuddered with revulsion. "How did you do it?"

"Meryl had given me keys. I snuck in the house a lot."

"I *knew* I heard things!"

"I'd watched you enough to know your routine, so that night I put the drug in your glass. You never noticed when you poured in the wine." He grinned. "It worked faster and better than I figured. I only had to hide for a little while. Then when you went out, I got that wagon from your barn and took you down to the pond." He turned his head to study her. "I thought for sure that'd spook you enough to get you packing. Didn't count on you moving in a man."

Fletcher whispered, "You drugged her, Granddad? After what Anna had been through?"

"This was different. I didn't do anything to her. Just put her outside. I even laid her down real gentle instead of just dumping her out of the wagon."

Maxi stiffened. "You bastard. How dare you? *You put me through hell!*"

"I never hurt you…then." Woody reacted to her antagonism with equal resentment. "Now I just might enjoy it."

Miles growled, *"You won't hurt her, Woody."*

"I'll do what I have to do."

The chains rattled loudly as Miles tried to fight loose, but he quieted again when Fletcher stepped forward…and in front of him. "Tell me the plan," he said while blocking Miles from view.

"I'm going to bury them both here." Woody nodded as if to convince himself. "They've done enough digging that no one will think anything of a little more loose dirt."

Being reasonable, Fletcher said, "I don't know if that's a

good idea. No one is going to believe she just up and moved away without selling the place."

"Most folks will think someone else got to them. The whole town's heard about her being hassled."

"By you," Maxi accused.

"Doesn't matter. No one knows it was me. Fletcher could say he saw a truck driving away with both of you. He's a cop, so they'd believe him." He asked Fletcher, "You remember telling me how many missing people are never found? It'd be like that."

Maxi watched in frustrated horror while they discussed murder as if it held no importance at all.

Fletcher nodded. "I remember, but we weren't talking about homeowners in the area. It's different from the idiots who'd sold dope to Anna."

"They *pushed* it on her, wouldn't let her get clean. With them around, she didn't stand a chance." Woody frowned. "You know that, right?"

Fletcher came a few steps closer. "Yeah, I'd had the same thought, which is why I almost beat them to death."

Satisfied, Woody took a stance in front of Maxi. "Sometimes, there's no other choice."

With one big step forward, Fletcher reached his grandfather and pressed the barrel down and away. "This time, there is. We don't have to hurt anyone."

"You said you came to help me."

"I did, but not like this." Fletcher tried to ease the rifle away.

"Lies!" Woody pushed him away. "They've turned you against me."

"No, Granddad." Fletcher caught himself and came forward again. "You know that's not possible."

"He does love me," Woody said...to himself? "But not enough? He doesn't understand. I'll make him see."

Puzzled, Fletcher said gently, "Granddad, are you okay?"

"I have to shoot them both."

"No." Fletcher's gaze never wavered from his grandfather. "That'd be too messy."

Maxi glanced at Miles. He appeared to be holding the chain in both hands now, his expression hard, alert.

Was there more slack in that chain?

"The blood will be on the hay," Woody argued, "and that's easy to burn."

"I have a better idea. Let's talk about it." Again Fletcher reached for the rifle.

"No!" Woody jerked it away, then slammed the stock against Fletcher's face. "I'm done talking." It was such a brutal hit that Maxi let out a short scream. Poor Fletcher staggered back, blood already gushing from his nose.

Woody took aim at Maxi.

He looked so dead set on shooting her, she froze.

"No." Miles suddenly launched forward, leaving the chain and handcuffs behind.

Woody turned to face the new threat, the rifle exploded—and Maxi's heart stopped.

CHAPTER EIGHTEEN

"Miles!" Panicked, Maxi jumped to her feet as he and Woody landed up against yet another support post with so much force the barn floor shook beneath her feet.

Fletcher yelled, "Don't hurt him," his voice garbled from blood.

Maxi pulled the gun. Breathing hard, fear squeezing her throat, she said, "Don't," while darting her gaze back and forth between the wrestling men and Fletcher.

Agonized, Fletcher held out a bloody hand to her. "Maxi, I'm here to help."

"I assumed, but you'll still stay put." She wasn't going to risk Miles again.

"He's almost eighty." He sounded choked with emotion when he repeated, "Don't hurt him, Miles. Please."

Miles landed one short jab against Woody's jaw. When the older man slumped, Miles lifted his hands and Woody dropped to the ground. Staggering a bit, Miles snatched the rifle from Woody's slack hand. Breathing hard, he faced her, his gaze going all over her. "Are you hurt?"

"No." She didn't move. She so badly wanted to grab him, but he looked ready to topple and she knew he had to be in pain.

He stared at her hard, as if he had trouble keeping her in focus. "You're sure?"

Eyes damp, she nodded. "You?"

"Fine."

No, he wasn't, but she knew him well enough now not to say so. He glanced around, saw the chunk of wood missing in the barn wall where the rifle shot, and slowly let out a breath.

Miles could have been killed—and she didn't know how she would have survived that. She started shaking and couldn't stop.

"I'm sorry," Fletcher said. The skin under his eyes had already discolored from an obviously broken nose. "I swear I didn't know."

Miles spared him a quick glance, then nodded. "I only hit him once, but he's out." Still unsteady on his feet, he retrieved his Glock from where Woody had put it. "Check him. Make sure he doesn't have any other injuries."

Fletcher nodded, rushing to his grandfather.

Even injured, Miles protected her, and dear God, she loved him so much it was strangling her.

Maxi realized she still had the revolver aimed at Fletcher, not that he was paying any attention to that as he knelt by his grandfather. She lowered the gun, setting it on the ground beside her.

Woody hadn't yet come around. She honestly didn't know which would be better, for Fletcher to lose him now, or to deal with all the ensuing criminal charges.

Miles stepped in front of her. Bracing one hand on the wall beside her head, he scoured his gaze over her as if looking for injuries.

"Not a scratch," she whispered brokenly. "I promise."

He appeared to be struggling, then he pulled her into his arms, crushing her tight, his face in her neck.

Her tears started. Everything added up and her knees almost gave out, she cried so hard. It was humiliating, the sobs loud and uncontrolled.

"Shh," Miles whispered, turning so he could see Fletcher and Woody while still keeping her tight against him. "It's okay now, babe. It's over."

She hated her own weakness. "Your poor head."

He smiled against her cheek. "It'll hurt less if you quiet down."

The sounds of a siren approaching convinced her to get it together. After three gulping breaths, she eased away from Miles just enough to wipe the wetness from her face. She sounded completely pathetic when she said, "I need a tissue."

Miles pulled off his shirt and offered the hem to her.

Why that made her laugh, she wasn't sure, except that she felt close to hysterics. She mopped her cheeks, then hugged him again. He was warm and strong, and by God, he was hers. "I was so scared."

"Me, too." He stroked his hands over her shoulders, down her back, up to tangle in her hair.

Fletcher lifted his grandfather's head into his lap. "I should have realized he wasn't well. Everything that happened with Anna really hit him hard. He hasn't been the same since. Then to lose Meryl…" He glanced at Maxi, then away. "I'm sorry."

"Why were you here?" Miles asked.

"I'm a good cop, regardless of what you think." His broken nose made his voice thick. "I knew you didn't want me on it, but I couldn't let it go. I had a feeling things were ramping up, so I was watching the house."

"You saw Woody get here?" Maxi guessed.

"Actually, no. The rain was so thick that I'd about given up and went to Granddad's to grab a cup of coffee—only, he wasn't there. I don't know why it clicked, but something made me look for his rifle. When I saw it wasn't in the gun case, I somehow...knew."

Maxi rested her cheek against Miles's chest, reassured by the touch of skin on skin. "Where is your sister now?"

"She lives in Cincinnati. There were too many memories for her here."

"She's doing okay?" Miles asked.

"Yeah, no more drugs."

"Good for her," he said, surprising Maxi with his compassion.

"It's been more than five years now and she hasn't touched anything, not a cigarette, not a drink, definitely no drugs." He smoothed his grandfather's hair. "He did save her, but it was the wrong way. And this..." Fletcher shook his head. "I don't know what to say. He had no right... He never should have..."

Neither of them could disagree with that.

When the sirens got louder, Miles picked up the revolver and put it in his pocket. "You okay?" he asked Fletcher.

"Yes. No..." He glanced up at Miles. "If only I'd realized sooner."

"We're damn lucky you showed up tonight. Thanks for that."

Fletcher's gaze skipped over Maxi. "Take care of her. And if there's anything I can do—"

"Look after your grandpa." Miles led Maxi out into the yard. He seemed steadier now, but she wanted him to sit down.

The rain had stopped, leaving behind mud everywhere. As she picked her way around a puddle, he said, "We need to plant some grass seed. Or maybe even lay some sod."

Her gaze shot up to his, but he was looking at the flashing lights growing ever closer.

Did he plan to stick around long enough to lay sod? She hoped so, because she wasn't about to let him go. She knew now that everything she'd thought was important wasn't nearly as important as him.

"How you handled the situation…" Maxi tried to find the right words, yet nothing could adequately convey all the things she felt for him. "I'm in awe of you, Miles. And I'm so proud of you."

"Proud?" He led her toward a patio table.

"You showed great restraint."

"Woody's an old man out of touch with reality. I couldn't pulverize him."

Yes, he could have—but he wasn't that type of person. Even in the heat of the moment, with adrenaline pumping and rage at the forefront, he'd thought of others. "You were very understanding with Fletcher, too."

"Don't remind me." As cars entered the yard, he laid down the rifle, revolver and Glock on the table, then took her with him as he backed away. "You know Fletcher passed me a key to the cuffs?"

So that was how he'd gotten free. "I saw him toss you something but didn't know what it was."

"He didn't want Woody to see, so his aim wasn't great. It took me a minute to find it in the hay. And good thing, too. I had one link nearly open enough to free myself, but I might not have managed it in time."

"Don't say that." She hid her face against him, breathing in his familiar scent, wanting, needing, to get even closer.

"Okay." His arms came around her. "As long as you don't ever scare me like that again."

"It wasn't my fault."

"That didn't make it any easier." He tipped up her chin. "The next few hours are going to be rough. Don't let anyone bully you, okay? Sahara should be here soon and she'll help."

"You think she'll come?"

His smile went crooked. "I'll be shocked if she doesn't."

Soon headlights off several different cars lit the yard like daylight. To get their individual stories, police separated them. Just as Maxi finished telling one person, another showed up and asked all the same questions.

Miles sat at the back of an ambulance while a paramedic cleaned the gash on his head and tested him for a concussion.

His gaze constantly sought her out, but then, she had a hard time looking away from him, too. This evening could have gone so differently. What if Fletcher hadn't shown up? What if he hadn't had a key to the cuffs?

What if Woody had just shot Miles instead of hitting him in the head?

Every time she thought of the various scenarios, she started to shake again.

It was a relief when, half an hour later, Sahara showed up, Brand with her. It was a dark, rainy night, and yet Sahara looked as fresh as she ever did. She wore skinny jeans, a sleeveless red silk blouse and nude-colored wedge sandals. Hair up, makeup on, attitude in evidence.

Maxi couldn't help but smile.

Sahara spoke with Miles first, even checked his head and, if she guessed right, lectured him a little. He quickly pointed her in Maxi's direction, where she sat in a chair on the front porch, her knees drawn up, her arms folded over them. Sahara started forward with a determined stride. Brand hung back with Miles.

Both men watched Sahara go, but their interest couldn't have been more different. Miles looked amused, and Brand looked...well, even from where she sat, Maxi saw the heat in his eyes.

When she got close, Sahara asked, "Are they still watching me?"

Fighting off a laugh, Maxi said, "Yes."

"Good. Sit tight and I'll be right back." Sahara went into the house.

"Okay." Not like she could do anything else with the chief of police now speaking to her.

"We'll exhume the bodies as soon as possible. And don't worry, we'll repair any damage done."

Maxi nodded. "Will someone be able to let me know before they get started?" It sounded ridiculous, but she said, "I have a lot of cats and—"

"I'm aware. I knew your grandmother. She was a good woman."

"Thank you." One thing about small towns—everyone knew everyone else.

"Why don't you give Hank Miller a call?"

"The vet?"

"He can maybe advise you on the best way to keep the cats calm during...excavation."

"Thank you, I will."

The chief looked up at the still drizzling sky. "We'll probably have to wait until the ground dries up." He gave her another uncomfortable glance. "Don't want to tear up your property any more than necessary."

So he'd leave dead bodies in the ground? Oh God, she was shaking again.

"Here you go." Sahara breezed out as if she dealt with near-death catastrophes every day. She handed Maxi a cup of coffee with sugar and creamer, then tucked a lightweight sweater around her shoulders.

She shouldn't have been cold, not with the thick summer night air, but she couldn't stop shivering.

"Now." Pulling a chair over close to sit beside her, Sahara sent off the officer with little effort, saying, "She's already answered everything and now she needs a break. If you think of anything else, you can speak with her again tomorrow."

Oddly enough, that worked. Maybe it was Sahara's air of command, or the no-nonsense tone she'd used, but the chief walked off, along with two other officers, and Maxi found herself alone with Sahara.

At first she just sipped the coffee and watched Miles as he spoke with a detective. Another ambulance took Woody away. He was alive, and arguing—with himself again. Fletcher, escorted by officers, went with his grandfather.

"I'd met him," Sahara said. "He'd seemed perfectly sane, if a little eccentric."

"I thought he was a sweet old man." Maxi couldn't pull her gaze off Miles. "I believe Woody loved my grandmother. If she hadn't died, she might have eventually married him and none of this would have happened."

"And you wouldn't be with Miles now."

Leave it to Sahara to cut to the heart of it all. "I might've sought him out for other reasons."

"But would he have forgiven you?" Sahara sipped her own coffee. "I think protecting you gave him the reason he needed to look past the rejection."

"I never rejected him." Not really. But she'd made so many dumb mistakes. "Mostly, I wanted to spare him from the craziness of my life."

"I doubt he saw it that way." Sahara turned thoughtful. "He won't go to the hospital, you know. I was concerned about it, but Brand, being another fighter with plenty of experience with injuries, agrees with Miles. The split on the back of his head isn't deep enough to need stitches. Apparently head wounds just bleed like the devil, but it's stopped now and all patched up. Rest is all he really needs." She tipped her head at Maxi. "Actually, he seems in better shape than you."

"Because I'm weak and he's not." It wasn't a bitter observation, just the truth. She told Sahara everything she'd already told to a dozen different officers. "He was hurt but pushed through it."

"Fighters learn how to do that, or so I've been told. It's one of those qualities that also make them excellent bodyguards."

Maxi felt certain that Miles would be excellent at anything he did. "He was enraged, but he didn't injure Woody any more than necessary to disarm him. He's been antagonistic toward Fletcher since he got here, but under these new circumstances, he was…kind." Damn it, emotion choked her up again.

"I'm not sure I'd employ an unkind man."

That sounded odd, given the employees were bodyguards who sometimes had to deal with lethal situations—like hers. "Really?"

"Of course. Being effective doesn't mean you can't also be thoughtful. I've seen cruelty, and it's reckless. I wouldn't want a reckless employee."

Wow. Sahara saw things that Maxi had never imagined, and it gave her such a unique perspective. "You must be very pleased with Miles because he's amazing. In all ways."

"True." Sahara shoulder-bumped her. "With a guy like that, you should probably ask him to stick around, right?"

"I want to." She used the crumpled tissue in her fist to wipe her eyes again. Getting the words out wasn't easy. "Do you know what a mess it's going to be around here? The chief said they'll dig up the three bodies, but he wants to wait until it's not so muddy. And they'll have to drain the pond, but that's okay. I want it gone. I think I'll fill it with dirt and put in a new one somewhere." She shuddered. "As long as they get them off my property, I don't care about mud."

"It'll be okay."

Putting her forehead on her knees helped Maxi to hide her misery and kept others from noticing her tears. "My poor cats

are going to be terrorized, so it's not like I can stay somewhere else while that's going on."

"Probably not."

"But you said it yourself, that Miles needs peace and quiet.
He deserves that, especially right now with his head injury."

"I plan to give him two weeks off."

Two weeks didn't sound like much to Maxi, but then, she
knew Miles. He might not take any offered break. When he'd
told her he liked to stay busy, he'd meant it. "I hope he uses
the time to recuperate."

"Away from you?" Sahara tsked. "Do you really think he'll
agree to that?"

Another bubble of emotion clogged her throat. "I don't
know."

Sahara said softly, "Maybe you should ask him."

"I can't. That'd be so unfair. I'm forty-five minutes away
from Body Armor. He needs to rest, then get back to work,
back to his life." She gave a pathetic laugh. "Hopefully his
next job will be easier than this has been."

"You don't know me very well, do you?"

Maxi stiffened. That was Miles's voice, coming from where
Sahara had been. She tipped her head to the side, just enough
to peek at him. With one hand he held an ice pack to the back
of his head, and with the other he gently tucked back her hair.

Blast. There he was, being amazing again while she whimpered like a weenie.

She made herself straighten, and by a sheer act of will she
managed to stem the useless tears. "I want to keep seeing
you." There, she'd said it.

His mouth quirked to one side. "You'll be seeing me, all
right." He cupped her face. "Or did you think I'd let you
walk out on me again?" Without giving her a chance to answer, he added, "I won't, you know, especially now that I
know where to find you."

Hope was a crazy thing, making her heart pump and scaring her at the same time. She turned her face to kiss his palm, then nestled her cheek against him. "It's going to be insane around here, but I was hoping I could come to see you when you're not working."

A strange look crossed his features. "And where do you think I'll be?"

"I guess...your apartment?"

"No." When Hero inched up onto the porch, Miles bent to lift him into his lap. The cat crawled up his chest, sniffed his chin, then butted his head against him.

Still one armed, Miles rearranged him on his lap and the cat started to purr.

Maxi waited, but he said nothing else. She cleared her throat. "I wouldn't expect you to make the forty-five-minute drive. For one thing, you're hurt. And once you're feeling better, you'll want to get back to work."

"I'm going to be here," he said, his attention on the cat. "So neither of us will have to travel far."

Her mouth went so dry, she couldn't swallow. "Here?"

Finally, he looked at her. "I love you, Maxi."

Every bone in her body melted. "Oh my God, *I love you, too.*"

"Don't start crying again." He leaned forward for a soft, brief kiss. "It devastates me."

She had to laugh. With everything they'd been through, *that* was what bothered him? "I love you," she repeated. And now that she knew he loved her, too, everything else was workable. "I can't ask you to travel that far for work, and I can't see a way for me to—"

"If I need to," he said, "I'll find a new job."

Sahara had been standing at least ten feet away in conversation with Brand, but she whipped around to glare at him. "No, you absolutely will not!"

Brand threw up his hands, following her when she marched over to them.

"I'm adding bodyguards," she said with a pointed look at Brand. "Not removing them."

Maxi felt terrible. "Of course he can't quit. He loves his job."

"I love you more," Miles said.

She melted again, then started breathing too fast. Knowing she'd never let him leave his job for her, Maxi scrambled for another idea. "Maybe I could find a caretaker, someone to live at the farm and tend to the—"

"No." Miles frowned at her. "You love it here."

Her smile trembled. "I love you more."

Sahara choked. "This is all so beautifully romantic and, honestly, a little melodramatic. No one needs to make a sacrifice, and that includes me. Miles doesn't need to be at the agency every day. Twice a week, in the case of meetings or for a new assignment, is often enough. We live in a cyber world, people. Nearly everything else can be handled online. Of course, there will be the occasional travel for clients who aren't nearby, but overall I can handpick assignments that are closer to where each of my bodyguards live."

She finished by beaming at Brand.

He frowned. "Let up, will you? Wrong time, wrong place."

Her smile didn't slip when she turned back to Maxi and Miles. "So, do we have a happy ending?"

"I'm happy," Maxi promised. So much so, she could barely contain herself.

"Getting there." Miles grinned, then said to Sahara, "I don't suppose you could handle the mess out here?"

Sahara flapped a hand. "Piece of cake. Why don't you both go inside and get cleaned up, change your clothes, share some kisses—whatever you need to do to put a pretty ribbon on the end of this day? I'll talk with the officers and get a schedule worked out so you know what to expect and when. I'll ensure that they wrap this up quickly and with as little fuss as possible."

Maxi's head spun after all that.

"Thank you." Miles stood, tossed the ice pack to Brand, who caught it, then handed the cat to Sahara. "This poor guy was part of Woody's plan and could use some TLC."

"Oh." Sahara hesitated but then cuddled the cat close when she heard him purring.

Miles took Maxi's hand and walked her inside. The second he got the door closed behind her, he turned her and pinned her to the wall.

"Tell me again."

"That I love you?" She stared up into his beautiful green eyes. "How could you not know that?"

"After you ran from me? When you only came back to me because you needed protection? When you—"

She touched a finger to his lips. "I love you. You are the most remarkable man I've ever known. I think I started falling in love with you about an hour after meeting you." She let out a breath. "Then we had sex, and I knew I was a goner."

Miles bit the end of her finger. "So I won you over with sexual prowess? Yeah, I can live with that."

She laughed. "You won me over by being you, so big and strong, gorgeous but still so nice. You're incredibly easy to talk to, plus you listen. You make me laugh without even trying. You're kind and hardworking. You have deadly skills, but you're so gentle with the cats. I know you're there to back me up, but you don't try to take over. You have great friends, and—"

"And the sex is top-notch?"

See now, how could she not love him? "There you go," she whispered, "making me laugh after our horrendous evening."

"I'd rather have a horrendous evening with you than a boring evening alone."

He'd said something similar before, after he'd gotten his arm stitched. And that hadn't finished healing before he got hit in the head. But he wanted her, and she more than wanted him.

And finally the danger was over.

Maxi whispered, "The sex is so incredible, I have no words."

"Now we're talking." He kissed her long and deep, then put his forehead to hers. "Sahara will find out how long it'll take to wrap up this mess, then we'll fix everything."

"And get my goats delivered?"

"Yes."

"And plant some sod?"

"Definitely."

"I want a new pond."

"Great idea." He kissed her again. "Plus, we'll remodel the kitchen and bathrooms, maybe make one of the bedrooms bigger—and just so you know, I have enough of my own money to do all that. Being a fighter was lucrative, especially since I'm good with finances."

"Is there anything you're not good at?"

"Resisting you." He kissed her again. "I suck at that."

"I'm glad."

He hugged her close, his mouth against her temple. "We have a lot to get done."

"Like getting married?"

This kiss was hungry, hard and fast. "Best idea yet."

"Really?"

He nodded. "And we'll live here, happily ever after, with my boss and friends occasionally visiting—and a lot of cats."

It seemed incredible, but the future looked very bright. "That sounds absolutely perfect to me."

★ ★ ★ ★ ★

Look for Brand and Sahara's sizzling story,
FAST BURN,
from Lori Foster and HQN Books!
Read on for a sneak peek…

CHAPTER ONE

Sahara Silver sat behind her enormous desk in her posh office on one of the upper floors of the elite Body Armor agency. Bright October sunshine splashed through tall windows. A large vase of fresh flowers, delivered that morning from a very content client, filled the air with sweetness.

For the most part, she was content.

She ran the most elite bodyguard agency in the area, probably in the whole country. She'd acquired a trifecta of studly employees, ex-MMA fighters with ability, competence and, her favorite, sexiness. Her agency was recently instrumental in solving a high-profile case, but she was no less satisfied with the outcome of other, more personal cases.

Body Armor saw results. Clients could come to her with a wide range of needs and know they'd be in good hands.

Yes, her life would almost be perfect...if her brother weren't missing, assumed dead by everyone except her.

Once she found her brother—because in her heart she knew he was still alive—he'd reclaim control of his company. He wouldn't be thrilled with the changes she'd implemented, but always, from the time she was a know-it-all preteen, he'd

encouraged her independence, her fearlessness and her confidence. Scott would understand why she'd had to put her
stamp on the agency once she'd inherited it.

Not that it mattered. She'd turn it all over in a nanosecond
to have him back. She'd live in a cardboard box on the street
if she could just hug her brother one more time.

"Brand Berry is here to see you."

Surprised, Sahara glanced at Enoch, her right-hand man
and very good friend. "Brand is here?" She immediately felt
flustered. *Absurd.* "I wasn't expecting him. Did I miss a meeting?"

"No." Enoch lowered his voice in a conspiratorial way. "He
said he only needed a minute of your time when you were
free, and since you're free right now—"

"Yes, of course. Show him in." Even as she said it, a tiny
unfamiliar thrill ran through her.

She'd made a point of surrounding herself with some of
the finest male specimens on the planet—professional fighters that she'd turned into prime bodyguards, each of them in
high demand. It was her vision for Body Armor, to get rid of
the stuffy "men in black" clones and offer instead *real* men,
with real muscles, certifiable machismo and lethal ability with
or without a weapon.

No, she didn't fire the previously established bodyguards;
that would have been disloyal to her brother, who'd hired
them. She simply reassigned them to the more boring cases,
and overall they were happy with that.

Anything to do with a celebrity, a dignitary or a politician,
her elite team now covered.

She desperately wanted to add Brand to that team.

Thinking she'd have a minute, she was just circling out
from behind her desk when Brand stepped in around Enoch.
Instead of waiting in the guest area, as a client would do, he
must have been hovering right outside her door!

Her toes curled in her high heels.

Enoch was on the small size, five-two, slight of build, with average brown hair and eyes. It was his keen intelligence and attention to detail that made him so perfect at his job.

But his size didn't really matter when he stood next to a man who made most everyone seem small, her included. Brand was big and badass with a solid steel frame of muscle all wrapped up in a cocky attitude.

Faded jeans molded to his thick thighs, going well with his running shoes and an ancient Aerosmith T-shirt that stretched over his chest and broad shoulders. Reflective sunglasses pushed to the top of his head made his golden-brown hair messy. Darker brown eyes held her captive as he murmured, "Sahara."

Leaning a hip against her desk, she drank in the rugged, virile sight of him. "Be still my heart."

Wary exasperation rooted him to the spot.

Yes, she always spoke her mind. Why not? She was the boss. Putting her hands together, her fingers extended to frame him in a square, she remarked, "A photo of you looking just like that could launch my new line of advertisement."

He crossed his arms. "Advertisement for *what*?"

"Bodyguards with ability and sex appeal." He'd look great on a billboard, maybe with a gun in his hand. She could already see it. Maybe she should ask Enoch to keep a camera at his desk for occasions like this?

When Brand just stood there, his expression amused, she smiled. "Tell me you've come to give me good news." She'd been after him for a few months now, constantly throwing out bait, trying to reel him in. He'd nibbled, but he wasn't caught. Not yet.

"I came to talk about that, yes."

Elation conflicted with disappointment. There were times

when she hoped they could take a different path from employer and employee, one more personal, intimate.

Even...sexually satisfying.

But in the end, the business came first. Always.

She hadn't given up hope for her brother, and when he finally returned, he deserved to find the company thriving.

She put her heart and soul into making that happen. There was no time for anything else.

"Perfect." She tried to be excited, but it wasn't easy.

"Actually," Brand said, coming to stand very near her, "I've got another fight lined up."

That gave her pause. She'd thought he was done with that for very difficult, personal reasons. "Oh? So how long do I have to wait for you to finish up—"

"It'll be my last fight, *but*," he said with gentle emphasis, "I'm not signing up as a bodyguard."

Her stomach bottomed out. This felt too much like losing, and by God, she did not lose. Determination had her straightening. "Tell me what it is you need. More money? Better benefits?"

Brand shook his head. "Truth is, Sahara, I can't see me working for you."

Wow. Now, that hurt. Peeved, she moved away from him to sit in her chair behind her desk. A power position.

She met his gaze without flinching. "I see." No, she didn't.

"You're too pushy." He smiled when he said it. "Too used to getting your way. And you love being in charge, but then, so do I."

Never in her life had she been so insulted. "Are you telling me you don't like me?" She rose from the chair again without realizing it, hands flat on the surface of the desk as she leaned toward him in challenge. "I got a very different impression."

"I like you," he confirmed but then added, "because you're

not my boss." He surprised her by mimicking her position until their noses almost touched over the middle of her desk.

She didn't know where to look. His eyes drew her, being so dark they were almost black, and always filled with wickedness.

Then there was his firm mouth set in that small, teasing smile that did crazy things to her.

And, oh, what that straight-armed pose did for his biceps.

She inhaled...and breathed in the scent of warm, musky male.

It seemed imperative to put some space between them, so she slowly straightened.

Brand's smile widened, and as he straightened, he murmured, "Coward."

"Oh, no," she corrected. "But I have priorities that take precedence over...other things."

He went back to crossing his arms. "Over me, you mean."

"Nonsense. You are a top priority right now. I want you on the team."

"The agency isn't a team, Sahara. It's you dictating and others following orders."

She said through her teeth, "I'm the coach. I give direction and encourage and—" bossed "—cheer. Rah-rah and all that."

He laughed.

Not with her, no. He laughed *at* her.

"Where did you work before you took over here?"

Was he genuinely interested, or just trying to move past her obvious irritation? Not that she'd stay irate long. It was a waste of time. She was more about manipulating things to get her way.

Or getting even.

But for now she'd work on that priority by answering his question. "Before Scott died, he often had me involved with the business. I learned everything here from the ground up."

"Describe 'ground.'"

"All right. When I was still very young, Scott let me sit in on meetings just to get a feel for things. When I turned eighteen, I worked as an attendant for the private elevator to his office."

"There was an armed guard even then?"

"You say it like it was the Stone Age." Feeling more confident, she again circled her desk, but instead of getting closer to him, she moved to the wall of windows to look down on the Cincinnati traffic. "I'm only thirty, so it was twelve years ago. And yes, Scott always had top-notch security at the agency, including an armed elevator guard."

"You escorted clients up to his office?"

"Yes."

Brand joined her, standing close at her back so that his scent enveloped her. "And I bet they got an earful before they ever reached your brother."

Dear Lord, was that a blush she felt on her face? She didn't embarrass easily—except that he'd nailed it perfectly. How many times had Scott remonstrated with her for being too pushy?

"Sahara?" Brand prompted.

She wished she hadn't worn her hair in her usual classic updo. With her nape exposed, the heat of his breath kept teasing her.

Brazening her way through the awkward moment, she flapped a hand and admitted, "I might have been a little nosy."

"And a little opinionated?"

"Maybe just a smidge." His closeness made her too edgy, so she again moved away, very casually in hopes that he wouldn't know he had her on the run. "Next I was a lobby receptionist."

"Fired from the elevator job, or was it a promotion?"

Damn him, did he really have such a low opinion of her?

Maybe he didn't like her. That wasn't something she'd ever considered. She got along great with the other guys, who were all friends with Brand.

Or…did they feel the same way, too? Did they only humor her in person while resenting her the rest of the time?

Disliking that possibility, she propped a hip on her desk and, doing her best to keep the frown off her face, said, "A lateral move, actually."

"Uh-huh. Did Scott tell you that?"

Scott had told her to quit harassing the clients—but Brand didn't need to know that. Although, seeing his expression, she'd bet he already did. He seemed to know her too well.

Better than anyone else, in fact.

"Scott told me he wanted me to experience every facet of the business."

"But you were never a bodyguard."

She took pleasure in saying, "Yes, I was."

Now Brand frowned, and she loved how intimidating he looked. He'd make an ideal bodyguard if only he'd realize it.

"Bullshit."

She tsked at the crude language, her idea of a reprimand. "Scott taught me to shoot. I'm actually pretty good at it."

"I've never seen you practice."

"Here, with my employees? Of course not." She had to maintain some mystique. "Scott owned his own range elsewhere and now it's mine."

"Where?"

She smiled. "It's private."

He countered with "Protecting a client isn't always about shooting."

"No, it's mostly about intelligent decisions, good planning and quick thinking." She let her gaze dip over him. "It's one reason I thought you would do so well at the job."

"Me, yes. But you?" His long, strong fingers circled her upper arm. "You're brilliant, Sahara, so no problem there."

The assurance that he didn't consider her stupid would have been nice, except that the moment he'd touched her, her thinking faltered. So did her breathing. And her heartbeat.

"I've never known anyone with a quicker mind than you," he added. "But when it comes to strength?" He lightly caressed her arm. "Physical strength, I mean. Does a woman like you, a woman who's always manicured and polished, have any?"

Just that simple touch, his warm fingers brushing over her bare skin, *on her arm*, and her priorities got all mixed up.

At five-eight, she wasn't exactly petite, but Brand still stood half a foot taller, and next to his chiseled bulk, she felt downright dainty.

Oh, this wouldn't do. Sahara cleared her throat and made herself stare up into his eyes. "Brute strength? I'm definitely lacking."

"Didn't say you were lacking. In fact, I'd say you're just about perfect, but not strong enough to tangle with someone intent on causing harm."

"When someone is smart enough and quick enough, there is no tangling." She gave him her best smug smile and pretended her knees weren't weak. "I worked for three different clients. One job was glorified babysitting for a three-year-old while authorities tried to find a failed kidnapper."

Brand's expression softened to real concern. "The child—"

"She was okay. Her father, Mr. Drayden, chased off the masked man before he got away with her."

"Thank God."

Sahara agreed. "Drayden wouldn't relax until he knew who the man was, why he'd tried to kidnap his daughter, and was assured he'd remain behind bars."

"Did they ever get the guy?"

Sahara wanted to turn away, but that would be too reveal-ing. "Yes. I shot him."

After the briefest pause, Brand clasped her other arm, too. "Tell me what happened."

"The sick bastard tried crawling in her bedroom window. He...had a knife. So I killed him." Brisker now, she explained, "He helped install the security system, so he knew exactly how to shut it down. He claimed the girl was his, that he'd slept with Drayden's wife. She denied it, of course, and to his credit, Drayden believed her. That turned out to be a good thing because they found out the psycho had made the same claim to three other children. Apparently he fixated on kids and convinced himself they were his even though he'd never touched the woman."

"Damn."

His hold was soothing, but the last thing she wanted from him, *from anyone*, was pity. "The little girl, Mari, screamed from the gunshot, but she never saw the body. Soon as the guy hit the ground I scooped her up and got her out of the room, telling her it was just a loud noise." Sahara could still remember the small arms clinging so tightly to her neck, the shaking of that small body and the soft sobs after the scream.

Until that day, she'd never thought about having children of her own. She missed Mari a lot.

"How long were you on assignment with the family?"

"Two months. But the time flew by, since I mostly played with the little girl." She twisted her mouth. "Afternoon tea with a G.I. Joe, a stuffed bear and a Barbie. Oh, the scraps Barbie and Joe got into. The bear and I would just watch in amazement."

Brand grinned. "You know, I can almost picture it, you in a tiny little chair sipping out of an empty plastic teacup with an audience of toys."

"Good times," she said, then tipped her head. "Can you see me killing a man?"

After briefly locking on her eyes, his gaze moved over her face and settled on her mouth. "Yeah, I guess I can. If it came to protecting someone you cared about."

Well, that was something anyway. "I had a shorter assignment with a twenty-three-year-old boy. At the time, I was only a year older and he had some serious misconceptions about the role of a bodyguard."

"How so?"

"I spent more time fending him off than protecting him. He got impossibly grabby."

Brand went back to scowling. "Your brother allowed that?"

"I didn't tell him! That would have been like admitting I couldn't handle the job, and it was an important one. He was a movie star's son being hassled by a radical group opposed to the star's last movie. Apparently they didn't understand fiction versus reality. They wanted to drive home their point by making his son miserable anytime he ventured into public. You'll understand that it was all confidential, so I can't give names or details."

"Sure. Tell me the part where you knocked him out."

She grinned. "We've already surmised that I'm not physically stout."

He agreed by saying, "You should have quit."

"I couldn't. Scott chose me for the job because I was close enough in age to blend in. The boy didn't want his friends to know he had a bodyguard. Guess it dented his macho pride or something."

"First, he's not a boy. At twenty-three, he's a man. And second, I hope you dented the hell out of his pride."

That was one of the nice things about Brand; he had a similar mind-set to her and they often agreed on things. "Of course I did. We were at a club with his friends. He kept trying to force me to dance with him. I knew where that would lead with the octopus, so I refused. I could keep an eye on him from the bar, but he wouldn't take no for an answer. He grabbed my wrist and wouldn't let go."

His expression darkening more by the moment, Brand asked, "What did you do?"

"I tripped him to the ground. That made him mad and he grabbed for me again."

"To do *what*?"

She shrugged. "I didn't want to find out, so I grabbed two fingers and twisted enough to break them."

"Ouch," Brand said with smiling satisfaction.

"He raged and decided it was time for us to go—with my wholehearted agreement. I had visions of the whole assignment going to hell, but it took an uptick when we stepped outside and the same group I was supposed to protect him from was there to mob him. That got him moving quickly to get in the car. On the way, I had to…ahem, assault a man who tried to drag my client back out of the car."

"Assault him how?"

"With my knee." She struck a pose, showing the knee she'd used and gaining Brand's undivided attention to her exposed leg. "In a place where no man wants to get hit."

Dragging his focus back to her face, Brand winced for real. "I gather that worked?"

"Like a charm." At least that night, she hadn't shot anyone. "When Scott heard the whole story, he tore into the client and his father and got me a bonus with an apology from the boy."

"Man."

"Man-boy," she compromised. "The third assignment was just a matter of escorting a local politician to and from a speech. It went off without incident."

"How come you never mentioned any of this before now?"

"Why would I?" She rarely discussed her backstory with

anyone, because those stories all centered around her missing brother and left her grieving from the loss. "My history with the agency has nothing to do with the reasons why you should sign on."

His eyes narrowed. "And you've been all about getting my agreement."

"Yes." She gave that quick thought and asked, "Does knowing it make you more inclined to—"

"Not really." Gaze intense, Brand slid his hands up her arms to her shoulders. "You've always amazed me, with or without the history report."

As he leaned closer—to kiss her, she was sure—she said desperately, "Work for me."

Without a single ounce of regret, he said, "No," and then his mouth was on hers, his lips pressing, his tongue touching until she opened.

The second she did, his tongue slid in and she melted against him.

God help her, it was incendiary.

If you enjoyed this book, you'll love
CAN'T HARDLY BREATHE, the next book in
New York Times *bestselling author Gena Showalter's*
ORIGINAL HEARTBREAKERS *series.*
Read on for a sneak peek!

Daniel Porter sat at the edge of the bed. Again and again he dismantled and rebuilt his Glock 17. Before he removed the magazine, he racked the slide to ensure no ammunition remained in the chamber. He lifted the upper portion of the semiautomatic, detached the recoil spring as well as the barrel. Then he put everything back together.

Rinse and repeat.

Some things you had to do over and over, until every cell in your body learned to perform the task on autopilot. That way, when bullets started flying, you'd react the right way—immediately—without having to check a training manual.

When his eyelids grew heavy, he placed the gun on the nightstand and stretched out across the mattress only to toss and turn. Staying at the Strawberry Inn without a woman wasn't one of his brightest ideas. Sex kept him distracted from the many horrors that lived inside his mind. After multiple overseas military tours, constant gunfights, car bombs, finding one friend after another blown to pieces, watching his targets collapse because he'd gotten a green light and pulled the trigger...his sanity had long since packed up and moved out.

Daniel scrubbed a clammy hand over his face. In the quiet of the room, he began to notice the mental chorus in the back of his mind. Muffled screams he'd heard since his first tour of duty. He pulled at hanks of his hair, but the screams only escalated.

This. This was the reason he refused to commit to a woman. Well, one of many reasons. He was too messed up, his past too violent, his present too uncertain.

A man who looked at a TV remote as if it were a bomb about to detonate had no business inviting an innocent civilian into his crazy.

He'd even forgotten how to laugh.

No, not true. Since his return to Strawberry Valley, two people had defied the odds and amused him. His best friend slash devil on his shoulder Jessie Kay West...and Dottie.

My name is Dorothea.

She'd been two grades behind him, had always kept to herself, had never caused any trouble and had never attended any parties. A "goody-goody" many had called her. Daniel remembered feeling sorry for her, a sweetheart targeted by the town bully.

Today, his reaction to her endearing shyness and unintentional insults had shocked him. Somehow she'd turned him on so fiercely, he'd felt as if *years* had passed since he'd last had sex rather than a few hours. But then, everything about his most recent encounter with Dot—Dorothea had shocked him.

Upon returning from his morning run, he'd stood in the doorway of his room, watching her work. As she'd vacuumed, she'd wiggled her hips, dancing to music with a different beat than the song playing on his iPod.

Control had been beyond him—he'd hardened instantly.

He'd noticed her appeal on several other occasions, of course. How could he not? Her eyes, once too big for her face, were now a perfect fit and the most amazing shade of green. Like shamrocks or lucky charms, framed by the thickest, blackest lashes he'd ever seen. Those eyes were an absolute showstopper. Her lips were plump and heart-shaped, a fantasy made flesh. And her body...

Daniel grinned up at the ceiling. He suspected she had serious curves underneath her scrubs. The way the material had tightened over her chest when she'd moved...the lushness of her ass when she'd bent over...every time he'd looked at her, he'd sworn he'd developed early onset arrhythmia.

With her eyes, lips and corkscrew curls, she reminded him of a living doll. *Blow her up, and she'll blow me.* He really wanted to play with her.

But he wouldn't. Ever. She lived right here in town.

When Daniel first struck up a friendship with Jessie Kay, his father expressed hope for a Christmas wedding and grandkids soon after. The moment Daniel had broken the news— no wedding, no kids—Virgil teared up.

Lesson learned. When it came to Strawberry Valley girls, Virgil would always think long-term, and he would always be disappointed when the relationship ended. Stress wasn't good for his ticker. Daniel loved the old grump with every fiber of his being, wanted him around as long as possible.

Came back to care for him. Not going to make things worse.

Bang, bang, bang!

Daniel palmed his semiautomatic and plunged to the floor to use the bed as a shield. As a bead of sweat rolled into his eye, his finger twitched on the trigger. The screams in his head were drowned out by the sound of his thundering heartbeat.

Bang, bang!

He muttered a curse. The door. Someone was knocking on the door.

Disgusted with himself, he glanced at the clock on the nightstand—1:08 a.m.

As he stood, his dog tags clinked against his mother's locket, the one he'd worn since her death. He pulled on the wrinkled, ripped jeans he'd tossed earlier and anchored his gun against his lower back.

Foregoing the peephole, he looked through the crack in the window curtains. His gaze landed on a dark, wild mass of corkscrew curls, and his frown deepened. Only one woman in town had hair like that, every strand made for tangling in a man's fists.

Concern overshadowed a fresh surge of desire as he threw open the door. Hinges squeaked, and Dorothea paled. But a fragrant cloud of lavender enveloped him, and his head fogged; desire suddenly overshadowed concern.

Down, boy.

She met his gaze for a split second, then ducked her head and wrung her hands. Before, freckles had covered her face. Now a thick layer of makeup hid them. Unfortunate. He liked those freckles, often imagined—

Nothing.

"Is something wrong?" On alert, he scanned left…right… The hallway was empty, no signs of danger.

As many times as he'd stayed at the inn, Dorothea had only ever spoken to him while cleaning his room. Which had always prompted his early-morning departures. There'd been no reason to grapple with temptation.

"I'm fine," she said and gulped. Her shallow inhalations came a little too quickly, and her cheeks grew chalk white. "Super fine."

How was her tone shrill and breathy at the same time?

He relaxed his battle stance, though his confusion remained. "Why are you here?"

"I…uh… Do you need more towels?"

"Towels?" His gaze roamed over the rest of her, as if drawn by an invisible force—disappointment struck. She wore a bulky, ankle-length raincoat, hiding the body underneath. Had a storm rolled in? He listened but heard no claps of thunder. "No, thank you. I'm good."

"Okay." She licked her porn-star lips and toyed with the tie around her waist. "Yes, I'll have coffee with you."

Coffee? "Now?"

A defiant nod, those corkscrew curls bouncing.

He barked out a laugh, surprised, amazed and delighted by her all over again. "What's really going on, Dorothea?"

Her eyes widened. "My name. You remembered this time." When he stared at her, expectant, she cleared her throat. "Right. The reason I'm here. I just... I wanted to talk to you." The color returned to her cheeks, a sexy blush spilling over her skin. "May I come in? Please. Before someone sees me."

Mistake. That blush gave a man ideas.

Besides, what could Miss Mathis have to say to him? He ran through a mental checklist of possible problems. His bill—nope, already paid in full. His father's health—nope, Daniel would have been called directly.

If he wanted answers, he'd have to deal with Dorothea... alone...with a bed nearby...

Swallowing a curse, he stepped aside.

She rushed past him as if her feet were on fire, the scent of lavender strengthening. His mouth watered.

I could eat her up.

But he wouldn't. Wouldn't even take a nibble.

"Shut the door. Please," she said, a tremor in her voice.

He hesitated but ultimately obeyed. "Would you like a beer while the coffee brews?"

"Yes, please." She spotted the six-pack he'd brought with him, claimed one of the bottles and popped the cap.

He watched with fascination as she drained the contents.

She wiped her mouth with the back of her wrist and belched softly into her fist. "Thanks. I needed that."

He tried not to smile as he grabbed the pot. "Let's get you that coffee."

"No worries. I'm not thirsty." She placed the empty bottle on the dresser. Her gaze darted around the room, a little wild, a lot nervous. She began to pace in front of him. She wasn't wearing shoes, revealing toenails painted yellow and orange, like her fingernails.

More curious by the second, he eased onto the edge of the bed. "Tell me what's going on."

"All right." Her tongue slipped over her lips, moistening both the upper and lower, and the fly of his jeans tightened. In an effort to keep his hands to himself, he fisted the comforter. "I can't really tell you. I have to show you."

"Show me, then." *And leave.* She had to leave. Soon.

"Yes," she croaked. Her trembling worsened as she untied the raincoat...

The material fell to the floor.

Daniel's heart stopped beating. His brain short-circuited. Dorothea Mathis was gloriously, wonderfully naked; she had more curves than he'd suspected, generous curves, *gorgeous* curves.

Was he drooling? He might be drooling.

She wasn't a living doll, he decided, but a 1950s pinup. *Lord save me.* She had the kind of body other women abhorred but men adored. *He* adored. A vine with thorns and holly was etched around the outside of one breast, ending in a pink bloom just over her heart.

Sweet Dorothea Mathis had a tattoo. He wanted to touch. He *needed* to touch.

A moment of rational thought intruded. Strawberry Valley girls were off-limits...his dad...disappointment... But...

Dorothea's soft, lush curves *deserved* to be touched. Though makeup still hid the freckles on her face, the sweet little dots covered the rest of her alabaster skin. A treasure map for his tongue.

I'll start up top and work my way down. Slowly.

She had a handful of scars on her abdomen and thighs, beautiful badges of strength and survival. More paths for his tongue to follow.

As he studied her, drinking her in, one of her arms draped over her breasts, shielding them from his view. With her free hand, she covered the apex of her thighs, and no shit, he almost whimpered. Such bounty should *never* be covered.

"I want...to sleep with you," she stammered. "One time. Only one time. Afterward, I don't want to speak with you about it. Or about anything. We'll avoid each other for the rest of our lives."

One night of no-strings sex? Yes, please. He wanted her. Here. Now.

For hours and hours...

No. No, no, no. If he slept with the only maid at the only inn in town, he'd have to stay in the city with all future dates, over an hour away from his dad. What if Virgil had another heart attack?

Daniel leaped off the bed to swipe up the raincoat. A darker blush stained Dorothea's cheeks...and spread...and though he wanted to watch the color deepen, he fit the material around her shoulders.

"You...you don't want me." Horror contorted her features as she spun and raced to the door.

His reflexes were well honed; they had to be. They were the only reason he hadn't come home from his tours of duty in a box. Before she could exit, he raced behind her and flattened his hands on the frame to cage her in.

"Don't run," he croaked. "I like the chase."

Tremors rubbed her against him. "So...you want me?"

Do. Not. Answer. "I'm in a state of shock." And awe.

He battled an insane urge to trace his nose along her nape…
to inhale the lavender scent of her skin…to taste every inch of
her. The heat she projected stroked him, sensitizing already
desperate nerve endings.

The mask of humanity he'd managed to don before reen-
tering society began to chip.

Off-kilter, he backed away from her. She remained in place,
clutching the lapels of her coat.

"Look at me," Daniel commanded softly.

After an eternity-long hesitation, she turned. Her gaze remained on his feet. Which was probably a good thing. Those
shamrock eyes might have been his undoing.

"Why me, Dorothea?" She'd shown no interest in him before. "Why now?"

She chewed on her bottom lip and said, "Right now I don't
really know. You talk too much."

Most people complained he didn't talk enough. But then,
Dorothea wasn't here to get to know him. And he wasn't
upset about that—really. He hadn't wanted to get to know
any of his recent dates.

"You didn't answer my questions," he said.

"So?" The coat gaped just enough to reveal a swell of delectable cleavage as she shifted from one foot to the other.
"Are we going to do this or not?"

Yes!

No! Momentary pleasure, lifelong complications. "I—"

"Oh my gosh. You actually hesitated," she squeaked.
"There's a naked girl right in front of you, and you have to
think about sleeping with her."

"You aren't my usual type." A Strawberry Valley girl
equaled marriage. No ifs, ands or buts about it. The only
other option was hurting his dad, so it wasn't an option at all.

She flinched, clearly misunderstanding him.

"I prefer city girls, the ones I have to chase," he added. Which only made her flinch again.

Okay, she hadn't short-circuited his brain; she'd liquefied it. Those curves...

Tears welled in her eyes, clinging to her wealth of black lashes—gutting him. When Harlow Glass had tortured Dorothea in the school hallways, her cheeks had burned bright red but her eyes had remained dry.

I hurt her worse than a bully.

"Dorothea," he said, stepping toward her.

"No!" She held out her arm to ward him off. "I'm not stick thin or sophisticated. I'm too easy, and you're not into pity screwing. Trust me, I get it." She spun once more, tore open the door and rushed into the hall.

This time, he let her go. His senses devolved into hunt mode, as he'd expected, the compulsion to go after her nearly overwhelming him. *Resist!*

What if, when he caught her—and he *would*—he didn't carry her back to his room but took what she'd offered, wherever they happened to be?

Biting his tongue until he tasted blood, he kicked the door shut.

Silence greeted him. He waited for the past to resurface, but thoughts of Dorothea drowned out the screams. Her little pink nipples had puckered in the cold, eager for his mouth. A dark thatch of curls had shielded the portal to paradise. Her legs had been toned but soft, long enough to wrap around him and strong enough to hold on to him until the end of the ride.

Excitement lingered, growing more powerful by the second, and curiosity held him in a vise grip. The Dorothea he knew would never show up at a man's door naked, requesting sex.

Maybe he didn't actually know her. Maybe he should learn

more about her. The more he learned, the less intrigued he'd be. He could forget this night had ever happened.

He snatched his cell from the nightstand and dialed Jude, LPH's tech expert.

Jude answered after the first ring, proving he hadn't been sleeping, either. "What?"

Good ole Jude. His friend had no tolerance for bull, or pleasantries. "Brusque" had become his only setting. And Daniel understood. Jude had lost the bottom half of his left leg in battle. A major blow, no doubt about it. But the worst was yet to come. During his recovery, his wife and twin daughters were killed by a drunk driver.

The loss of his leg had devastated him. The loss of his family had changed him. He no longer laughed or smiled; he was like Daniel, only much worse.

"Do me a favor and find out everything you can about Dorothea Mathis. She's a Strawberry Valley resident. Works at the Strawberry Inn."

The faint *click-clack* of typing registered, as if the guy had already been seated in front of his wall of computers. "Who's the client, and how soon does he—she?—want the report?"

"I'm the client, and I'd like the report ASAP."

The typing stopped. "So this is personal," Jude said with no inflection of emotion. "That's new."

"Extenuating circumstances," he muttered.

"She do you wrong?"

I'm not stick thin or sophisticated. I'm too easy, and you're not into pity screwing. Trust me, I get it.

"The opposite," he said.

Another pause. "Do you want to know the names of the men she's slept with? Or just a list of any criminal acts she might have committed?"

He snorted. "If she's gotten a parking ticket, I'll be shocked."

"So she's a good girl."

"I don't know what she is," he admitted. Those corkscrew curls…pure innocence. Those heart-shaped lips…pure decadence. Those soft curves…*mine, all mine.*

"Tell Brock this is a hands-off situation," he said before the words had time to process.

What the hell was wrong with him?

Brock was the privileged rich boy who'd grown up ignored by his parents. He was covered in tatts and piercings and tended to avoid girls who reminded him of the debutants he'd been expected to marry. He preferred the wild ones… those willing to proposition a man.

"Warning received," Jude said. "Dorothea Mathis belongs to you."

He ground his teeth in irritation. "You are seriously irritating, you know that?"

"Yes, and that's one of my better qualities."

"Just get me the details." Those lips…those curves… "And make it fast."

CAN'T HARDLY BREATHE—available soon from Gena Showalter and HQN Books!